PENGUIN BOOKS

T0358019

THE
DEEP

Kyle Perry is a drug and alcohol counsellor based in Hobart, Tasmania. He has grown up around the Tasmanian bush and seas, with the landscape a key feature of his writing and his spare time. He loves the sea, and his entire leg is covered in ocean tattoos.

His debut novel, *The Bluffs*, has been translated into five languages. It was shortlisted for the Dymocks Book of the Year, the Indie's Debut Fiction Book of the Year and Best First Novel at the International Thriller Writers Awards, and was longlisted for the Australian Book Industry Awards' General Fiction Book of the Year.

ALSO BY KYLE PERRY

The Bluffs

THE
DEEP

KYLE
PERRY

PENGUIN BOOKS

PENGUIN BOOKS

UK | USA | Canada | Ireland | Australia
India | New Zealand | South Africa | China

Penguin Books is part of the Penguin Random House group of companies,
whose addresses can be found at global.penguinrandomhouse.com.

First published by Michael Joseph, 2021
This edition published by Penguin Books, 2022

Cover design by Adam Laszczuk © Penguin Random House Australia Pty Ltd
Cover images courtesy Sirachai Arunrugstichai/Getty Images (cliffs) and
Maximillian cabinet/Shutterstock (waves)
Typeset in Sabon by Midland Typesetters, Australia
Printed and bound in Australia by Griffin Press, an accredited
ISO AS/NZS 14001 Environmental Management Systems printer

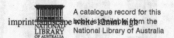

A catalogue record for this
imprint ... book is available from the
National Library of Australia

ISBN 978 1 76104 819 7

penguin.com.au

Ryan Barber,
wouldn't have made it without you.

I pay my respects to the traditional custodians of country, the Paredarerme, who are the custodians of Teralina and Turrakana – also known as Eaglehawk Neck and the Tasman Peninsula. I pay my respects to elders past, present and emerging.

I acknowledge today's Aboriginal community on all Lutruwita, who are the custodians of this island, and I recognise their continuing connection to land, waters and culture.

Black Wind at morning, sailors take warning.
Black Wind at night, death is in sight.

Maritime saying of the Tasman Peninsula

The sirens of the Tasman Peninsula are known to be evil creatures who lure sailors to their deaths . . . Their songs were reported to be haunting and beautiful, sweeping many people into the deep . . .

From *Folktales of Tasmania*, by Cheryl Stirling

When first I heard the sirens' song,
'twas out upon the sea.
Their gaze was hot, their hunger high.
A coward, I did flee –
terror, I flew, to my domain.
But she did follow me,
far from that misty bounding main,
the Black Wind of the sea.
Now ever I must flee,
there is no peace for me.

Dr William Ashbury, circa 1850s

PROLOGUE

Pirates Bay, Tasmania

The boy gasped for breath, hair in his mouth, before the next wave slammed him back against the bottom. He tumbled, the fizz of bubbles around him.

Back to the surface. Another desperate breath. Stinging eyes searching for land. In the pre-dawn light the ocean was a roiling grey, the dark gumtrees so close . . .

Knocked under by another wave, bull kelp tangling around his limbs. He clung to it as the current sucked him away from shore. His hands were so cold he couldn't grip the kelp, but he wrapped slick loops of it around his wrists, adrenaline and fear giving him strength.

The water receded in a rush of whitewash and for a moment his head and torso were above the water.

'Help!' he called, voice raw.

A crash and he was under again. He held his breath, wrists locked in the kelp, until the rushing water had passed.

Above the sound of the wind and the waves, a dog barked.

The boy pulled himself forward. He could feel sand beneath his feet.

When the next wave came he let it carry him forward in the swirl of sand and silt. He spun, over and over. Arms tangled in kelp. Forehead scraping rock.

The water pulled away, but he rolled until he found a crevice in the coarse rocks on the shore. He gasped for salty air, the sound of breaking waves close by. He wasn't out of danger yet. He dragged himself forward, grazing skin, all strength gone from his legs, the wind cold against his bare back.

A German shepherd splashed into the rockpool beside him, barked, nudged its nose under his arm.

The boy dug bleeding fingers into the rock as the waves surged over him again, the dog yelping.

Rough hands seized him under his armpits and picked him up.

'I've got him!' the man shouted. 'Here, he's still breathing!'

The dog shook its fur and licked the boy's bleeding shins, its barks mixing with human voices. They were crowding him now, carrying him off the rocks, onto the sandy beach. The man laid him on his back, putting an ear to his chest.

The boy opened his eyes, crusted with silt and sand.

'He's alive,' said a woman. 'Thank God, he's alive.'

She was right in his face and he pulled away, coughing, scrabbling on hands and knees, backing himself against the panting dog. The stink of wet fur and seaweed.

Still these people crowded around him. 'Easy, mate, easy,' said the man.

The boy's grazes stung, his body ached. He shivered from the cold, his heart pounded. He needed to *run* . . .

The sight of the woman holding out a towel broke through his panic, and a new thought reached the surface of his mind.

These people have come to rescue you.

You need their help.

He forced his struggling breaths to slow.

'Thank you,' he croaked. His throat and nose burned raw from the salt water.

Then he turned and buried his face in the dog's fur. 'Thanks, Zeus,' he whispered to his dog. 'You did it.'

'Bloody hell. Look at his tattoos,' said the man.

The boy knew he was a desperate sight. Short, thin, shaggy blond hair. Covered in kelp and sand. He wore only a pair of board-shorts, the cuts and puckered scars all over his skin rising from goosebumped flesh.

'No, it can't be . . .' gasped the woman. 'After *seven years*?'

Tattooed across his scrawny shoulder blade, which dripped icy sea water, jagged words read:

THIS IS FOREST DEMPSEY
BE CAREFUL WHAT YOU WISH FOR

CHAPTER 1

AHAB

Ahab Stark burst out of the bay with a gulping breath, speargun in his hand, an underwater torch dangling from his wrist. He pulled his diving mask down to his neck, coughing. Cold water matted his grizzled beard, the salt water stinging ice-blue eyes long since used to its bite. He bared his teeth in a grin; he'd pushed that dive a little too far.

The sky still had a dusting of dawn stars – no clouds in sight – but under the surface of the water he had heard the vibration of the drone and felt the cross-current. It was easy to feel it here, around the isolated reefs that spired out of the bay, and he had seen a school of Australian salmon flee to deeper water.

The Black Wind was on its way.

He floated in the dangerous silence that preceded it. Of course, the ocean is never quiet, but to Ahab this was true silence. Natural sounds, constant movement around him, waiting with bated breath. He looked up at the lightening sky, content.

'I'll take my time,' he told it.

Eventually, when the cold and the wind had seeped deeper into his blood, he kicked his matte-black fins, swimming over to his anchored rigid inflatable boat. He climbed up the ladder, naked skin dripping water. His fishing haul was in the catch bag attached to his waist – enough king flathead to offer a fish-of-the-day special at his pub. He dropped his mask and snorkel, speargun and torch, slid off his fins.

His diving partner, Ned, was floating on the other side of the boat. Ned wore a ripple-patterned wetsuit – even in the middle of summer, the younger man found the water too cold. 'Fish have disappeared, Ahab,' he called. 'Reckon it's coming? Black Wind?'

'On its way,' Ahab called back.

Ned hurriedly climbed into the boat himself, shivering as he peeled his wetsuit off his lanky frame. A boat was like a footy change room – no one cared if you were naked. Ned dried his mullet and checked it in his phone camera before he towelled the rest of himself dry.

'Let's get out of here,' said Ahab, once they were both dressed.

'Look,' said Ned, zipping up his thick coat. 'Another boat.'

It was visible – just – through the peaking waves.

'They'll be right,' said Ahab. 'They'll see the signs.'

He glanced at the sky – still clear of clouds save for some high horsetail wisps, which caught the first blush of the sunrise. The truth was, there weren't any signs, yet. Sometimes the Black Wind came with little warning. And there were always out-of-towners on these waters.

Ahab let out a sigh. 'Better have a look.'

He fired up the engine and they headed towards the other boat, slicing through a sea of dark interlocking waves, tinges of the pink sunrise now catching in the liquid peaks.

As they drew closer, Ahab identified the other boat, and he backed off the throttle. It was the abalone motherboat, the *Absconder*, a 60-foot Westcoaster, with a flybridge and live abalone tanks, and a crane on the rear deck. It belonged to the head of Dempsey Abalone – Davey Dempsey, his cousin.

Ahab tied his RIB to the side of the *Absconder*.

'I'll stay here?' said Ned.

'Get ready to leave in a hurry,' Ahab said softly, as he pulled himself up through the dive door and planted his feet on the deck.

Davey stood at the stern with his second-in-charge, Chips, and spun at the sound of someone coming aboard his vessel. He cut an impressive figure – a dark-haired, muscular man, in a business shirt but with his sleeves rolled back to show his distinctive tribal tattoo sleeves. He had a rugged face that was, as Ahab had heard Ned sulkily describe it, 'unfairly good-looking'.

He smiled wryly at Ahab's entrance. 'Alright, cuz. Come right aboard.'

Chips wore warm hi-vis, for comfort not style, her sandy hair in a long ponytail under a blue baseball cap. She gave Ahab a deferential nod. A long time ago, when she'd dropped out of high school, Ahab had been the one who'd given her work, then put her name forward for the Business.

She had never forgotten it. Ahab wished he could take it back.

'To what do we owe the pleasure?' said Davey, leaning back on the rail. He was wary of Ahab, with good reason, but tried to hide it.

'Black Wind is on the way,' said Ahab.

Davey grimaced. 'How long 'til it hits?'

'An hour. Maybe two.'

Davey sucked his teeth, then turned and looked out over the water from the bow. Ahab followed his eyes. The aluminium tiller-steer boats were just in view. 'An hour . . .'

Abalone fishing was a strange business. It required divers, who were down there under the water now, to hunt for what were technically sea snails. The thick inner layer of their spiral shells was a source of iridescent, colourful mother-of-pearl, but it was their flesh that was the prize – delicious raw or cooked, it sold like gold in Asia. Tasmania supplied about 25 per cent of the world's yearly abalone harvest.

On those smaller boats all around the *Absconder* were deckhands, staying above wherever the diver was fishing below. The divers prised abalone from the rocks and sent them to the surface in catch bags, on shot lines with underwater parachutes filled with air from the divers' regulators.

Catch bags full of abalone, but other things too, as Ahab well knew . . . things that were left out here, for Davey to pick up, bring back to shore, and sell on, right under the nose of the law.

'It'll still be there later,' said Ahab.

'Always plenty in the sea,' agreed Davey. 'But we've got a quota. Business stops for no one. I'll signal the divers later.'

'You really want to risk it?' said Ahab.

Davey straightened. 'Don't forget who you're talking to.'

'I know exactly who I'm talking to.'

Chips shuffled her feet. She glanced between the two men, uneasy.

Davey laughed, breaking the tension. 'Don't worry, Chips. We respect the elders that have gone before.'

He might really have intended to be respectful, but all it did was wrench Ahab's chest. There was no way to change the past . . .

Ahab gave a wordless salute as farewell and climbed back down to his boat. Ned turned the wheel, pushed down the throttle, and set them towards Shacktown.

One of these days, he would have to tell the police about the Business. But could he really do it? Ruin Davey's life, Chips's life, the lives of countless others . . .?

But what about the lives *they* ruined?

Angrily, he pushed the thought aside. As he'd done so many times before.

He couldn't do anything – not yet. As much as it goaded him, sometimes to the edge of insanity, Ahab was a man of his word.

But his self-control had its limits. One day he would find a reason to break his promise.

As they neared the sea cliffs, mist from Devils Kitchen caught the pink dawn like smoke. Devils Kitchen: a huge, deep trench in the cliffs of Pirates Bay, where the water and wind had eroded a chasm, forming a dangerous swirl of waves and fury, turning the swells of the Great Southern Ocean into a boiling cauldron. It was gigantic, magnificent, and dangerous as hell. But that wasn't where it got its name – early European settlers in the area had seen this mist rising and claimed it was the Devil, boiling his meat pot.

Now the buildings of Shacktown came into view, spreading across the wooded hills to the stark cliffs, spilling right down to the beaches. Ahab surveyed it all from his boat, the beach mansions and the holiday shacks and all those in between, waiting in the she-oaks and banksias and sands.

As they rounded the point, heading towards the huge maze of wooden piers that made up the marina, they saw red-and-blue pinpricks of ambulance lights and police cars, far in the distance, down on the northern beach.

'What's gone on there?' called Ned over the sound of the engine.

'We'll find out soon enough,' said Ahab.

Shacktown residents were notorious gossips, and even this early the marina was stirring.

Ned eased them into their berth, and Ahab left him to moor the boat, jumping onto the slick timber pier, catch bag in hand.

He approached a huddle of fishermen who were talking among themselves, dressed in thick waterproof gear.

'Ho!' called Ahab. 'A no-go today, boys! Black Wind's on its way . . .'

'Ahab!' said one of the men, as the others broke apart. 'Have you heard?'

'What's happened?'

'They found Forest. *Forest Dempsey!*'

Ahab dropped the catch bag.

The fishermen edged away from the look in his eyes.

CHAPTER 2

MACKEREL

Sucking on his vape, Mackerel Dempsey stood far away from the entrance to Shacktown Police Station, as was polite. The grape flavour of the vapour filled his mouth and burned his throat, tasting like Nerds lollies. The cloud hovered in front of him before slowly dissipating in the faintly menacing breeze. The station had been renovated to seem friendly and inviting, etchings of seabirds swirling along the windows to make tourists feel safe.

An early-morning tour bus rumbled by, a red double-decker, the top open to the elements. It was full of wide-brimmed hats and cameras. A sunburned woman waved at Mack, cheerful. The side of the bus read: SEE TASMANIA? SEA TASMANIA.

He waved back and took another puff. He always put off entering the cop station as long as he could.

A narrow isthmus of land, Eaglehawk Neck was 50 kilometres east of Hobart and halfway down the Tasman Peninsula. Swamping that land, engulfing it like umbrellas on a crowded beach, was Shacktown. The area offered stunning views, unique geology, the tallest sea cliffs in Australia and some of the largest sea caves ever explored – and plenty that were unexplored. There were green parks and white beaches, shops and cafés, danger and folklore. Shacktown had something for everyone. Worth the drive.

The Shacktown locals were a large part of the appeal, their attitude towards tourists one of fondness. They opened their homes as Airbnbs without qualms, invited strangers on the beach back to the cafés for lunch, forced travellers to sign their guestbooks, or, if they didn't have them handy, gave out their address and insisted on postcards from their next destination or a Facebook friend request.

But underneath it all, unseen by most, was the influence of the Dempsey criminal dynasty. And Mackenzie – known by most people as Mackerel – its outcast. Crooked nose, tattoos. Large enough to be intimidating yet for some reason always the butt of people's jokes. His father had once said it just oozed out of him – like he was asking to be bullied.

The automatic door to the police station opened and an old man in a ripped puffer jacket and stained trackpants walked out. He nodded to Mackerel, wandering over for a chat, already lighting his cigarette. 'Hey, Mack. How's the day looking?'

They saw each other every day – every damn day. They had the same daily sign-in conditions and they both chose to get it over with first thing in the morning. The old man stank of body odour, was always drunk, and no one ever stopped to chat with him – which was why Mackerel always went out of his way to do so.

'Looking good, I reckon!' said Mack. 'Just heading out on the boat. First day's work I've been able to land in a while. How about you?'

'Sorry to break it to you, mate, but I heard in there that the Black Wind is on its way.'

'No . . .'

Mackerel couldn't afford another day without the meagre

income he made from the only fisherman in town – his best mate – who still gave him work.

'Just go home and get high,' advised the old man, stretching his back. 'Weird feeling in the station today. I think some kinda shit's gone down. Hope you weren't involved, mate.' He took another puff and walked off with a lazy wave, the smoke caught in the breeze.

Out on the ocean, that breeze would soon become a droning wind. The Black Wind. Mackerel had been caught out in the Black Wind once, and it still gave him chills to remember it. It twisted and pulled at the waves like a cyclone. The rage of it, the chaos, the feeling that death was just a bee's dick away and there was nothing you could do but hold on and pray . . .

Mackerel flicked the vape off – five quick taps of the trigger – and slipped it into his pocket. As he stepped into the foyer of Shacktown Police Station, his mind turned and turned. Subconsciously he made slight adjustments to his stance and walk, trying to appear as non-threatening as possible. He had a fresh face and big blue eyes, and he'd been told he had a nice smile. A bit goofy, a bit endearing. These days, he needed every shred of endearing he could manage.

Even in the station, he had to keep on his toes. It was common knowledge that Mackerel had been run out of town five years ago – for very good reason – and should never have returned. But only those with ties to the local underworld knew what this 'very good reason' was . . .

'Morning, Constable Linda . . .'

'Yeah, morning, Mack,' said Linda. She pulled out the bail sign-in registry, jotted down his name, the time and date, and spun the book around for him to sign. There was a briskness to it, and his heart sank. That usually meant it'd be an interrogation day.

How's your health and temper?

How's the job hunt going? How's the psychologist going? Who have you been seeing? What have you been doing? Anything illegal? C'mon, Mackerel, tell me the truth . . . What have you been doing?

Anything you want to tell me now before I find out later?

This daily sign-in was a constant reminder of everything he'd lost. His dignity, the respect of everyone he knew, the ability to ever be more than twelve hours away from Shacktown, even just being able to work his old job. All Tasmanian fishermen have to be of good character and be a fit and proper person, so when he went to prison he'd lost his FLAD – Fishing Licence (Abalone Dive). That meant he couldn't even dive for a living, the one thing he was good at.

Linda glanced up from the work she was doing on her computer, confused to still see Mack there. 'I'm sure you have places to be?'

She seemed distracted. He noticed now the absence of other officers. Where were they all?

'Yes, ma'am.' Mackerel turned and walked out as quickly as possible.

No interrogation today!

That was a good sign.

Yet instantly his mind was back to his upcoming court case. His rehabilitation. What he could do to fix things.

I could go to church . . . No, too transparent. Maybe a religious girlfriend? That'd look good.

While prison loomed? Who'd possibly have a relationship with someone like that?

Someone looking to save a lost cause, that's who.

He felt a pang of fear. If he went back to prison – which was the most likely outcome of his upcoming sentencing – he'd be alone again. He didn't want to be alone again.

These were the unhappy thoughts in his head as he limped to the chemist, the gulls cawing overhead. There was the smell of roasting coffee from a van set up in a little park, and he could hear the shouts of children on the swings there. Sunshine beamed. You'd never know the Black Wind was on its way, except for those rippled clouds blowing in from the horizon.

A couple of local men saw Mack limping past and spat at their feet. This attitude was why no one else in town would give him a job. He tried not to mind. It was just lucky that he could work on Big Mane's boat as a deckie, on the few occasions his best mate actually had the work for him.

'Morning, Mackenzie,' said the pharmacist, the bell jingling as he walked in the door. Fishing lures and glass floats dangled from the ceiling and caught the light. She opened the safe and pulled out his Webster pack, pressing the two pills and a sublingual strip into his hand, which he had to put in his mouth in front of her.

'Want some water today, darling?'

He liked the pharmacist for lots of reasons, but mainly because she was nice to him.

'Not today, thank you, ma'am.'

One antidepressant. One painkiller. One opioid replacement, called Suboxone – he'd become hooked on that, in prison. Well, he had been the one who was dealing it to the others in prison, but still . . .

'How's your day been so far?' he asked.

'It's been good, thank you, Mackenzie. You're not out on the boat today? You heard the weather report?'

'Yes, ma'am. No boat for me.'

'Oh good.' She nodded, a crease of concern between her brows. 'I know how you like to take risks.'

Risks like drug dealing.

Risks like returning to Shacktown even though he'd been warned what would happen if he did.

Risks like getting his hopes up that he might have a normal life one day.

He laughed. 'Not anymore. I've taken enough risks for one lifetime. They didn't pay off.'

And he meant it.

He hoped it came across like he meant it.

He smiled, then limped towards the door. Lately the pain in his knee seemed to be getting worse, but the process for getting more painkillers was too much work for someone like him. As it was, he could only have his daily dose at the pharmacy – they had to be kept in a safe, under lock and key and restriction and regulation, and he wasn't allowed to take them home.

'Have a good day, Mackenzie,' called the pharmacist.

'Thank you, ma'am, you too. Let me know if you need me to get anything in for you . . .'

They both laughed. It was a bad joke. A drug dealer joke. That wouldn't look good for him in court.

Once he was outside, he grimaced in pain. Being reformed hurt – the old Mack could've sourced better painkillers by other means.

Don't think about that. Chin up.

He looked again at the sky. Rippled clouds were forming with speed. The faintest drone filled the air, something visceral and haunting that raised the hairs on Mack's neck.

With his morning ritual complete, and nothing to do until his 8 pm curfew, he could head home and get out of the wind. He set out in that direction, ducking around a gaggle of tourists in big sun hats who were crowding the entrance to the surf shop.

If only he had a job that wasn't dependant on Big Mane and his boat.

A burst of ideas and potential surfaced in his mind. All the jobs he could do if he had money, people working for him.

He slammed the thoughts down. Or tried to. His mind never stopped. Anxiety and post-traumatic stress. Pre-traumatic stress. He was sorry for what he'd done, he was trying to rehabilitate, he didn't want to go back to prison, with all the noise and the politics and the . . .

Focus on the future.

All he wanted in life now was a house of his own, a wife he could love, maybe a pet dog. To be allowed to dive again, bringing in a good honest income. Not driving a third-hand hatchback that was almost as old as he was and struggled to make it up Shacktown's hills. Not dependant on opioids just to get through the day, or pain-killers he'd built up a tolerance to.

Who was he kidding? There was no use planning for the future. He couldn't do anything until his court case. Until he, most likely, returned to jail. And then he would have to wait until he was released. Which might be six months, or it might be seven years. It all depended on the mood of the judge on the day, and it's not like anyone in his family was going to put in a good word for him . . .

And the prosecution had already told him they were pushing for as much prison time as possible.

No. *Shut up.* *Just be happy with what you have.*

There was no one to see him, but he forced a smile onto his face. Bright. Firm. Real.

Endearing. He was Mackerel Dempsey, and he was reformed.

He limped towards Big Mane's house, head held high, even though no one ever looked his way.

Big Mane's house was squat and flat, made of dirty red brick, enclosed by conifer trees. Sleek A-frame beach homes ran alongside it, fresh and clean by comparison, but here in Shacktown a medley of different styles was commonplace. Rich and poor and everything in between, all were welcome in Shacktown.

Save for the mansions up in the hills, the neighbourhoods didn't fall into easy categories. As the name suggested, it had begun as a town of shacks, and those shack owners were still fiercely protective of their real estate, even as the town grew around them and land prices rose.

The rising hills of the peninsula meant that seaside views were plenty, yet in certain locations around town there were sweet spots – postcard views of land, sand and sea all together. Rather than huddling in one area, the wealthy sea changers who came to Shacktown spread throughout the town, hunting these sweet spots.

These days, most of the old holidays shacks that had given the town its name had been renovated into year-round dwellings, some of which were so artsy and inviting they drew their own Instagram followers and Airbnb pilgrims.

Mackerel entered through the back door. He could hear Big Mane playing Xbox deeper in the house.

'I'm home,' shouted Mack.

'You heard about the weather?' shouted Big Mane.

'Yeah,' Mack called back. 'Doesn't matter, though.'

'Oi, I know that's bullshit,' Big Mane called back. 'But I'll have another day's work for you soon, I promise.'

'Thanks, bro,' he called, stepping into his own room, tidy and small.

'Thanks, bro,' he repeated, softer.

He would be forever grateful to Big Mane, his best friend since primary school. For putting him up, for posting his bail, for giving him *his own room* . . . Sure, it was cramped and falling apart. The bunk bed he slept on was there to be used by Big Mane's nephews when they visited, and it creaked as he tossed and turned every night. But it was safe and clean and quiet.

He kept his areas of the house as spotless as he could, and tried to make it up to Big Mane by doing the laundry, cooking, cleaning, the lawns – far more than his fair share around the house. Sure, the bathroom could do with a better scrub, and the vacuum had been broken for a while. And Mack wasn't great at cooking anything other than steak, veggies and fish, and Big Mane ordered pizza four nights out of seven . . .

Be positive. You have to be positive.

He lay on his bed, looked up at the underside of the bunk above. He wiped bleary eyes and forced another smile onto his face.

When I was in prison, I was in control. I was like a caged dog, but I had everything I wanted. Everyone respected me, I was rich . . .

Now I'm still like a caged dog, but I've got fuck-all to show for it.

His smile was so tight it hurt. A single slow tear rolled down from the corner of his eye.

I'm trying. Can anybody see that I'm trying?

Big Mane's footsteps rumbled down the corridor, and his big frame burst into the room without knocking. He had the weathered face of a fisherman, but it was flushed with excitement in a way Mack had never seen. His phone was in his hand.

'Mate! You're not gonna believe it. They've found your nephew! They found Forest!'

CHAPTER 3

AHAB

Ahab sat on the balcony of his private attic suite, above his inn, The Mermaid's Darling. The Black Wind howled up from the beach and set the whole building to creaking, the sky now dense with low rippled cloud. It ruffled his beard, damp on his cheeks. Out here, a man could really feel the brunt of it, looking out over the white-tipped waters of Pirates Bay, the changeable ocean, the surface dotted with red buoys like berries, which would soon disappear below crosshatch waves.

The beaches weren't empty – locals and tourists alike found the wave patterns like a fireworks display, even as they huddled under jackets and blankets.

He wondered how many of these out-of-towners knew, or cared, that Forest Dempsey had been found.

The phone rang, just inside the door to the balcony. A landline, old school, enamel red. No mobile phone for him.

He leaned his chair back on two legs, perfectly balanced, and plucked the receiver off the hook. 'The Mermaid's Darling,' he said, eyes on the ocean, deep in thought.

'I'm sorry, I can't get you in to see him yet,' said Constable Linda.

'You know I have to,' said Ahab.

'Ahab, it's tricky,' said Linda. '*She's* got involved.'

He ground his teeth. 'Of course she has. At least tell me what Forest is saying.'

'Same as before. Nothing at all. One thing is clear, though: the kid is bloody terrified.'

'I'm family. He'll talk to me,' said Ahab.

'*She's* family too.'

'What about Alexandra? Jesse?'

'No sign of the parents. We're all out looking, but nothing so far. And with the Wind come in, it'll be hard to search the water.'

'And Forest hasn't said anything about them?'

'He's a *damaged teenage kid* who's been *missing* for *seven years*,' said Linda, slowly, as though spelling it out for him. She was one of few people in Shacktown who spoke to Ahab without any deference.

'What will it take for me to get a chance to speak to him?' said Ahab.

'Davey has the legal guardianship . . .' Linda sucked her teeth. 'Which means, again, you'll need to talk to . . .'

'Her.' Ahab's grip on the handset tightened. 'I'll make sure to do that.'

'Good luck,' said Linda, and hung up.

Ahab tapped the phone against his chin, looking out over Pirates Bay. The ocean was now a pebbled grey-blue, with the beginnings of that white criss-cross wave pattern that only formed during the Black Wind. It was known as a cross sea, and it was wickedly dangerous. A massive percentage of sunken ships the world over were attributed to cross seas – ships fared best when taking waves head-on, but in a cross sea that was impossible, as no matter which way you were facing, a wave could take you out from the side.

And here, in Pirates Bay, the Black Wind created the fiercest localised cross sea in the natural world. White crests forming at the base of the distant rocky outcrops. If you were near them, the sound of the sucking whirlpools created by the cross waves was enough to chill even the saltiest blood.

The ocean was changeable and unpredictable, that was her nature. But a cross sea offended Ahab's sense of fair play.

Watching the water, Ahab's mind hummed like an outboard motor.

What to do about *her*?

A knock on the door. 'Ahab?' called Ned.

He replaced the phone on its hook and walked through his little suite, towards the narrow doorway to the inn below. He patted Keegan on the way, who wagged his tail lazily against the sunbed without opening his eyes. He'd recognised Ned's voice at the door, or his reaction would have been very different.

'No sign of Jesse or Alexandra, but Forest has been taken to the Royal Hobart,' said Ned.

'Thanks, lad,' said Ahab.

'What's the plan?'

'I have to go see *her*.'

Ned winced. 'Do you . . . do you need me to come along?'

Ahab appreciated Ned's bravery.

'All good, mate.' He headed down the stairs.

'Roger,' Ned called after him, relieved.

Ahab's mind turned back to her.

Ivy Dempsey.

Aunty Ivy.

She was the mother of Jesse, Davey and Mackenzie Dempsey. She was the richest woman in Shacktown, and also the most corrupt.

She was as dangerous as the tides. In fact, he'd give himself a better chance of surviving the cross sea than an encounter with her.

He grabbed his coat.

Ahab walked the trail down to the Tessellated Pavement, another popular tourist spot. The Pavement was a flat stretch of rock reaching into the ocean, covered by a latticework of rectangular saltwater pools, so geometrically precise they looked man-made. Were siren-made, if you believed the legends.

Here the Black Wind was a steady hum, and the waves crashed and sucked at a beach covered in tree bark and stones. Strong wind, beating sun, and people everywhere. Music played somewhere but it had no chance with the wind in the trees and buffeting the buildings further up the shore, the waves on the rock, that melancholy drone. A huddle of people watched a storm petrel dip and coast in the wind. Birds loved the Black Wind.

He walked along the Pavement and down onto the sand, footsteps crunching shells, dried cuttlefish backbones and gumnuts. He looked beyond the storm petrel, to where the sky opened up over the bay, making a mockery of the weathered cliffs and hills that tried to contain it.

Weathered. Ahab knew that every seaside, the whole ecology of coastal life, existed because of erosion and the forces of the wind and sea. But here in Shacktown the weather beat down on the coastline more than anywhere else he'd visited. And he felt it himself today – like the place might finally be wearing him down. It sure seemed that way if he was honestly thinking any good would come from a chat with Ivy.

Her house was just up ahead. A beachside mansion, it was set among grounds cleared of the hillside grasses, bordered by gumtrees but still ever-so-lucratively close to the sea. The front of the house faced a quiet street, but the rear offered a private, well-trodden staircase that ran down the harsh slope to the beach.

He climbed the steps, built of gumtree roots and driftwood, to the recycled-timber gate. Fragments of sea glass were set in a glistening mosaic in the wood. The name of the mansion – Safe Harbour – signposted the gate, the theme continued by the red-and-white life rings that lined the sandy path beyond. The back door was surprisingly simple and seemed too small for its casing, but it was surrounded on both sides by giant floor-to-ceiling windows that angled slightly backwards, like the prow of a ship.

Like many buildings in Shacktown, Safe Harbour had begun life as a shack – structures built back in the forties and fifties by owners who had no skill in construction, just glorified tents erected to claim free land. In Tasmania, the name 'shack' carried with it suggestions of a lifestyle of simplicity and escape – shack towns had grown to become holiday communities that flooded in the summers and turned into ghost towns in the winter. You could have a surgeon living next to a docker next to a receptionist, all enjoying their time off, drinking together around campfires, mixing in circles that would never form in real society. Shacktown grew from this ideal, and held to it stubbornly.

For her part, Ivy Dempsey was the matriarch of the criminal dynasty that was Shacktown's protector.

He didn't go past the gate of Safe Harbour. He'd been told in no uncertain terms what would happen if he ever did again.

Not that he was scared. He just wasn't stupid.

'Ivy!' he shouted.

Movement behind those windows. The door opened and Ivy stepped down onto the path, brushing down her apron, which was smeared with flour and dough. For a grey-haired, round-faced, sixty-something woman in a tartan dress, it was strange how Ahab found her more dangerous than a great white shark.

'Ahab,' said Ivy, making her way along the path. She stopped a few paces from him, tapping her foot impatiently. 'I've got something in the oven. What have you heard?'

'Same as you.' He kept his voice carefully neutral. 'Forest won't say what happened to him. No sign of Jesse or Alexandra.'

Ivy nodded, pulling a wooden spoon out of her apron pocket. Ahab couldn't say for certain that it was just a prop, as it was covered in flour, but he mistrusted it all the same. Something in the oven? Just another mind game.

She was a decade older than him. His own dearly departed mother, Miriam Dempsey, had married a Stark, whereas Ivy had married into the Dempsey dynasty. When Jesse, Ivy's eldest son, disappeared, the multi-million-dollar family business had fallen to her next son, Davey.

But if Jesse Dempsey ever returned – as seemed suddenly possible – he would surely resume his position as head of Dempsey Abalone, and the drug smuggling business. And everyone knew what Jesse was like with his possessions – if he felt Davey was a threat to the Business, he wouldn't hesitate to get rid of even his own brother. Permanently.

From the look in Ivy's eyes, Ahab wondered if she was thinking the same thing. Davey was by far her favourite son; Jesse was a lunatic, and Mackenzie was the child she wished had never been born.

She examined Ahab now, waiting for him to speak, to make his move. Where Ahab's mind hummed like a motor, hers worked like a giant chessboard. She patted the wooden spoon in her hand, flour puffing into the air. She *knew* what he wanted. She just wanted to hear him say it.

Finally, Ahab said, 'I need to speak to him.'

'Oh? Oh, *that's* what you've come to ask?' Ivy gave a soft chuckle. 'Dearie me, no. Stay away from Forest. Until someone finds Jesse and Alexandra, we have guardianship of him.'

'Ivy, you need to let me talk to him.'

'*Need* to?' she said, tasting the word. 'I *need* to . . .'

'Please,' said Ahab, feeling as though the word was wrenched from him.

'Now, isn't that nice? Using manners.'

His aunt turned around and headed back into Safe Harbour.

'*You* don't have custody of him,' he called after her.

She waved the spoon in carefree dismissal before she stepped inside, which set Ahab to burning anger. He pulled a cigarette out of his pocket, lighting it against a cupped hand, and studied the closed door.

Davey Dempsey was Forest's godfather. Davey had legal guardianship, not Ivy.

But that might as well have been the same thing; Davey wouldn't do a thing without Ivy's approval.

There was more at stake than just the boy. He tapped his ash on the other side of the gate and headed back onto the beach.

CHAPTER 4

MACKEREL

There she was. Should he talk to her? Or should he pretend he hadn't seen her?

Seaglass Café was set back from the beach, beside a park of scrubby gumtrees and a little wooden playground. The café had a large verandah, but inside it was cosy and eclectic, decorated as though a maritime museum had been plundered: hanging glass floats and semaphore flags and thick rope.

The table in the back corner was Mackerel's favourite place to sit and think – and after the news about Forest, he really needed to think. He sat here in his usual cushy blue armchair, a lambskin rug beneath his feet, a faded Australian flag limp in the corner and, best of all, a clear path to the side exit.

The owner of the café, Salvatore, treated Mackerel well, often giving him free coffees. Mackerel sometimes tried to pay, but Salvatore made a big show of refusing, drawing attention to both of them, until Mackerel had stopped trying. Salvatore had once been a money launderer for the Business, but had given it up years ago, and he saw in Mackerel a kind of kindred spirit. Both of them were people who had left the drug game behind.

Mackerel's coffee sat forgotten on the table. He was watching the short woman at the counter intensely. She had frizzy blonde hair, high heels and a blue designer summer dress. Shelby Dempsey. A tall, good-looking teenage boy stood beside her, scowling with impatience – her son, Kane.

Mackerel was caught in the agony of decision paralysis, so much so that he found himself sweating, his stomach clenched.

Shelby ordered some food and she and her son took a seat in the takeaway waiting area.

If he wanted to know what was happening with Forest, there was no one else he could ask. His brother, Davey, wouldn't tell him anything. His mother, Ivy, wouldn't even look at him.

But there was a chance Shelby would speak to him. She was Davey's wife, but he hadn't seen either her or Kane since he'd come back to Shacktown. There was the possibility they didn't hate him. But he'd have to decide soon, before her food was ready and she was gone.

The trouble was, if Davey found out Mackerel had spoken to Shelby, he'd beat him black and blue.

The story Ivy told everyone in town was that Mackerel had tried to kidnap Davey for ransom. The truth was different but, in Mack's mind, just as bad: in drug-fuelled psychosis, he had tried to take over the Business.

Davey should've killed him for mutiny, but instead he'd exiled him. A sign of brotherly affection, but Mackerel was still paying the price. The ache in his leg was testament to the beating he'd received.

After that, he should never have returned to Shacktown, but it was obvious to all that Mackerel wasn't a threat to anyone anymore, least of all Davey. While his mother ensured Mackerel was disdained by most of the town, at least Davey was merciful enough to understand that if Mackerel hadn't come back to Shacktown, he'd be in prison right now. There was no other place for him.

Mackerel watched a local woman approach Shelby, give her a big hug. Shelby hugged her back, nodding at whatever the woman said. He knew that they must've been speaking about Forest. He licked his dry lips – he wanted to speak to her, but he knew he shouldn't.

He had agreed not to make contact with Shelby, or Kane. His brother felt that Mackerel would corrupt his son, or slip up and say something to Shelby about the Business – he kept that side of his income secret from his wife. Or he feared that, just by being around Mackerel, whose criminal history was available to anyone who wanted to google him, Shelby would put two and two together and grow suspicious.

As if Mackerel would ever tell. Family business stayed family business. No matter how far Mackerel fell, he still had standards. He still followed the code. Shelby wouldn't find out about the Business from him. Not even with his dying breath.

He may have broken the code once, when he tried to take over the Business, but he had been a different person back then.

Right now, with Shelby in the Seaglass Café, still speaking to that local woman, was as close as he'd been to her in years. But what would he do if he approached her and she flinched away from him?

Now he saw a waitress bringing her a paper package – probably takeaway fish and chips. He couldn't wait any longer.

He knocked over his coffee as he rushed towards her, startling a tourist family and prompting the waitress to come dashing over with a tea towel.

He didn't have time to apologise, his mind was on this one chance.

'Shelby,' he called, too loudly.

She pulled off her Ray-Bans. Her hazel eyes widened. '*Mackerel? What on earth . . . I thought you were in jail?*'

She hadn't even known he was in *town*?

Belatedly, he gave her a wide smile. 'No, I . . . I'm out on bail. Have been for three months.'

'Three *months*? Have you told Davey?' said Shelby.

'Yeah,' he said. 'He knows. Listen . . .' He glanced around at the people watching the scene he'd caused. Why did he always cause a scene? His shoulders hunched up to his ears. 'Can we step outside?'

Kane looked up at him with vague recognition. Fourteen years old now, he was the spitting image of Davey. He carried the same easy weight of wealth, and had the healthy glow of a child who was loved and nurtured.

There was an awkward silence. Shelby fiddled with the paper wrapping of her food and then walked out onto the café's verandah. Mackerel followed, into the heavy wind.

'Are you okay?' he blurted. 'About Forest?'

'It doesn't feel real,' said Shelby instantly. 'I can't . . .' She rested her hand against the back of Kane's head, gently combing his hair with her fingers, and he pulled away. 'Little Forest has been missing for this long, and then to just . . . He'd be a teenager now. Thirteen. I wonder what he looks like? No one can tell us what's happened, no one knows what's going on . . . It doesn't feel real, Mack. What are we supposed to feel? What are we supposed to *think*?'

'What's Davey think?'

'I don't know, I can't get a hold of him. Kane and I were on the way to Hobart when we heard. We came straight back, but Davey isn't answering his phone. Ivy thinks it's because he must be involved in the search for Jesse and Alexandra. There's search parties combing up and down the bushland near the northern beach now. We're just picking up some lunch to head around to Ivy's. Are you joining the search?'

Mackerel would've loved to, but if the search parties were made of locals, he wouldn't put it past them to corner him and give him a touch-up. It had happened a couple times when he'd been out alone. 'No, not this time.'

Shelby looked at the food in her arms. 'Well, we better get going —'

'Thanks, Shelby. Really good to see you,' he said too quickly. 'I guess I'll see you around.'

'No, Mack, wait.' Her face softened, eyes kind. 'Don't you want to come with us?'

'To Ivy's?' he said frankly. 'Are you insane?'

Shelby's eyebrows snapped down. 'This is a big day for our family. Ivy would want you there. We all do.'

'You *are* insane. No way, Shelby.'

'Please?'

It was the way she said it. Her voice cracked, though she coughed to try and hide it.

The poor woman was terrified. Of what?

Of my psychopath eldest brother, he realised.

He hadn't even considered that. If Jesse *had* returned, then Dempsey Abalone reverted to his control, and who knew what he'd do about Davey? Even though she didn't know about the Business, Shelby had been around long enough to know what Jesse was capable of.

Mackerel shuddered. Old cigarette burns on his arms started to sting.

'Okay,' he said. 'I'll come.'

CHAPTER 5

AHAB

Ahab pulled his LandCruiser up at Davey Dempsey's mansion. He slowed to a crawl and wound the window down, the crunch of thick tyres on blue-grey gravel as he came to a halt in the turning circle around a gushing fountain.

This was Homeward. A true mansion. Iconic, set high on the hill and visible from the sea, glittering among manicured gardens. It offered a picturesque, unparalleled view of the ocean, cliffs and Shacktown.

Gleaming glass and local timbers, the main structure looked out over the water, box-like and unflinching in brick and concrete, but Shelby had instructed the landscapers to put in climbing plants to cover the walls and hedges to border the property. It now had a rooftop garden that spilled out over the edge, a backyard playground better than any in the local parks and a riot of rainbow-coloured sculptural art in the front, commissioned specifically by Shelby to look like local fish and octopus. A strange, captivating blend of old fort chic, marine art gallery and Royal Botanical Gardens, it screamed wealth.

Although Ahab hated the Business that had funded the upgrades to the building, he knew that it hadn't *all* been dirty money. Abalone diving was lucrative enough to pay for this place – otherwise no one would've believed the Dempseys' wealth. And while it seemed incredible, as far as Ahab knew, Shelby had no idea of her husband's dealings.

Years ago, abalone licences had been worth nothing. 'Nobody likes the stuff. Nobody buys it. Too much hassle to get it.' People had bartered the licences away for a carton of beer. But only so many had been given out, and no more were being issued. When demand went up in the Asian markets, and diving technology improved, the licences were suddenly worth *millions*. One of the strangest Cinderella stories of all time. Earlier generations of Dempseys had used their licences to dominate the industry, and allowed Shacktown to flourish.

That made Davey, the steward of this abalone kingdom, beloved by everyone. Prince Charming.

Not the king, though. That title was still held by Jesse Dempsey, should he ever return to claim it.

And maybe he had.

Ahab knocked on the black steel door louder than he intended, then rang the doorbell.

No answer.

Ahab was not in a patient mood today.

He checked under the doormat, then up on the sill above the door. He inspected the crevices of the bricks, then examined the line of potted plants seated along the front of the house. One by one, he tipped them back.

There it was: a spare key.

If he guessed right, Shelby would have left it here. Davey would have had a fit if he knew there was a spare key lying under a pot plant, but that was the trouble with not telling your wife the dangerous circles you moved in.

He let himself into the house.

'Davey?'

Their entranceway was a blocky tunnel of shelves and alcoves, coloured glass and stucco, a line of local pinot on a shelving unit. He took off his boots and padded onto the tiled floor of the kitchen, part of a wide open-plan living space at least two storeys high, giving the impression there were no other floors.

'Davey?' he called again, voice echoing off the gleaming kitchenware. 'It's Ahab. Twice in one day. You'd think the sirens' curse had come early.' He laughed humourlessly, voice echoing. The place smelled like scented Huon Pine candles and coffee. 'We need to talk.'

The kitchen faced a huge lounge area, all gleaming white and lush carpet, with a sunken square seat in its centre. Large windows overlooked the bay and the bushland.

He pressed his fingers into the abalone shell that was embedded in the kitchen bench. He knew that, if his mother hadn't lost her mind to the drugs, *he* might've lived somewhere like this. He wasn't bothered, preferring his attic suite to a place like this. But the irony of the same drugs taking everything from his mum and giving such power to his cousin was not a happy thought.

He'll get his day. The curse will take him too.

But there was no happiness in that thought either. He hoped, desperately, that he was wrong.

He paused as he trailed his fingers along the counter. There was a half-drunk coffee on the bench. He wrapped his fingers around the mug: it was still warm, and it smelled of a dash of whisky.

He turned quickly, putting the bench at his back, looking over the space again. He slowed his breathing and listened.

Nothing.

Perhaps he wasn't alone.

He slid a knife out of the knife block and padded off into the house. Kitchen knives were not good weapons, but back in the day, before Ahab had left the Business, he'd learned enough to make even a blunt blade dangerous.

He came to the timber stairs and headed down into a large rumpus room: fraying couches, a giant Tasmanian oak TV cabinet spilling out cables from various gaming consoles.

He walked back up the stairs and to the top floor. The first bedroom he entered was the master bedroom, again with floor-to-ceiling windows overlooking the breathtaking beauty of the bay. He flipped his hold on the knife, then looked around the room. Right away he saw that there was a note on the bedside table. A folded page. Someone had written 'Shelby' on the top.

Ahab hesitated. There was a difference between investigator and voyeur . . . but with the tip of the knife, he turned the page over.

'*Tell Jesse I'm sorry.*'

Blood rushed to Ahab's head.

I knew it . . .

He picked up the note. He read it again. He turned it over, looking for anything else.

I knew it . . .

He couldn't remember walking back down the stairs, but his whole body felt on fire.

I damn well knew it!

Davey *had* been involved in the disappearance of Jesse, Alexandra and Forest.

Ahab would find him. Of that much he was sure.

Now his steps were deliberate again. Never before had he been so aware of the cursed Dempsey blood boiling in his veins.

He wasn't a murderer. But he came from a family of them.

CHAPTER 6

MACKEREL

Mackerel sat in the front seat of Shelby's Jeep, all of his senses on edge. The cherry air-freshener gave him a headache. Awkward silence, clenched jaw, the drone of the Black Wind seeming to grow louder by the second. The bumpy road made his stomach roll.

They passed the triple-storey Mermaid's Darling inn, the domain of his cousin Ahab, tourists milling about the front, in jackets now that fine rain had begun to fall across it all. He wondered how Ahab was taking the news. Probably doing his best to take control of the situation, as usual.

They reached Ivy's house. Safe Harbour. They parked on the street, outside the garden gate, an arched hedge wreathed with stained-glass fishing floats of red and bottle green.

Shelby gushed, 'I'll just go in and check with her first. Let her know you're here, just so there isn't as much . . . unpleasantness.' She slipped out of the car, and Kane quickly followed.

Mackerel wanted to wait in the Jeep, but he felt that was too cowardly. He climbed out and looked – for the first time in a long time – upon Safe Harbour.

His sprawling childhood home looked different these days. Cabbage gums that were taller and wilder, more grey and white in their bark. A cleaner coat of paint covered the wooden walls, golden metallic finishes along the window frames. A vegetable garden where Dad's maritime paraphernalia had once been.

And then Shelby was back at the gate, with *her*. His mother, Ivy, wrapped in a cardigan, handbag across her shoulder. She took Mackerel in with one glance. 'Oh Shelby, you didn't tell me *he* was the one you wanted to bring with us. No, dear. Not him.'

'Mackerel needs to come,' said Shelby firmly.

'And I said no,' said Ivy, adopting her tone.

'Without Davey, Mackerel is the closest blood relative. Which is what they'll want,' said Shelby. 'Unless, of course, we grab Ahab?'

Ivy's nostrils flared. 'You know I don't like being manipulated, dear.'

'We *have* to see him, ASAP.' Shelby's voice trembled. 'He's *back*!'

'What are you talking about?' said Mackerel.

'We're going to Hobart, to the hospital, to see Forest,' said Shelby. 'Don't you want to come?'

There was guilt in her voice, but it was her eyes that were pleading with him.

She'd tricked him. Manipulated him. That should've made him angry, but some other feeling was more pressing.

'You *want* me to come?'

Of course he wanted to see his nephew. Jesse may have been a nightmare, but Alexandra and Forest were a part of the family – Forest with his wide, curious eyes, Alexandra with her bright laugh, quick wit.

When they disappeared, everything had changed overnight. Davey took over the Business, Kane lost the only cousin he had. Ivy became even harder on Mack. All those wedding photos with Jesse and Davey as each other's best man . . . those happy moments had turned into sad memories.

Forest was back. Could any of that be recovered? Could those absences be filled? And where did Mackerel fit into it? He didn't even belong in Shacktown anymore, let alone the Dempsey family . . .

'See, Shelby? He's slow as ever.' Ivy tutted. 'Bring this dimwit if you must, but I'm not responsible for him.'

'What about Kane?' said Mackerel dumbly.

'Constable Linda is here to watch over him,' said Ivy, speaking to him directly for the first time. 'What, you think we'd leave him alone? In these circumstances?'

Mackerel felt his face grow hot. 'No, I didn't.'

'Come on, Shelby,' Ivy said. 'Forest is waiting for us.'

The women had a conversation in the front of the car that didn't include him.

Mackerel was used to it.

He faded into the back seat and watched the view through the windows. The rise and fall of the landscape, the sun peeking out from the clouds the further they drove from Shacktown, the drone fading behind them.

By listening in on Shelby and Ivy, Mackerel was able to pick up a few important things. Like that Forest wasn't willing to say what had happened to him. That Forest had horrible tattoos on his back. That Forest was scared and broken.

Kunanyi/Mount Wellington appeared in the distance, then the sweeping curves of the Tasman Bridge. They'd be at the hospital soon.

Mackerel felt nervous about seeing the state his nephew was in – he didn't want to have a full-on breakdown, not in front of Shelby.

———

The Royal Hobart Hospital was a multistorey building taking up an entire block right in the city. Square windows and clean floors – Mackerel hated it. He was no stranger to institutions, that oppressive sense of all those floors above pressing down.

They'd had to provide ID at the reception desk to prove they were family. Outside Forest's room, they met a sharp-featured, black-haired woman. She was sitting on a chair by the door, reading *Women's Weekly*. She stood up and ran her hands over her pin-striped suit and black tie. 'Hey there.'

'We're here,' said Ivy. 'We're Forest's next of kin.'

'I'm Detective De Corrado,' said the woman, then turned to Mackerel. 'And I guess you're Davey Dempsey?'

'No. I'm M-Mackenzie Dempsey.' He stumbled on his words.

'Where's Davey?' said De Corrado with a frown. 'He's the next of kin.'

'This is Davey's wife, Shelby,' said Ivy impatiently. 'Can we go in, dear?' She clutched her handbag.

The detective eyed her up and down. 'Ivy Dempsey, I presume? I've heard a little about you.'

Her voice was charming, but Mackerel felt the deeper meaning behind the words.

'I'm flattered, dear,' said Ivy with a smile.

The detective wasn't fooled. She turned to Shelby. 'You're Davey's wife?'

Shelby nodded, eyes on the door. 'How's he doing?'

'As comfortable as we can make him.' De Corrado turned her gaze on Mackerel. 'You're the one out on bail?'

He shifted uncomfortably. 'Yes, ma'am.'

'Has Forest said anything else?' said Ivy.

'Not yet,' said the detective. 'Why don't you come in?'

Ivy held Shelby's arm and stepped into the private room.

Mackerel trailed behind.

A uniformed police officer stood by the window. He watched the three of them intently. In the other corner of the room was a German shepherd, curled up on a mat.

And in the hospital bed was a thirteen-year-old version of the Forest he'd known as a kid.

His sandy hair was long and rangy, startling blue eyes looming out from under that shaggy fringe, gauze covering a wound on his forehead. He was dressed in a hospital gown, huddled against the bedhead, an IV drip in his hand, his thin arms around his knees, fingers wrapped in bandages.

Here he was.

Mackerel's nephew.

The boy who'd been ripped away from them. Who'd missed out on seven years of family Christmases, birthday parties, fishing trips. Each one a hollowing out. Seven years of the same question. *What happened to Forest, Jesse and Alexandra?*

Shelby froze when she saw him and gave a soft gasp.

Anger boiled in Mackerel's stomach. Forest looked malnourished, weak, neglected. Whoever had tattooed those words on his back was going to pay. They were going to regret they'd ever messed with a Dempsey.

Ivy rushed towards Forest, arms outstretched, and drew the boy into in her arms. They held each other for a moment, before Ivy pulled back.

'Hello, dear,' she said, sounding shaken. 'I'm your grandmother.'

'Hello,' Forest whispered, voice raspy. His eyes took in Shelby, then flicked to Mackerel.

'I'm Mackerel . . .' He drew closer. 'I'm your uncle.'

'I know.' Forest's words were followed by a wince as he put a hand to his throat. He swallowed painfully. 'I remember.'

Mackerel's fingers itched. He was longing to do something, anything, to take away the boy's pain.

'I'm Shelby. I'm married to Davey, your other uncle. We're . . . we're your family.'

'I remember you all.' Forest nodded politely. 'Thank you for coming to see me.'

Ivy brushed the fringe out of his eyes. 'Forest . . . what do you remember?'

'Glimpses.' Those unnerving eyes turned back to Mackerel. 'I remember Uncle Mack, and Uncle Davey, and you.' He smiled timidly at Ivy. 'When I turned six, you gave me a backpack shaped like a jetpack. I wanted to be an astronaut, and you told me I was born to be an astronaut.'

'How could you possibly . . .?' said Ivy. Mackerel thought she might faint. 'I did . . . I did tell you that.'

'Do you remember anything . . . about why you were in the ocean?' said Shelby.

At this, Forest's face darkened. He looked down. He reached a hand towards the dog, and it obediently pulled itself to its feet and trotted over, climbing onto the bed beside him in a scrabble of claws. It curled up, head in his lap, and Forest stroked its fur. 'Please don't make me talk about it.'

'Dear . . . it's important,' said Ivy.

Forest shook his head. 'I can't. Please.'

Mackerel caught De Corrado's eyes. She was studying him. She held his gaze for a moment before returning to the boy.

'It's your family, Forest,' she said. 'They just want to make sure you're safe, and find out what happened to your parents.'

'I know. I wish I could help. I'm sorry . . . I'm sorry to let everyone down . . .' He buried his face in the dog's fur. He didn't move.

De Corrado gestured for them all to leave.

Mackerel almost refused, wanting to take his nephew in his arms and comfort him, but he obeyed.

———

Mackerel, Shelby and Ivy sat in a nearby room, a cramped nurse's office full of files, old hospital equipment, and the sharp smell of antiseptic. De Corrado and a skinny balding psychiatrist called Dr Joseph sat across from the Dempseys.

'. . . and so we can't even broach the topic with him. He begins to apologise, and then blocks us out. Covers his eyes, his ears, puts his face in the dog's fur like you just saw,' said Detective De Corrado. 'He's terrified of whatever happened to him.'

'He's dissociating from the event, and from reality, right now,' said Dr Joseph. 'This dissociation is an armour. Of course, he could also be in shock. He's been underfed, he's covered in bruises, and those tattoos are infected.'

'You need to find who did this to him!' said Shelby angrily.

'Yes, we *know*,' said De Corrado. 'What we need from you is to help Forest relax enough to open up about what happened.'

'His mind is still sharp,' said Dr Joseph. 'He remembers everything we say to him. Every now and then he asks questions about people from his past. We think he's trying to find emotional anchors to orient himself. That's a good sign. If he can anchor himself, he might feel safe enough to open up. It's good all of you are here. What he needs is his family, who love him, to welcome him back. If he can find enough emotional anchors to his old life . . . well, the sooner the better.'

'So far he's recalled things like the colour of his bedroom walls,' said De Corrado. 'Toys he had, names of schoolfriends, teachers . . . we're convinced he is who he says he is.'

'You didn't believe him? You *interrogated* him?' said Shelby, outraged.

Ivy put a hand on Shelby's knee. 'It's okay, dear. They had to. Forest is the heir to a multi-million-dollar business. When he comes of age, he will have a greater share in Dempsey Abalone than Davey.'

Disgrace churned in Mackerel's stomach. He, of course, had no part in the inheritance anymore. But he didn't mind; he'd give everything he owned to his nephew if it'd help him even a little bit.

'We'll still need to run a DNA test and compare it against yours, Mrs Dempsey, or yours, Mackenzie,' said Detective De Corrado. 'As unlikely as it is, we still need to make sure.'

Ivy frowned. 'What? Didn't you just say he's the real deal? Surely he's been through enough.'

'It's standard procedure,' said Detective De Corrado. 'You just said yourself that he's the heir to a —'

'Forest answered all your questions,' interrupted Ivy. 'He knew the colour of his *bedroom walls*!'

'Mrs Dempsey, your family's is a large fortune —'

'I know perfectly well what Forest means to this family,' said Ivy. 'We're *not* running a DNA test.'

'Let me be clear. I don't need your permission,' said Detective De Corrado. 'As far as the law is concerned he's an unidentified minor.'

Ivy turned to Dr Joseph. 'Could you leave the room, please? We have family business to discuss.'

Dr Joseph huffed and disagreed, but the detective nodded and dismissed him from the room.

'And Shelby, could you be a dear and check on Forest?'

Her daughter-in-law looked like she had a mind to disagree, but Ivy fixed her with a warm smile and she gave in.

Only Mackerel and Ivy remained with the detective.

'Well?' said Detective De Corrado. 'What's the big secret?'

'There won't be a DNA match between us and Forest,' said Ivy. 'Because Forest was adopted.'

Mackerel's mouth dropped open but he quickly closed it.

What?

'That . . . isn't in his records,' said Detective De Corrado. 'And clearly *you* didn't know,' she said to Mack.

'Yes, I did,' lied Mackerel, his mind turning.

'And yet, it's all true,' said Ivy. 'It was very hush-hush.'

'You'll have to explain, please,' said Detective De Corrado.

'I'll explain nothing,' said Ivy. 'Forest doesn't even know himself. He has no reason to. There will be no change to his record, and you'll tell no one else. Am I making myself clear?'

'Some of the other detectives told me your family had crooked dealings,' said Detective De Corrado, eyes on the old woman. 'Was this one of them?'

Ivy straightened in her seat, letting the aura of her wealth gather around her – a subtle change in the way she spoke, disdain in her eyes, her handbag falling to the floor, discarded.

'If you ever make a comment like that about my family again, in private or in public, I will ruin your life. The same money that brought Forest into the Dempsey bloodline can bring your world to an end. Crooked dealings? I'm sure you know that it doesn't take much to bribe a few dirty cops to corroborate a story of your corruption. Or hire a couple of drug dealers to pay a visit to your family, your friends . . . I'm not above putting a bounty on a detective.'

Ivy's face betrayed no emotion.

'I am grateful for all you're doing to help my grandson. But if I ever hear a word about Forest's adoption, I will know it came from you. *Do you understand?*'

Mackerel said nothing, studying his hands. Long experience taught him Ivy always meant what she said. It was no use doubting her.

Detective De Corrado's eyes were narrow. 'Oh, I understand,' she said, but her voice had a mocking edge. 'Crystal clear.'

Ivy took no note of her tone. 'You can call Dr Joseph back in now,' she said dismissively. 'And retrieve my daughter-in-law.'

'Certainly. Happy to help. This has all been *very enlightening*.'

De Corrado left the room, moving lazily.

A moment later the psychiatrist wandered in, glancing curiously between them, perhaps picking up on the energy in the room. Then Shelby came in, and Ivy simply patted her on the arm.

'What will be done with Forest now?' said Ivy to the detective when she came back into the room, as though their previous conversation had never occurred.

'He'll be kept in for observation,' said De Corrado, her voice falsely cheerful. 'The hope is he might cooperate with us. Really, the best way to help him recover will be through love and care and assurances of safety. And I'm informed you've paid for a private therapist and nearby therapeutic accommodation in the city, once it's appropriate for him to leave the hospital?'

'Forest will be afforded every expense,' said Ivy graciously.

'And eventually he can come stay at mine, at Homeward,' said Shelby. 'Davey is his godfather, after all.'

Ivy smiled warmly. 'Very good idea, dear.'

'Yes, that's a very good idea. Friendly surroundings, safe faces. It may take some time before he's up to moving, however,' said Dr Joseph. 'Undoubtedly there may be some pharmacological interventions required, and depending on what the detectives decide about . . .'

Mackerel's attention wavered as he thought of Forest staying with Davey and Shelby. If Forest stayed at Homeward then Mackerel wouldn't be allowed to see him. But he shouldn't feel sad – it was the best place for him. He'd be taken care of, he'd have his cousin Kane there, he'd be safe . . .

'Then let us know the moment he says a thing, and anything we can do to help,' said Ivy, dragging Mackerel's attention back into the room. 'Very well. Goodo. Carry on. Let's go back in and see him.'

Shelby reached out and Ivy gripped her arm tightly as they re-entered Forest's room. Mackerel stood up to follow them.

'Poor kid,' Detective De Corrado murmured.

Mackerel wasn't sure whether she meant the trauma Forest had suffered or the fact that Ivy now had her talons in his life.

CHAPTER 7

MACKEREL

Over the next hour, Forest still wouldn't speak about what had happened to him, and wouldn't say anything about Alexandra or Jesse. He talked haltingly about times before he went missing, asking lots of questions about each of their lives. Mackerel dodged most of those questions, too embarrassed to admit he was out on bail, due for sentencing in seven months.

But then Forest lost energy, right in front of their eyes, slipping into longer and longer bouts of drowsiness, until he fell completely asleep. They left with a muted farewell to avoid waking the exhausted child.

Ivy wanted to stay in the city, close to Forest, so Shelby and Mackerel drove back to Shacktown alone.

It was mid-afternoon and the traffic was heavy, reminding Mackerel why he preferred the quiet of Shacktown. Shelby had no issues navigating the city, lane switching as they made their way over the bridge. He remembered that Hobart was her home town, before Davey had swept her off her feet.

Davey, who still hadn't answered his phone. Every missed call put Shelby more and more on edge.

'Have you ever known Davey not to answer his phone?' she said.

Mack shrugged. 'Maybe he dropped it in the water? Maybe he —'

'Why did Ahab blame Davey for their disappearance, seven years ago?' she asked. 'No one would ever tell me. Not the truth, anyway.'

Mackerel shifted in his seat. She was bringing up things he couldn't talk about with her.

He could hardly say, *Because Ahab suspected Davey of getting rid of Jesse in order to take over the Business. He was furious that Forest and Alexandra had been swept up in it. But Ahab wasn't thinking clearly – he blamed the Business for bringing in the ice that killed his mother. He wanted to go to the cops to bring it all down . . . until Ivy intervened. Like she always does.*

'What did Davey tell you?' said Mackerel.

'Don't,' said Shelby. 'You always do that. All of you Dempseys. Dodge questions, say stuff that doesn't mean anything. And I *hate* how you roll over for her!' She pounded the steering wheel. 'You barely said a word in there. You need to stand up to her.'

Mackerel was confused. 'Stand up to who? Ivy? Shelby, I know it's been a big day, but you're talking crazy.'

'It's not funny, Mackerel.'

They fell into silence for a while longer, and she again pounded the steering wheel. 'See? You did it again! You deflected my question.'

'You're the one who brought up Ivy.'

'Stop! Just answer the question!'

Mackerel stayed silent. He watched the window.

Shelby said, 'When Jesse went missing, Davey got everything. Now Forest has returned, and with what those tattoos say, and with Davey missing, I'm worried, Mack. I'm really, really worried.' They'd reached the end of the worst traffic and she accelerated the Jeep. 'Do I have reason to be worried?'

'Why would you say that?' said Mackerel.

What did she know? How much did she suspect?

'Stop dodging, Mack, or I'll pull over and make you walk.'

He swallowed. If he had to hitchhike, he might not make it home in time for curfew.

'There's a reason no one believed Ahab,' said Mackerel. 'Davey loved Jesse. You know that, you saw that. Davey loved Alexandra and Forest, too. He wouldn't have done anything to hurt them. And you know that, or you wouldn't still be married to him.'

'Don't talk about my marriage like you understand it, Mackerel,' said Shelby.

That shut him up. He turned away and looked out the window, at the long sweeping curves of the highway through the hills outside Hobart. Davey had brought him out here, years ago, on one of his first driving lessons. Davey was the only one in the family who'd given up time for him. Driving lessons, kicking the footy, teaching him how to tie a lure, how to pick up girls . . .

'Davey will be fine,' said Mackerel. 'Davey is always fine.'

'Did you and Jesse *ever* get along?' said Shelby.

'You know the answer to that question,' said Mackerel angrily.

'So that's a no?' said Shelby.

'No,' said Mackerel. 'Jesse was a bully.' *And I was his favourite thing to torment.*

'A lot of people loved him.'

'A lot of people love Ivy, too,' said Mackerel.

The final stretch into Shacktown was enclosed by bushland, the road rising and falling through the mountains that bordered the sea. They came over the hill and into town. From above, Shacktown looked like it had been reclaimed by the bush, the black peppermints and banksias and eucalypts hiding houses and yards and streets – until you saw that gigantic marina and the boats moored there.

Then, if you looked closely, you could make out the mismatched houses sticking out of the trees – the cottages, townhouses, villas, container homes, mansions, caravans, tents. Everyone was welcome here, at the edge of the world.

The white foam waves, crashing against the base of the cliffs, were so distant and large they looked to be moving in slow motion. The crosshatch waves brought a shiver to Mackerel's spine. Beneath it all, the drone of the Black Wind.

They headed for Ivy's house. Gumtree branches covered the street like a canopy, moving and pitching in the wind.

'You should come in,' said Shelby when they arrived.

Mackerel hadn't unbuckled his seatbelt. 'I might just wait here,' he said, eyeing his childhood home.

'Come on, Mack.'

'I don't want to go inside.'

She leaned across and unbuckled his seatbelt for him. 'Don't be a scaredy-cat.'

Taking deep breaths, he climbed out of the Jeep and followed Shelby inside. The outside of the house may have changed over the years, but the inside looked almost identical to what he remembered. The nautical artwork in the corridor, varnished timber struts, high ceilings with skylights. That smell . . . the smell of Ivy's perfume and the wood and the cooking. His childhood.

He hated it. He wanted to leave.

'Constable Linda?' Shelby called into Ivy's house. 'Kane?'

Mackerel paused to study a wall of family photos. Weddings, school photos, baby photos of Kane and Forest. Really, he was looking for pictures of himself, and he was surprised to see his face in a few of the group shots, and in one solitary portrait from his high-school farewell dinner, chubby and goofy-looking.

So she hadn't thrown all his portraits out, as she'd told him she had.

Kane appeared in the hallway. 'Can we go home now?'

'Have you spoken to Dad at all?'

'No? Where is he?' said Kane.

Constable Linda came up behind Kane. 'Good kid you've got here, Shelby. Didn't get a peep out of him.'

'That's only because Ivy has an Xbox,' said Shelby. She planted a kiss on Kane's head.

Kane rolled his eyes and strolled out to the car.

Perfect kids. Perfect mansion. Perfect life. Mackerel wondered what it must be like. Something inside of him was annoyed that Davey was evidently a good father. Where had he learned that? Their own father, Joel Dempsey, had been a shit dad.

Then the answer came to him: Ahab. Ahab had been more of a father to them than their own.

'We'll have officers patrolling your house tonight, Shelby,' said Linda.

'That's okay, I thought Mack might come and stay with us tonight. Is that okay, Mack?'

His heart plummeted.

'He won't be able to stay, Shelby. This one's got a curfew,' explained Linda. 'I'll make sure the officers are there.'

'I'm sure it won't matter if Mack stays just for one night. It'd be good for him to be around family.'

Mackerel didn't laugh, that would've been rude. Shelby had no sense what his life was like, but how would she? She had no way of knowing that some days he'd get home at 7.55 pm and the cops would be waiting for him, hoping to catch him even one minute late. Still, what she wanted was family, and it warmed him that she thought of him that way.

'It doesn't work that way,' said Linda. 'The courts set the rules, not me.'

'Alright . . .' said Shelby.

'I'll see you soon. You've got my mobile, yeah? Give me a call any time.' She headed out.

'It's not fair you can't stay at ours,' said Shelby.

'Davey will be home soon,' said Mackerel. 'I wouldn't worry about it.'

'And if he's not? Having the cops outside is all well and good, but right now, I won't feel comfortable in there without anyone but *family*.'

'Well, you know, you could ask Ahab . . .?'

'If Ivy found out, she'd disown me.'

He snorted. 'So it's okay to invite me along, but not Ahab?'

'I'd rather fight for you than Ahab.'

Mackerel's cheeks warmed, and he looked away. 'Honestly, I'm sure Davey will be back soon. Nothing to worry about. You know Davey's always right wherever he needs to be.'

'So you won't come?'

'Shelby, if he finds me in your house . . . Look, I'm sure he'll be back soon.'

She threw up her hands. 'Fine, I'll go call Constable Linda then, shall I? Tell her we still need her to babysit?'

She stalked from the room, leaving Mackerel alone. He headed for the back door, hands in his pockets, before he had too much time to think.

Mackerel descended the back steps and headed along the windy beach, sand in his eyes, the stink of kelp and a rotting seal carcass in his nose. It was hard to walk on the sand with his limp, but he walked the beach whenever he could. A few tourists still stood on the shore, taking photos of the cross sea, oblivious to him. He navigated around them, still thinking about why he'd turned Shelby down, wondering if he'd made the right choice.

Afraid of Davey. Afraid of Ivy. Letting Shelby down . . .

He made his way to the Seaglass Café and took his usual place in the back.

A minute later, Salvatore was there across from him, arms folded. He brought Mackerel his usual flat white.

'What's wrong? You're pale.'

'Just . . . family stuff.'

'It's *always* family stuff with you Dempseys. And *you're* always looking back. You think I didn't see you leaving with Shelby Dempsey? The way she held on to you for support?' He leaned forward. 'If this isn't the moment for reconciliation, when *is*? You should be ecstatic!'

'I am! I'm . . . Forest is *alive*! But . . . I just have to tread carefully, Sal. You know how it is. You know they don't trust me.'

'Bloody hell, Mack, we both know how things are in the drug world, and so does Davey. Everyone knows you weren't in your right mind four years ago. The only issue is that the crew you ran in Brisbane – you were *too* good at it. That's why Davey's mad. He realises that if you'd pulled off the mutiny, you would've been a good bloody captain. Davey is too perfect, too good, he talks too well – it makes him hard to follow as a leader, and arrogant as fuck. The crew would follow you. You're more at their level. They'd respect you.'

'Yeah, thanks, Sal,' muttered Mackerel, 'I really want to be told I'm at the same level as a crew of drug smugglers.'

'You're missing the point! You need to look forward.' Sal forced him to look up. 'What's the first rule of scuba diving?'

That question caught him off guard. 'Don't hold your breath?'

'Exactly. Keep breathing. Keep swimming, Mopey Fish.'

'For what? In seven months I'll be back in prison —'

'Stop whining! Prison isn't set in stone! Can't you see it?' Salvatore threw up his hands. 'Ah, it's no good talking to you.'

'What can't I see, Sal?'

'I really hoped you would've thought of this yourself.' Salvatore reached for Mackerel's coffee, which hadn't been touched, and drank. 'Your nephew returning is your *chance*. Seven months . . . imagine what you could achieve in seven months. Imagine if *you* found out what happened to Forest Dempsey. If *you* solved the mystery. No judge would sentence you to prison after that.'

Mackerel hesitated. 'I'm not going to use Forest's suffering for my own needs. He's got enough people poking at him and crowding him.'

'Imagine what your *family* would do if you solved the mystery . . .' continued Salvatore.

That was tempting.

He shook his head. It was stupid, there was nothing he could do. Why was Salvatore trying to get his hopes up like this?

'Fine, how about something else . . .' Salvatore's voice was serious. He gestured at Mackerel with the coffee cup. 'Something only *you* can do, to protect your nephew.'

'What are you *talking* about, Salvatore! Spit it out.'

'Listen to me carefully, Mack . . .' His voice lowered to barely a whisper, so much so that Mackerel had to strain to hear. 'Blackbeard is coming.'

Mackerel's blood ran cold.

'Impossible. Davey always keeps —'

'Yes, yes, I know, your big brother Davey Dempsey and his incredibly well-oiled drug machine keeps Blackbeard away . . . But now that Forest has returned, half of Dempsey Abalone will return to him. Don't you see? If Davey has only half the business, half the money, half the legitimacy – half the power – that's not enough to hold the Business forever, to maintain a foothold in Shacktown. Blackbeard will find a way in. He's been trying for years.'

Now Mackerel felt panic rise up. Why had no one told him? He thought of Forest, and Shelby, and Kane. He thought of Big Mane.

No. It wasn't his job to fight Blackbeard. That's why Davey made the big bucks.

'No, Salvatore. I'm staying out of it. Davey will handle it.'

'Are you sure he can?'

There was something about Salvatore's tone.

'Salvatore . . .' said Mackerel slowly. 'How do you know all this?'

'If you repeat what I'm about to tell you, I could die a very unpleasant death,' said Sal, his voice dropping again.

'He's contacted you, hasn't he?' said Mackerel. 'Blackbeard has already made contact with you.'

'He sent one of his lackeys this morning.' Salvatore swallowed and wiped a sheen of sweat off his brow. 'Blackbeard wants me to launder his money. Or he'll burn down this café.'

Mackerel winced. All those customers, living their happy lives, blissfully unaware of the criminality all around them. And why would they notice? They'd never crossed that line. Not like poor Salvatore. He was just like Mackerel, desperately trying to get out of a world that you could never truly leave behind.

But that was a bold move from Blackbeard, showing himself so soon.

'Forest was only found this morning. Why's he moving so fast?'

'Davey hasn't been seen since returning to shore this morning,' said Salvatore meaningfully.

Mackerel stood up in a rush. 'What do you know about Davey?'

'Sit back down,' hissed Salvatore. 'And lower your voice!'

Mackerel stayed standing. 'Davey wouldn't abandon us to Blackbeard.'

'That's not what I'm saying! But *no one has seen him*. And that's an awfully big ocean out there . . .'

Mackerel felt sick. In his mind's eye, he saw the sunken boat, the words 'THE SIRENS CURSE' on her prow.

All men of Dempsey blood were cursed to find incredible fortune, followed by incredible misfortune. Ahab, Mackerel, Jesse . . . they'd all been struck by the curse, as his father had. Davey was the only one who had escaped it. So far.

'No. Davey will keep him out,' said Mackerel woodenly. 'He knows what he's doing.'

'And if he can't?' Salvatore gestured around his café. Mackerel saw the sweat marks under his arms. 'Without Davey, you're the only one who can help.'

'Are you trying to keep me *out* of prison or send me *back*?' cried Mackerel.

Now people were turning to look at them. Salvatore stood up and went to attend to his customers.

Mackerel slumped back down into his chair. If something had happened to Davey, then . . .

No. Davey was fine. He always was.

Something caught his eye. A little red-crested robin had flown in through the open windows. It fluttered against the nearby glass, desperate to get out. Mackerel lurched back to his feet and limped over to open the sliding door.

It made him think of Shelby, trying to beat through a barrier she couldn't even see, a whole industry right under her nose. It financed her lifestyle while trapping her in a cage. What were her and Davey's conversations like? Did Davey get lonely, keeping that secret? The most dangerous thing in that life wasn't the drugs, it was the secrets you keep from those you love.

Listen to you. Getting philosophical.

He needed to go back to Big Mane's and stop pretending to be anything other than a rehabilitating ice addict with a nightly curfew.

He fled through the side exit, pulling his hood over his head.

The Dread Pirate Blackbeard. Here, in Shacktown.

Blackbeard was a drug lord with a reputation for fierce violence and cruelty. Even in the criminal world, he was considered the lowest of the low. As close to pure evil as Mackerel could imagine. His moniker was taken from Dread Pirate Roberts, the infamous man who had captained Silk Road, the first black market on the dark web. His name, in turn, had been taken from *The Princess Bride*, which featured the original Dread Pirate Roberts – a feared pirate whose name was passed down to his successor so he could continue to reign with terror even after his death.

This Dread Pirate Blackbeard was the same. No one knew who he was or where he'd come from, but he'd ruthlessly taken over other operations all around Indonesia and South-East Asia, and even New Zealand. He ran business in every illegal trade: drugs, weapons, human imports, body disposal. He'd been wanting to find a way into Australia for years and, of course, the rumours said his sights were set on Tasmania as the way in.

When he lumbered through the front door of Big Mane's place, he yelled out, 'Hey, bro! I'm back.'

Big Mane wandered in from the lounge room, wearing footy shorts and a cardigan, and wrapped Mackerel in a stiff hug.

'You okay, bro? I've ordered us pizza and I've got a shit ton of beer in the fridge. I figure you and I both need to get maggot drunk. Where have you been? You weren't answering my calls.'

'Sorry, I didn't even hear it ring,' said Mackerel honestly. 'I'm just gonna have a shower first, let me know when the pizza's here.'

'Roger.'

In the shower, Mackerel's mind turned back to Blackbeard. It was wise, to start with the island of Tasmania. That's how he'd do it, if he wanted to start a criminal operation in Australia. The Tasman Peninsula was the perfect place to make landfall – open to the seas but isolated, offering Blackbeard a bottleneck of land to control, a direct sail to New Zealand and proximity to Hobart.

He wondered how Davey and his crew had been able to keep Blackbeard out so far. The usual ways, he supposed. Actively working to uncover any of his agents, likely bringing them into the fold through slick politics, or more often making a brutal example of them.

They held all the infrastructure, and with Ivy's uncanny ability to find the right cops to bribe, Dempsey Abalone would make it hard for any competition to muscle in.

'Someone else will take care of it,' Mackerel said aloud. 'I'd only screw things up.'

Pounding on the bathroom door. 'Pizza's here, bro. Let's get shitfaced.'

Mackerel dried himself on a towel that definitely needed a wash.

He thought of Shelby again.

She deserves to know.

CHAPTER 8

FOREST

Forest stood at the window of his hospital room, still in his gown, watching the cars on the street below. He'd woken from a restless sleep to find it was early evening. He rested an arm against the frame, deep in thought.

Exhaustion dragged at his body. The world felt like it was tumbling around him. Like he was still in the ocean.

'I'm in over my head now, Zeus,' he said.

Zeus lay asleep on Forest's bed – at first the authorities had wanted to put the dog in a kennel, but Dr Joseph had agreed his companionship would be good for Forest, provided the dog didn't leave the room and enter the rest of the hospital.

Forest was grateful Dr Joseph had intervened – the hospital room, as nice as it was, felt like a prison. Uniformed police waited outside. To protect him, they said.

There was a knock, and a nurse entered. 'Hi, Forest,' she said. 'How are we feeling?'

'Fine, thank you,' he said. He sat down in the chair, holding out his arm so she could check his blood pressure. 'How are you?'

'Better than you, I imagine. Anything you'd like me to tell the police?'

'Not right now, thank you.'

They were relentless. He stayed silent for the remainder of her checks.

When the nurse made to leave, she hesitated at the door. 'Anything else you need?'

'I . . . well . . . n-no. No, it's fine.'

'Forest, if there's anything I can do for you . . .'

He licked his lips. 'I don't want to make extra work for any-one . . .'

She let the door swing shut and crossed her arms. 'Don't be like that, Forest. How can I help?'

'C-could I have a milkshake?'

Her face softened. 'Of course, sweetheart. I'll go find one for you. What flavour?'

'Thank you . . . strawberry, if they have it?'

She left and he returned to the window, watching the moving cars.

He had to get out of here.

He had to make contact with Huck, before Huck did something stupid. What was the best way to get out of here, and back to Shacktown?

He was lost in these thoughts until, a while later, the door opened. He turned, expecting to see the nurse, but it was someone else. A younger-looking woman with tight brown curls and a wide, cat-like face. She had two pink milkshakes in her hands.

'Hello, Forest.' She held out one of the glasses to him. 'My name is Frankie.'

He nodded, accepting the milkshake. The glass was cool to the touch. 'Thank you.'

'That's quite alright. Can I take a seat?'

He hesitated a moment too long, then nodded.

'Thank you.' She sat across from him and sucked from her straw. She looked slightly doll-like, made even younger by the way she drank her milkshake with childlike enthusiasm. 'I've been asked by your grandmother to come chat with you. I'm a counsellor.'

Ah. He froze, and instantly changed his assessment of her. That childlike enthusiasm now looked very much calculated.

So, the games had really begun.

Ivy, it seemed, was desperate to know about the fate of her eldest son and daughter-in-law.

Understandable.

He felt that familiar guilt.

'Thank you for coming,' he said politely.

'That's okay, Forest. I won't take up much of your time. How about I just stay however long it takes us to finish our milkshakes. Deal?'

Damn. Now if he drank too fast, or too slow, she'd read something into it. He took a sip and nearly sighed with pleasure. It was good, nice and thick and cold. Lots of ice-cream. Too much ice-cream. It was so thick, it would be hard to drink it quickly.

Was this planned? Or was he being paranoid?

Damn.

'This is my dog, Zeus,' he said.

'Yes, I've heard,' she said. 'But I'm interested in you, Forest.'

She'd dodged his deflection. Double damn.

'You've had a very long day,' she continued.

'Yes, I'm tired,' he said. 'I'm not sure I'll be up to talking for long.'

Clumsy. But he wasn't at his best right now. Now was not the time to match wits with a counsellor who looked barely old enough to be out of high school, let alone university.

She sipped from her milkshake. 'Just until we finish our drinks.'

He took a sip. She watched him, letting silence fill the space.

Had it gone on too long now? Was it awkward? Should he say something?

'How is Ivy?' he blurted, to fill the silence.

'She's worried about you. Are you worried about her?'

'Yeah.'

She nodded, making an affirming noise. 'I would be too. It's a lot to take in at her age. Her grandson, appearing after seven years. If I was her, I'd be feeling a lot of different emotions. What do you think you'd feel, if you were her?'

'I'm not sure.'

'Do you find it hard to put yourself in her shoes?' She sipped her milkshake slowly.

So did he, matching her pace.

'When will I be able to go back to Shacktown?' he said. 'To stay with Davey and Shelby?'

'I don't know, sorry. I can try and find out for you. It'll be up to Dr Joseph, and Ivy as well, as your guardian. She's paid for some special rooms here in Hobart for you, with twenty-four seven support. Much better than Shacktown. Less dangerous. Why do you want to go back to Shacktown?'

'I want to stay with family,' he said. 'I don't like it here.'

'Why don't you like it here, Forest?'

'I feel trapped.'

'Mmmm. I'd probably feel trapped too, I guess that's a normal feeling. Can I ask what makes you feel trapped?'

'Four walls and a locked door,' he said evenly. He took a long drink of the milkshake.

Frankie drank hers more slowly, still observing him.

He wiped his mouth. 'This is very good. Thank you. Can I speak to Ivy?'

'Yes, of course,' said Frankie. 'She'll be in tomorrow morning.'

'She's staying nearby? I'd like to see her tonight.' *And get you out of my room.*

'I'm sorry, but it's been a big day for her too. She said she doesn't want to be disturbed. She's an old woman who needs some rest. She'll be here first thing in the morning. Unless it's urgent? I'm not sure what it'll do to her health if we wake her up, but I suppose if it's urgent . . .' She put her milkshake to the side and pulled out her phone.

'No. No, it's not urgent.'

'Okay.' She put her phone back in her pocket, but left her milkshake where it was. 'Is there anything you'd like to talk to me about?' She put her hands lightly in her lap.

Enough of this.

Forest's glass fell out of his hands, smashing onto the floor. Pink milk went everywhere, thick with unmelted ice-cream.

He leapt to his feet, knocking over his chair with a crash. 'I'm sorry! I'm so sorry!'

Zeus leapt from the bed and began to lick the milk up.

Forest pulled him back, not wanting the dog to lick up shards of glass.

Frankie calmly rose to her feet and headed into the bathroom for a towel. 'It's okay, Forest.'

The door flew open and Detective De Corrado stood there, pushing her jacket away from her gun holster. 'What is it? What happened?'

'He dropped his milkshake, detective,' said Frankie with a raise of her eyebrows.

'What? You mean he actually —' De Corrado stopped herself before she finished her thought.

He'd actually what?

'I think he scared himself,' Frankie said meaningfully, then nodded to him. 'Do you need me to stay, or would you like me to leave?'

She suspected I'd drop the glass. She knew I'd want to end the conversation!

No. That doesn't tell them anything. Don't worry about that.

Both women were watching him. Shit.

'I just want to sleep,' he said. 'I'm sure I'll see you again, Frankie.'

'I'm glad you agree to keep seeing me,' she said swiftly. She smiled as she walked out the door.

'Well? Anything you can tell us, Forest?' said De Corrado without any preamble.

Zeus didn't like her tone. He growled softly.

'Shoosh, you,' she said.

'No,' said Forest frankly. 'Please, I'm so tired. Can I sleep now?'

'Of course,' she said, 'but I'm not happy about it.'

She foraged in a cupboard and found a broom, sweeping up the milky glass shards.

'Forest, I'm on your side, you know.'

He put his head in his hands. 'I'm sorry, I just . . .'

'Oh, don't do that. Stop, Forest. I'm not pushing you for answers, I just want to do everything I can to help you. Throw me a bone, kid. What am I supposed to do with you?'

He climbed into bed, pulling the blankets over him. 'How about let me sleep?'

She sighed. 'Okay, kid. I'm sorry. I just . . .' She wanted to say something, but she stopped herself.

'Say it,' said Forest.

'Was Davey involved?' she asked.

Davey? That was an angle he hadn't expected.

For a moment he forgot himself.

'Why would you say that?' he asked, sitting back up.

'Because he hasn't been seen since this morning.'

Something lurched underneath him and De Corrado caught him before he slipped off the bed. Zeus began to bark.

You missed something! he thought, shaking her off. *Why has Davey gone missing?*

'I need to sleep,' he said loudly, pulling the covers up to his neck and putting the pillow over his head. 'Thank you for your hard work today, detective! I'll see you tomorrow! Goodnight!'

CHAPTER 9

AHAB

It was early evening and Ahab stood behind the bar of The Mermaid's Darling, pulling a pint of stout for Ned. There were few things like the heady smell of ale, the gleam of a Tasmanian oak finish, a fireplace burning in the corner against the chill of the Black Wind. In the beer garden, strung with lights, twenty-somethings were out in the ringing wind, drunk as skunks.

'Big day,' said Ned.

'Too right,' said Ahab, handing him the pint.

'Forest Dempsey. Can't believe it.' He slammed the glass onto the bench. 'Black Wind, too. Almost enough to make me *believe* in your sirens' curse.'

Ahab grunted. He walked up and down the bar, serving both locals and tourists, and, as it turned out, the odd journalist. He engaged the latter in polite conversation, underscored by a slight tone of menace. They soon backed off. Ahab had that effect on people.

As well as tourists, the Darling attracted all types of locals: fishermen, farmers, snooty business people, unemployed bludgers.

There were even a few of the mainland Australians who moved to Shacktown and drove an hour and a half to Hobart every day for work. To a Tasmanian, such a long commute was unheard of, borderline insane. To someone from Melbourne or Sydney, it was a pleasant morning drive on a scenic coast.

His eyes were drawn to a dark-haired woman who entered through the heavy timber doors. She was dressed in a pantsuit and dragging a small suitcase behind her. She took in the whole room at a glance, identifying all of the exits. The draft coming through the closing door lifted up the hem of her jacket, revealing a firearm in a holster.

She smiled at someone, and Ahab followed her gaze. It was Constable Linda – off duty and drinking with her girlfriends – who raised her glass to her.

The newcomer sat by herself at a table in the far corner, beneath a wired dolphin skeleton. She caught Ahab's eye, raised an eyebrow, and tapped the table.

He slung his tea towel over his shoulder and nudged Ned out of a conversation with a pretty blonde tourist, whom he was trying to convince to come dirtbiking with him. It was time for Ned to take over the barman duties.

He walked over to the dark-haired woman. Detective, he guessed. She watched him all the way, her expression wary.

'Welcome to the Mermaid's Darling,' said Ahab. He pulled a chair out from the table and turned it backwards, sitting down with his forearms resting on the back.

'Master Publican,' she said.

'Hey, Ahab,' said Constable Linda, wandering over. She patted Ahab on the shoulder. 'I see you've met Detective De Corrado.'

'We hadn't got to names yet,' said Ahab.

'She's working your cousin's case.' Linda leaned closer to Ahab, her touch on his shoulder slightly possessive. 'Everyone at the station took your advice. Thanks for that. I've told her she can rely on you.' She gave De Corrado one last smile, then walked off towards the bar.

'You're well liked by the local cops, you know?' said De Corrado.

'Small town,' said Ahab. 'And this is the best pub in it. Most people know me.'

'There's a difference between being *known* and being *liked*, Ahab Stark,' said De Corrado. 'Particularly for someone of the Dempsey dynasty.'

Ahab bowed his head. 'At your service.' Then added, 'Out of interest, what *do* the local cops think of the Dempsey dynasty?'

'Oh, whatever Ivy pays them to think, I imagine,' said De Corrado.

Ahab was saved from answering by a man in fisherman's overalls, who approached, slightly tipsy. 'Crazy, isn't it, Ahab? The boy is back . . . can't imagine what you must be feeling. Here for you if you need anything, mate. But don't hog all the women, scallywag. How you going, darling?'

'Thanks, mate,' said Ahab, nudging him away. 'I'll come talk to you later, yeah?'

'Alright, Ahab, I'll leave you to it.' He gave a roguish wink before he staggered off.

'Charming town,' she said.

'We get all sorts in here.' He stood. 'I can tell you're busy, so I'll leave you be. But if there's anything you need – a guide, someone to help you find information – let me know.'

'What can you tell me about the disappearance of the three Dempseys?' said De Corrado, shamelessly direct.

'How would you like me to answer? The story Ivy pays people to tell, or the one she pays people *not* to tell?'

He noticed her shift in her seat, adjusting what she thought of him. 'Let's start with the answer that I'm expecting.'

'So the story we tell the tourists . . .' He spun the chair the right way, sat back down and leaned back. 'Seven years ago. Jesse Dempsey, head of Dempsey Abalone and the wealthiest man for miles. Alexandra, his dear sweet wife. And their son, little blue-eyed Forest. The three of them went for a sail on their private yacht and were never seen again. The yacht was found the next day, crashed onto the rocks further up the coast. Signs of a struggle onboard. Everyone assumed pirates.'

'I bet the tourists love that part,' said De Corrado.

'Some do. Others love the next bit: that it was Jesse's second-in-charge at Dempsey Abalone who was behind it all. The man they called Donny – Jonah Donnager. Most of the locals thought Donny wanted the business for himself, or that Donny wanted to kidnap Forest so that his odd little son Huck would have a friend forever . . .'

'Fascinating. Where is Donny now?' said De Corrado.

'Who knows. I was hoping you might be able to tell me.'

He gestured to Ned for a drink, who waved him off – *soon, soon* – still trying to convince the tourist to come dirtbiking.

'One part of the story most people don't tell is that his son, little Huck, went missing that same day. It's not quite as captivating – he wasn't rich, he wasn't well known. If you ask me, there has to be some connection, although beats me what it might be. Back then, the locals turned on Donny, and once the police cleared him as a suspect he left town as fast as he could, half-mad with grief or guilt, no one ever knew . . . But what does it matter? Now Forest is back, all that changes, right? He can tell us everything we've wanted to know these last seven years.'

'Yes,' said De Corrado slowly, 'Forest's return *should* change things . . . If it makes you feel any better, we've been looking for Huck Donnager all this time too. But most people assume Donny knows where he is, that he took his son with him to keep him safe. There's a rumour Jesse knew some dangerous people.'

'You already know the story, then,' said Ahab, wondering how much she *did* know. Jesse himself was plenty dangerous.

'I wouldn't be a very good detective if I didn't know the story, Master Publican,' she said. She smiled as Ned approached with a beer for Ahab and a menu for her. 'Hi, I'm Detective De Corrado.'

Ned smiled, introduced himself, took her order of a gin and tonic, and headed back to the bar.

De Corrado watched him go, then said to Ahab, 'How does Forest's return change things for Ivy?'

He spat out his beer as she startled to chuckle. 'You're no fool, are you, detective?'

She winked.

'Would you like to see something?' said Ahab suddenly.

'I suppose so,' said De Corrado. 'Can it wait until after I've eaten?'

'Only if you don't mind me joining you,' said Ahab.

'How could I refuse?' She cocked her head. 'Is this a *keep your enemies closer* kind of thing, Master Publican?'

'You tell me,' said Ahab. 'I'm sure you didn't choose to stay in my inn for the night just for the charming clientele.'

'The clientele is growing on me,' said De Corrado, with a rakish grin. 'But what makes you think I'm staying the night?'

Oh, this woman was good. Ahab would have to stay on his toes.

After their dinner of battered flathead and chips – on the house, of course – Ahab led De Corrado up the rickety bent stairs that spiralled through the innards of the Mermaid's Darling, past two other landings, until he reached the attic. He knocked on the door and heard his dog stir and snarl inside, before his voice – 'it's me, Keegan' – set him at ease.

'Guard dog?' said De Corrado with resignation. 'Dogs don't like me.'

'If anyone but me or Ned comes through that door, they'll be leaving bloody,' said Ahab.

'Always dogs. Why can't any of you people have a pet cat?'

Ahab walked in and petted Keegan, De Corrado following behind. Keegan gave a little snap at her, but she knew enough about dogs to not flinch away. 'Stop it. I'm not hurting you.'

Then De Corrado lifted her gaze and swept it around the room. He was sure she wouldn't be too impressed – his room was rustic, filled with old books and boating and fishing gear. It was just one wide space that had everything in it – including the shower and toilet in full view, the toilet seat up. She paused at that.

'So, you're working with a team of investigators, I take it?' said Ahab, leading her over to the far wall.

'Yeah, a big team.' She walked around a pile of fishing magazines. 'And they know I'm here. Plus enough people in the pub saw me follow you up the stairs. So if you're thinking of killing me off, you won't get away with it.'

'You watch too many movies, detective,' said Ahab. 'Do you know my favourite type? The ones where they have a corkboard up, with photos and strings connecting them, the little notes that have dates and times. Trying to piece it all together. Do you like those movies?'

'You'd be surprised how often investigators use that exact same technique,' said De Corrado. 'Personally, I find it a bit naïve.'

Ahab walked up to the huge timber cupboard that covered a good portion of the wall and swung open the door.

Inside was a large corkboard, covered in photos, notes, maps. Strings of different colours connected the different elements. Photos of Jesse, Alexandra, Forest . . . Donny, his son Huck . . . the entire Dempsey family – Shelby included. There was a large map of Tasmania with coloured pins, a map of the local waters, a smaller map of mainland Australia . . .

'Well, you did ask . . .' murmured De Corrado, unabashed. She walked over to examine it. 'Shoosh, Keegan,' she said as the dog rumbled a warning. 'Bad dog.'

'There's been unconfirmed sightings of Donny all over Tasmania,' said Ahab. 'Primarily in drug houses. There's been a few in Queensland, but I don't trust them.' Ahab's eyes were drawn to the string that connected Forest and Davey Dempsey.

'What's this?' De Corrado leaned closer to an underwater photo of a sunken ship. A name was written across the prow: *THE SIRENS CURSE*.

'Unrelated.'

'You're a terrible liar.'

Ahab stepped back. Every time he stood to look at the board, it seemed impossibly big.

'I asked around about you, you know,' said De Corrado innocently, still taking in the details of the board. 'The Mermaid's Darling. When you inherited the inn, you changed its name from the The Siren's Curse to The Mermaid's Darling.'

She clearly didn't like it when he didn't answer her questions.

'What does any of that matter?' said Ahab. 'Forest has returned. Once he's in the right state of mind, he can answer everyone's questions.'

'You're right,' said Detective De Corrado slowly. 'Because that's all he's good for, right? To answer your questions? Who cares what he's been through?'

Ahab had no response to that.

'But because you've been so kind as to show me this very disconcerting but highly informative board, I'll tell you this: there's a chance he won't,' said De Corrado. 'Answer your questions, I mean. Inconvenient, I know.'

Ahab imagined he could hear the ringing of a ship's bell. His eyes flicked to the photo of the sunken ship. He should've known the sirens' curse wouldn't release its grip that easily. 'And why won't he answer questions?'

'As I learned today from a very talkative psychiatrist, trauma affects the brain in different ways,' said De Corrado. 'And clearly Forest is severely traumatised. I know Linda has been giving you updates – so you know that Forest is not saying anything. But the truth is, he might *always* shut down when confronted with those questions. Or he could have no memories of that time – who knows what he's repressed in order to survive? The psych thinks if he's around familiar things from his past, he might *anchor* himself enough to stop repressing it all, but there's no guarantee.'

Ahab began thinking of ways he could hasten that process, his mind turning to the next cupboard, full of photo albums that might do the trick, but then he caught the way she was looking at him, like she knew what he was thinking.

He sighed. 'I'm not . . . I'm not going to push him too hard. I *am* happy he's back. Even if he never gets his memories back, or never wants to speak about it again, it's good he's here, but . . . Alexandra suffered, under Jesse . . . If Forest's returned, there's a chance she's still alive, too. I didn't do anything, back then; I want to do something now. And maybe the clock is ticking.' He rested his finger on the string linking Alexandra's photo to Forest's.

'You think Davey's involved, don't you? Isn't that why Ivy won't let you on her property?'

'You *have* done your research,' said Ahab. 'You would've had to dig deep to find that tidbit.'

'Ivy's not as powerful as you think she is.'

Yes, she is that powerful, thought Ahab.

'I used to think Davey was involved. But he's since convinced me he didn't knock Jesse off,' said Ahab. 'I'm satisfied now, alright? I had other things happening in my life at the time. I was distracted.'

'Yes, your mum's ice addiction. Miriam. It's almost like you were taking your anger out on Davey.'

His anger flashed and he turned on her. 'Be careful, detective.'

'Of course,' she said, a smile in the corner of her mouth.

He had to stop losing his temper every time someone mentioned his mother.

He closed the cupboard with a thud. 'I'm happy Forest is back. Really happy. Let's go and toast to his return.' He gestured to the door.

De Corrado studied Ahab. 'Why did you show me this board, Master Publican?'

'It's a good conversation starter,' he said. 'Come on, let me show you the room you'll be renting.'

It was late at night, after closing time, and the pub was empty save for Ahab and Detective De Corrado. He had promised to tell her about the curse, but that required the right atmosphere – an oil lantern set between them gave their conversation a conspiratorial air.

The detective had asked if she could bring a colleague, but Ahab had refused. 'You can tell them the important bits.'

'Tell me the story then, Innkeeper,' said De Corrado. She took a sip of a fresh gin and tonic. Detective De Corrado, to her enormous discredit, was not a fan of whisky.

'You know the Tessellated Pavement?' said Ahab.

'I went for a little sight-seeing earlier to orient myself,' said De Corrado. 'Those rocks – the lines in the stone look like they've been ploughed with a tractor.'

'Or something more ancient,' said Ahab. 'Sacrificial altars built by the sirens of Pirates Bay.'

'. . . Mermaids?'

'Common knowledge. There's sirens in the bay. Wickedly dangerous,' said Ahab, with deadly sincerity. 'They're the ones who send the Black Wind. They hunger for the souls of sailors. That drone is their singing. If you hear it out on the sea, it really does sound like a song . . .'

De Corrado played with the straw in her gin. 'You're teasing me.'

'Sometimes, at night, you can even see them. Their witch lights, deep below the surface, or in the caves . . . the *caves*. They're hidden in rubble of stones that make up the Black Shore, or in the fallen dolerite pillars, or burrowed deep under the cliffs. Here we have the largest system of sea caves in the southern hemisphere, maybe even the world – it hasn't all been explored yet.'

His voice trailed off, letting the wind rattle the panes. The Black Wind.

'A wind that springs out of nowhere and leaves just the same. Can't be predicted, can't be forecast. A wind that sets the ocean into strange currents, crossing over themselves like a contradiction. Criss-crossed just like the Tessellated Pavement. These seas *drone*.'

He went quiet again, so they could hear the sound of it. 'Out at sea, all you can do is race back to shore as fast as you can. There's no sailing it, no living with it. And . . . it can draw things out of you. Things you don't want. Things that lure you into the deep.'

'What do you mean?' said De Corrado. Her voice was mocking, but her eyes belied her interest.

He sipped his whisky.

'Let me recite a poem:

> When first I heard the sirens' song,
> 'twas out upon the sea.
> Their gaze was hot, their hunger high.
> A coward, I did flee –
> terror, I flew, to my domain.
> But she did follow me,
> far from that misty bounding main,
> the Black Wind of the sea.

Now ever I must flee,
there is no peace for me.'

'. . . Unsettling,' was all De Corrado had to say to that.

'Dr William Ashbury, written around 1850. He was caught in the Black Wind, out at sea, and became obsessed with siren lore. Claimed they followed him, called to him, even in his sleep. Some say he smashed his head open with a rock to get rid of the song . . . although don't believe everything you're told.'

'How does that prove that the mermaids are real?' said Detective De Corrado.

'*Sirens*. There's a difference. Mermaids are sweet natured, sirens are hungry and cruel. It's a cautionary tale – never anger the sea. Leave it be, and hope it leaves you alone . . . But the Wind. The Wind is not of the sea. It's above it, where *we* live.' He shook his head. 'Where can you run from the wind? Where can you run from the sirens' song?'

She tapped for another gin, which he poured. The sirens' song rattled the windows. 'Good story, Innkeeper,' said De Corrado. 'Now, you promised to tell me about a curse?'

'The sirens are part of it. But the night is young. We'll get there. I think I'd like to keep you waiting.'

'Fine. In the meantime, tell me more about your family.'

Ahab leaned back. 'Ah . . . the great Dempseys of old . . . Begged, borrowed or stole all the abalone licences they could. And now the town itself is a monument to that history. The end.'

'That was longer than it was enlightening,' said Detective De Corrado.

'I didn't realise this was an interrogation.'

She raised her eyebrows to indicate that it was.

'You already know how it happened,' he said.

'Well. I'm a little more interested in the complexities of your *immediate* family tree,' said De Corrado.

'And what are you offering in return?' said Ahab.

'I didn't know we were bargaining.'

Ahab raised his eyebrows to indicate they were.

'A chance to meet with Forest, face to face,' said Detective De Corrado. 'A privilege not currently afforded to you.'

Damn. She really was good.

'Yes. Thanks to dear Aunty Ivy.' Ahab hesitated, rolling the bottom of his glass on the table, his eyes on hers. 'And what do I have to give you, exactly?'

'I want you to answer every question I have,' said Detective De Corrado. 'No detail left out. Why certain members of the Dempsey family aren't involved in the abalone business. Why all you received from the inheritance was this inn, and why you changed its name. And why the previous name is the same as that boat on your corkboard. Why your mother, Miriam, died a pauper, cut out of the inheritance. Why Mackenzie Dempsey is ostracised.'

'Mackenzie is the best of the lot,' murmured Ahab.

'Yet his criminal record is a mile long.' Detective De Corrado leaned in closer. 'When Jesse and his family disappeared, everything went to Davey. Nothing to Mackenzie, nothing to *you*.'

'Nothing sinister there. Davey was next in line, and Forest's godfather.'

'But you were more of a father to those boys than anyone. *You're* the one who drove Davey to his first date, not Joel Dempsey,' she said. '*You're* the one who taught Mackenzie how to scuba-dive, not Joel. I know you treated Jesse like a son, too. So why weren't *you* Forest's godfather?'

'You've been watching us for a while, haven't you,' said Ahab, realisation dawning. 'There's no chance you could've gathered all that in the last day. The way you think, the way you talk . . . it has a bit of *Canberra* about it. Are you AFP?'

'You couldn't save your mum, so you're trying to save Alexandra. Is that it?' said De Corrado, ignoring his question.

'*Don't*,' he warned, 'talk about my mother.'

'Why? Where does she come into the story? You can't intimidate me into silence, Ahab. I'm not scared of the Dempseys.'

'Fine. You want to know about the curse?'

'Yes,' said De Corrado, 'I do.'

'Remember the hubris of the *Titanic*? The company claimed that "God Himself could not sink this ship." They challenged Him, and the story goes that He sank it. A testament to that age-old truth: *don't mock God*.'

His voice grew soft.

'My great-great-grandfather did the same thing to the sirens. He named his boat *The Sirens Curse*, claimed he wasn't afraid of them. He sauntered across their water, plundered their goods, laughed about it with his mates. And then he was killed in the fiercest Black Wind in history, only a mile off shore. Ever since then, there's been a trend: every Dempsey man will find great success and fortune, only for it to be followed by incredible misfortune, when all of that success turns to ash.'

'And what was your fortune?'

'Turned to ash,' said Ahab dismissively. 'And in return, I lost my mother.'

'She was addicted,' said De Corrado, her voice gentle for the first time. The interrogation was over. 'You couldn't have stopped it.'

'I could have. I know it, and the curse knows it too.'

She sipped her drink, and Ahab sensed her mood drop. 'So, is there a way to break the curse?'

'Yes,' said Ahab. 'Once us Dempseys stop plundering the sea, the curse will be lifted.'

'And how do you know that?'

His mind tipped back there now, to his mother. No longer safe in her hut by the sea, but in a hospital bed. Hair like straw, face like a skull, swept up in the psychosis that hit every Dempsey caught up in that drug.

'We can only break the curse if we stop plundering the sea, Ahab. It's the only way . . .'

'I'm gonna end the Business, Mum. I'm gonna burn every one of their boats to the waterline.'

'You can't turn on your family. Promise me you'll always be there for family . . . Swear to me.'

He shook his head and brought himself back to the present.

'It doesn't matter,' he said to De Corrado. 'I want to answer every question you have, but there are promises I have to keep.'

'Then I can't get you access to Forest. I'm a woman of my word.'

'I'll find another way,' said Ahab.

'I'm sure you will . . . Can you make me a promise, then? Answer the questions you can, and tell me before you start lying to me? It'll make my job easier.'

They held each other's eyes for a moment too long.

'I promise,' said Ahab eventually.

He doused the oil lamp.

'Right. Time for bed. Big day tomorrow.'

'You really believe you're cursed?' said De Corrado into the sudden dim.

'I know I am,' said Ahab. 'And so is that boy in the hospital.'

CHAPTER 10

MACKEREL

Mackerel turned over, the sound of buzzing by his bedside. A phone call.

'Shelby?' he croaked, bringing the phone to his ear. 'What time is it?'

Her voice was hushed. 'Mackerel . . . *There was someone in the roof.*'

Mackerel sat bolt upright, and smashed his head on the bunk above. He swore, dropping the phone, then scrambled for it.

'Mackerel? Are you there? The police were patrolling, and they're getting more officers down here, but . . . can you come out?' said Shelby. 'Please . . .'

'Shelby, I'm on curfew . . . if the cops see me they'll put me back in prison.'

'Surely they'd understand,' said Shelby. Her voice was trembling.

'I'm not the man you need . . . you should call Ahab.'

'But the intruder . . . he said something about . . .'

Mackerel hit his head on the underside of the bunk again. Wincing, he said, 'Wait, you *saw* the intruder? It wasn't Davey?'

'No, of course it wasn't! I *told* you. There was someone in the ceiling!' she said. 'Mack, are you drunk?'

'No,' he said, heart pounding again. 'Who was it? Who was in your roof?'

'Don't worry about it, the cops want to talk to me now.' Her voice was frosty. 'But you're right, I'll call Ahab instead.'

She hung up the phone.

Mackerel dressed himself and ran to the door. He was grateful he hadn't drunk as much as Big Mane had intended them to. He'd been so tired he'd crashed out early and gone to bed.

He opened the door and . . . hesitated. Should he risk it?

Here it was. What kind of man did he want to be? He stood there, the Black Wind around him.

He could easily be back in prison by morning.

He could get bashed for being on Davey's property without his permission.

Or . . . he could help Shelby.

Shivering, he scrambled to his car.

CHAPTER 11

AHAB

Ahab had not expected the phone call from Shelby Dempsey in the middle of the night – why would he? – but with De Corrado in tow, he'd driven straight to Homeward.

The local police were already out and working the scene, calling loudly to each other to be heard over the Black Wind. While De Corrado met up with them, Ahab decided to walk his own lap around the expansive mansion. The local cops acknowledged him and called him over, but he kept to himself, his torch beam crossing with theirs, the blue and red of the police lights setting the whole scene flickering.

His mind kept turning. He was concerned by what Shelby had told him – Davey was still missing. Forest's reappearance had left Ahab in an impossible position – he needed to work with the police while keeping Davey's drug business secret. Unless . . . should he tell De Corrado? Would it help bring Alexandra back?

No. Shelve it until you've spoken to Forest.

Ahab knew the criminal world, knew how it twisted and turned. If he revealed the Business right now . . . It would cause more harm than good, even if he could get through the layers of bribed cops Ivy had in place. What a bloody mess.

He ignored the rational voice at the back of his head that told him he was just making excuses because he wasn't ready to break his promise to his mother yet.

And why had he promised to *tell* De Corrado when he was lying? What good would that do *anyone*? He half suspected her of dosing his drink. How had he dropped his guard like that? And now he'd said it, he couldn't back down.

When he'd completed his lap, he returned to the side of the house. While most of the architecture was monolithic, there was a small alcove here, somewhat disguised by a trellis and climbing plants. To Ahab's eyes, the trellis's slats were a much heavier wood than Shelby's landscapers had used elsewhere. And he knew why.

His torch beam caught a bundle of broken leaves, then followed a path of destroyed greenery up to the roof. Someone had climbed this trellis, the broken stems marking out long strides.

He flicked off his torch, glanced around to make sure no one was watching, and began to climb, keeping to the same line, holding tight as the wind tried to pluck him off.

The roof of Homeward was a timber addition that reached right over the edge of the building, providing a spectacular entertaining area. There were a couple of police officers there right now, looking for footsteps in the rooftop garden beds.

Ahab knew the timber roof housed something else Davey had commissioned during its construction.

Staying as close as he could against the external wall, hoping no one saw him, he reached the slats of the gabling. Testing each, he found a disguised door. He pulled it open on its swinging hinge. Inside, he found a small enclosed area.

A drug dealer's bolthole.

He clambered inside, closed the door behind him and had a look around. A ceiling fan in the floor shone light up into the room.

It was like a miniature bomb shelter in there. It was carpeted, and there was a sleeping bag on top of a mattress. The room was stocked with canned food and water bottles and, hanging on the wall, a sawn-off shotgun and a Glock pistol. Since the firearms were in place, presumably Shelby's intruder hadn't found this room.

Ahab assumed that's why the intruder was in the roof: looking for the bolthole. Looking for Davey.

The space was dusty and smelled of soap. A peek through the ceiling fan showed that it was directly above the master bathroom. A rope was coiled in a heap beside the casing of the fan, attached to a support beam with a pulley mechanism. That would've been the way in from the house. Clever.

He froze when he heard another voice up in the roof. There was no way into this bolthole from the rest of the roof space, but someone was just on the other side of the dividing wall.

'Baz? Can you hear me? Am I near Shelby's bedroom?'

It was De Corrado's voice.

But who was Baz? It must've been her colleague, down in the house.

If he told them about this bolthole, then they'd know Davey was crooked . . .

No, he didn't need to tell them.

The intruder hadn't made it into the bolthole, and Davey wasn't there either. Then he thought of the warm coffee with the whisky, and something occurred to him – had Davey Dempsey been in here when Ahab had come calling?

It was time to get out of there. Checking the area was free of police, he swiftly climbed back out onto the trellis. The trapdoor swung shut behind him. Now he climbed down, his mind turning furiously.

Tell Jesse I'm sorry.

Davey Dempsey knew *something.*

So where the hell is he?

CHAPTER 12

MACKEREL

Mackerel stood on the gravel driveway, next to a huddle of neighbours drawn to the commotion at Homeward. All around them the Black Wind hummed.

He listened in as a woman spoke to her friend. 'Are you sure? I heard it was a peeping Tom, but Davey saw him and chased him off. Now both of them are missing —'

'No, I talked to the officer, he told me it was a journalist trying to get the scoop on Forest. The poor family. They've been through enough.'

'Why don't you all head home?' came a voice, causing the neighbours to jump. Mack spun to see Constable Linda, who flicked her torch back on. 'We've got this under control. Everyone go home. Except for you, Mack.'

Mackerel wished she hadn't said that in front of the neighbours. He was sure he was being added to the story being spun even as they walked back down the drive.

'You know I have to report any breach of your curfew,' Linda told him.

'Yeah, but . . . Shelby called me . . . I thought I could help.'

'I find that hard to believe.' Constable Linda had never been friendly with him, exactly, but finding him here had changed something in her tone. She stood there appraising him. 'You know, your brother hasn't come home all night.'

The accusation was clear in her voice. After all, the whole town thought Mackerel was jealous of his brother.

'I didn't do anything,' he said. 'I haven't seen him.'

'Your brother disappears, Shelby reports someone in the roof of their house, and now you're here . . .' She took a step towards him.

'I saw him show up, Linda,' came Ahab's voice. He approached and stood between the two of them. 'I can vouch for him.'

Linda nodded to Ahab. 'Right you are.' She turned to Mackerel. 'You're on thin ice, Mackerel. Don't blow it.'

'How about you leave seeing Mackerel out of your report, lass,' said Ahab. 'For me?'

'Don't call me lass,' said Linda. 'And if I do that, you owe me free drinks for a week.'

Once she'd left to continue her duties, Ahab gripped his shoulders. 'Are you okay?'

Ahab wasn't part of Mackerel's life anymore. He used to be, but Mackerel had to side with Davey when Ahab turned.

Truth was, Mackerel was proud of being related to Ahab. His cousin was fiercely respected by everyone in town but, more than that, he'd been deeply involved in the Business and yet had managed to get out. If Mackerel could've been like anyone, he'd want to be like Ahab.

'A lot has happened,' said Ahab, ice-blue eyes locked on him. 'I'm trying to help, Mackenzie. I have to understand what happened to Forest. Can you help me?'

'Ivy wouldn't —'

'Mackenzie,' said Ahab firmly. 'Look around you. *Look*, man.'

Mack dropped his eyes. He wondered how he must appear to Ahab right now, failure of a man that he was. Did Ahab think back to the chubby teenager he'd taught to scuba-dive, or taken camping, or given his first rifle? Did he regret wasting that time on him?

'Something is going *on* here,' said Ahab. 'Forest has returned, Davey is missing, there's an intruder in the house. If you hear anything about Forest – if he says anything to you – you have to tell me.'

'Okay. I will. I promise.'

'Good. You'd better get out of here, before Linda changes her mind.'

Ahab turned and walked away.

Mackerel watched him go, filled with a desire to chase after him and tell him about Blackbeard. But he stopped himself.

Ahab does everything he can to stay clear of the Business these days.

A moment later, Shelby barrelled into Mackerel's chest, hugging him tight. 'You came!'

Mackerel put his arms around her, holding her tight.

'Davey's still not home,' she whispered into his chest. 'Mack, I can't do this.'

'Shhh, it's okay.' He rubbed her back in small circles.

It felt strange to be holding a woman. Comforting her.

Back in Queensland, when he'd been running his crew, he'd been just as popular as Davey, just as charismatic. Maybe even more so. He'd been at the top of an upper-class drug ring, for fuck's sake. This brought back those memories. He liked that feeling.

Detective De Corrado walked towards them. Mackerel grimaced.

'Come inside and out of the wind, you two,' she said, not unkindly. 'We've found nothing in the area. I need to ask you some questions, Shelby. Maybe Mackenzie here can support you while you answer them.'

———

De Corrado and another detective, Barry Smith, now sat across from Shelby and Mackerel in the lounge.

The inside of Homeward smelled exactly how he remembered it, like honey candles and clean carpets. (Did clean carpets have a smell? He was sure they did.) The furniture had changed, the art on the walls had changed, the whole kitchen looked like it had been renovated, but the feeling inside was still the same. And even with the shitstorm of police officers everywhere, right then, inside his fancy mansion, on the couch beside Shelby, Mackerel had never felt more jealous of Davey in his life.

Kane sauntered in from outside, hands in the pockets of his flannelette pyjamas, looking down his nose at the officers in his house. He looked just like Ivy when he did that.

He sat down on the other side of Shelby, looping his arm in hers. 'I called Nan, she said she was gonna come back from Hobart, but I told her to stay there and be close to Forest. I told her we've got *enough* people looking after us, and that Uncle Mack was here to take care of you.' He gave Mackerel a grateful nod.

'I bet she was happy about that,' said Mackerel.

Kane shrugged. 'I told her you were brave to break your curfew. I think it's good you risked going back to prison to come look after Mum, and I told Nan that, too.'

Mackerel had to wipe the grin off his face.

Kane stayed on the couch with them as the detectives showed Shelby photos of shoeprints found in the dust in the roof. Mackerel resisted the urge to point out they didn't match his. They asked questions about the intruder, his tone of voice, any accent, did Shelby get a look at his face, would Shelby be able to pick him from a line-up?

With Mack and Kane on either side, she began to gather herself, detailing for the first time the full story.

Shelby had heard footsteps in the roof – they'd woken her up.

She'd rushed up to the rooftop garden to investigate, found no one, so ran back into the house. She flicked on all the lights, only to find a tall man with a balaclava just outside Kane's room. He'd seen her, and asked her where Davey was.

'He was so arrogant. Like he owned the house,' said Shelby, bristling.

'So what did you do?' said De Corrado.

'I didn't want Kane to come out, so I kept my voice down and told him the police were on their way. He called me a bitch and then scampered.'

'Always "bitch",' De Corrado said as an aside. 'When will they come up with a better one?'

'I could've taken him,' whispered Kane to Mackerel. 'I wish I'd heard them outside my door.'

'I bet you could have,' agreed Mackerel.

'So he was looking for Davey . . . any potential enemies in Davey's world?' said Detective Smith.

'What do you mean by his "world"?' said Shelby.

'His work sphere,' said Smith with a lazy grin.

'What do you mean by *his world*?' she said again. Shelby was too smart by half. 'What the hell are you implying?'

Mackerel's mind turned back to what De Corrado had said in the hospital. If she knew something about the Business, she had no way of proving it. And no one local would corroborate her story, not with Ivy having played defence for so long.

But De Corrado had no way of knowing Shelby was not involved in the slightest. He had to let her know. This was the last thing Shelby needed to find out tonight.

Behind Shelby's back, he caught De Corrado's eyes and shook his head an inch.

Smith had opened his mouth to reply, but De Corrado put a hand on his arm. 'I think it's best to let Mrs Dempsey sleep. She had a long day yesterday, and no sleep tonight. Mackenzie, allow me to escort you back to your premises. I believe you're in breach of your bail curfew. Mrs Dempsey, Detective Smith will remain here for the night. I noticed you have around 103 spare guest rooms, I'm sure he could stay in one.'

'It's a good idea,' said Mackerel to Shelby. He squeezed her arm. 'I'll talk to you tomorrow. We'll come up with something.'

'Why do you have to leave?' she said. 'You've already broken the curfew. What does it matter now?'

'Rules are rules.' He hugged her and, taking a risk, kissed her softly on the head. 'Take care of her,' he said to Kane.

Kane nodded, eyes on his mother. 'Do you want me to sleep in with you tonight, Mum?'

Mackerel let De Corrado lead him out of the house. He took two bottles of pinot as he walked by the shelves near the doorway – Davey wouldn't notice them missing.

Their footsteps crunched on the gravel as they walked to an unmarked BMW, parked right next to his third-hand hatchback.

'Sit in the front if you want, Mack,' she said. 'I'll get someone to drop your car off tomorrow morning. For now, I think you and I need to have a good little talk.'

He gave her directions to Big Mane's and she pulled away from the house.

'Talk to me, man. What do I need to know?'

'"His world",' said Mackerel to the window. 'Interesting phrase.'

'Can we skip the part where you lie to my face and I pretend to believe you? I'd like to get to where you give me some subtle clue that may or may not implicate your family.'

'I'd never implicate my family,' said Mackerel.

'Ah, so they *are* up to something?' countered De Corrado.

'No, not at all. Never have been, never will be. You'll not find a more upstanding family than the Dempseys of Shacktown. But . . . if they *were* involved in something . . . I promise you, Shelby would know nothing about it.'

'*Is* Davey crooked?' said De Corrado bluntly.

'No, of course not,' said Mackerel. 'But if he *were* . . . do you really think a woman like Shelby would have stuck around?'

'You actually sound like you believe what you're saying,' said De Corrado. 'I've seen the worst of human nature, Mackenzie. You'd be surprised what people will compromise on, in order to keep what they have. Look at that mansion, all that glittering finery. How far would you be willing to go to protect that? When you have it all – a big house, a family, respect, a smoking hot husband . . . don't give me that look . . . Mack, people will go a long way to protect their pretty things.'

'I've seen the worst of human nature too, detective,' said Mackerel softly. 'And Shelby isn't like that.'

They pulled up outside Big Mane's place – it was only a short drive from Homeward. He hoped Big Mane hadn't stayed up for him. He'd taken his role as Mack's best friend very seriously, and fretted about him whenever Mackerel took risks. Like breaching curfew.

She turned the car off. The wind blew so hard the car rocked, giving the inside an almost cosy air. 'You know, you talk a lot more when you're not around your family,' said De Corrado. 'Back at the hospital I thought you must've had a speech impediment or something. But listen to you, you speak beautifully.' She was patronising him.

'I'm used to talking to cops,' he said. 'There's something about never being believed that I find fun.'

'You know that if your brother is up to something, I'll find out,' she said.

'That's just a bluff,' said Mackerel. 'You're here about Forest, not Davey.'

De Corrado looked at him intently, her face softly illuminated by the streetlight. 'The problem is you're so good at lying, you're even lying to yourself.'

'Heard that one before,' he said. He passed her one of the bottles of pinot. 'Want one?'

'I don't take bribes, so if you tell anyone I accepted this, I'll lie,' said De Corrado, taking the bottle from him and admiring it.

She nodded towards the house. 'Sounds like Ahab got you off the hook for breaching your bail conditions. A man with that kind of power in a small town, it makes you wonder, doesn't it? Well, anyway, I wouldn't count on him being there to save you if it happens again.'

'Thanks for the ride, detective,' said Mackerel, undoing his seatbelt. 'Remember what I told you about Shelby.'

'*You* remember what I said about Shelby,' she said. 'And all those stories you have to tell? When you learned how bad human nature can be? If you ever want to sit down over a beer and talk about them, let me know. I'd be fascinated to hear what you saw in Brisbane. Full disclosure, it's mostly so I can build up a better picture of your family. But I reckon you'll know how to manipulate the conversation to keep me in the dark on the important facts.'

'And you get to claim the cost of the beers as a work expense,' said Mackerel.

'You *have* been around the traps, haven't you?'

'Sweet dreams, detective,' he said, and stepped out into the wind.

His smile faded as he walked in the front door, kicking his shoes off. He couldn't stop thinking about what she'd said. *A woman like Shelby.*

The smell of Big Mane's house – that male musk and deodorant smell – contrasted so much with Shelby's honey candles. The wallpaper, peeling and bubbled and a startling shade of pale green. Threadbare carpet with a path worn down the middle.

He didn't care. It was home. He was glad to be there with Big Mane. But there was no denying it was worlds away from Homeward.

Lights flicked on in the hallway and Big Mane came stumbling out of his bedroom, wrapping a dressing-gown around himself. 'You good, bro?'

He rested a hand on the wall. He was still a bit drunk – although Big Mane could drink all day and all night and never so much as get a headache.

'Let's get those beers going,' said Mack. He held up the pinot. 'I need to get blind.'

Big Mane grinned. 'I thought you'd never ask.'

He and Big Mane settled down in the lounge room, the Xbox powering on and a carton of cans on the floor in front of them, Big Mane's tunes already pumping from the speaker.

Still Mackerel thought of Shelby. She wasn't just some trophy wife, she was smart – he knew she'd gone to university and studied chemistry, she could've gone far with it if she'd chosen to – she loved her husband, spoiled Kane, helped run junior footy, gave back to the school community.

Davey, like all the Dempseys, was an *excellent* liar. Sometimes that's all it came down to.

'Whatever it is, stop thinking about it,' said Big Mane, pouring them each a generous glass of the pinot. 'You said you were getting blind tonight.'

What was it De Corrado had said?

Sometimes you can get so good at lying, you lie even to yourself.

CHAPTER 13

MACKEREL

'Mack . . . wake up.'

Mackerel was hungover – blinking against the light, he had an instant headache.

Big Mane crouched beside him, shaking his shoulder.

'Mane . . . I don't think I can work today,' said Mack.

'I'm sorry, bro,' said Big Mane. 'I've . . . I've got news.'

'Wha—'

'They . . . they found your brother . . .' Big Mane caught himself. 'Bro, I'm so sorry. They found him floating in Devils Kitchen. He's . . . he's gone, bro.'

Mack lurched upright, the nausea fighting the headache for his attention.

'Who? Jesse?'

'No . . . no, they've found Davey.'

'Are they helping him?'

'Mate, it's not . . . they can't . . .'

'Who's running the rescue?'

'Mack, the Black Wind – there's no way boats can get down there, never mind a chopper. It's no good, bro.'

'I'm going,' said Mackerel.

Mackerel forced himself to the front of the crowd at the viewing platform. He looked down, down, down at the swirl of dangerous water at the bottom of the cliff, whipped into a nightmare by the Black Wind, and felt his hangover nausea roll. Waves the size of boats sloshed against the rocks, shooting up spray, followed by a monstrous sucking sound as whirlpools formed in their wake.

He noticed who stood beside him. It was Chips, twisting her baseball cap in her hand, tears rolling down her cheeks.

He couldn't understand why she was crying. Davey wasn't dead yet. He had his scuba gear. He would be fine.

Big Mane, moving in Mackerel's wake, took a pair of binoculars off a nearby teenage girl. 'It's his brother down there,' he said, and she immediately drew back. A bubble of space opened around Mackerel, Chips and Big Mane. Even the locals made space.

Why were they all being nice to him all of a sudden?

'I really thought he'd live forever,' said Chips.

Mackerel, his hoodie whipping in the pitch of the wind, took the binoculars and focused on the point of colour down there, swallowing another rush of nausea as his eyes disagreed with the shift in perspective.

A lifeless form was being tossed around in the waves, buoyed by diving gear.

The tiger-stripe wetsuit had been ripped to shreds by the rocks, blood frothing pink in the white foam. Davey's distinctive Mares Phantom wetsuit had yellow and black stripes, designed to scare off sharks. And it was his custom diving gear: glinting gold, shipped in from South America. And there, where the sleeve was ripped from his arms – those were his tattoos.

It was definitely Davey.

'There's no way they'll be able to retrieve the body,' said Big Mane. 'I'm sorry.'

Mack tore his eyes away, pushing the binoculars into Big Mane's chest, and ran towards the police officers as fast as his limp allowed. They were making a vague attempt at crowd control, Constable Linda at their head, dark rings under her eyes – she looked as though she'd slept about as well as Mackerel had.

'What's being done?' he demanded.

'Mackerel . . . I . . .' Her face fell at the sight of him. Gone was the hard tone of the night before. 'There's no way we can safely retrieve the body. I'm so, so sorry. We'd just lose —'

Big Mane jogged up behind Mackerel.

Mackerel pushed him towards his car. 'Take me to your boat.'

Big Mane went pale. 'No, mate, you can't possibly think of going in there.'

'Just get me as close as you can and then I'll dive. The deeper you go, the weaker the cross-current.'

'Mack, you'll be killed!'

'He's my *brother*!'

'The police have divers, let them do it!'

'They won't risk it with the Wind like this, but they don't know this water like I do. I'm twice the diver they are. I'm doing it, with or without you.'

'Mate, I don't think you are,' said Big Mane. 'You're not thinking straight. You drank a shitload last night. This is nuts! No one's gonna take you out there.'

'I will,' said a voice.

It was Ahab.

Big Mane ducked his head.

'My whole life, I've met maybe five people who move better under the water than they do above,' said Ahab, eyeing Mackerel, 'and Mackenzie is one of them. Let's go, cousin.'

On the water, the drone of the Black Wind was louder. It snatched and thrust across the rigid inflatable, the only type of boat that could withstand the cross-seas for any stretch of time. And, fortunately, it was already primed for scuba diving.

Ahab, dressed in full scuba gear, his mask around his neck, stood at the controls. He was calm, even in the Black Wind. He knew how to navigate it – there was no finer skipper in all of Pirates Bay, as far as Mackerel knew. The only way through the Black Wind was with a small, manoeuvrable boat like this, and it only worked if you stayed near the cliffs, where at least one side of you was safe from waves.

Even still, there was only so much Ahab could do in mitigation of the risk. There was every chance they'd roll or sink. That's why he was wearing his dive gear too. It would be no picnic, but if they sank, he could swim back to the shore along the bottom of the ocean, where the currents weren't as strong and the seaweed offered hand-holds whenever the water tried to suck you away.

Mackerel was already in his own wetsuit and gear, the weight of his buoyancy control device vest – the BC – a familiar pressure across his chest. He was comfortable with the boat pitching and rolling under his feet, but he was eager to be in the water, his true home.

They stopped just short of the opening to Devils Kitchen. Rugged formations soared above Mackerel's head, like the columns of some Egyptian temple.

'Go!' called Ahab.

Mackerel put his regulator into his mouth, made the okay symbol with his hand, and fell backwards into the ocean.

At first he floated on the surface, immediately feeling his muscles relax at the touch of the water, icy cold trickling down through the seal around the back of his neck and sending a shiver through his body. He released air from the BC and began to sink, the water line covering his mask and head in a moment.

He was under.

Down and down.

Breathe in, bubbles out.

He equalised as he went – blocking his nose and blowing to release pressure in his ears.

The cool, soft sea accepted him as it always did. As though he were just another creature of the salt water.

Calm. Peace.

Focus.

They said you could become addicted to the bubbles of scuba diving. It calmed all his senses. Forced him to focus on the moment. It made him feel alone in a way that he didn't mind.

Stuck in prison, Mackerel had missed diving the most. He'd tried and failed to explain to his cellmate how it made him feel. The meditative state of it, how all his problems stayed behind on land.

Breathe in, bubbles out.

The pressure-cool expanse of everything that drives our blue planet. The loud rush of bubbles, the hiss of the regulator, the clicks of the water. The ever-rolling movement of ocean and light. He felt the push against his fins, the pull of the weight pouches built in to his BC. He was expert at modulating his buoyancy, using the BC vest or even just by breathing in and out.

He dived deeper through a sway of brown bull kelp, away from the turmoil of the surface. He heard the thud of Ahab's motor above, powering away, back to safety.

Now Mackerel really was alone. It was stupid to dive without a partner, but Mackerel wasn't afraid.

Once he got to Davey, his escape plan was a wide underwater tunnel that moved through into the base of Tasmans Arch, which had a shallow shelf where Mackerel could wait and be winched to safety.

It was not a pretty plan, but it was the best he could come up with in a hurry. On land, it had seemed barely possible. But here, under the water, it seemed perfectly sane.

He swam forward, through another curtain of the giant kelp and past the crag that signalled the opening of Devils Kitchen, a flurry of opal-coloured parrot fish swimming the other way. The suction from the ocean was less the further he descended, but the sound above was still ferocious, the water slamming and thundering against rocks.

Breathe in, bubbles out.

He powered on his diving light, angling through the slanting bubble foam and torn shreds of floating seaweed.

Then he saw it.

A diving rope, lined with reflector strips. It ran from an opening in the kelp-lined wall that signified one of the many submarine tunnels, right up to the surface of the Kitchen.

He pulled the rope, trying to haul it towards himself. The current spun him around – without something to brace himself on, he didn't have a hope.

He swam for where the line reached the cave and set himself inside, bracing his fins on the rock, then began to reel it in.

It was tough work, the rope fighting his pulling. He dragged it towards the cave entrance, focusing on calm breaths, his arms straining against the resistance of the water, releasing air from his BC to compensate.

The sea shifted and danced, silt and sand stirred up by the wind. Through the haze he saw something approaching him, tied to the end of the rope.

It was someone. A person.

He yanked again.

Closer now . . . a glint of gold. A tiger-stripe pattern.

It was Davey!

He wasn't moving. His tattooed arm was limp.

It was Davey's body.

Davey was dead.

Breathe in . . . just breathe in . . . no, no, no, please, God, don't take my brother away . . .

He had a rush of memory, of diving this exact place with Davey. Spear-hunting fish, the comfort of each other under the sea, sharing their kills on a smoky driftwood fire under a brilliant Milky Way sky . . .

His brother was dead. No matter what good Mackerel did now, no matter how he tried to change his life, he would never have those moments with his brother again. He'd fucked that up, hadn't he? Like he fucked everything up. Now his brother would never be able to say he forgave him. His brother would never be able to tell him he loved him.

Suddenly he sensed a strange shift in the pressure. Mackerel's instinct kicked in. Something had been in the tunnel behind him. Now it was coming for him.

He dodged just in time to see a hand dart past him, a diving blade glinting in its grasp.

Mackerel spun and twisted, pushing himself away from the cave entrance as hard as he could. He used slimy yellow kelp as a hand-hold as the swell moved in and around him, his vision obscured by seaweed and silt, light and foam.

He caught a glimpse of Davey's body shooting back to the boiling surface, the line still holding him in place.

The figure from the cave followed him, mirroring Mackerel's movements, but then paused. The man's diving mask was tinted – Mack couldn't see his face.

Mackerel pulled out his own diving knife. He wanted to see this man's face before he killed him. Because surely he was the one responsible for Davey's death, putting his body on display. He would be willing to kill Mackerel to keep his identity secret. It'd be a fight to the death.

So why wasn't the man moving?

Breathe in, bubbles out.

The man's face tilted, glancing up at Davey's body, then back at Mackerel. He held out his knife to signal his aggression.

Underwater you could make no demands, couldn't curse or threaten. This was just hunting. This was fishing.

Mackerel considered the knife in his own hand. If he could dislodge the assailant's mask, he'd have the upper hand – it was hard to see underwater without a mask.

It'd be easier to aim for the man's breather, but he didn't want him dead and drowned. He wanted answers.

Mackerel felt water gathering behind him, a surge. He sensed the pressure as it approached and released his grip on the kelp, letting the water propel him towards his assailant.

The man, rather than bringing his own knife to parry, tried to twist away.

But Mackerel was quick. His knife clipped the man across the forehead, missing the mask and digging into his diving hood, drawing a deep cut.

He'd only had that one shot. Now the current was sweeping him away. Mackerel hooked his arm around the line holding Davey's body and sawed it through with his knife. He released some of his own buoyancy, letting his weight drag him deeper into the trench, away from the surges close to the surface, dragging Davey's body down with him.

He swam for the tunnel to Tasmans Arch. His escape route.

Then he felt the resistance on the line loosen.

Davey fell past him like a rock, his BC burst and spewing bubbles, disappearing into the kelp, down into the crevasses that made up the floor of the trench. Down there at the bottom the current moved and tumbled in and out of a hundred rocky channels. Davey's body would get shredded to pieces as it was sucked out into the depths.

Davey . . . no . . .

Mackerel looked up.

The assailant was floating, perhaps three metres away, but not drawing closer.

Mackerel had one thought.

Get him.

He took a full breath to change his buoyancy, sensing the movement of the current, seeing the swirl of the kelp, and again launched himself towards the man, kicking with all his strength.

The assailant turned and swam away. He headed for the entrance to another tunnel, which Mackerel knew would lead him into one of the many systems of sea caves, here in the cliffs. But Mackerel knew those caves intimately; he had practically grown up in them.

But this man clearly knew them as well. *And* the other man was stronger than Mackerel, faster.

Now Mack sensed something else, a different kind of pressure building behind him. A new twisting shift in the current, one he hadn't felt before.

A feeling of terror broke through the calm of the bubbles.

The waves crashing against the cliffs were forming a whirlpool.

Mackerel had just forced his arms in through the opening tunnel and wedged himself in a frond of rock when he felt the pull of the whirlpool sucking his legs back out, twisting one of his fins like a broken rudder. Mackerel unlatched it from his foot, before his ankle was broken, and the fin was sucked away into the dark below.

He wedged himself in tighter, forcing himself to stay calm.

Breathe in, bubbles out.

His ears hummed with the change in pressure, silver baitfish and shreds of kelp flying past, the sound of the whirlpool deafening, until finally the current stabilised and Mackerel felt the backwash flowing into the cave. He lunged forward, letting himself be carried along, reaching for the next safe recess in the rock.

He knew this tunnel, and now, the further he got from Devils Kitchen, the weaker the pull of the whirlpool behind him, his diving torch lighting the way through the murky dark. He couldn't panic – if he panicked, he'd become disoriented and be lost in there for good.

With each surge and each ebb, he had to wedge himself into new holes. Slowly, slowly. But not so slow that he would run out of air. His rapid breathing had been using it up at an alarming rate. The whirlpool's roar was terrifying.

Finally he reached the end of the tunnel, where the current barely moved, a little place to rest before the cavern opened out into Waterfall Bay.

But his assailant was in here, too, curled up near the exit.

Breathe in, bubbles out.

The man saw Mackerel and fled, leaving behind a rush of bubbles from his flippers and regulator.

Mackerel struggled to swim with his single fin. He didn't have a chance of catching him.

Once he was out of the tunnel and into Waterfall Bay he was swept up again. He breached the surface. He had to orient himself, but the cross-hatch waves were like a washing machine. He struggled to hold his mask and regulator in place.

This wasn't the way out he had planned – the water was much wilder here – but he had to track down Davey's killer. He knew a place where he could leave the water and he did his best to head that way, ducking under the waves rather than over the top of them.

He was heading to the near side of the bay, where there was a shelf of rock which sloped up out of the sea.

But when one wave caught him by surprise and lifted him high in its crest, he saw his destination – his assailant was there, clambering out of the water onto it.

This man had to be a local, to know about that shelf.

Mackerel dived back under and swam, lopsided and kicking against the current, mostly in vain. A heavy wave crashed right above him – it must have been a white wall – and his regulator was wrenched from his face.

Another giant wave forced him down, pulling at his remaining fin. He unbuckled it, the calm he'd felt earlier quickly evaporating, as he was smashed down again and held under.

His mask gone now too, he grabbed his spare regulator – calm breaths – and put air into his BC, shooting himself to the surface.

He kicked and kicked, straining already depleted muscles, trying to get closer to the shelf, where the cross-waves couldn't push him back out to sea. He had the regulator, he had his BC, he was fine . . .

He searched for the shelf, panic threatening to swamp him. And then, finally, he caught the right wave, as the cold water pulled back and then threw him forward.

He slammed against the shelf. Scrabbling, he clung his fingers to the rocky clefts as the water tried to suck him back. Exhausted, he slipped out of his BC vest, relieved to feel the weight fall off him, letting all of his gear go.

Where was his assailant? He was nowhere to be seen.

No, there he was. Halfway up the cliff.

He was climbing a rope ladder, hoisting it up behind himself as he went so Mackerel couldn't follow.

Mackerel was stranded. It wouldn't be long before one of the white-wall waves crashed onto the shelf and sucked him away.

He pushed himself up against the cliff face as a wave slammed onto the shelf and sucked away his BC.

He shouted up at the assailant, curses and murder. The man still wore his hooded wetsuit and scuba mask. He wasn't taking any risks – he didn't want Mack to recognise him.

Whoever he was, he'd intentionally put Davey's body in Devils Kitchen, for everyone to see. It made no sense.

Mackerel clung to the cliff. Without the calm of the bubbles, he was just a normal bloke. Scared shitless and waiting to die. One big wave and he was done.

But when the assailant reached the top of the cliff, without even looking back, he threw the ladder back down.

For Mackerel.

Mackerel wasted no time, shimmying up the rope latter as fast as his dud leg allowed, a terrifying ascent as the ladder swung in the wind, scratching his arms on the rough rock, the Black Wind whistling through his ears and sucking at his breath.

Finally, he reached the top.

His assailant was long gone.

Mackerel slumped to the ground, pulling in breaths, clinging to the earth. Dry land. Safe.

And all around him, the Black Wind hummed her song.

Davey's dead . . .

He broke.

CHAPTER 14

AHAB

It was late afternoon at Ivy's house and Ahab stood inside, for the first time in years. He leaned against the doorpost of the corridor, peering into the lounge room, itching for a cigarette. The room was filled with family – distant cousins, aunts, uncles, from both Joel's side and Ivy's side – who spilled out of the open double doors and onto the timber deck.

Dempseys were big on having family nearby in times of crisis. Because Ahab had played a role in the attempt to retrieve Davey's body, Ivy tolerated his presence, if only for a short time. Ahab was sure it was only to save face. She paced near the doors, walking inside and out, inside and out, biting the head off anyone who looked at her. She'd been the same at the memorial service for Jesse, Alexandra and Forest, when they'd been declared legally dead.

Forest had returned to the family yesterday, filling a hole. Now Davey had been wrenched away.

Jesse and Davey. Two sons. Both of them claimed by the sea . . . and, Ahab suspected, by the Business.

He felt sorry for Ivy. Imagine being in control of everyone around you, and yet still losing that which was most precious. It was unimaginable . . .

It had been many years since Ahab had buried his own son. The boy had only been six months old when Ahab watched that little coffin get covered with dirt, but he felt the loss of all the years his son hadn't lived just as keenly as if the boy had died at age thirty. To have to do that not once, but twice . . . well, that's why Ahab and the boy's mother had broken up – he could not go through that again.

Some people recovered from that pain. But some people weren't cursed.

And when little Forest had disappeared, it had nearly broken him all over again.

He's back. Forest is back. You don't have to grieve him ever again . . .

Ahab hated grief. He hated being around it. He wanted to get out of there, return to his inn and his dog. And he felt guilty, because as much as he was sad for Davey, he felt another emotion . . .

Frustration.

Now he might never know why Davey had written that note . . .

Tell Jesse I'm sorry.

Davey had known something about Forest's reappearance, and the wording implied he suspected Jesse was still alive. Was *he* responsible for Davey's death? Ahab wondered how Ivy would react if that was the case; losing one son for another.

Mackenzie, Shelby and Kane were huddled together in the middle of the lounge room's huge L-shaped couch. Shelby's face was dull and flat, wet with tears and sweat. Kane had his head in her lap, looking like a young boy again, crying enough to break any man's heart. Mackenzie sniffled, drawn into himself, shaking. His hair was still wet from the ocean. Ahab felt a stirring of fierce satisfaction – Mackenzie had made him very proud today.

But why would Davey go scuba diving when the Black Wind had been blowing all day and all night? He wouldn't, not unless he'd lost his mind.

So who put Davey in Devils Kitchen?

Ahab needed a cigarette.

He looked around until he caught sight of Detective De Corrado, a beer in her hand, talking to one of Ivy's cousins. He should break his promise and tell her about the Business.

He *really* needed a cigarette.

He stepped outside but stayed on the far side of the porch, leaning against the corner of Safe Harbour. The crashing waves nearby, the call of seagulls, and a calmer sea breeze. The Black Wind had stopped. The sea had returned to normal, as though it had accepted Davey as a sacrifice.

Even now, police divers were trying to retrieve his body. From what Mackenzie had hinted at, Davey's body had sunk into the crevasses of the rocky ocean floor and been swept out by the current. He doubted they had any hope.

A few minutes later Ahab saw Mackenzie step outside, vape in hand, heading down towards the shoreline.

'Mack,' Ahab called.

Mackenzie turned, dazed. It seemed as though he had no idea where he was, what he was doing, where he should go . . .

'I'm just going to have a vape,' said Mackenzie, holding it up. 'Is that okay?'

'You don't need my permission, son. I just wanted to say I was proud of you, for what you did today. Going after your brother.'

Mackenzie's face screwed up. He turned away. 'I failed him.'

'You couldn't have saved him . . .'

'Ahab . . .' Mack's voice lowered. 'Someone else was down there with me.'

'What?' Ahab pulled Mackenzie away from the house so they wouldn't be overheard. 'What are you talking about?'

'There was someone down there. They attacked me!' Mackenzie furtively sucked on his vape. 'Davey was all tied up, and then out of a tunnel . . . I couldn't see his face! His mask was all . . . Ahab, I think Blackbeard is here. Sal – at the café, Sal told me that h-he's making a move. I think Blackbeard got to Davey.'

The Dread Pirate Blackbeard? Here in Shacktown?

Here in my town.

Ahab released a breath, puffing out his cheeks. If Blackbeard was in town, or at least someone trying to *be* Dread Pirate Blackbeard – the whole point of the moniker was to introduce an element of confusion and uncertainty – then Mack was right. There was every chance he'd murdered the local drug kingpin. Poor Davey. It would have been like a knife in the dark.

'I'd always hoped Blackbeard was just a myth,' he said, lighting another cigarette. 'Salvatore is sure?'

Mack nodded, sucking on his vape. A weight had left him – he looked at Ahab with complete confidence that his cousin would now take care of the situation.

'So you think Blackbeard put his body there as a . . . as a what? As a sign that he's here? As a *warning*?' said Ahab.

'Maybe.'

For now, Chips would be able to keep the Business running, but if Blackbeard really was making a move, she'd be too short on respect and experience to hold power for long.

And why did Blackbeard strike right when Forest reappeared?

'You need to tell someone,' said Ahab. 'You need to tell the police.'

'No,' said Mackenzie, a Dempsey's default response to any mention of the police. 'Ivy would kill me! And Shelby . . . the truth would ruin her.'

'It's already ruined her!' Ahab said sternly. 'She deserves to know why her husband died. As far as she's concerned, he was a law-abiding citizen. She *deserves* the truth. And she needs to know that the money she's been relying on for so long is about to dry up.' A realisation hit him. 'Mack, if the person in her roof was one of Blackbeard's men . . .'

'N-No, Ahab,' said Mackenzie. 'We can't do this to her. *Please*.'

He looked terrified. Ahab couldn't blame the poor man, but the reality was he'd have to learn to adapt, and fast.

'Mack, you need to think way bigger picture. With Davey dead, you're next in line for the throne.' He made Mackenzie meet his eyes. 'All of Dempsey Abalone will be passed down to you.'

'No, it won't,' said Mackenzie desperately. 'It all goes to someone else.'

A great wave of weariness rolled over Ahab. 'You're right,' he said. 'It falls to Forest.'

CHAPTER 15

FOREST

It was dinnertime in the Royal Hobart Hospital, and Forest was sweating.

He sat at the cramped bedside table, across from Frankie, who was observing him closely with those cat-like eyes. She'd brought dinner up to his room, roast chicken and gravy potatoes, and insisted on eating together. She'd done the same thing at breakfast, when Ivy had planned to visit but had instead 'returned to Shacktown for an emergency'.

An emergency . . . Forest hoped that Huck hadn't done something stupid.

Eating dinner under the harsh lights of the hospital room, he wondered how Frankie knew that mealtime was such a weak point for him. After so many days of starving and countless missed meals, he could never bring himself to turn down food – and that made it hard for him to keep his defences up while he ate.

So he ate as fast as he could, hating the knowing look that came into her eyes as he did so. What was she reading into it? He was rambling about something – he checked back into himself, the words rolling off his lips like a script. Ah, he was talking about primary school.

The only consolation he had was that, whatever it was she thought of his responses to her questions, whatever analysis she was forming, it was wrong.

But that didn't mean she couldn't complicate things for him.

'How was that?' said Frankie, the instant he took the final bite of potato. She had left half her meal uneaten.

'Good,' he said around that last mouthful. 'Thank you.'

'Well, Forest . . . I have some news you need to hear . . .'

He put his fork down. 'What is it?'

'I'm sorry to be the one to tell you this . . . but your uncle, Davey, was found dead this morning.'

What . . . ?

The lights grew brighter. A ringing began in his ears.

'Forest?'

'How did he die?'

'Drowned. A scuba-diving accident.'

A weird sensation went through his body. He felt like all his limbs belonged to someone else.

He avoided Frankie's eyes. He couldn't deal with her being here, not right now. X-raying him, peppering him with questions.

'I'd like to be alone now,' he said.

Zeus sensed his unease and climbed off the bed to put his head in Forest's lap.

'Hmm . . . first I'll need something new I can tell the police.' She said it matter-of-factly, with full certainty he'd provide what she was asking for. She'd almost caught him out with that trick twice already – she'd wait until he was caught off-guard, then ask for information with such confidence that he almost obliged without thinking.

'I don't have anything,' said Forest. 'Goodnight, Frankie.'

'They're still after information – they need to know something new, Forest.'

He stood up, still feeling that weird sensation, and walked over to the bed as best he could. He climbed under the covers and Zeus jumped up beside him.

'Alright. I understand, Forest. Thank you, Forest. Goodnight, Forest,' she said.

The dog wagged his tail once.

Frankie flicked off the lights and closed the door behind her without another word, leaving the room in darkness save for the city lights filtering through the hospital blinds.

Davey was dead.

Did his death have something to do with Forest's return?

It had to. The coincidence was too great.

Which meant Forest had killed him. However indirectly, he was responsible for a man's death.

He had to get out of there – he wouldn't learn a thing from this hospital room.

And he had to get to Huck.

He counted to one hundred before climbing out from under the covers. Underneath his bed, neatly folded, were a black hoodie, jeans and sneakers. He'd had one of the nurses bring them to him that morning – he'd spun her a story about how vulnerable he felt in his hospital gown, how naked, and how he would feel better in some clothes that were his favourite colour, black. Maybe something with a hood, so he could pull it over his head when he felt scared, some comfy shoes . . . She'd eaten it up.

Quickly and quietly, he got dressed, putting spare pillows underneath the doona.

'I'll be back soon, Zeus,' he said. 'Sorry I can't bring you with me. I'll try to be back before dawn. Just go to sleep.'

Zeus wuffed.

This would be the tricky part. The bathroom window was small, but it was set right beside a fire escape. The main window, out in his room, was too far from the fire escape, and they'd notice right away if he knocked out all that glass . . .

He wrapped his fist in a towel and smashed the glass, trying to get as many of the tinkling shards to fall inside the room as possible. When that was done, he climbed up on the toilet, laid towels around the window frame and squeezed himself through.

The drop to the street was dizzying, and the warm smoky-salt smell of Hobart in the summer hit him hard after the antiseptic scent of his room. He curled his fingers around the side of the fire escape and clung on with all his strength, climbing around to the other side until he could hop down onto the landing.

His impact on the metal made a clang that froze him in place. Voices stirred from inside a nearby window. He scurried down the stairs and onto the street.

He pulled his hoodie over his head, shoes slapping against the footpath.

Free.

And no one was coming to save him. He was in this alone.

He could still walk away from it all. He could go anywhere, do what he wanted. There were no nurses checking in on him, no police, no Frankie trying to pry secrets from his head. No one for him to disappoint.

In fact, no one even looked at him. Strangers passed without a second glance. People ate inside restaurants, living whole lives that had nothing to do with Forest. Cars drove by and didn't stop. No one out here cared what he did or didn't say, what he did or didn't do. It was tempting, there was no denying it. But there was something he had to do.

He jogged all the way to St David's Park. Scabs on his legs cracked open, but he didn't care.

He made his way to the oak tree, the sight of it etched in his memory. He climbed, the rough bark tugging at the bandages on his fingers, until he reached the hollow: the bum bag was exactly where he'd left it.

He let out a massive sigh of relief. He'd half expected it to be gone.

He checked inside – it still had all the cash he'd saved up, plus a detailed map of Shacktown and surrounds.

As he made his way down to Salamanca, his mind flicked through everything he'd learned about the Dempseys. He mentally rehearsed every trick he'd need to get through to each of them.

When he got to the square, he hailed a taxi. He'd stashed away more than enough cash to pay the fare all the way to Shacktown.

CHAPTER 16

MACKEREL

Night had fallen and heavy rain pounded on the roof of Safe Harbour, echoing everyone's emotions. Some of the family were still there, but most had long gone. Davey's memorial would be held in a week, when they promised to return.

Mackerel sat alone on the deck, just under the awning, watching the rain pooling on the timber slats, reflecting the houselights. Curfew was closing in – he'd need to head back to Big Mane's soon.

He nursed a can of beer that had grown warm in his hands. He didn't want to feel anymore, but he didn't want to be hungover in the morning either. He blamed his hangover on why he hadn't been able to stop the assailant in Devils Kitchen. It was his fault that Davey's murder would go unsolved.

He felt weird in his head – with everything that had gone on, he'd missed his meds for the day. No painkillers. No opiates. No antidepressants. The worst day of his life was not a good time to be missing his meds. Maybe that's why he was out here alone, trying to get fresh air. He couldn't stand being around so many people. Without his opiates, his mind went a little screwy. He should really try to detox, but the half-life of Suboxone made coming off it harder than coming off heroin.

He wasn't really listening to the rumble of the voices inside the house, but now they rose. He heard his name. Ivy was speaking.

'. . . an ice addict! He once thought there was a transmitter in his ear and a Mafia sniper on his trail,' she said. '*Drug psychosis*. Another time he was hospitalised because he tried to dig an imaginary tracker out of his forearm. You wouldn't believe the mess. *Then*, he turned on his *brother*.'

'That's ancient history. He's family!' Shelby was defending him. 'Someone should've told me he was out of jail, that he was here in Shacktown!'

'*All* he's ever done for our family is cause problems. There's a reason that runts don't survive out in the wild.'

'We're *not* animals,' said Shelby. 'I can't believe you'd talk about your own son like that! He's the only one you've got left!'

'Don't remind me,' snapped Ivy. 'I'd happily exchange him for either!'

'You don't mean that,' said Shelby after a long pause.

Mackerel stood up, stepping out into the rain.

Yes, she did.

He was too tired for tears. He didn't care anymore. It was time to go home – maybe he *would* get absolutely maggot drunk. He sculled the rest of his beer and crunched the can, leaving it on Ivy's lawn.

Runt of the litter. Black sheep. Weak as piss. Embarrassing little fat Mackerel. To survive in the underworld, you had to be hard. That's what Ivy had taught him, back when he was first inducted to the true nature of the family. Everyone agreed that Mackerel was too soft. Too weak. Too stupid.

They all made it their mission to make him hard. For his own good. He couldn't remember when exactly it had turned to cruelty.

He liked to think that Ivy had loved him, once. But somewhere along the way she'd played the part of delivering tough love so well that she just kept going.

That's what he told himself. It helped him not to hate her. Somewhere, deep down, his mum loved him.

If he could give himself up to bring back Davey, or even Jesse, that psychopath, he would. If only so, just once, he could have done something right for her.

The rain was cold and heavy, running down the back of his neck. It reminded him of being under water, sea water trickling into his wetsuit. For the briefest moment he thought about walking up to Devils Kitchen and jumping in. Then he faced the other way and limped down onto the beach, stopping to listen to the waves and the slap of raindrops in the gumtrees. He began the slow walk up to Big Mane's, wishing that the ocean would rise and sweep him away.

Mackerel stared at the bunk above. He was warm from the shower and feeling dizzy from the beer, the pain in his knee finally masked. Big Mane had picked up on his mood the moment Mack walked in the door and knew to leave him alone. He'd stumbled straight into the shower, stopping only to bring a six-pack with him.

Mack wished he had his own place. Somewhere he didn't have to talk to anyone. It was tricky living with Big Mane, being bailed and curfewed here. He always felt like he owed him something, when the last thing he wanted was to owe the world another debt.

But Big Mane knew that, and respected it.

You're lucky to have a friend like that. You don't deserve him.

Even as he was thinking that, Big Mane appeared at the door to his room. He looked pale but excited. Big Mane had looked just like that the day before, when he'd told him Forest had been found.

'What have you got to tell me now, Mane?' he asked drunkenly.

'Bro . . . you're not gonna believe this . . . Forest Dempsey is here?'

Mackerel sat up, his vision swimming. 'Huh?'

And suddenly there he was. Forest Dempsey. Hair drenched by the rain, wearing a black hoodie, blue eyes in a gaunt face.

In Mack's *bedroom*.

Big Mane pulled the door shut as he left.

'W-What are you doing here?' said Mackerel. He was hallucinating. He was too drunk . . . The missed meds were messing with him . . .

Forest sat cross-legged on the floor, pulling his hoodie off, his blonde hair still too long. He looked sad and defeated.

'Hello, Uncle Mack.'

Forest's return to the world was a little glowing coal of hope in the depressing shit that surrounded Davey's death and Blackbeard's arrival. So why did Mackerel want to cry, just looking at him?

He scrambled under the bed, looking for another beer. His hand seized on one and he cracked it open. He couldn't cope with all of this right now. He chugged most of it in one go.

'Sorry,' he said, wiping his mouth. 'Why are you here, buddy?'

'They were keeping me locked up in that hospital.' He shivered and folded his arms around himself. 'I *won't* be locked up again.'

Locked up. Tattooed. Beaten. Tortured?

'Why are you *here*?' Mackerel said. 'H-how did you *get* here?'

'I stole some money. I hired a taxi.'

'You *stole* —'

'You're the only one I can trust,' Forest said. 'The . . . the shells told me.'

'What?' Mack stood up, banging his head on the bottom of the bunk above *yet again*. He swore loudly, spilling beer.

'You're the only one I can trust,' repeated Forest, careful eyes on Mack. 'And I'm so, so sorry about Uncle Davey.'

Mackerel sometimes thought of what he'd say to Jesse and Alexandra if they ever returned. Not often – he spent most of his life trying to repress their absence, and the part of him that was guiltily relieved Jesse was no longer around. But never, not once, had he thought about what he'd say to Forest.

Now the boy was here, and Mackerel was *fucking drunk again*.

Mack didn't know how to respond, thoughts foggy. He dimly heard the doorbell ring.

'Okay . . .' he said. 'Just . . . just stay here. I need to get some water . . . I need to sober up.'

As soon as he closed the door to his room, he tumbled into Big Mane, who looked flustered.

'I've gotta call Ahab,' said Mackerel.

'We've got other problems,' said Big Mane. 'The cops are here. Bail check.'

Mackerel froze. What to do?

Family business stayed family business.

So he couldn't let them find Forest Dempsey in his house . . .

'Call Ahab. Tell him Forest is here. He'll know what to do.'

'Mack? Are you here?' shouted Linda's voice from the doorway.

'Yeah, I'm here,' he said.

The door was flung open, and three police officers piled in. Constable Linda and the two detectives, De Corrado and Smith.

'Mackerel, can you step into the bathroom, please,' said Linda. She'd rediscovered her professional tone since this morning. 'We need to UT you.'

Mackerel nodded, keeping his eyes on the detectives. Why were *they* here?

In the bathroom, he unzipped his pants and pissed into the cup, Linda standing close so she could see the urine leaving his penis. He was used to it by now, but that didn't mean he didn't wish they could bring a male officer to do this part.

She put on rubber gloves and he handed her the cup. She dipped a testing cartridge in, took it out, then waited. Five minutes, they waited. Linda seemed certain something would eventually show on the cartridge.

Mackerel finished the rest of his piss in the toilet, flushed, closed the lid and sat down. There was no point leaving until the urine test was done.

Finally Linda looked up. 'You're clean.'

Mackerel bristled at her tone. 'You're not supposed to use that language anymore. It implies drug users are dirty.'

'Watch it,' she snapped. She tipped the rest of Mackerel's urine down the sink, wrapped up the cup in her glove and put it all in the bin.

Mackerel washed his hands and followed her out into the lounge room.

The two detectives stood in the middle of the lounge, chatting to each other. Big Mane hovered at the doorway, looking between them and Mack. Mack felt bad for bringing all this into his life – the uniformed officers were one thing, but these two city detectives in their tailored suits were something else again.

Before they could explain their presence, Ahab appeared at the open front door. Big Mane had called him, then.

'Why are *you* here?' said De Corrado to Ahab. She frowned. 'Don't tell me you followed me from the inn?'

Ahab snuck a glance at Mackerel. Mackerel shook his head, trying to get the message across. *No, don't tell them he's here, it'll look bad for me.*

'Because Forest Dempsey is here,' Ahab said anyway.

Mackerel put his head in his hands.

'Forest Dempsey? *Here?*' De Corrado scrambled through the house. 'Forest? Forest!'

———

They all gathered in the lounge. Big Mane had hurriedly moved some dirty jocks off the couches so Mackerel and Forest could sit. He didn't offer Linda a seat.

Forest sat beside Mackerel, Ahab rocking impatiently in an armchair. De Corrado and Smith perched on chairs taken from the dining table. Linda leaned against the wall, arms folded.

'You're drunk, Mr Dempsey,' observed Smith.

'His brother just died,' snapped Ahab.

Smith inclined his head to indicate it was a fair response.

'And Forest . . .?' said Detective De Corrado. 'How did you get here? Why did you come to Shacktown?'

Mackerel noted with interest that she hadn't yet called Ivy, given the conversation they'd had at the hospital that first day. But he didn't like the tone she took with his nephew, and slung an arm around his shoulders protectively.

'I heard Davey died,' the boy said. 'I wanted to be with family, so I came to Mackerel's. Seeing as no one would let me come.'

'I'm sorry, but things have to . . . happen in the right way, Forest,' said De Corrado.

She was struggling to find the right words, and Mackerel had a sudden suspicion that De Corrado didn't know how to talk to kids. That thought made him start to grin, but he quickly wiped it off his face. This was not the time to be smiling. Shit, he needed to sober up fast.

'I know it's tough right now, but you're what we call a "key witness" in a pretty important criminal investigation,' De Corrado said.

'I know what a key witness is,' said Forest dryly.

'The . . . we want to catch the person who did this,' continued De Corrado. 'There's lots of people working to make that happen. Does coming here have anything to do with what happened to you? Is there anything you want to tell us, no matter how small?' She held

Mackerel's eyes. 'Or, if you like, do you want to tell your uncle, who can pass it on?' She smiled at Mack.

The boy shrugged under Mack's protective arm. 'I just wanted to be around family. I'm sorry if that was the wrong thing to do.' His voice was innocent, but there was a hint of veiled criticism there.

'It's not wrong, but you have to understand that it's not safe for you. Mentally or physically. Dr Joseph hasn't discharged you yet. I'm sorry, but we'll need to take you back to Hobart.'

'No! *No!*' Forest leapt off the couch and sprinted from the room.

'Forest!' called Mackerel, cursing his limp as everyone else beat him to the door.

Forest was crouched on the front steps, taking heaving breaths like he was choking. His hand was scrabbling at his throat. Everyone crowded around him.

'Call an ambulance!' said Linda.

'No.' Mack gestured for the others to hang back. The boy was having a panic attack – Mackerel knew the signs all too well.

He pitched his voice low. 'It's alright, Forest . . . it's okay . . . you're safe, no one is going to lock you up . . .' He sat down beside him. 'You're going to be safe . . . you're going to be fine . . .'

Forest gave a sad chuckle, speaking through gasping breaths. 'If only . . . you knew . . .'

Mackerel heard movement behind him, the detectives drawing closer, wanting to hear what Forest was saying. Mackerel turned on them. 'Give him some space! It's alright, he's not going anywhere. Just give him a moment.'

'Do you know what you're doing, Mackerel?' said De Corrado.

'Yeah,' said Mackerel. 'I do.'

He'd seen a lot of panic attacks in prison. He'd learned that soft voices and reassuring words made a difference, or were anyway far better than prison guards yelling at you.

'Call an ambulance,' insisted Linda.

Mackerel and Forest sat by themselves on the cold stone steps, soaking wet. Fifteen minutes had passed and Ahab had brought them both blankets to keep them warm, if not dry.

Forest's breathing had eased, and he warily watched the detectives, who were having a conversation by the gate. He huddled deeper under his blanket.

'It feels like I'm letting them win. I wish there was a way I could stay.'

'You're not losing anything,' said Mackerel. 'The hospital is probably better for you.'

'Not you, too,' sighed Forest.

Mackerel chuckled at that. 'You're older than you look, aren't you?' Flashing lights were coming down the hill. 'How do you feel?'

'I don't want to go, Uncle Mack.'

'I know,' said Mack. 'I'm sorry. It won't be forever.'

'Can you come with me?'

'I don't think they'll let me,' said Mackerel.

The ambulance pulled up, and a paramedic climbed out. The detectives walked to meet her.

Forest stood up, letting the blanket drop. 'I'm not going without Mackerel,' he called.

'I'm sorry, but he can't leave,' De Corrado called back. 'He's got a curfew.'

'Then I'm not going,' said Forest, sitting back down.

'How about if I come, boy?' said Ahab. He stood under the corner of the roof, smoking a cigarette, the end glowing red in the dark of the night. 'Would that be okay?'

Forest stayed silent.

'He's safe, Forest,' said Mackerel. 'You can trust Ahab.'

Forest pulled himself back to his feet. He looked at Mackerel one more time, then stepped into the ambulance. Ahab nodded back to Mack, grateful, and the ambulance took off.

Detective Smith went to his unmarked car and followed after the ambulance, a police light flashing in the windshield. Why was he going? Surely they weren't going to question Forest tonight?

Everything was making him unreasonably mad, and the alcohol was wearing off, pain returning to his knee.

De Corrado and Linda tried to escort Mackerel back into the lounge room, but his temper was fraying.

'I'm going to bed,' he said.

'I want to know why Forest was here,' said De Corrado.

'Because he heard about Davey and wanted to be with family!' Mackerel's voice rose.

'I doubt that,' said Linda. 'Why would he come to *you*?'

'What's *that* supposed to mean?'

'You need a night in the cells to cool off?' retorted Linda.

'You owe us answers,' said De Corrado.

'I owe you *nothing*!' Mackerel was shouting now. 'You think you can just walk into my home, piss-test me, humiliate me, ship my nephew off to somewhere he doesn't want to go, *and* talk to me like I'm scum beneath your boot? Threaten to lock me up? My *brother* just *died*!' He addressed that last comment to Linda. 'You boys in blue are the biggest gang on the planet. You think you own the fucking world!'

'Don't use that tone with *us*, Mackerel,' she warned.

'I'll use whatever fucking tone I fucking like!' shouted Mackerel, feeling his old self creeping back. The one who'd walked the streets of Brisbane in expensive clothes and made a mockery of the police every chance he got. He'd never forget all those off-the-record interviews, in the back of cop cars or the stations, where they turned the cameras off and gave him a good bashing to get their own back. 'Fuck off, *pigs*. I'm going to bed.'

He made to slam the front door in their faces, but paused when he caught De Corrado's eye.

'Except for you,' he muttered. 'Sorry.'

Then he slammed the door.

In the hallway, he nearly barrelled into Big Mane, whose eyes were wide, as though seeing him for the first time.

Mackerel felt a rush of shame, which only made him angrier. He ducked his head and fled to his room.

It had felt good seeing that surprise in Linda's face, but he couldn't even lose his temper with the police without apologising. Where did that leave him? The old Mack really was gone.

CHAPTER 17

AHAB

The ambulance rumbled and pitched, bringing Ahab's mind back to memories of this exact scenario with his mother. How many times had she overdosed, and he'd had to come with her to the hospital? He tried to push those thoughts away.

Beside him, Forest lay on the gurney, eyes closed, shivering from the cold. Ahab grabbed another blanket and put it on top of him.

The kid was so much thinner than Ahab had expected. Seeing him in Big Mane's lounge was the first time he'd actually set eyes on the boy, and now he was struck by how malnourished he looked. Big dark lines around his sunken eyes. Like the effects of sleep deprivation had become permanent. Those sunken eyes looked just like his mother's had in the grips of her addiction. Just what had been done to this boy?

Forest's forehead wrinkled and a steady burn rolled in Ahab's chest. He thought of the tattoo getting buzzed into Forest's back. Who would be evil enough to do something like that to a child?

Jesse was. He'd been a cruel, cruel man.

Then it came to him. *Blackbeard*. Blackbeard was evil enough to do it, too.

Was it cause and effect, some connection he couldn't see yet? Or was it simply that Blackbeard had been waiting for the right time?

What happened to you? Ahab wanted to ask. He wanted to take Forest's shoulders, shake him . . . *What happened to all of you?* But he wouldn't. This boy deserved better. And he would *get* better. That this could happen to Ahab's own family was inexcusable. In Ahab's town! He'd spend the rest of his life trying to make it up to the boy, if that's what it took.

As though reading his mind, Forest's eyes opened and locked immediately on Ahab's. They were a startling shade of aqua. Just like his father's.

'We haven't really had a chance to chat,' said Ahab. 'Do you remember me?'

'You're my dad's cousin. But you were more like a second father to him,' said Forest without hesitation. 'I remember.'

Ahab steadied himself against the side of the compartment as they turned a corner. That may have been true, but not in the later years. Jesse had always been volatile, but near the end he'd really begun to lose it, the paranoia taking over. It happened to all Dempseys who used ice. And when you were dealing it, you had an easy supply.

Ahab had his own problems by then, dealing with his mother, so he'd started removing himself from Jesse's, Davey's and Mackenzie's lives. Not a day went by that he didn't regret that, but at the time it felt like he didn't have a choice.

'So you made your way to Uncle Mackenzie's,' said Ahab. 'Clever lad. How did you even find his house?'

'Promise you won't think I'm crazy . . . The shells told me where to find him.'

What? The boy can talk to shells?

Ahab tried not to show any emotion on his face, but the boy was too sharp.

'You hear them too?' said Forest, sitting up.

'No.'

'You do. You hear the shells too! I'm not crazy!' He threw the blanket from himself and tried to get off the gurney. 'Let me out! Let me back to the ocean! I'll prove it.' He shook off Ahab's hands. 'No, I can prove it! *Let me back to the ocean* and I'll prove it!'

The paramedic climbed into the compartment from the seat in front. 'Forest, it's okay, I need you to calm down.'

'Don't even think about it,' warned Forest as she reached for the sedatives. He lay back. 'I'm fine.'

'Are you sure?' said the paramedic.

Forest reached out for him and Ahab took his hand in his own, feeling the hard scabs on the boy's fingertips.

'I'm sure,' said Forest.

Everything that had been on the tip of Ahab's tongue dried up. Every question he'd been about to ask, every strategy he'd thought to employ to get his answers.

They went over a pothole, and Forest's grip tightened briefly. It was sweaty. Or was *Ahab's* hand sweaty?

He can talk to shells . . .

Alarm bells sounded in his mind.

No, he's a Dempsey. We learn how to lie from the cradle. It doesn't mean anything.

Ahab thought back to everything that had happened. He was missing something. He reviewed the facts, and kept coming back to the same conclusion: no one now stood between this boy and full control of Dempsey Abalone.

'Why was Davey scuba-diving in a Black Wind?' asked Forest.

'Nobody knows,' said Ahab. 'Maybe he was looking for your mum and dad.'

Forest bit his lip. 'Was it the curse?'

Ahab felt a little bit of his tension dissipate. Of course. The sirens' curse. With a family curse, coincidences made perfect sense. He shouldn't read more into it than that. He was going down the wrong path.

There was *no way* that this boy could be involved in Davey's death.

Was there?

Ahab moved a finger up to rest against the pulse inside Forest's wrist. It was pounding. The boy was definitely nervous. 'Have you ever seen *The Princess Bride*, Forest?'

Forest frowned. 'No. Why?'

'It was one of your father's favourite movies,' lied Ahab, feeling for any change in his pulse. 'He loved the main character, Westley. Also known as the Dread Pirate Roberts.'

He watched Forest's face.

'Pirates? I thought Dad hated pirates,' said Forest.

No sign of recognition.

Of course Forest isn't working for Blackbeard. You're being paranoid, old man.

Forest picked up on his mood. He frowned at Ahab, then turned away. Soon he closed his eyes and began to doze, his hand dropping out of Ahab's grasp.

Why did he have this feeling that he was asking all the wrong questions?

Forest didn't wake until the ambulance arrived in Hobart. Ahab had squandered his chance.

A thin young woman with curly brown hair greeted them the moment the ambulance doors opened. 'Forest! Your grandmother is *worried sick!*'

'Hello, Frankie,' said Forest darkly. 'Can you stay with me, Ahab?'

'No, he can't,' said Frankie. 'Your grandmother has expressly forbidden it. A good night to you, Ahab.'

Ahab ruffled Forest's hair. 'I'll see you soon, boy. Rest up and hurry back to Shacktown as soon as you can. We've all missed you.'

His mind was full of theories and thoughts. The problem with being a Dempsey was that you saw enemies where there were none.

Or maybe he was just rattled because the boy was in worse shape than he thought.

Whoever had done this to him was going to pay.

CHAPTER 18

FOREST

Early the next morning they moved Forest to a new building, on the waterfront in Battery Point, the old and expensive part of Hobart. A new bed, windows that didn't open. He'd noticed that the mood of the nurses had turned against him after his escape the night before. It was probably best to be moving on. He knew better than to stay where he wasn't wanted.

This new room was spacious and furnished in antiques and heavy blue curtains. Zeus sprawled across his lap, wide awake. The bed was so big and soft he thought the big dog might sink into it and disappear.

The heavy timber door opened and Frankie stepped inside.

My old nemesis, he thought, his face calm.

Zeus growled softly.

'Shh,' said Forest, rubbing him under the chin. 'I'll let you bite her later.'

'Is it okay if I take a seat, Forest?' said Frankie.

'Yes, of course! Free country,' said Forest brightly. 'Apparently.' He looked over at the sealed windows.

She raised an eyebrow. When she took a seat nearby, Zeus sat up and growled more loudly. Frankie quickly leapt off, then laughed. 'Maybe I should sit over here?' She perched on the end of a suede couch.

'Maybe you should,' said Forest, patting Zeus's head. 'Good boy.'

She raised both eyebrows at that. A half-smile. 'So we're not even trying to be subtle anymore, Forest?'

'I've no idea what you're talking about,' he said.

'You know what?' She stretched out on the couch, looking around the room, nodding to herself. 'I've realised you don't know much about me. We always talk about you, Forest, but never talk about *me* . . . so what should I tell you? Hmm . . . well, Ivy hired me. And I specialise in cases like yours. So you can relax – I can see that you're tense right now.'

She wasn't even looking at him. Forest relaxed his body, and then, feeling his guard drop, immediately tensed right back up.

'You gave everyone a scare last night,' continued Frankie. 'Do you wanna tell me about it?'

'I thought we were talking about you,' said Forest.

'Sorry. Habit. What do you want to talk about, then?' said Frankie.

'Not what *you* want to talk about,' countered Forest.

'Yes, well, you *know* what I want to talk about, but you never seem to want to go there. What happened to you? Where are your parents? Who gave you those tattoos? Et cetera, et cetera . . . I don't know about you, but I'm getting tired.' It was a lie – she'd ask him again the moment he relaxed. 'So, again: what do you want to talk about?' said Frankie.

'When will I be able to go back to Shacktown?' he asked.

'Well, you see, Forest . . . now that Dr Joseph has discharged you, that decision is entirely up to Ivy, as your guardian. And, I'm afraid, she's put that decision down to *me*. So . . .'

Zeus growled, echoing Forest's mood.

What to do? How should he play this game?

'Alright,' said Forest, releasing a massive breath. 'Let's talk about it, then.'

She leaned forward an inch. 'Yes?'

'Let's talk about the trauma.'

'Good. Let's talk about the trauma.'

'But . . . I mean, if you specialise in . . . what did you say? *Cases like mine?*' She gave him an encouraging nod. 'How can I be sure? Like, what can you tell me?' He smiled innocently. 'Before I say anything, I mean. I *am* a traumatised boy, after all.'

'Which would make sense,' said Frankie easily. 'See, trauma can really ruin your body, but it can also ruin your mind. Turn even the sharpest little mind into complete mush. Mushy, like soggy mushrooms and rotten potatoes. No matter how clever you think you are. No matter how many people might get hurt.' There was a bite to her voice. 'But sometimes it's good to talk about it. Sometimes people, like me, are even *trained* in talking about it. But, if it's too much for you, we can talk about something else. Anything else, really.'

'I want a different counsellor,' said Forest.

'I'm afraid, in this case, I'm all you've got,' said Frankie, with a sad smile. 'But I hope that, in time, you'll learn to trust me. That's all you have to do. Just trust me.'

'I'd trust you a lot more if you let me go back to Shacktown.'

'Really, is that so?' Frankie leaned forward again. 'Convince me.'

CHAPTER 19

MACKEREL

Mackerel had signed into the station for the day, gaining a frosty reception from the officer on the desk – Linda must have given them a report of his words last night. Then he'd gone to the pharmacy and taken his meds, *finally*. He felt better already. And, even better, the pharmacist had given him the briefest of hugs and expressed her condolences for Davey.

Now he was walking back to Big Mane's house to get ready for a day working on the boat. There was no spring in his step – the loss of Davey was still an all too fresh wound, and there was still the problem of Blackbeard – but at least today would be better than yesterday.

At least, that's what he thought until he saw the Mercedes SUV parked out the front of Big Mane's.

Ivy.

She stepped out of the car and beckoned him closer. She looked haggard from grief; he doubted she'd slept.

He limped over.

'Tell me everything that happened last night,' she commanded.

He answered quickly and obediently, not taking his eyes off her black sandals, but left out the fact that Ahab had been there.

'*You* were the one he came to see? *You're* the one he trusts?' she scoffed. 'Heaven help us, I'll never understand males. And you told the police nothing?'

'No,' he said, glancing up at her.

'Of course not.' She bit her lip in thought. 'Good. Now, obviously, you will not speak to Ahab again. I don't care if he appears on your front doorstep on the verge of death, you don't let him in. He made his choice: he's not part of this family. I'm disappointed in you.'

He ducked his head lower.

Without another word, she turned away and climbed back into her car.

Mackerel made to head inside, anxious to get away from her, but she rolled down her window and snapped, 'Come on, then.'

'Come where?' said Mackerel.

'To Hobart, dimwit. If you're the one Forest trusts then you need to be there to get something out of him. We have to find out what happened to Alexandra and Jesse, and if it's related to what happened to Davey. Forest is the key to it all!' There was strain in her voice. 'And, seeing as my useless contractor isn't getting a peep out of him, maybe you can get him to open up. So hurry up. Davey deserves the best from us.'

'But I . . .'

The words died on his lips. Big Mane had work for him today – another day's work, to make up for the shift he missed yesterday. And it would do him good to be out on the boats, to be in the water, help take his mind off the grief.

'I said hurry, dimwit,' said Ivy. She rolled up the window.

Another day's income lost. Another friend let down.

Another failure in a long tally of failures.

There was one redeeming thought that Mackerel kept coming back to: *Forest trusts me.* That thought warmed him, gave him hope.

But Big Mane was already at the boat waiting for him. He shot him a quick text, explaining that his mother had come for him – a whole paragraph of apologies.

Then he climbed into Ivy's car.

For the whole drive to Hobart, there was no music, no conversation. Just his mother staring straight ahead, resolute. The same anger she'd shown yesterday in the face of Davey's death.

They pulled up at a big house in Battery Point, with the names of doctors and psychologists listed on the sign out the front. Ivy had her knitting bag and a picnic basket, both of which she forced into Mackerel's arms. He followed her into a reception room, and then was led down a gleaming, varnish-scented hallway to a large timber door. She pushed it open, Mackerel trailing behind.

Forest lay on a massive bed, flipping idly through an old magazine. He looked up as they entered and then cried out in delight.

Ivy swept the boy up in her arms.

An ageing psychiatrist entered the room and had a brief chat with them – Mackerel wasn't sure what had happened to Dr Joseph, but this new woman seemed very cold. The psychiatrist was followed by another, far warmer young lady called Frankie, who had some other kind of 'therapist' title. He noticed Forest stiffen when Frankie walked in.

When the psychiatrist left, Frankie and Ivy had a chat in the corner. Mackerel sat down beside Forest, and the boy mumbled, 'Thanks for coming.'

'How did you recover after last night?'

Forest shrugged. 'You've gotta convince Ivy to let me come home.'

'You'll learn, little one,' he said wisely, ruffling Forest's shaggy hair. 'No one convinces your grandmother of *anything*.'

Frankie left, and the three Dempseys made themselves comfortable. They spent the next few hours talking about inconsequential things. Ivy described the renovations made to Safe Harbour since Forest had been a child, and Mackerel spoke at length about the work he did out on the ocean for Big Mane. Talking about the sea, at least, gave him a little sense of calm, and he grew into the conversation as the day went on.

Forest was good at asking questions. Ivy, now sitting in the corner and crocheting, nodded in what might have even been encouragement as Mackerel spoke, drawing interest from the boy.

But while for the most part Forest listened attentively, occasionally asking a question about some detail or other, he offered nothing of his own. Mackerel did have to wonder what had happened to that animal skittishness he'd seen in the hospital room two days ago. This boy looked almost at ease.

No. No, that was wrong. Whenever Forest didn't think anyone was watching him, his face went tight and his shoulders hunched. He could put on a good act, but Mack still felt like one wrong move might send him scurrying for cover.

Later that afternoon they were joined by De Corrado and Smith, but the detectives got nothing out of Forest. Ivy smiled wanly when De Corrado looked her way.

When De Corrado left, she winked at Mackerel, which made him feel better about his outburst the night before. Although he was glad Ivy didn't catch it – he didn't want her thinking he was mates with the cops.

After they left, Frankie joined the room. Forest gave her such a sincere smile that Mackerel had to assume it was fake.

After that, Mack had a nap on Forest's bed while he and Ivy went for a walk around the grounds. When they returned, Mackerel was called into another room, where he sat down for a debrief with Ivy, Frankie, the new psychiatrist and Detective De Corrado.

'Honestly, I'm getting nowhere with him,' said Frankie to Ivy. 'Whatever happened to him these last seven years, he's fully dissociated from it. And I think being in this facility, nice as it is, isn't helping. He's longing to go back to Shacktown. I say we let him.'

'Based off Dr Joseph's notes, I'd agree. Time for a new direction,' said the psychiatrist. 'But only if there are appropriate supports in place in Shacktown. And if you feel able to care for him following the events of yesterday.'

'Don't you worry about me, dear,' Ivy told her, eyes glittering. 'Forest should be around family now.'

'We support that,' said De Corrado. 'He'll be close to our investigation, and he's obviously willing to break a window or two in order to make his way to Shacktown. Moving him there mitigates the risk of that going wrong, should he attempt it again. But I'm proposing some form of round-the-clock guard. We still don't know if he's at risk or if someone still means him harm.'

'I'd like to see them try,' said Mackerel angrily, before he could stop himself.

The women all looked at him like he was a cute but slightly irritating dog, yapping uncontrollably. He held their gaze for a solid moment before dropping his head.

'Then we all agree he should return to Shacktown with Ivy,' said Frankie. 'He keeps asking to. Maybe being in Shacktown will set him at ease, unlock some memories . . .'

'It's a tricky tension we are balancing here,' agreed the psychiatrist. 'We want to keep him safe and clear, but he needs to start moving on with his life.'

'Stirring up memories sounds good to me,' said De Corrado. 'We need some kind of way into understanding what happened to him. We're getting nowhere.'

'Okay, but it would be remiss not to also discuss the risks,' said the psychiatrist. 'For example, what if . . .'

The women kept talking, deferring to Ivy, who would make the final call. Mackerel left the room and only De Corrado noticed.

He walked to Forest's room, where the boy stood near the window, looking down past the lawns, where you could just see the water and the yachts.

'Hi,' said Mackerel, taking a seat on the bed.

'They're deciding my fate, then?' said Forest, not turning from the window.

'Something like that,' said Mackerel. 'Between me and you, I think it's heading the direction you want it to.'

Forest spun. 'I'm going home with you?' A wide grin broke out on his face.

'Don't tell them I told you.'

Ten minutes later, Ivy came into the room. She looked at Mackerel and rolled her eyes. 'I'm guessing he told you, then, Forest?'

'Told me what?' said Forest, with the perfect amount of confusion. 'All he said was that I had to wait for you.'

'Well, then I hope you're happy. You're coming back to Shacktown, dear,' she said, beaming. 'You'll stay with me for the time being.'

Forest's eyes grew watery. He hugged her tightly. 'Thank you, Nan. You're a lifesaver.'

Over her shoulder he caught Mackerel's eye and winked.

'"Grandmother",' she corrected.

Mackerel chuckled, rubbing Zeus's belly.

CHAPTER 20

FOREST

Forest lay on top of the covers in his new bedroom at Safe Harbour. There was a four-poster bed, with the canopy and everything, and it was made up with silk sheets. They made his skin itch – Ivy had told him they were new. Even this bed had only been bought today. Zeus lay just outside the glass doors that led out onto the garden, whining. Ivy said she didn't have many rules, but she had insisted the dog stay outside.

That evening, in a gleaming dining room around a massive table made from a gigantic piece of dark-brown driftwood, they'd eaten a six-course dinner, provided by a catering company she'd called in just for the two of them, including a waitress who filled up his glass and cleared away the plates as he finished each course.

As they ate, Ivy implored him to make himself at home. He should let her know anything he needed. She wanted him to be safe, but she danced around what she really wanted to say: she wouldn't ask what had happened to him, but she was cautioning him to make sensible decisions. Then, she gave him a gold-tinted credit card.

She told him with a wink that it had a ten-thousand-dollar limit –
enough for him to buy 'essentials'.

Now, lying on the bed, looking around at the room, he had the
overwhelming sense that she was trying to dazzle him with wealth.

It made him realise that it was past time he went to see Huck.

As quietly as he could, Forest slipped out of bed and got dressed,
finding an oversized jacket in the wardrobe Ivy had prepared for
him. He swiped a fancy metal pen off the desk, and brought the
credit card with him, too.

As he walked out the door, Zeus rolled over onto his back, paws
in the air, whimpering.

'*Stay.*'

Zeus wagged his tail once, but he didn't change position.

Forest stayed low and moved quietly through the muggy, moonlit night. He knew that the police were keeping an eye on the house,
but he had always been very good at sneaking around. He picked
his way through the grey saltbush that separated Safe Harbour from
the neighbouring property, then crept down their root-strewn staircase to the beach. The salty air, dense with heady eucalypt, buzzed
with insects. The sky above was a fountain of stars.

Forest padded along the sand until he reached a park with a playground and swings. Here he climbed a cabbage gum, retrieving his
bum bag, having stashed it here the night before. This time he took
only the map of Shacktown, leaving the remaining cash hidden inside.

He began the long walk around the curved beach, keeping to
the shadows and avoiding the late-night beach walkers but still on
edge. At one point the cry of a penguin in the beach laurel by his feet
startled him into a yelp, and he nearly bolted for the water. Fighting
to bring himself back to a sense of calm, he continued on. The next
sound he heard – a bolting trio of deer – caused him to drop to the
sand, making himself as flat as possible, until he worked out what
they were.

Finally he reached a line of boatsheds right near the marina. Lit up by the marina lights, all of these sheds were in varying stages of repair – some of them looked as though they were still in regular use, but the tideline clearly reached right up under their foundations and made upkeep look difficult.

The small one in the middle with the peeling pastel-blue paint had its door boarded up with fence palings, with a rotting sign that simply said 'ASBESTOS'.

Bingo.

Forest climbed underneath the shed's raised foundations and slithered along the damp sand, covered in shells and slimy seaweed, and followed the upwards slope towards the floor. There he found a hole in the floorboards, and he hauled himself up into the shed.

He caught a brief look at the dim interior – the flickering glow from a tiny campfire revealing a sleeping bag – before a weight knocked him over and pinned him to the ground, pressing his face hard into the floorboards.

'I oughta break your nose,' said Huck.

Forest laughed, trying to heave the older boy off him. 'Huck! You're here.'

'Shut up.' Huck had him pinned by the wrists, knee digging into his back. Then he pushed Forest's shirt up. 'Shit, it's true. Who did you get to tattoo you?'

'Someone who sucks at it,' said Forest. He took the opportunity to slide out from under Huck and sprang into a crouch. He held out his hand to the tall, lean boy; looked into those green eyes, lank brown curls falling around his suntanned face. 'It's good to see you.'

Huck knocked the hand away, pushed him in the chest until he had Forest backed against the wall. 'What the hell kind of a game are you playing?'

'C'mon, you knew I was gonna try it.'

'I didn't think you were *serious*! You swore an oath!' said Huck.

'Are you kidding?' Forest stood straighter. 'Two birds, Huck. I'll clear your name, and your dad's, plus I just became the richest boy in Tasmania!' He flashed the gold-plated credit card.

'I wanted to put Forest's ghost to rest! This is doing the opposite! It's . . . it's a bloody mockery of his memory!' Huck took a deep breath through his nose, turning away. 'You swore an *oath*.'

'I didn't break it.'

'Not yet.' Huck pounded the side of the shed. Forest hoped the sound didn't carry. 'How long do you think you can keep this charade up?'

'Forever, Huck. You said you trusted me.' Forest rolled up his sleeve, showing a raised scar. 'Under the full moon.'

Huck rubbed his own forearm, then pounded the wall again, harder than before. 'I know you. You don't give a shit about money. Why are you doing this?'

'Everyone gives a shit about money, Huck,' said Forest. Sometimes he wondered how the older boy survived out here on his own – even though they'd both come from the same world, Huck's sense of right and wrong were like a small child's.

'Answer my question,' said Huck.

'You answered it yourself: I swore an oath. Huck, you're the only friend I ever had who I trusted. You and me against the world —'

'This isn't one of your books! This is *real life*!'

'Huck, you deserve better. We both do. And I'm gonna make it happen.'

'And what about Forest's family? What are you doing to *them*?'

Forest's mouth twisted, his heart sinking. But . . . sometimes you had to make tough calls. The real world was full of tough calls, and you had to choose what mattered most. And Huck was what mattered most.

'We . . . we can't focus on that, Huck. What you deserve matters more than . . . it just matters more, okay! You should see them. You should see how happy they are —'

'No, don't. Don't act like you're being noble. None of this is even *real*!'

'They're *happy*!' Forest showed him the credit card again. '*I'm* happy! *You* can be happy! I'm trying my best, okay? I'm fucking *trying*, Huck!'

Huck was silent for a few moments, pretending not to see Forest wiping his eyes. 'I can't be happy with this. What I *want* is to let the ghosts of the past rest. Not for you to wake them all up and call them down our heads.'

'You're right, Huck . . . Forest's ghost needs to be laid to rest.'

'Don't do that. Don't talk down to me. You haven't seen the shit I've seen —'

'I'm doing this so you can be happy. You can have your life back *and* we can *finally* put Forest's ghost to rest.'

Huck, as he'd hoped, hesitated at that. 'What do you mean, put his ghost to rest?'

'Yeah,' said Forest, 'now I've got your attention, don't I? Listen to me. As Forest Dempsey, I've got access to *everything*. The family, the abalone company, his old house, the police . . . I can find out what *happened* to him. And then,' he prodded Huck in the chest, 'Forest's ghost won't haunt you no more.'

Huck grimaced, then sat down against the wall, folding his legs.

'No,' he said simply. He pulled out a packet of cigarettes from the pocket of his shorts and lit one. 'No. I'm going to the mainland. You've drawn way too much attention to us. This place won't be safe for me anymore.'

'Forest's ghost will follow you there. You know it will.'

'I don't *care!* This is all going to go wrong!' Huck's face was set off by the glow of the cigarette tip, the smoke escaping from the side of his mouth. 'All I want to do is stay the hell away from it.'

'What you want is to prove your dad wasn't involved,' said Forest. 'You want to be more than a teenage runaway, camping in fucking *boatsheds*. What you *want* is your own life back.'

Huck puffed on his cigarette. 'And if I believe you? If you really can put Forest to rest?'

'Then I need you to take me to the cave,' said Forest.

'No,' said Huck instantly. 'Fuck off.'

'The one where Forest died.'

'No,' said Huck.

'You have to,' said Forest.

'*No*. I'm not going back there.'

'I'm not asking you to go back there! I just need you to tell me where it is.' He pulled out the crinkled map. 'If anyone else ever finds the cave . . . if I, *Forest Dempsey*, don't know where it is, my story is blown.'

'That's not my problem.'

Forest pulled up his sleeve. 'An oath.'

'And I made a promise that I would never tell anyone where that cave was. *Ever*.'

'You're not telling me. You're not even *showing* me.' He flashed the pen he'd brought. 'I'll hold the pen, and you just . . . guide my hand to the right spot.

Huck sat there, thinking about what Forest was asking of him. Thinking about the past, too, probably. What he'd escaped and what still haunted him.

'How does this lay Forest to rest?' said Huck. 'Seems to me like you'll just rile him up more.'

'I need to know where it is. Just in case. As insurance, while I solve the mystery of what happened to him. You should *see* Ahab's room, Huck. He's got a whole corkboard full of photos and pins. He'll help me work it out.'

'So I'm just helping you trick these poor people.'

'Huck, look at me . . . look me in the eyes. Everything I'm doing here, I'm doing for you, alright? You've trusted me before. You've gotta trust me now. No matter who else gets hurt by this, *you* won't get hurt. All of your hurt is gonna go *away*. I *promise*.'

Huck stared back at him. So grown up, so jaded, and yet still so childlike . . .

'Fine,' said Huck. He slid the lighter and packet of cigarettes across to Forest. 'But no one else in the Dempsey family gets hurt.'

Forest breathed a sigh of relief. 'I give you my word.'

At least Huck hadn't made him promise not to go visit the cave.

He lit up one of the cigarettes and inhaled. Then he laid the map in front of Huck.

CHAPTER 21

MACKEREL

The setting summer sun burned bright and hot in the cloudless sky, but not as hot as Mackerel's anger.

'Look, don't be mad at *me*,' said Big Mane.

'Oh, we're well beyond mad.' Mackerel paced around Big Mane's lounge room. His face was itching, a tempest swelling up inside him. 'You had *no right* to give her my bank details!'

'Shelby's just concerned about you.' He held his hands up in placation. 'That's three days you haven't been able to work. She knows you've got court fees and debts you're repaying —'

'And who told her *that*?'

Big Mane's face went red as a buoy and he shook his head. 'I dunno?'

'I can carry my own weight, mate!'

'Well, can you?' said Big Mane, dropping his hands back into his pockets. 'Can you really?'

'Do you *know* how much she gave me?' Mackerel pulled at his hair. 'With Davey dead, she can't be giving this kind of money away!'

'I dunno,' said Big Mane again, with a shrug that implied he didn't much care. 'Maybe he had life insurance? No disrespect to the dead.' He awkwardly crossed himself. 'Mate, I think you're being pig-headed here. You deserve a break.'

'No, I fucking don't,' said Mackerel. He stormed out of the door, into his car and up to Homeward.

He was still in a foul mood when he arrived, slamming the car door shut.

Shelby was already out the front door and heading towards him, wearing a polka-dot skirt, ruby red sandals, and a face so determined her jaw jutted out like a ship cutting through waves. He supposed her new motion sensors and security cameras had let her know the moment he'd pulled into the driveway.

'I don't need handouts!' he shouted.

'What aren't you telling me about Davey?' Shelby countered.

That pulled Mackerel up. 'I . . . I'm here to talk about the money!'

She searched his eyes, as though looking for a lie, and then she looked him up and down. He realised he was wearing dirty trackies and the same hoodie as yesterday.

He had still been in the shower when his phone pinged with the notification of a bank deposit. When he saw what it was, he'd thrown these clothes on, not thinking straight, still smarting from the way Ivy had dismissed him the moment Forest came home with her.

He felt a ridiculous urge to apologise to Shelby for his dirty clothes, which he quashed.

'You're not coming inside if you're going to cause a scene,' said Shelby. 'If you can act like an adult, I'll make you dinner.' She turned, skirt flicking, and walked back to the front of the house.

Limping, he rushed to catch up with her. Why did it seem like all the women in his life had a Master's degree in throwing him off balance? 'You can't just send me money without asking.'

'Also,' said Shelby casually, 'you'll need to explain this.' She pulled a pistol out of the pocket of her dress.

In the space of a breath Mackerel knew that Shelby must've found one of Davey's hidden weapon caches. He lunged for it and she twitched it out of his reach. 'Careful,' she warned, holding it away from him. He saw now that her lips were drawn tight in fury. 'I don't want any *accidents*.'

'You can't just flash that around!' he whispered. 'What if Kane sees it?'

She stood on the front step and folded her arms, holding the pistol far too casually. 'We need to talk about a few things.'

'Shelby, pass me the gun,' said Mackerel.

'Oh relax, Mackerel, it's not loaded. My dad used to take me to the rifle range – I probably know as much about guns as you do. Let's recap.' She held up her fingers, counting. 'First, they find Forest, but Davey is missing. Then there's a man in my ceiling, presumably looking for Davey. Next day, Davey goes diving in Devils Kitchen, which makes no sense, and he . . . he's dead. Now, I find a gun *strapped under the shelf of my husband's bathroom mirror!* Why? That doesn't make sense either. None of it makes any sense.'

She put up a finger to stop Mackerel from interrupting.

'And so then I tear this whole house apart, looking for something, anything. And what do I find? Hidden in Davey's side of the wardrobe, in a shoebox beneath a pair of smelly old runners?' Her voice rose. '*More* guns, Mackerel!'

'. . . They're mine,' said Mackerel.

'Don't lie to me, Mackerel! Tell me honestly: was Davey dodgy?' This new grief tearing her voice was different. She sounded like she was drowning.

'Not a chance,' he said. 'Davey was as straight as they come.'

'"Tell Jesse I'm sorry" . . . Forest comes back . . .'

'Tell Jesse I'm sorry?'

'It was on a note Davey left me. A note which is now missing, by the way. I found it just before you and I met at Seaglass.'

'Maybe the man in the roof took it?' said Mackerel.

'I was hoping you might help me make some sense of it all, but I was wrong, hey? Family business stays family business?' Shelby's eyes glittered with tears. 'I'm starting to put two and two together, here, just so you know.' She wiped her nose. 'How long ago did you and Davey deal drugs together? Was he doing it when I married him?'

'Shelby, the money you gave me . . .' said Mackerel, trying in vain to get things back on track.

'Come back when you're ready to talk.' She slammed the door in his face, taking the gun with her.

Mackerel sat in his car in Homeward's driveway. The panic he'd felt at the sight of Shelby holding a gun still had him on edge. It wasn't right for her to be exposed to Davey's world.

He looked up at the house, a memory of childhood laughter in his mind.

I'll own a mansion of my own, one day, said Davey. He would have been about ten, but he already had the swagger of a good-looking youth, swiping at seaside grasses with a stick.

We'll have enough for ten mansions, said Jesse, with all the confidence of being the oldest. He strutted ahead of the other two, feet crunching in the sand.

Me too, said Mackerel, the youngest. Chubby and clumsy, following behind, carrying an armful of cuttlefish backbones. *I'll have the biggest mansion out of everyone.*

You? Jesse scoffed. *You'll be lucky to get a rowboat.* He laughed cruelly. Davey followed suit, although he looked back at Mackerel guiltily.

Mackerel had just grinned, his only real defence at being the butt of Jesse's jokes – the butt of everyone's jokes. But he must've felt defiant that day, or excited by the idea of his own mansion, because words leapt out of his mouth. *I'll have the most money of all the Dempseys.*

At this Jesse had turned and knocked the cuttlefish out of Mackerel's hands. *You? You won't get a cent. Dad hates you and Mum thinks you're useless. You're an embarrassment to the Dempsey name.* He pushed Mackerel over and laughed, encouraging Davey to join in. *Fatty little Mackerel, you'll die homeless and drug-addicted like Ahab's mum will. Everyone knows it.*

You're wrong, he'd said.

Jesse had punched him in the face so hard Mackerel's whole world became dizzy stars. When he came to, Jesse had strolled on ahead, up the stairs to Safe Harbour, but Davey was helping Mack sit up, hand on his shoulder. *It's alright, Mack. You can live with me in my mansion. I won't let you go homeless.*

Later, with all that time in prison to think about what had happened, Mackerel put that moment down as one of the things that had motivated him to start building his own drug dynasty. What Jesse had said was one thing, but Davey's offer of charity had confirmed it. They both assumed Mackerel would grow up to be a failure.

And now, even if by some miracle Mackerel ever made something of himself, Davey would never be around to see it.

He drove back to Big Mane's. Back to his real life.

CHAPTER 22

FOREST

Forest had 'borrowed' a child's bicycle he'd found leaning against a back fence – it was a BMX with pegs, and slightly too small for him. But it had a light, which was what he needed. By moonlight bright and clear, and this butter-yellow torchlight, he followed Huck's map to the cave. He had to be sure.

It was a good 3 kilometres away. He pedalled along suburban streets until they gave way to a gravel track that ran up the hillside, framed by short, wiry bush pea scrub. Rising from the seat to pedal against the slope, he rode up the track until he was taken in by the taller Tasmanian blanketleaf and she-oaks. Now he was away from prying eyes, but he was against the clock – at any moment Ivy might angle open the bedroom door to check on him.

He kept his eyes on the track – the larger rocks thrown into jumping shadows by the bike's headlight – always pushing against the ever-rising slope, sweat stinging his eyes. Finally the track dipped down and the trees gave way to moonlit water, a tangy salt breeze and, like toppled gravestones, a field of fallen dolerite pillars.

He slowed to a stop and left the bike in the bushes, bringing the headlight with him, and walked out to the patch of fallen pillars. He was closer to the shore than he realised, and the breeze whistled through them.

'So this is where I died,' he murmured.

A sharp memory made him flinch. A back-alley tattooist buzzing those words into his shoulder. Once Forest had given him the money, the man had insisted on first going out and buying cocaine, snorting half the bag by the time he was done with the tattoo.

Forest pulled his hand away from his shoulder and the fresh memory of pain.

Don't look back. You know what to do.

He scrambled up to the closest boulder. Nothing at all grew on these, so his shoes scrabbled for purchase and he scraped open the scabs on his knees. After that he held the light under his armpit, crawling to the top.

Like a Jurassic world, the boulder field stretched all down the shore, dotted with a nearby copse of gnarled-looking she-oaks, eerie in the dark. Huck had said the entrance to the cave was marked by a fallen pillar, like a crossbeam, covered in tree roots. He scanned these trees with the lamp but could see no crossbeam stone. An answering light came from a boat out on the water, and Forest quickly cupped the lamp, then uncupped it. To hide now would look suspicious. Even if they could see him, he was just a lad doing some exploring.

In the middle of the night? he thought with a snort. *Not suspicious at all.*

He picked his way along more boulders, searching for trees out here, wishing he'd thought to bring a more powerful torch. He saw now that caves dotted all of these pillars, where they'd fallen from whatever cliff once stood here, forming crawl spaces that weaved in and out of the rock.

He shuddered, imagining faces in there, peering out at him. He wished he didn't have to do all this alone.

He headed for a tree that stood higher than the rest, trying to avoid lingering near the cave entrances. As he drew closer, he saw it was a stunted native currant tree. He picked his way closer through a gully between the stones, splashing through a puddle of stinking briny water that wet his shoes. Back up out of the gully, he puffed and panted as he crawled up to the tree, using its roots as handholds.

That was promising.

He strained, feet slipping, until he finally dragged his weight to the top.

This might be it. Tree roots gathered between the pillar he stood on and the next, and the rock in-between *could* be considered a crossbeam. Beneath it, the maw of one of those cave entrances.

This has *to be it.*

Now that he was here, he didn't want to go inside. The thought nearly suffocated him. Terror made him want to run – to the water, away from this cave, any direction that led away from whatever lurked inside.

Suddenly he heard a sound, a stone's throw away. A scrabble of footsteps as somewhere above him a man slipped and stumbled, then a soft curse.

True terror hit him now. Forest flicked his light off and flattened himself against the stone, sliding noisily into the opening of the cave.

He shook so hard he thought he'd throw up. How had he been followed? *Stupid!* He'd deserve to be outed for not paying more attention!

He stayed in the mouth of the cave, scanning the tops of the nearest boulders. The sound of the wind and waves rose and fell in irregular rhythm. Insects buzzed right beside his ears.

A tall silhouette appeared on a nearby pillar, framed against the moonlight: a man rising from a crouch, standing up straight to scan the surrounding rocks.

Forest moved deeper into the cave, eyes on the figure. His heart pounded hard in his throat. What would he do if he was caught? Who was this man? Could he talk his way out of it? Fight? Beg for mercy?

Finally the man moved on, out of view.

Still, Forest stayed in his hiding place a long time, until he was cold and cramping. He climbed out of the cave slowly, taking a sharp rock with him. Not much of a weapon, but better than nothing.

Not wanting to risk the light, he found it hard-going to get back to the path. He was all scraped forearms and bruised knees, but at least he hadn't made any gasps of pain. Eventually he found the grave track and, crouched among the scrub, finally allowed himself to flick the light on every now and then, looking for the bike.

Suddenly it was there, right in front of him. It had been moved – out of the bushes and onto the path. Impossible to miss.

A piece of paper had been folded and wedged between the hand-brake and the handlebars.

Forest's fingers fumbled as he scrambled to turn off the light. He froze for a good two minutes, looking all around, ears straining for any sound, the smell of ocean and bush coming with every shallow breath. Finding no sign of the man who'd been searching the rocks, he slowly approached the bike and plucked out the paper.

A nearby voice snuffled, as though waking from a doze, and rasped, 'Forest?'

Forest hardly realised what he was doing, but before he knew it he was flying back up the gravel path on the bike, pedalling with the fire of adrenaline and terror.

It wasn't until he was back beneath the streetlights of Shacktown that he ditched the bike, leaving it where he'd found it. He sprinted down to the beach, away from the streets.

He had to rest, then, panting and coughing from the exertion.

The fear was too much. What was written on that note? A threat?

Stopping under a streetlight he pulled the paper from his pocket and unfolded it.

> SOMEONE'S LYING.
> OVEREEM'S DIVE CENTRE, PUMP SHED, 10 AM
> DAY AFTER TOMORROW.
> COME ALONE.

He stood there for a long minute, reading the note again and again. Fighting to breathe.

He scrunched up the paper.

Someone was onto him.

He had to leave.

He had to leave *now*.

He ran back to Ivy's, but when he tried to slip over the fence he was too clumsy, too loud. Torchlight shone bright in his eyes, and he backed away with a whimper.

'*Forest*?' came a terse whisper. '*Why aren't you inside?*'

It was a female voice, but not Ivy's. The light moved, and he could see again. It was Linda.

'How did you get out without us seeing you?' she demanded. '*How long have you been gone?*'

Forest was caught off guard. The note. *Where was the note?* He looked down – still crumpled in his hand. He couldn't let them see it.

'Forest? What happened? Are you okay? *Did someone take you from Ivy's?*'

'No,' he said, fighting to show her the beaten boy she expected to see. It wasn't hard tonight – he was rattled.

He closed his eyes.

'I went for a walk,' he said. He put his hands behind his back, slipping the letter down the back of his shorts. 'I wanted to . . . what's the point being free if I can't walk around my home town?'

'What do you mean, *free*?' she said. 'Were you kept locked up before?'

Shit. He didn't want to give them any hints that they might take too seriously. Unless . . . could he use this?

'I . . .' *Think, Forest. Think.* 'I feel safe in Shacktown. Not like Hobart. That's a . . . bad place. I didn't like being stuck in Hobart. I had to get out of that city, I had to run away . . .'

'*Hobart?*'

'Please,' he whispered. 'I want my grandmother.'

'Yes, okay,' said Linda gruffly, dragging him to the door. 'Stick by me, can't have you running off again.' He heard Zeus barking, and then the dog came bounding up to him. Lights in Safe Harbour flicked on.

The immediate threat averted, Forest's mind returned to the note he'd been given. And who it was he might have seen down by the boulder field.

CHAPTER 23

AHAB

Ahab sat on his balcony, smoking a cigarette, his morning swim complete. He shared the view with a bleary-eyed De Corrado, who was sipping a coffee.

The lights of Shacktown shimmered in the rising twilight, the roof of the Mermaid's Darling creaking as it warmed up.

'So they've all just left?'

He'd watched a number of unmarked police cars drive out of town – the inn was on one of the major thoroughfares.

'Not all of them, but most,' said De Corrado. 'We're not beat cops, we're CIB. Given how the boy has relaxed after coming back to Shacktown, it suggests being in Hobart was causing him all that distress we observed. That means Hobart's the place to pick up the trail, and so that's where the resources are going.'

She pulled her knees to her chest, resting her heels on the seat of the chair, her black hair tangling in the wind.

'I just hope being here and feeling safe means Forest will open up soon. I still think that's how we solve what happened to him. But we can't have one of ours with him all day. Although even when there *is* a detective or a uniform with him, Ivy keeps getting in the way.'

'She has a right to,' said Ahab.

'You're defending her?'

'I'm a realist. Forest can clearly evade the police whenever he wants to, and he's never going to relax if you're shadowing his every move. That'll do more harm than good. Don't you learn anything about psychology at the academy?'

She gave him a withering look, then rose, straightening her shirt. 'Enjoy your rooftop, Innkeeper.'

He let her go, watching the town from his vantage point. It was a hive of activity. Out on the water were coloured fishing boats sailing in and out of the marina, making up for the days lost to the Black Wind. A van pulled up below – a group of twenty-somethings pooled out. That would be the big booking for the inn today.

Forest was clearly a Dempsey to his bones; Dempsey boys knew how to keep secrets. When it felt safe enough to extend the boy his trust, he'd share all he knew. He'd been thinking about it all night, and it was the only way – tell Forest about the Business, and then together they would come up with a plan to take the criminal side out of it.

If Forest agrees.

He was young. He was traumatised. But . . . there just wasn't any other way. Besides, Jesse, Davey and Mackenzie had all been brought into it at a younger age than Forest.

In the meantime, he had to make sure the police didn't investigate Dempsey Abalone too closely – the Business was good at hiding its tracks, but without Davey at the helm . . .

Chips knew what she was doing with the day-to-day operations, and she had Ivy to look after the bigger picture, but between Blackbeard and the cops, they were more exposed than they'd ever been . . .

Ahab sighed.

I'll have to help out the Business. Just this one time.

Ahab waited near the boatsheds by the marina, sitting on a bench rusted by sea spray. When Chips showed up, he saw that she was carrying two bottles of beer. A football jersey exposed her ropey fisherman's arms, her sandy hair pulled back into her familiar cap.

'I got your message,' she said. She passed him one of the bottles and slumped down next to him. Her face was drawn, her eyes sunken. 'Have a beer with me. For old time's sake.'

He hesitated before he cracked it open. 'For old time's sake.'

Ahab had given years of his life to the operation, but when his own mother had fallen prey to ice, he could lie to himself no longer. But that didn't mean he hated those still involved. He remembered what it was like, to feel like you were just a businessman. The world of drug dealing was alluring – the money, the adrenaline, easy access to whatever you wanted.

But when he'd left, he'd fallen out. Hard. Blaming Davey for Jesse and his family's disappearance had been a stupid mistake, but you couldn't take mistakes back.

'I know you, Ahab. I know what you're thinking.'

'I don't think you do, lass,' said Ahab.

'Davey is gone. Forest is back. You're thinking you can help Forest turn Dempsey Abalone legit.'

Damn. He'd forgotten just how bright she was – that's how she'd worked her way up to becoming Davey's 2IC.

He looked at the cigarette butt pinched in his fingers, then threw it to the ground.

'We know the writing's on the wall, Ahab. Ivy will make sure the Business goes to Forest, and I imagine he'll run it just as she wants. Still, things might change for us. Maybe you'll get what you want.' The light in Chips's eyes faded. 'But the Business may not exist long enough for that to happen. Blackbeard knows too much.'

The words fell from her lips like stones dropped off the pier.

'So it's true. He's here?'

In answer, she sculled the rest of her beer in one go.

'Tell me everything,' said Ahab.

'You'll only use it against us to bring the Business down.'

'What does Blackbeard know?' insisted Ahab.

'Everything, Ahab. He knows the chain of command. He knows how we operate – we've seen strange boats at a few of our old drop sites.'

'Then he's bought off one of your crew.'

'It's worse than that. He's made contact with some of our old suppliers. The only people who know our suppliers are Davey, me, and . . . well, you know.'

'Jonah Donnager,' said Ahab.

'No. Jesse Dempsey.'

Ahab thought back to Davey's note to Shelby. *Tell Jesse I'm sorry.*

'I'll tell you one more thing, Ahab, and then you and I go our separate ways. Jesse was supposed to return one day. He told Davey to look after the place until then.' She paused, turning the empty beer bottle in her hands. 'But then a few days ago Forest shows up, looking the way he did . . . Now we're all thinking that you were right, all those years ago: Davey *did* do something to Jesse and his family. We think he must've paid someone to abduct them, kept them chained up, for all we know. But then Forest escapes, and now Blackbeard is here . . . We think maybe Blackbeard is Jesse.'

Ahab's mouth went dry. He drank from his beer to hide his dismay.

'So,' said Chips. 'The crew is divided. Half want to defect to Blackbeard, half want to fight back.'

'Why did no one ever *tell* me any of this?' said Ahab.

'Even Ivy doesn't know that Jesse chose to leave, as far as I can tell,' said Chips. 'Davey only told a couple of us, swearing us to secrecy on Jesse's orders . . . I don't need to tell you how nasty he could be if you didn't follow orders. None of us are game to tell her – if she finds out we knew all this and didn't tell her, she'd kill us herself.'

'So Blackbeard's going to win.'

'He will if you insist on Dempsey Abalone going legit,' said Chips. She gestured for a cigarette.

'Since when do you smoke?' he asked.

'Since I recently became very stressed.'

She struggled to light it with shaking hands – he helped her, and she smiled in gratitude.

'You sure you don't want to come back and lead the Business?'

'No.'

She rested a head on his shoulder.

'I don't regret it, you know?' she said. 'I'm glad you introduced me to his world. Wouldn't change it for anything.'

If she meant that to be comforting, it had the opposite effect.

CHAPTER 24

MACKEREL

Against all odds, Mackerel had been invited to Ivy's for dinner. He'd used some of the money Shelby had given him to buy a nice new shirt. Now he wished he'd washed it, as it was scratching at his neck.

Even though he'd dressed up, he still didn't fit in. The dining room at Safe Harbour was gleaming and airy, with ocean views, real silverware and that giant dining room table.

Across that dinner table, Forest Dempsey was newly calm and assured. He held his own in conversation. He'd become less gaunt since his rescue – he'd eaten his dinner twice as fast as anyone else, and was already eating his second helping – but there were still those dark bags under his eyes.

But then, it wasn't surprising the poor boy couldn't sleep. He thought of the tattoo. He thought of the fact that someone would've had to hold him down while they buzzed those words into his skin.

Shelby, Mackerel noticed, was also watching Forest like a hawk. She was at least being civil to Mackerel, which was nice. But he remained nervous – she would still want more from him than he was willing to tell.

Davey's absence hung in the room like a dark cloud – their family had been drastically reconfigured in the space of a few days. Kane was in complete denial: poking at his food, snapping at any question sent his way, taking things personally. At least Forest's dog, Zeus, had his head on Kane's lap, the boy feeding him almost half of his own serving.

And Kane and Forest kept stealing looks at each other. The cousins seemed equally fascinated by the other.

Mackerel desperately wanted to participate in the conversation – to make it better, fill it with warmth and light. He used to be a great conversationalist, but these days he always felt like he couldn't find a way in. Even *Forest* was better at it than he was, although it soon became apparent to all that Forest was falling asleep at the table.

When the boy's voice stumbled to a halt more or less mid-sentence, Ivy whispered to Shelby, 'I can't imagine the *culture shock* of all this. Poor thing.' There was a surprisingly bitter tone to her voice.

Mackerel heard a fork clatter to the table and then Shelby had her face in her hands. Kane rushed to her side, and Mackerel rose to follow. Shelby waved them both back to their seats. 'I'm fine,' she said.

Kane stayed by her, rubbing her shoulder. 'It'll be okay, Mum.'

Shelby reached up to rest her hand on his.

'Alright, enough of this farce, then,' said Ivy. 'Bedtime. You two can stay here tonight. Kane, dear, you'll share Forest's room.' The way she said it, with a sharp look at Forest, now dozing at the table, made Mackerel think he was missing something. 'And you, Mackerel. Curfew soon, I imagine?'

The dismissal stung, particularly when Kane shot him a look of blame, as though it was his fault he couldn't stay and help comfort his mother.

But it *was* his fault he had curfew.

He said his goodnights, with Forest stirring awake and giving Mackerel a sleepy wave, and he walked out onto the deck. The sky sparkled with stars. The sound of the waves; the smell of jacaranda. A buzz of insects.

He pulled his vape out of his pocket and sucked in a cloud.

'How did you like dinner, dear?' Ivy appeared at his side, startling him.

She looked at the vape, then held out her hand. 'Give it here.'

Obedient, he passed it over. She examined it, took a couple puffs, then handed it back with a cough. 'What are you, twelve years old? It tastes like lollies!'

Why was she out here? What did she want? He and Ivy didn't *do* small talk.

He tried to speak, but his throat had closed over.

'What did you think of Forest, dear?' said Ivy. 'Did he look okay to you?'

'He looked tired. I don't reckon he's been sleeping.'

Ivy grunted. 'You obviously haven't heard. Good, that means the police know how to keep their mouths shut. For your information, Forest snuck out last night, evaded a police guard – *which I did not authorise* – and went for a wander around Shacktown.'

'*What*? Did anything happen to him?' gasped Mackerel.

'Yes, sadly Forest got abducted all over again, and is currently being held captive . . . Dimwit, clearly nothing happened!'

Mackerel tried to respond but Ivy spoke over him.

'I'm arranging for Frankie to stay in town and have daily sessions with him. We need Forest on an even keel – he needs to start answering our questions. This can't go on forever. Of course, I'll breathe easier now that the CIBs are gone, but . . .' She sucked at her lip. 'How much does Shelby know about Davey?'

'She's suspicious. She found some of his guns yesterday.'

'I figured as much. Before you arrived she was . . . *questing*. You didn't tell her anything?' Her eyes narrowed.

'Of course not.'

'Don't take that tone with me.'

'I'm not – I didn't —'

'Good. Because, heaven help me, you're the last person I can still trust,' said Ivy. She watched the sea through the trees, the breeze causing her curls to dance. 'What a mess.'

Mackerel's eyes bulged – did she just say she could trust him?

'With Davey gone, the crew will need another leader. Can you do it?'

'Do what?'

She opened her mouth angrily, then calmed herself with visible effort. Her nostrils flared as she breathed deep. 'Dear, I made myself quite clear. This is going to be a long conversation if you can't follow simple logic. *Can you lead the Business, yes or no?* I know that's what you want. At least you've proven that you're not completely useless at the work.'

'I . . . I don't think . . . No, I'm not . . .'

'Stop stammering. They didn't put you in prison because you were bad at what you do, they put you in there because you were *good* at what you do.'

That was almost a compliment. Mackerel felt like his eyes were going dark, his hearing becoming muffled. For some reason his memory was returning to one of the many beatings he received from Jesse, as though that would help him make sense of his mother, for the first time, *complimenting* him . . .

'Do you think I wasn't paying attention? I read every article, followed the case notes. I can't fault the work you did up there – you won clients over, stayed ahead of the police, built up your business. You didn't do anything wrong. *Dogs* are just an occupational hazard.' She spat that word. People who spoke to the police, anyone who snitched, were known as dogs in the criminal world. In the Dempsey family, any dog-like tendencies were quickly bred out of you. 'I imagine you trusted people too easily. You always were gormless and gullible.'

'You'd trust me with Dempsey Abalone?' said Mackerel.

'Until Forest comes of age, yes. Without Davey, the crew is adrift. That hussy, Chips, couldn't turn a profit selling bananas to Queenslanders. And . . . there's rumours of another player come to join in our game.'

'Blackbeard.'

'You've *heard*?' There was real surprise in her voice. She paused for several breaths. 'Well, I'd sooner you take over than Chips,' she said. 'And it keeps Forest safe.'

'How?' said Mackerel.

'Dimwit! Forest is the heir to everything. He has a target on his back! I *don't* want him sucked into the drug game at his age. Isn't that much obvious?'

She caught and held Mackerel's eyes.

'Will you take over the Business? You'll have to earn their trust, but I'll vouch for you. We'll have to move quickly, before Chips does irreparable damage.'

Worlds clashed and warred inside of Mackerel, even as he struggled to comprehend what was being asked of him.

Mum wants my help? he thought.

That showed how weak he was – he made it a rule *never* to call her Mum, not even in his own mind.

'Joel was a bastard,' she said, meaning Mackerel's father. 'My only regret is he never knew how much I hated him until the hour that he died.'

As always, she knew what to say to disorient him.

Mackerel knew that Ivy had never loved his dad. It wasn't until he was sixteen that he found out an even worse truth – Joel wasn't Davey's father. Davey was the result of an affair Ivy had had with her true love, but she refused to give up the life Joel Dempsey's power and influence afforded her. If Joel had ever discovered Davey's true heritage, things would've been different for Mackerel. *He* might've been the favourite, and Davey would've been in the background. That's what rankled Mackerel the most. Joel had teased and bullied and beat up Mackerel more than he ever had Davey, and far more than Jesse. Jesse, the soldier. Capable, ruthless – a leader. And Davey, the golden boy. Strong and smart and handsome. Davey, who wasn't even a Dempsey by blood.

Maybe that's what had made Mackerel want to take over the Business five years ago, drug-addled as he was. The Business was *his* birthright.

'But even though you're half Joel's son, you're also half mine,' continued Ivy. 'Maybe that half will be enough to get the job done.' She eyed him with clear dislike. 'I dare say you'd enjoy that, wouldn't you, Mackerel? Finally get a taste of what you've been embarrassingly desperate for all this time?'

I'd have status again. People wouldn't spit at me on the street. I'd have power. Money . . .

He imagined himself as he was, in the warm Queensland air, dressed in nothing but a towel and a thick gold chain around his neck, standing on the balcony of a penthouse suite watching the sun rise, a beautiful woman still asleep in his bed.

Then he remembered the banging of the prison-cell doors, the contempt of the guards, the hard seats of the courtroom.

'Curfew,' he choked. 'I've gotta go!'

'Of course. Run away. I should've known better.'

'I'll give you an answer tomorrow, Ivy,' said Mackerel, backing away from her, his hands up as though she'd levelled a gun at him. 'Don't write me off just yet!'

CHAPTER 25

FOREST

The next morning Forest opened the pantry in search of breakfast, baffled at the variety of foods inside. He looked up at the different boxes of cereals, their bright colours, and swallowed.

'Need some help?' said Kane.

Forest tried not to be angry with the other boy – it wasn't his fault Ivy had put them in the same room. It wasn't his fault that she'd cut off his chance to sneak away unseen to meet up with Huck.

'No, I'm okay,' he said.

'Cool.' Kane reached past him to take down the box of Weet-Bix, fixing himself a bowl and then taking it to the lounge room. Once he was gone, Forest took down the Coco Pops.

This morning he was supposed to meet the stranger at Overeem's Dive Centre. He'd thought long and hard about it all through the night. He *had* to go. Because whoever it was, they knew he was lying. But also . . . well, after examining the photographs of Ivy's family all over the house, he thought perhaps he knew who had left him that note.

'Want some help?' said Shelby, breaking through his thoughts.

Forest spun, arms rising.

'Shh, it's okay . . .' Shelby smiled. She gestured for him to take a seat at the kitchen table and opened the box for him, pouring out the cereal.

Hesitating, Forest sat down.

Shelby put the bowl of Coco Pops in front of him. 'Where's Zeus?' she asked.

'Outside, enjoying the sunshine,' said Forest, forcing his voice to be friendly.

The bowl she'd made him was overfull, and as he took a first tentative spoonful he felt . . . *bliss*. He quickly shovelled more in his mouth. Why did these people ever leave the house, when there was such wonderful food available all the time? Then he wiped his mouth, and looked longingly at the carton.

Shelby reached out for the box – he'd thought she was just staring into space while he ate, her mind miles away, but she must have been watching him closely. 'You want another.'

Forest shook his head. 'I'm going for a walk.'

'Where are you going?' said Shelby, putting the box back into the pantry.

'The beach. Just to clear my head,' Forest said, already headed towards the door.

'Are you sure you should be out there alone?' said Shelby. 'I'll come with you.'

'No,' he said, too quickly.

Silence filled the space between them. He studied her closely now – last night she had seemed messy, fragile as an already-broken egg shell. Now she wore make-up, had her hair curled, wore nice clothing . . .

He took a breath. He had to get to the dive centre by 10 am. What would Forest Dempsey do next?

'I won't be alone, I'll have Zeus. I'm fine.'

'Dogs don't count,' she said.

'Okay . . .' He thought through his options. 'Call Uncle Mack to come pick me up.'

'Mackerel?' said Shelby.

Forest sat down at the table. 'Yes. Will you please call him?' He smiled, showing all of his teeth. 'I'd like to spend the day with Uncle Mack.'

'Alright . . . I'll see if he's free.' Shelby went to make the call.

Why did she sound so suspicious? Surely it wasn't suspicious that he wanted to spend time with his uncle? Had he missed something?

Some part of him felt guilty, but it was a genius idea, making Mackerel the cure-all for Forest Dempsey's anxiety. The man seemed the easiest member of the Dempsey family to manipulate, the weakest link. Now he just had to really win Mackerel over to his side. And he knew just how to do it.

CHAPTER 26

MACKEREL

Mackerel felt like a terrible human being, because his main concern as he drove towards Ivy's house was that this was *another* day of lost income.

If Forest needs you, you need to be there, he thought. *You're the only one he trusts.*

But that hadn't made letting Big Mane down feel any better. Mackerel wiped his sweaty face – he hadn't slept well, and that always made him anxious – and he also had this suspicion that Ivy would be waiting, ready to put her question to him again . . .

I can't go back to that world, he thought. *I'm no good at it anymore.*

That was a lie, and he knew it.

I'm a normal citizen. That's all I want.

That was still a lie, but with a better shape.

Lost in those thoughts, before he knew it he had pulled into the tree-covered street and came to a stop outside the front gate of Safe Harbour.

Mackerel rolled down the window. The day was looking to be a scorcher – the flowers buzzed with bees.

Forest was waiting just on the other side of the gate. When he saw Mackerel he waved, then ran over to climb into the car.

'Where's the dog?' said Mackerel.

'Thought it'd be good for him to spend some time with Kane,' said Forest. 'And I wanted some time alone with you.'

Mackerel felt a smile growing at the corner of his lips. He pulled away from the kerb before Ivy appeared. 'How are you doing, kid?'

Forest shrugged. 'Take a guess.'

'Pretty shit?' Mackerel shifted in his seat. 'Anywhere you wanna go today?'

Mackerel was suddenly much happier about spending the day with Forest – hell, with the money Shelby had given him, they could drive to the other side of Tassie and back. As long as he was back in time for curfew. The thought of leaving Shacktown was suddenly very, very appealing.

Then he paused. 'Ivy said last night that you have to talk to Frankie every day?' She really was set on that counsellor – she'd even put her up in a local Airbnb.

'Frankie.' Forest was grimacing. 'You can drop me off there later. Right now, I want to go to the beach.'

The sound of waves and wind, gulls cawing, children screaming and laughing in the waves. The beaming summer heat.

Mackerel left his shoes in the car, tiptoeing across the hot asphalt of the carpark and onto the hot sand. He took a deep breath, listening to someone's music playing nearby.

Forest walked ahead, right down to the tide line, water up to his ankles. The boy looked much more alive here, away from Safe Harbour – Mackerel thought again of how much Forest seemed to hate restriction.

Mack was still filled with anger about whatever had happened to the boy, but that emotion was less strong than it had been. All of his emotions felt burned out now: grief for Davey, fear of Blackbeard, anger about Forest, confusion over what to say to Shelby . . .

Anyway, here at the beach, he could let it all fade.

He stepped into the ocean and gave a sigh as the cold sea water reached up around his ankles, cooling his feet.

Forest crouched, playing with the wet sand from under the waves. Then he picked up a shell. He looked out over the ocean for a moment longer, then returned to Mackerel, holding out the shell. It was an Adelaide top shell, with its leopard print.

'Here. Hold it in your hand,' said Forest.

Mackerel took the shell in his right hand but Forest quickly took it from him and pushed it into his left hand. 'No. *Vena amoris*, the vein of love. It runs into your left hand, from your heart. Your heart's blood is salt water. It works better in your left hand.'

'What does?' said Mackerel.

'I want to show you something. It's . . . it's a bit strange, but pretty cool.'

'What is it?' said Mackerel.

'Our family . . . our relationship with the sea . . .' Forest looked out over the ocean. 'Sometimes, shells speak to me. The ocean speaks to me.'

'Shells speak to you?' Where had Mackerel heard that before?

Forest stepped to the side. 'Bring the tip of the shell to your mouth and clearly tell it a secret. You have to look out to the ocean as you do.'

Mackerel chuckled. 'You just want me to look like an idiot.'

'Uncle Mack . . .' Forest's voice was deadly serious. 'Just let me show you. But you have to take it seriously: it doesn't work if the secret doesn't come from your heart.'

Mackerel looked towards the ocean. 'You're not playing a joke on me?'

'No.' Forest walked away, feet sloshing in the waves, until he was completely out of earshot, the rumble of the waves masking the sounds between them. He motioned for Mack to stop looking at him – to look out over the waves.

Mack focused on the horizon.

He thought of a secret. One from the heart. It took him a while to even gather the strength to say it to a shell, but he spoke it clearly.

'Neither of my parents ever told me that they love me.'

He turned back to Forest and the boy approached, taking the shell from Mackerel and holding it to his ear.

He closed his eyes.

'The shell says . . . it's *certain* your mum and dad love you.'

Mackerel's mouth dropped open, and now cold sweat broke out all over his body.

No, no, no . . . I'm going crazy.

Now he remembered where he'd heard about shell-speaking before. Mad Aunt Miriam.

In her ice-induced psychosis, Ahab's mother had talked to shells as well. Had it *been* psychosis?

Forest slipped the shell into his pocket.

'How?' choked Mackerel.

The boy shrugged. 'I told you. Sometimes, the shells speak to me. And . . . there are other things I can do.'

'Like what? Show me!' said Mackerel.

'First, take me to the dive centre. The one with the aquarium.' He bent down to the sand, picking up three more shells and putting them in his pockets. He held his hand in the water, then stood up. He turned to Mackerel. 'I want to get close to the fish.'

Overeem's Dive Centre was a large complex of concrete and wide glass windows, built near the ocean's edge but backing onto scrub.

The place was something like a public square for Shacktown, with an open and airy entrance hall, home to a café, and today there were temporary market stalls set up on the wide tiled area out the front.

The main attraction was the aquarium, one of the biggest in Australia, rivalling Sydney's and Melbourne's, but there was also a deep saltwater pool where diving and snorkel classes could run. The dive centre had been one of the first big things that brought the tourists to Shacktown.

Sitting in his car, Mackerel realised that the market stalls meant today must have been Saturday – he'd lost track of the week. There were journalists circling like sharks, filming stories or speaking to the bustling locals.

I can't handle the media on top of everything else, he thought woefully.

He reached into the back seat and found a baseball cap and a large hoodie. 'Put these on?' he said to Forest.

The hoodie was way too big for him – it was like a dress – so Forest bunched up the sides and tied a knot, then rolled back the sleeves.

'Trendy,' he said with a straight face.

The shells spoke to him . . .

'Sunnies?' said Mackerel, giving him an old pair from his glovebox.

With the cap and sunnies hiding his face, Forest trailed after Mackerel. They walked quickly around the square, avoiding most of the journalists, and through the big glass doors that led to the café area. The food and drinks menu was written out on diving slates – usually used to communicate underwater with waterproof markers – and they caught Mackerel's eye.

'Do you want a coffee?' he asked Forest.

'I . . . I've never had one.'

At first he felt alarmed – what a stupid thing to ask! How could he keep forgetting Forest didn't have a lifetime of normal experiences? But if he always handled him with kid gloves, surely that would only make the boy feel worse . . .

No. He couldn't feel guilty for asking questions. This was exactly the sort of thing Mackerel should be helping Forest to discover.

Yeah. Treat him like a normal kid. Don't think about the shells. You're not crazy.

'You're gonna love it.' Mackerel ordered them both a flat white, but asked for a caramel shot in Forest's – he'd discovered at dinner last night that Forest had a serious sweet tooth.

The barista, a man named Chase, whom Mackerel had gone to high school with, glanced over at Forest. He leaned in close. 'That's Forest, yeah?'

'Yeah,' said Mackerel.

'Nice disguise. Had those journos in here earlier. The news is finally beginning to break – they removed the embargo.' Chase put his hand to his chest and tutted. 'Poor little sweetheart.' He watched Forest with a morbid fascination.

'Thanks,' said Mackerel.

Chase patted him on the shoulder. 'No problem, babe. Actually, once you've had your coffee, I might come with.'

Chase made their coffees, then disappeared into the kitchen to get changed.

'I hate that *everyone* gets to know my story, even though I don't want to talk about it,' said Forest bitterly. 'All these people have come here to try to *break* me.'

Mackerel paused at that. Forest had a point – the embargo would have to be lifted eventually, but then Forest would struggle to walk down the street without people begging to know what had happened.

But . . . well, the boy presented himself so well now. Surely it wasn't unreasonable for people to assume he could speak about what happened to him? How bad could it really be if he was functioning so well?

'Don't look at me like that,' said Forest.

'Like what?'

'I don't need you feeling sorry for me. I'm fine.'

He took a sip of his coffee, and that at least made him smile.

'Oh man. This *is* good.'

Chase returned, having shed his apron. 'I told the shift supervisor I'm gonna be tour guide for you guys. He said that's okay. Because *I'm* the shift supervisor.' He crouched down in front of Forest. 'I'll be honest, little buddy, I have no fucking clue how to act around you. Sorry if I say the wrong thing.' He stood up and sauntered off towards the aquarium entrance.

Chase was a great tour guide, although Mackerel wasn't sure those were *really* the names of every single fish they passed. He had been through the aquarium enough times, and he found it more interesting to watch Forest. The boy was the perfect audience. He walked around with an open mouth. He was fascinated by the tank with the rays, the touch pool, the jellyfish, the octopus.

Cuthbert the Cuttlefish seemed to grab Forest's attention the most. He stopped for a long time beside the tank, reading the description, watching Cuthbert change colours. He put his fingers on the glass and closed his eyes, as though listening.

Chase sidled up to Mackerel. 'What's he doing?'

'I think he's listening to the fish,' said Mackerel.

Chase laughed. 'No, seriously, what is he doing?'

Mackerel stayed silent.

And then they moved into the room with the seahorses, a large space with a number of cylindrical tanks, well lit and colourful.

Here Forest's wonder became almost tangible – he walked around light on his feet, like a breeze circling the room.

'Our pièce de résistance,' announced Chase. 'The Land of the Seahorse.'

Forest approached the tank in the middle. The sign read: *Weedy Seadragon.*

These seadragons had long snouts and bodies that moved and waved like the seaweed. They were a dark red, with flashes of colour, blending in with the kelp.

'They're local, around here,' said Chase. 'Fascinating little creatures, the weedy seadragon, the way they blend into their environment. They're masters of mimicry.'

Forest read the description slowly, then went down on his knees, holding both hands on the tank. He pressed his forehead against the glass and began to quietly cry.

'What do we do?' whispered Chase, looking alarmed.

'We just let him be,' said Mackerel.

Forest's fingers were drawing patterns on the glass.

'Alright, well . . . I better get back to the café.' Chase squeezed Mackerel's shoulder. 'I was so sorry to hear about your brother, babe. He was a good man. Shacktown is a worse place without him. Let us know if there's any way we can help.' And he was gone.

Mackerel sat down cross-legged beside Forest.

'You alright?' said Mackerel.

Forest wiped his eyes and nose. 'Yeah. I'm fine,' he said softly. 'I'm going to the bathroom. I'll meet you back here.'

Mackerel watched him go, then looked back at the patterns he'd marked on the glass. They looked like a word.

They'd drawn plenty of attention from the other patrons, but he ignored their strange looks and breathed on the marks.

The condensation brought up the marks Forest's fingers had made. It was a word, but it had been crossed out:

~~WEEDY~~

Mackerel stood up and followed Forest.

Forest hadn't walked to the bathroom, he was ducking out through a side exit.

Mackerel trailed him at a distance, but he'd waited a moment too long before slipping out the exit himself – he couldn't see Forest anywhere along the service-way alley.

He followed the lane, footsteps splashing in puddles from leaking pipes, to where it opened out onto a wide grassy area that led right into the bush, blocked off on one side by the giant concrete wall of the above-ground dive pool. It was empty save for a shed the size of Big Mane's kitchen, which was labelled as the pump room.

Where had Forest gone?

He tried not to panic. The only place he could've gone was the bush or the pump room. He made his way to the door of the pump room, but stopped short. Over the loud hum of the machines inside . . . voices. Mack pressed his ear against the door. The metal was thin. He heard every word perfectly.

'. . . carefully about what you're about to say. Your brother is waiting for me in the aquarium, and . . .'

Mackerel fell away from the wall. *Impossible*. He quickly pressed his ear against the door again.

'. . . no, not even my family. No one can know I'm alive. If you keep my secret, Forest, we can help each other.' It was a deep, familiar voice.

'I know exactly who you are. I recognised you from the photos at Ivy's house – you passed right by me out at the boulder field. Why were you following me?'

'I was watching the house, trying to find a chance to come knock on your door, but the police were everywhere. Then I saw you sneak out – I lost you near the boatsheds, but then I saw you take that bike a little later.'

'So you want me to trust you even though you were stalking me? And no, I don't forgive you. Not yet,' Forest paused. 'But you can make it up to me.'

'Forgive? I had nothing to do with it, Forest!'

It was definitely his brother's voice.

Davey.

Davey was still alive.

He couldn't make sense of it. He'd seen Davey die! Davey was *dead*!

You didn't see his face. All you saw were his tattoos . . . it would take work, but if you found another body . . . not impossible in Davey's line of work.

'I'm so *sorry*, Forest! I don't know what could have happened! You were supposed to be safe!'

I'm not crazy, I'm not crazy, this might really be happening . . .

But it can't be happening!

Mackerel had to keep his focus on the conversation.

'You can make it up to me,' Forest was saying. 'You can help me avenge Mum.'

'What happened to Jesse? *Tell me*,' said Davey.

'What happened to *him*? Do you know what they did to *me!*' shouted Forest.

Mackerel pressed his ears so close to the metal it was painful. Tears sprang up in his eyes.

If Davey was alive, then everything would be fine.

He felt dizzy. He felt sick.

His brother was alive.

'Please don't tell my family. If Blackbeard knows I'm alive, he'll kill me.'

'Who the hell is Blackbeard?' said Forest.

Mackerel's heart lurched. The elation he'd felt a second ago collapsed into pieces.

Blackbeard. Blackbeard is after Davey.

That's why Davey wanted everyone to think he was dead.

Oh shit . . . oh shit, oh shit, oh shit.

'Blackbeard is already in town. He wants Dempsey Abalone all to himself. And I just . . . I thought you were safe. I need you to remember that I warned you, and then vouch for me when the time is right.'

A flicker of movement. Someone was coming around the main building. Mackerel quickly moved around the side of the shed, keeping himself out of view.

Then he realised he needed to get away. If someone saw him acting suspiciously, they might come over and find Davey hiding in the shed . . . and then the news would be out . . . and Blackbeard . . .

He limp-hobbled back inside the aquarium. Back to the Land of the Seahorse. He'd have to work the rest out later.

Forest was drenched in sweat by the time he got back.

Mackerel, sitting on a bench bolted to the wall, grabbed his shoulders. He could feel the boy trembling. 'I was this close to calling the police. Where the hell did you go?'

Forest pushed him away.

'Mackerel, you're not gonna believe this . . . your brother is alive. I had to be sure that . . . I just had to be sure. But if he hasn't left yet, he might still be there, and together we can . . .'

Forest really does trust me, thought Mackerel. A renewed protectiveness for the boy settled firmly across his shoulders. *Better not tell him I was spying on him.*

Mackerel hurried behind Forest as they approached the pump shed.

Forest opened the door and they both stepped in. It was damp and dusty, full of cobwebs and the smell of chlorine, and a loud rattling came from the big pump right at the end.

'Davey?' Mack called.

There was no one inside.

They stepped in further, peering into the darker depths, where crates and boxes were stacked beside pipes leading down into the ground.

Scuffling sounded in the bushes outside, and the door slammed shut, followed by the sound of a heavy bolt.

'Davey!' shouted Mackerel, running back to the door. 'Bro!'

'I thought we could work together, Forest,' called Davey. 'I guess not. Now I've really got to get out of town.'

'Davey,' called Forest. 'I didn't call the cops, it's just me and Mack! Let us out of here. Mack can help us with the Blackbeard problem! *You owe me.*'

'Davey. Davey, please . . . please . . .' said Mackerel.

There was no response, just the sound of footsteps running away.

Mackerel held his phone in his hand, wondering who to call, still reeling.

'You're sure it's Davey?' he said suddenly. Maybe the boy had made a mistake in the dark of the shed.

'Of course I'm sure,' said Forest wearily. 'His photo is everywhere in Ivy's house. But there's a big cut on his forehead, runs from here to here,' said Forest, pointing it out on his own head. 'Doesn't look like it's been stitched up properly.'

From Mackerel's diving knife.

Davey had been the assailant in Devils Kitchen?

That's why he left the ladder for me.

'But why would he fake his death and then come to you?' said Mackerel.

'Because he had something to do with my abduction, and he knows that I know,' said Forest.

'You think he had something to do with you and your parents going missing? Bullshit. Not Davey. There's no way. *No way.*'

'He did, Mackerel. He had something to do with it.'

'You're lying. You've no idea what you're talking about. Davey is . . . He wouldn't . . .'

'Then why did he fake his death the moment I returned?'

'Because of Blackbeard?'

No, that doesn't quite make sense. There's something I'm missing.

'Who the hell is this Blackbeard?' said Forest.

'The real question is: what *happened* to you?' Mackerel's voice rose. 'All those years you were missing?'

Forest flinched away, then shook his head. 'Please. Not you, Mack. You're the only one I can trust. Don't turn on me.'

'I'm not turning on you, I just want to know!'

'I can't tell you. Please, Mack. Please don't be like them . . .'

'Okay . . . okay, I'm sorry . . .'

Mackerel stopped himself from saying more. He tried to put himself in Forest's shoes right now. A dead man had just made himself known to him . . .

'How did he let you know to meet him here? Do you have some way of contacting him?'

'No.'

'C'mon, kid! My brother is *alive*! I need to talk to him!'

'Just tell the police, then!'

Mackerel laughed, but it was humourless. 'We can't tell the police.'

'Why not?' said Forest with genuine confusion.

So Forest truly had no idea about the Business. That should've been comforting, but right then it just made everything harder.

'I'm sorry,' said Forest. 'I should've told you why I wanted to come here . . . it's just . . . it's so hard to know who to trust. Everyone seems to want something from me, or want me to be something I'm not.'

'I have to tell Shelby. She has to know,' said Mackerel.

'No,' said Forest. 'That is a *terrible* idea.'

'I know,' said Mackerel, 'but it's the right thing to do.'

Mackerel paced the shed. The constant chugging of the pump and the smell from all the cleaning chemicals was giving him a headache. He needed alcohol. He needed weed, but that would show up in his urine test. He needed ice – that'd give him the mental edge required to work out what to do.

Davey was alive and Blackbeard was here.

Forest sat on the ground, baseball cap pulled low, arms across his knees. He hadn't spoken a word since Mackerel had called Shelby.

Finally there was a knock on the door that sent a clang through the whole shed. 'Mack?'

Her voice snapped him back to reality. He didn't need ice. Stupid thing to think.

'Shelby!' Mackerel ran to the door. 'I think there's just a deadbolt.'

'Yes, thank you, Mack, I do have eyes.'

Shelby unbolted the door and opened it. Sunlight streamed in, haloing her like an angel. Mack covered his eyes.

'Where is he? Where's Forest?' She stepped inside. Her eyes held unshed tears.

'I'm here.'

Shelby studied Forest closely. 'Are you okay, Forest?' She said the words very calmly, but the implication set Mackerel's anger to boiling. He fought to bring himself under control – now was not the time.

'I'm fine,' said Forest. He stepped closer to Mackerel. 'Thanks to Uncle Mack.'

'What the hell is going on? Enough is enough. Tell me *everything!*'

'I will,' said Mackerel. 'But not here. I know a place.'

The three of them sat at the back of the Seaglass Café, in Mackerel's favourite spot. He faced the rest of the café, to ensure no one came close enough to overhear. Three hot drinks sat on the low table in mismatched clay mugs – a flat white for him, a chai for Shelby, and a hot chocolate for Forest.

The smell of the café, with its salty sea air, cooking oil and coffee, was already calming him. He needed to be calm, for what he was about to do.

Mackerel had been thinking it through the whole drive over. How do you tell someone their husband was still alive?

'I know that you're going to find this hard to believe,' he ventured. 'I know you're going to think I'm joking, or crazy, or . . .'

Shelby opened her mouth to interrupt, but he raised his hand.

'Let me finish, Shelbs. Just let me . . .' He swallowed. 'The truth is . . . Davey is still alive.'

Her eyebrows rose, then snapped back into a sharp frown.

'He faked his death. He's still alive, Shelby.'

She leaned forward. 'Why the hell would you say that?' Her eyes flicked between his, fast, searching for something. She turned to Forest, who nodded.

'He's telling the truth,' said Forest. 'I saw him, too.'

'What are you trying to do? It's not funny.'

Slowly, struggling to find the right words, Mackerel explained to Shelby what had happened under the water. That the body must have been a double, that *Davey* had attacked him under the water.

Shelby leaned back, still angry, but also showing frank disbelief in her face, in her folded arms.

Mackerel realised he had muddled his explanation. It happened when he was anxious – he stuttered and said the wrong thing . . .

'Have you been using again, Mack?'

'No! I haven't!'

'Do you think there are people out to get you? Are voices telling you that —'

'It's not psychosis, Shelby! This is really happening!'

'No, it's not. *Why* would he fake his death?'

Why?

Mackerel took a deep breath, maybe the deepest breath he'd ever taken in his life, filling his lungs for whatever he might encounter in the stormy sea he was about to dive into . . .

'Because Davey runs one of the biggest drug-import operations in Australia.'

Shock, followed by amusement, followed by confusion, followed by . . . fury.

'Bullshit,' she said.

Forest's own eyes had grown wide. '*What?*' he whispered.

It couldn't be helped. Forest had to know, for his own protection. They both needed to know.

'Dempsey Abalone is the front for a drug-smuggling business. It has been for years. Jesse was in charge last, now Davey runs it. Ivy's involved too.'

Shelby bit her lip so hard that little drops of blood had gathered under her teeth. 'He's alive.'

'Yes, Shelby,' said Mackerel. 'He's alive.'

'My gun-hiding bastard of a husband is a drug dealer . . . and he's alive. Swear to me you're not making this up. *Swear to me.*'

'I swear.'

Forest looked at his hands, shaking his head softly, muttering to himself.

Shelby reached for her chai, raising it to her lips with shaking hands, then put it back on the table without taking a sip. Forest stood up and began pacing beside the window, close enough that he could still listen.

'You looked me in the eyes, two days ago, and told me that Davey wasn't dodgy,' said Shelby. 'You lied to my face.'

'I was trying to protect you,' said Mackerel, as he thought about the next thing he had to say. 'But now you need to know, because you and Kane could be in danger.'

'Danger?' said Shelby instantly.

'Another drug baron has come to town. The Dread Pirate Blackbeard.'

'The . . . *what*?'

'He's a crime lord . . . and a very bad one at that,' said Mack. 'The way I first heard it told, he was born on the east coast of New Zealand, his father a drug lord who killed for fun. No one knows who they were, but the rumours are that Blackbeard killed him before he turned fourteen, and took over his father's business. And went hard . . . in trafficking. In all sorts of trafficking.'

'That all sounds completely made up,' said Shelby.

Mackerel knew he was rambling, botching another explanation, but he needed Shelby to understand. Forest stopped pacing and sat back down at the table, next to Shelby, so he could study Mackerel's face. He did his best to explain the way the Business used the abalone diving as a cover, trying to make her understand how it all worked, the threat Blackbeard posed now that Chips was left in charge . . .

'So my husband is a coward, too?' said Shelby. 'The moment another drug dealer shows up, he fakes his death? Leaves me and Kane to fend for ourselves? That's not the Davey I know.' She laughed once, loud and humourless. 'But I suppose what you're say-ing is I didn't really know him at all?'

'No, he's not a coward. There's something else going on,' said Mackerel. 'I just don't know what.'

'You should've told me. I deserved to know.'

'Shelby . . .' How could he make her understand? 'It was better that you weren't involved. Davey always wanted it that way. This just isn't a woman's world . . .'

'Are you serious? I can't believe . . . for a start, if both Ivy and Chips are involved – they're women.'

'Yeah, but . . . look, it takes a *special kind* of woman to . . .'

'Just shut up, Mack. Stop talking.' She drank from her chai, turning away from him. 'Davey is a drug dealer.'

'Yes,' said Mackerel. 'But not like your normal drug dealer. He's a lot more successful than —'

'*That doesn't make me feel better, Mackerel!* So, Davey is alive, but he's a criminal.'

'Yes.'

'And no one ever told me because, and I repeat, *it isn't a wom-an's world?*'

'No, Shelby, that's not the only reas—'

'Go to hell.' She breathed deliberately through her nose, her shoulders rising and falling with the effort of keeping herself under control.

'Shelbs, it's not like that . . .'

'*Go to hell.*' She took him in. 'You and Davey both.'

She dashed out of the café, her handbag swinging.

'It was the right thing to do,' said Mack, even though Forest hadn't spoken. 'She deserved to be told the truth.'

'You know what you have to do now,' said Forest, his voice shaking. 'Go follow her.'

CHAPTER 27

FOREST

Dempsey Abalone is a front for a drug syndicate.

Forest's ears were ringing. He could taste metal.

I've walked right into the middle of a gang war . . .

No. He realised it had all begun the moment he'd appeared.

Did I cause all of this?

'Do you want another hot chocolate?' asked the owner of the café. 'That one looks like it's gone cold.'

'Yes please.'

'Okay,' said the owner, but he didn't leave. Instead, he took a seat in the booth opposite Forest. 'I'm Salvatore, a friend of Mack's. He and Shelby sure left in a hurry,' he said conversationally.

'Yeah,' said Forest. He felt like he was adrift. He had no idea what to do next.

He realised the man was still there, studying him closely.

'Poor little Forest,' said Salvatore. 'I watched the conversation. I couldn't hear it, but I can guess what it was about. You and Shelby just found out, didn't you? About the Business?' He leaned forward. 'We will do what we can to protect you from Blackbeard.'

Forest didn't say anything to that. Instead he lurched to his feet and ran out the door. Even the café owner knew more than he did. Did *everyone* know?

Some conman he was! He'd convinced everyone he was the heir to Dempsey Abalone, not realising it was a front for a criminal enterprise!

His footsteps pounded down the street, stirring a flock of cockatoos into flight from an acacia tree. He'd spent months rehearsing how Forest Dempsey would respond to every conceivable scenario, but he had no idea how to respond to this.

He had to talk to someone who *knew* Forest. He had to talk to Huck.

It was daylight, so Huck wouldn't be at the boatshed. Too much risk of being caught trespassing. At this time of day he'd likely be fishing for his dinner.

He headed down to the main beach and walked along the sand, footsteps sinking, dodging bright beach tents and groups of holiday makers enjoying the summer heat. The Black Wind was a distant memory. Even that weird vibe from the death of Davey Dempsey wasn't hanging in the air anymore.

Davey Dempsey. Nope, he couldn't think about him right now. If he thought of Davey, and of this dangerous Blackbeard, he wanted to run and hide. And he couldn't. He had to do this for Huck.

Off in the distance, at the rockier end of the beach, he saw a group of fishermen, evenly spaced along the rocks. A smaller figure sat on a pillar at the end of the line.

Huck.

By the time Forest reached him, he was drenched in sweat and his face felt sunburned. 'Caught anything?' he asked.

'Not yet,' said Huck. He chewed on a cigarette, watching his fishing line where it entered the waves. He turned Forest's way, his long hair catching in the wind. 'You okay? You look upset.'

Forest saw the concern in Huck's face and it made him feel ashamed. Huck would only worry about him more if he told him about the Business. But if Jesse had been running the drug business, then it might well be connected to Forest's death.

Suddenly he felt a bit lighter. He was right – pretending to be Forest *had* unearthed a clue about the real Forest's death! He just couldn't share it with Huck yet.

'I found the cave. I need you to tell me again what happened to Forest Dempsey – every detail.'

'You *went* there?' cried Huck, dropping his cigarette.

'I didn't go inside!' said Forest hurriedly. 'I just went to have a look. I needed to know how to get there, without the map, in case it ever comes up.'

Huck pulled another cigarette from his pocket. 'Well, you know what there is to know. I don't like talking about it. Jesse Dempsey trapped me, his wife and his son in that cave. The tide rose, they drowned, I escaped.' He shivered. 'And now Forest's ghost follows me everywhere.'

Forest nodded. It was tough getting Huck to open up about this sort of stuff, to say the least. It was no good rushing him.

He sat himself down on the rocks beside his friend, watching the waves as they swelled around the rocks. In the pool beside him a crab crawled, picking its way over the rock face. Forest imagined being trapped in a cave as it slowly filled with water, as Alexandra and the real Forest had been. It spoke to some deep fear inside him – the terror of it threatened to suffocate him. He hoped he never had reason to actually go inside that cave – he didn't think he'd be able to manage it.

'And you don't know where Jesse went after that?' Forest asked.

'All I know is that me and Dad got blamed for what happened.'

'But what about the other cave? The Treasure Cave?'

'Don't talk about that!' snarled Huck. 'It's cursed.'

'But that's part of it, right? You said it was why Jesse tried to kill you three?' He thought of what he'd just learned. Was it part of the drug operation? Perhaps Alexandra Dempsey had had a moment just like the one Shelby had today, discovering that her husband was a drug dealer. 'Did he . . . store something in that cave?'

'I dunno, do I? He tried to *kill* me. I was hardly going to stick around to figure out why.'

Huck shivered, glancing around him. Forest had the disconcerting sense that Huck could hear something that wasn't there.

'When are you gonna give up this act? You need to stop pretending to be Forest.'

'Not until your name is cleared,' said Forest sharply. 'So it'd help if *you* helped.'

'Never asked you to do this.' Huck tugged on his rod. 'It won't be good if people see you talking to me.'

'One last question, then. Have you ever heard of Blackbeard?'

Huck frowned. 'No. Should I?'

'No. I guess not,' said Forest.

He held out his hand so he could take a drag of Huck's cigarette. He watched the fishermen nearby, one of whom was giving them weird looks. Buckets of bait sat beside them. He wondered what Huck was using for bait.

'Huck . . . have you got any bliss salts with you?'

'Yeah,' said Huck. 'Of course. You want some?'

'No,' said Forest, 'just wondering.' He watched the waves as he took another puff. 'But you remember the house, yeah? You ever wonder where they got it all from?'

'No,' said Huck, 'the one time I asked, I got belted. You're not thinking of trying to *deal* here, are you?'

'No,' said Forest. 'Got all the money I need as Forest Dempsey.'

'Ahuh. Just be careful hanging around with Mackerel too much,' warned Huck.

'Yeah,' said Forest heavily. 'But I like spending time with him. He's different from the rest of the family . . . and he went nuts over the shell-talking! You should have seen him! I've got his complete trust, I think.'

'I thought you were gonna save that for emergencies?'

'No, I was gonna save it for a strategic time,' said Forest. 'It was a strategic time.'

'You were always a better conman than me,' said Huck. 'You and the Witch could've done very well for yourselves if things had gone differently . . .'

Forest took another drag of the cigarette, his heart low. He thought he'd escaped the world of drugs. Now it looked like he was right back in the middle of it.

Well, at least it was a world he understood. If he had to revert to the boy he used to be, and use all the skills the Witch had taught him, then so be it.

He extinguished the cigarette and stood up. 'They'll be wondering where I am.'

'You'll come back and see me soon?' said Huck.

'Whenever I can,' said Forest.

CHAPTER 28

MACKEREL

Mackerel saw Shelby's Jeep leave the Seaglass's gravel carpark and take off down the street in a screech of tyres. He followed swiftly after her in his own car, praying she wasn't headed for the police station.

Instead, she drove along the boulevard and up the hill towards Homeward, speeding the whole way, overtaking other cars even on narrow streets. Bark had been blown off the gumtrees during the Black Wind and now blanketed driveways.

He rolled down his windows as he caught up to her on the switchback road that led up to Homeward – a strong salty breeze clacked through the eucalypt leaves overhead, a quartet of seagulls riding the air.

They arrived at almost the same time. He parked alongside her just as she was climbing out of her car.

'Shelby, wait!'

She ran to the door.

He followed as fast as he could.

She hesitated on the doormat, her hand on the doorhandle.

'He won't be here, he'll be long gone,' said Mackerel as he caught up, puffing.

'You're wrong. He'll be here,' said Shelby. She pushed inside, the hinges giving a heavy creak.

He followed her as she ran straight for her laptop, which sat on the waxed-timber dining room table. She logged in and opened up the security camera program. 'The new cameras have been shut down. It's all gone. All the footage.' She slammed the laptop closed, eyes scanning the room. 'He's been here. Only Davey knows my password.'

Mackerel didn't hesitate. 'Let's split up and search the house,' he said, moving deeper inside. He knew exactly where to look.

But Shelby was too discerning. 'Oh no, brother-in-law, I'm following you. You've got that look in your eye.'

Mackerel briefly considered trying to lose her, but he discarded that idea. He led her up the staircase, lined with photos of their good-looking family. They could've been straight out of a film. He moved through the master bedroom into their en suite.

'He's not here,' said Shelby. But he didn't move, and so neither did she.

The window was too small for anyone to get through, some of it taken up by an exhaust fan. Mackerel looked at the ceiling. There was no manhole, but there was a large extractor fan there too.

Davey's bolthole.

Shelby followed his gaze. 'You think he's in the roof?'

'See that small ring, welded onto the side of the casing?' said Mackerel. He began looking around. 'See if there's some kind of a pole with a hook.'

'You've *got* to be kidding me. That fan has never worked. Davey kept trying to reconnect it, but then he gave up and installed the one in the window.'

The two of them searched the bathroom until Mackerel found a mop that lived behind the door. Just as he'd thought: there was a plastic hook at the end of the handle.

It didn't take much to hook the ring on the casing of the ceiling fan. Mackerel yanked and the whole thing dropped out, dangling from a heavy rope, interspersed with climbing knots, that disappeared up into the hole.

'That's it,' said Shelby, already gripping the rope. 'I'm gonna kill him.'

'Wait —'

But she'd already started scurrying up, quickly disappearing into the bolthole.

Mackerel followed her up the rope, no mean feat given his weight and dodgy leg, but he couldn't fit more than his head through such a small opening.

He watched as Shelby crouched, turning on the torch on her phone. The bolthole was in a corner where the roof cavity met the outside, but it was closed off from the rest of the roof space by a wall. The rope that held up the fan casing was attached to a spring-loaded pulley system, like the ones service stations had for the tyre pumps. There was a trapdoor to the outside and another through the wall, leading into the rest of the roof space. Hooks sat on the wall – Mackerel recognised that Davey would have stored guns there.

'Most drug dealers have a place like this,' he said. 'A safe room, or an escape route. We call it a bolthole.' He tried to pull himself further in but gave up. Awkwardly squeezed his arm above his head. 'This was what your intruder was looking for.'

Shelby pushed at the door to the outside. It gave just slightly before slamming shut again. They heard a shuffle from the other side.

Both of them went very still and quiet, then Shelby pressed her ear against the door.

'Davey?' she called. 'Davey! Don't . . . don't go. Don't run. Please . . . whatever it is, we can do this together.'

A deep, heavy sigh came from the other side.

'Please, Davey,' said Shelby. 'They're telling me you're a drug dealer. If you are . . . that's okay . . . I just need to . . . Please, Davey . . . please.' She pushed against the door, but it wouldn't move. 'Help me, Mack!'

Mack again tried to squeeze through the hole, but he couldn't, he was just too big.

And for the second time that day, Mackerel heard his brother's voice.

'Shelbs . . . I'm sorry.' Davey's voice was muffled, heavy. 'This isn't a world that you'd understand. It'll be better if you let me go.'

'Never,' said Shelby. 'I won't, ever!'

'Don't tell anyone I'm alive. It's safer for you and Kane. Don't come looking for me.'

'Where are you *going*?' she said. '*What about us?*'

'Blackbeard is going to take over this town, Mackerel!' Davey's voice rose. 'Blackbeard's already *here*. There's nothing I can do to stop him. He'll kill me if he finds me. If he finds out I'm alive, he'll take Shelby hostage, or torture her, or . . . He still thinks I'm a threat, even though the whole crew have turned on me.'

'The crew is loyal to you!' said Mackerel. 'You know they are.'

'Not anymore. When Forest returned the way he did, in that state . . . the whole crew think I've been lying about what happened . . . if one of them finds me, it'll be just as bad as Blackbeard.'

'What are you talking about?' said Mackerel. 'You're not making any sense.'

'Wait, you *did* have something to do with Forest's abduction?' said Shelby.

'No,' said Davey heavily, 'because it wasn't an abduction. Jesse took Alexandra and Forest and they all left town willingly. I don't know where, I don't know why. He didn't want anyone to ever find him. But obviously something went wrong. Now the crew think I've been lying all these years. After Jesse vouched for me, they think I must've betrayed him. Like you tried to betray *me*, Mack. They'll kill me if they find me. I'm not safe *anywhere*.'

'Jesse took them away? But . . .' Mackerel didn't understand. Jesse had left voluntarily? But then, what had made it all go wrong? And why hadn't anyone told *him*? Back then, Mackerel had still been part of the family . . . From the sounds of it, even the crew knew.

Family business is supposed to stay family business!

'Stop holding the door, Davey!' cried Shelby.

Davey gave a watery chuckle. 'I've protected you this long, babe. Let me keep doing it a while longer. If I'm dead, the crew won't take it out on you or Kane. And Blackbeard can't use you against me. An eye for an eye, all that.'

'I can help!' Shelby's voice had risen to a desperate scream. 'Just tell me what I need to do!'

'Let me disappear. Blackbeard is a plague – get out of Shacktown, all of you. Please.' He gasped with the pain of the moment. 'Goodbye, Shelbs.'

'No!' She pounded on the trapdoor. '*No! Davey!*'

Mackerel tried to climb back down to intercept Davey, but he'd forced himself in too far. He was trapped.

'Move, Mack!' screamed Shelby, trying to push him down.

'Wait!' said Mackerel, his sides chafing at the edges of the fan casing. His armpit was caught.

Skin tearing, blood running down the inside of his shirt, Mackerel squirmed himself free and scurried down the rope, twisting his bad leg. 'Fuck!' he cursed, pain shooting up his side.

Shelby climbed down past him and raced out the door.

He limped out after her, heading down the stairs, following the sound of Shelby's voice as she ran laps of the house, shouting Davey's name.

When he finally caught up with her he grabbed her close.

'Let go of me!' she screamed, trying to fight her way free.

'Stop shouting his name! Nobody can know he's alive, Shelby! Nobody can know . . .'

He held her until she stopped struggling, eventually breaking down and burying her face in Mackerel's shoulder.

Mackerel thought of Davey, and all the respect and wealth he'd gathered – gone, just like that. He knew what that felt like.

That was the thing about being king of the jungle. You're only king while you're *in* the jungle.

Shelby sat on the counter in the kitchen, drinking expensive red wine straight from the bottle. Her make-up was gone, her hair limp from the shower, where she'd spent the last half an hour. Between sips that left her lips ruby-red she looked into the distance, out of the picture window and to the sea beyond.

'You've gotta run away,' said Mackerel, pacing back and forth even as he limped, the side of his shirt stained with blood where he'd grazed it coming out of the bolthole. 'You have to take Kane and run, leave Shacktown for good.'

Shelby took another swig, face unchanging.

Mackerel was worried at the sight of her. 'Shelby . . .'

'I hate Davey,' she said.

'You don't mean that,' said Mackerel.

'I'll kill him myself.' She took another swig. 'How dare he put his little drug hole above where I shower.'

'Shelby . . .'

'Don't say my name like that,' said Shelby, voice cold, still staring into the distance. 'Don't pretend like you care about me. My husband ran a criminal business and you did nothing to stop him.'

'I'm sorry, Shelby.'

'No, you're not. Shut up, Mackerel. I want you to get out of my house.' But she didn't say it with much gusto, and she didn't complain when Mackerel didn't leave. Instead she kept drinking the wine, absently wiping at her tears.

'He's right, though,' said Mackerel. He reached out to take the bottle from her but had to dodge away when she took a swing at his head.

'Don't touch my wine,' she said dangerously. 'And don't *ever* say that Davey is *right*. Davey is *not* right. Davey gave up any permission to be right ever again.'

'Okay! But you really should listen to him and leave Shacktown.'

'Don't talk to me like that!' said Shelby. 'Don't talk down to me!'

'It's not safe.'

'This is my *home*.'

Mackerel hesitated, trying to find another way to convince her. 'Look, Shelbs, you can't afford this place anymore. Abalone has been dying out for years, and . . . with Blackbeard around . . . the money won't be enough.'

'I'll get a job myself. I'm more capable than you think, Mack. I've got a Master's degree in chemistry, did you know?'

'Of course I know,' said Mackerel.

'You know, but you never *cared*. You all couldn't imagine that I was anything more than "dreamy Davey Dempsey's" wife.' She snorted. 'Drug Dealing Davey Dempsey. The Dickhead. Davey the Despicable. Davey the Deadweight. The Deceiving . . .'

'Alright!' said Mackerel. 'That's not fair. He was trying to protect you.'

This time he had to leap aside as the bottle came hurtling towards him, smashing onto the kitchen tiles and spilling red wine.

'I don't *need* protecting.' She still spoke calmly, at odds with her furious red face.

She hopped down from her perch to retrieve another bottle from the wine rack.

'Davey,' she said slowly, 'the Divorced.'

'Smash all the bottles you want, but the fact remains that he just walked away from everything he loves in order to protect you,' he said irritably.

'It's not heroic, Mackerel!' said Shelby. 'It doesn't count when he's the reason we're in danger in the first place! Don't romanticise this!'

She unscrewed the new bottle and took a big swig, and Mackerel, frustrated, pulled a bottle of honey-coloured whisky from the liquor cabinet. He poured himself a glass and leaned against the wall. The drink was smooth and fiery. His mind flicked through options. What to do?

'Maybe I'll just kill Blackbeard and put an end to all this myself,' said Shelby. She held the bottle halfway to her lips, frozen, wine dribbling out onto her dress. 'I could kill Blackbeard myself,' she said again.

She put the bottle down and turned her bloodshot eyes onto Mackerel.

'How do you kill a drug dealer?'

'What?'

She came around the bench and stepped towards him. 'How do you kill a drug dealer?'

'You can't —'

'You're a coward too,' said Shelby.

'You're drunk. You're sad. You're in shock. You're not thinking straight. Besides, Blackbeard is way too powerful to even get close to.'

'Aha! So you have to get close to them to kill them. That makes sense.'

'Shelby,' said Mackerel, worried about how serious she sounded. 'You *really* can't tell anyone Davey's alive. It puts you at risk.'

'Can you stay here the night, Mack?' she said, changing the topic. 'Please . . .?'

He was getting whiplash from the way Shelby turned conversations whichever direction she wanted them to go.

'I can't. I'm bailed to Big Mane's.'

'What if we changed your bail address to here?' she said.

'You really don't want to do that,' said Mackerel.

'Oh, I really do.'

'You don't know what you're asking.'

She laughed, harsh and humourless. 'No, apparently I don't know much at all. You must think I'm an idiot for not knowing the truth. All those years . . .'

'You couldn't have known, Shelby,' said Mackerel. 'He worked hard to keep you away from it all.'

She drank more of the wine. 'I need you here, Mackerel. I can't do this alone.'

Though her hair fell over her face, and her eyes were red, that didn't change the serious intent in her expression. She spoke those words with such conviction.

He took a deep breath.

He didn't want to be bailed here. He didn't want to be trapped in a house full of his brother's things, the family portraits, the grieving son. He didn't want to be around Shelby, who was such an expert in throwing him off balance, and who made him feel guilty. Because she was right: he *had* just sat by while her husband ran his dangerous second life, putting her family at risk and now leaving a gaping hole where the Davey she thought she knew used to live.

He liked living with Big Mane. He liked having some semblance of control over his life.

And he didn't need to get mixed up in everything.

But did he have a choice? Shelby had no one else. She might do something stupid. And Kane didn't have anyone else either.

'Say yes, Mackerel. I need you to say yes. Promise me you'll say yes.'

'Pour out that wine and I'll think about it.'

Without taking her eyes off him, Shelby threw the bottle into the sink, where it, too, smashed. It was probably worth what Mackerel earned for a full day's work.

'Promise me you'll say yes,' she repeated.

He looked at the clock on the wall – it was already well into the afternoon. 'It's too late to vary my conditions today. We'll have to put the change of address before the judge tomorrow.'

'That's not a promise, Mackerel. *Promise me.*'

'Okay, okay, Shelby. I promise.'

Shelby nodded, tension leaving her shoulders like a balloon deflating. She began to wobble and Mackerel raced over to catch her, half carrying her over to the lounge and onto a couch. She leaned back, holding a cushion as though to stop the world from spinning.

'And Ivy really knows everything?' asked Shelby. 'It all makes sense now. The way you boys always do exactly what you're told.'

'She and Dad taught us everything we know. It was expected we'd help Jesse.'

'And that's why Ivy is always harping on about keeping everything private. Family business stays family business,' said Shelby. 'I married into a criminal dynasty.'

'I wouldn't call us that,' said Mackerel uneasily.

'Do we tell her about Davey being alive?' said Shelby. Her words had become slurred, and she curled up on her side, closing her eyes.

'If Davey hasn't told her himself, we need to trust his judgement,' said Mackerel slowly. 'So no . . . we shouldn't tell her.'

'She'll kill us if she finds out we kept this from her,' said Shelby.

Mackerel shrugged.

He didn't tell Shelby that Ivy had already asked him to run the Business.

Which, of course, was out of the question if he moved in here.

He realised that Shelby had begun to softly snore. She'd passed out, probably as much from the emotion of the day as the wine. He took a throw rug from the back of the couch and laid it over her.

Why *didn't* he want Ivy to know Davey was alive?

Because my loyalty is to Davey first. And if Davey hasn't told her, I won't tell her.

Besides, Davey probably has a plan. He organised to meet Forest, so he must have a plan. He'll fix everything. That's what Davey does . . .

Right?

CHAPTER 29

FOREST

Walking back to town from Huck's fishing spot, Forest's mind turned over what he'd been told.

What had happened to Jesse Dempsey? If he'd killed Alexandra and the real Forest – he only had Huck's word to go on, but why would he lie – then he was still out there somewhere. He'd known from the start that Jesse was dangerous – a murderer – but if he was a drug lord, that changed things. A little shiver of anticipation rolled through Forest. Would he want to reclaim what used to be his? Now that the media embargo was up, if Jesse saw that his son had returned . . . would he come finish the job?

Or Jesse knows I'm a fake, so he doesn't care. It's probably better for him that I'm here – I'm the perfect cover for his son's death. If I'm around, no one will ever come looking for a body.

As long as I keep my mouth shut. I can't tell anyone anything, otherwise Jesse will kill me. Or maybe Blackbeard will.

He reached a path that ran away from the beach, through the low yellow button scrub. He missed his dog, and he wanted to lie down. Instead, he had to go see Frankie. His nemesis. He might as well get it out of the way now, while his mind was sparking after his interaction with Huck. It was better to deal with Frankie when he was alert.

The path turned into a potholed street, where he passed some vaguely hostile local youths on bikes and skateboards. When he reached Frankie's fancy Airbnb – Ivy was paying, after all – the door was wide open. Jacaranda trees stood either side and a creeping vine ran across the purple wall.

He cracked his neck and stretched his arms, as though gearing up for a game of football. He couldn't afford to let his guard down even for a moment.

Frankie had chosen a spacious, light-filled room that faced the ocean through big windows. He took a seat in a plush recliner while she finished typing something on her laptop. When she was done she came over and handed him a sequined pillow, one of those where you rubbed it back and forth and it changed patterns. Incense burned in the corner – vanilla spice.

'What's with the pillow?'

'Helps you calm down. It's sensory. When you've been through things like you've been through, your senses can be raw . . . this way, the senses have a chance to be soothed.'

Forest nodded, rubbing the pillow's sequins back and forth. 'What do you want to know from me today?'

'Nothing in particular. Whatever you want to tell me,' said Frankie.

'And if I still don't want to talk about it?' said Forest.

'Well, I guess I'll have to pick myself up off the floor from surprise. But that's also fine. Things happen when they happen. We've got other things we can do. Breathing exercises. Special little personality tests that can tell us what job you might be good at when you grow up.'

'Why would I need any other job? I'll be running an abalone business.'

'And that's all you want to do?'

'It's what I'm supposed to do,' said Forest. 'Part of my legacy.'

'*Supposed to do*,' she repeated. 'Are you looking forward to that?'

'Of course,' said Forest.

'If I was you, I'd feel a bit trapped by that,' said Frankie.

'I'm used to being trapped . . .'

Frankie leaned forward so quick, Forest thought she would hurt herself.

Ah, trapped. He shouldn't have said that.

'What do you mean by *trapped?*'

'Nothing,' he said.

'Do you feel reminded of that place when you're in here?'

'Yes,' said Forest, refusing to make eye contact. 'And it just sucks, because it makes me feel like I can't trust you.'

'Maybe we could go somewhere else?' she said.

'No,' said Forest, 'I'm liking these pillows . . .'

Frankie nodded, and said nothing else. She simply watched him, leaving a silence for him to fill.

Time for another approach. Forest leaned forward himself. 'Sometimes . . . I keep thinking this is all part of the plan. That you're just another test. *Are* you another test? Who are you working for?'

He saw her mouth press into a line for a brief moment, then she said, 'I'm working for *you*, Forest. You're safe now. I'm here to help *you*.'

Forest let the tears pool in his eyes and allowed them to roll down his cheeks. 'Frankie, I really wish I could believe that.'

If those words rang with a greater peal of truth, well, so be it.

'Let's talk about something else, then,' she said, instantly steering away from the topic. 'Why don't you tell me about the things you've enjoyed since you've been back.'

Forest paused. That was an unexpected question.

'Honestly . . .' he lied. 'I really like the silk sheets.'

Frankie nodded and made a small affirming noise, as though saying *keep going*.

'Yeah, and being able to walk by the beach . . . and being around people that seem to want what's best for me . . .' He grew stern, pointing at the laptop. 'You can't tell anyone I don't trust them. I think I trust Ivy. It's just . . . it's in my head.'

She nodded, made another affirming noise. 'How about you just talk, and I'll just listen.'

The session completed, Forest had asked Frankie to call Mackerel for a lift. He waited in silence, Frankie working away on her laptop. He was mentally drained, his temples soaked with sweat.

It was hard, pretending the whole time, when all he wanted was to talk through all of this with someone. Especially because of that thing she did where she leaned in and really listened. It gave off a really nice feeling . . . like she cared about him. But he couldn't trust her.

It's all a trick. Don't drop your focus, even for an instant, or you'll lose it all.

You can't trust anyone.

When Mackerel finally pulled up outside, he saw that his face was pale. He wondered how he'd gone with Shelby.

What a shitstorm this is all turning into . . .

No, head in the game . . . Dodge all his questions. Ask him questions instead.

He left without saying goodbye to Frankie, relieved to be sliding into the front seat of Mackerel's car.

'I don't like coming here, but Frankie's really good at what she does. She just listens the whole time,' he said unprompted.

'You didn't tell her about Davey?' said Mackerel instantly.

'No,' said Forest. 'Hey, listen, can we go do something else? I don't want to go back to Safe Harbour just yet.'

'Okay,' said Mackerel. 'There's a retro van near the lookout – you can smell the coffee before you see the van, it's that good. We can sit in the car and watch the view.'

'You really like coffee, don't you?' said Forest.

Mackerel was silent for a moment, before he said, 'When I was a kid I always saw normal people drinking coffee. I thought that's what it meant to be a proper part of society.'

He drove up the hill, the tyres crunching over gumnuts as they slowed down for the lookout. The coffee van was situated in the perfect spot, with little tables set out, and tourists and locals alike spilling out everywhere, enjoying the afternoon sun.

Once they had ordered and returned to the car – Mackerel obviously wanted to talk where they wouldn't be overheard – Forest went on the offensive, asking questions before Mackerel could. 'What was prison like?'

Mackerel raised his eyebrows, wrinkles forming across his forehead. 'No one has ever really asked me that before,' he said. 'It's . . . boring. But stressful. And full of politics. And loud – clanging doors, shouting . . . cellmates that snore . . .'

'Tell me more,' said Forest. And Mackerel, sensing that maybe for the first time he had a receptive audience, began to regale him with stories.

'One time this guy was gonna jump me, because he'd heard about what I tried to do to Davey . . . he was involved with the Business at some stage, and so knew my name, figured he'd try and get some points with Davey, maybe get him to pay for a better lawyer. But because I was dealing the Suboxone in there, I had a few people who I paid to protect me. Well, two of them got bashed, but by the time he got to *me*, the screws had caught up to him.

Threw him in solitary. See, the screws – that's what we call the guards – the screws liked me. Because I paid them off, but also because the Suboxone kept a lot of the inmates nice and sedated . . .' His voice trailed off. 'Then the screws upped their asking price, and my contact couldn't get the Subies to me anymore, and . . . everything went to shit.' He brightened. 'But for a time, there was no one more popular than me in that place.'

'Wait, wait, wait,' said Forest, struggling to get Mack to stop. 'Why were you put in there in the first place?'

Mackerel sighed.

'It . . . started fairly young. Drugs were always around at home. Jesse, Davey and I knew how to get eccies – ecstasy – and coke, even straight MDMA. When I was younger the party scene was bigger around here, now it's all ice . . . I got into the ice, too. Went hard . . . lost my mind.'

He gave Forest a look that made clear he wasn't joking.

'Literally, I lost my mind. Drug-induced psychosis. I should let you know that . . . psychosis kinda runs in our family. I was in that state when I tried to take over the Business . . .'

The memory of Davey gave him pause.

'So I'd burned all my bridges down here, but I pulled myself out eventually and moved up to Queensland. Bigger party scene up there. I was moving lots of eccies, making good money, but then someone I knew asked if I'd move some ice for him, and that money was even better. It's easier to find ice users than to sell party drugs, and there's less competition, so I just kept doing it. I got a "real" job in insurance, but even then I'd still move the ice. I'd rock up in my company car and my suit. People liked working with me, I was a professional, not some dropkick addict. That's why I got trusted with more, and from there . . .'

'What does it look like, when you get trusted with more?' said Forest, genuinely curious. He also felt a simmering guilt. He was lying to this poor man, winning his most intimate confidence by making him believe they were family . . .

'Maaate,' said Mack, with a small smile. 'We *lived* in hotels. Ate fancy dinners every night. Bought expensive cars and gold chains and designer clothes. Had whatever we wanted. I've been in every penthouse suite on the Gold Coast. I've dated famous people, Forest. People you'd recognise.' He paused and grimaced. 'Actually, maybe you wouldn't.'

'Your clients would come into the hotels?' said Forest. The early part of Mack's story was all too familiar, but this was definitely different from the drug world he'd known. 'You kept the drugs *there*?'

'Nah, mate,' said Mack, his eyes shining, lost in memory. 'We had the stuff in a car, parked a few blocks away. By then I was only doing deals that had been prearranged, generally through Snapchat – harder to track. I'd have the right amount in the boot of the car, in a gym bag. They'd rock up to the hotel, give me the money, I'd give them the keys, they'd go get the product and leave the keys in the boot. It was a good system.'

'And then you got caught, and sent to jail,' said Forest.

'Yeah,' said Mackerel, but his eyes were still lost in the memory of the good times.

Forest didn't like that look – there was a hunger there. He took in Mackerel's tattered appearance with fresh eyes. Fraying hems on his shirt, stains on the collar, a cheap haircut that he'd probably done himself . . .

But even though he didn't look like much, from what he'd just told Forest, the man was very capable.

If not for me, Mackerel would be the next in line for Dempsey Abalone. Assuming Davey stays hidden.

And he's not nearly as stupid as I thought he was.

CHAPTER 30

MACKEREL

Early the next morning, Mackerel called his lawyer. He was a good enough lawyer, as things went. You didn't always know who you'd get when they were appointed with government aid.

The lawyer thought it was a very good idea to have Mackerel's bail address moved to a respectable place like the Dempseys' mansion. It spoke of restored family relationships, and demonstrated how he was helping his sister-in-law. But since Mackerel was almost certainly going back to jail in seven months' time, the lawyer wondered if it was really a good thing for Kane. He'd just lost his dad, and then he'd lose his uncle too, just as he got to know him . . .

But Mackerel had to do it. He'd already promised Shelby. And his gut told him she would do something stupid if he wasn't around. That look in her eyes, he'd seen it before: out on the street. Desperate people were willing to do desperate things for a fix.

An hour's drive into Hobart. An appearance before the judge that took next to no time at all – he suspected that, considering the tragic circumstances of his brother's death and the grief of his widow, his lawyer had had something to do with that. There was a fee to pay for changing the conditions, which he paid from the money Shelby had already transferred to him, and then . . . he was driving back to Big Mane's to pack up his belongings.

In a daze, he knocked on Big Mane's bedroom door. 'Hey, we should talk . . .'

Big Mane opened the door, wrapped in his shower robe with a console controller in his hand, gaming headphones over his ears. 'Why? Everything okay?'

Mackerel hadn't wanted to say anything unless his bail change was approved, but now that it had . . .

'The good news is, you won't have to see my ugly mug so often . . . my bail address got changed.'

'What? Where are you gonna go?'

'I'll be staying with Shelby.'

The visible relief on Big Mane's face hurt him.

'Am I that hard to live with?' said Mackerel in a small voice.

'Nah, mate. I think that staying with Shelby is a bloody good idea. It can't be good for her to be rattling around that big house, just her and the kid. And now I won't feel guilty when I leave after curfew and you're stuck here alone. Plus, no more cops banging on the door at all hours of the night.'

'You said you slept with ear plugs!'

'Bro, I lied so that you wouldn't feel bad. I just didn't want you feeling worse than you did. You already feel guilty about too much stuff that isn't your fault.' He put the controller down and started getting changed. 'Only problem is, who's gonna cook and clean for me now? Are you saying I've gotta get a missus?'

Mackerel chuckled. 'Or learn to cook for yourself.'

Big Mane started pulling empty suitcases out from under his bed, chucking one to Mackerel. 'Let's get your shit packed up, then. Hurry up and get out of my house and into your fancy mansion.' He laughed, making it clear it was a joke.

'You know . . . I'm really grateful for —'

'Yeah, I know, mate, you've told me a million times. Especially when you're drunk – then you're even noisier about it. I love you, mate. I believe in you. I think you've got what it takes. And I'm honoured to call you my best friend.'

That was too much. Mackerel looked away, blinking very hard.

'What days are you gonna come over to play Xbox?' said Big Mane. 'Or are you gonna ditch me entirely?'

Mackerel pulled himself back under control and said, 'Lock it in for every Friday. Xbox Fridays. And . . . if you'll still have me, I'll still work for you.'

'What's this *if you'll still have me* bullshit? You're one of the few competent blokes out there.' They were in Mackerel's bedroom now, pulling clothes out of the drawers. A lot of them were Big Mane's old clothes, but some of them Mackerel had paid for with his own money. 'Besides, it wouldn't be the same without you out there.'

'One day, I want to be as good a man as you,' said Mackerel.

Big Mane grabbed him by the shoulder and crushed him in a quick hug. 'Fucken idiot. You're already a good bloke, bro. Don't forget it.' He pushed him away, wiping at his eyes. 'Ah, finish this yourself, ya flog. I'll see what's yours in the laundry.'

Mack parked next to the fountain and dragged the suitcases to the front door, looking up over the creeping plants. He pressed the doorbell. A moment later, Shelby opened the door. She wore a red dress, her make-up done, amber drops hanging from her ears, a glass of wine in her hand. She looked like she was hosting a dinner party.

'Hello, Mack. Good to see you.' She pushed the door open. 'Welcome home.'

Mackerel said in a rush, 'You don't understand how much disruption this will bring to your house. So the moment it gets too much, let me know. I'll find somewhere else to live.'

'Listen, Mack, I want you here. Kane barely even knew you existed, but now that he does, *he* wants you here. You're good with kids. Everyone likes you.'

Mackerel was floored. 'Everyone likes me?'

'You're easy to bully, but you're a likeable guy . . .'

He was speechless. He rubbed his eyes.

She grabbed his hands and pulled them away, but he wouldn't meet her eyes; he wasn't sure he'd be able to handle her pity.

'Just warn Kane not to get close to me,' he said. 'I'll probably be back in prison in seven months' time.'

'Yeah, I was thinking about that. My friend Fiona's a lawyer, so I invited her around for dinner – she's here now. Maybe she can help.'

It always astounded Mackerel how straight folk didn't understand how the legal system worked. It wasn't like going to your GP, where if one doctor didn't know the answer you just needed a second opinion. Navigating the legal system was a tangled mess. It was like organising a school concert combined with a work trip, mixed with applying for a job that you needed to get a university degree for first. Except you had to pay a friend to study the degree *for* you because all the textbooks were in another language, but your friend couldn't read so you had to read out the foreign words to *them*, and then hopefully they gathered all the right information to tell *you* how to pass the job interview. And sometimes the interviewers were grumpy from lack of sleep, or were getting sick, or didn't like the way you looked. Or they had already decided who they wanted for the job. And even if they hadn't, it all still just came down to luck and money.

But there was no use explaining that. So he grimaced, nodded and followed Shelby into the house. There was Fiona, with black hair in a ponytail, square glasses, very red lipstick and a blue dress. She looked Mack up and down, making it clear she wasn't at all impressed with what she saw. He'd seen her at Ivy's the day Davey had 'died'. She had been identified to him as Shelby's best friend, but honestly, that whole afternoon had been a blur . . .

Mackerel walked past her, dragging his bags up the stairs and into the room that would be his. It was the size of Big Mane's lounge room, with plush white carpet, a king-size bed, its own sparkling en suite, and fancy abstract art on the walls.

He looked around, open mouthed, catching his reflection in the floor-length mirror. He looked like an intruder – he didn't belong in here.

Too intimidated to unpack his stuff and claim the space as his own, he fled back to the kitchen.

Shelby was a brisk and professional host, busying herself around the kitchen and by the heavy dining table, with Fiona in a support-ing role. They were preparing a three-course meal, with prawns as an entree, a steamed-duck main, and chocolate gateau for dessert. Various bottles of expensive alcohol would accompany the meal.

Shelby went to get Kane, and Mackerel and Fiona sat down. The lawyer's eyes bored through Mack and he shifted uncomfortably until Shelby and Kane returned.

The food was incredible. Mackerel had to fight not to stuff his face, desperate to prove to Fiona that he wasn't the animal that, from the way she kept glaring at him, she clearly thought he was.

The two women talked about everyday things, with Shelby intentionally asking questions to bring Mackerel into the conversa-tion. He, in turn, tried to bring Kane in. The boy was surly, didn't want to be there, kept whining about the food, twitching unhap-pily. When Kane complained about the parsnip puree one too many times, Mackerel said, 'I know what you mean. Mashed potatoes are one of the only things they give you to eat in jail. One time, one of my mates tried to snort some up his nose, just to prove it wasn't really potatoes but powder mixed with water.'

'Up his *nose?*' said Kane. 'I don't believe you.'

'Maybe don't talk about prison at the table,' said Fiona sternly.

Mackerel ignored her, seeing now the fire in Kane's eyes. He knew Shelby was a great mum, but surely the kid also needed someone to meet him on his own level now and then? Especially if Mackerel was going to be living there.

'Yeah,' he said. 'And we had to have plastic forks, because if you have metal ones, you might use them to stab someone.' He reached across and took Kane's hand, using Kane's fork to stab a carrot, a bean, a piece of meat.

Kane wryly watched him do it, rolled his eyes, then ate his forkful. 'I'm not a kid. You don't have to pretend the fork is an air-plane.' He swallowed. Then he said eagerly, 'What else happens in jail?'

'Well . . .' began Mackerel slowly, 'there's fights *all the time.*'

'I don't think this is good for him to hear, *Uncle* Mackerel,' said Fiona. 'I mean, prison is the reason you've been away from your family this whole time, right? You've been locked up?'

Shelby didn't say anything. Her eyes were on Mackerel's whisky glass, which was empty. She leaned across and poured him some more.

'Yeah, I was . . .' said Mackerel forlornly, although in a way he was enjoying the glare that Fiona was giving him. 'I deserved it . . . I deserved what I did. I sold drugs, which are *bad for* you. I used to sell the drugs to the drug dealers. They were bad people, but I'd get lots of money out of them. Like, *millions* of dollars.'

'Really?' said Kane, then caught himself. 'That's not impressive. Dad is . . . was a millionaire . . .' His voice dropped off.

'Enough, Mack,' said Shelby, checking back into the con-versation.

But he was on a roll now. 'The hardest part about having so much money is finding someone who loves you for *you*, and not just all the money you have,' said Mackerel sadly, watching Kane's eyes grow interested again. 'You know the singer from Pine and Ocean?'

'Atlanta Parks?' said Kane.

'Yeah, we dated for a while. But at the end of the day she just wanted me for my money. At least, I think she did . . . she took off when the cops started looking at me.'

Mackerel let his face fall, which wasn't hard. That particular betrayal *had* hurt.

'*You dated Atlanta Parks?*' said Kane, then looked indignantly at Shelby. 'And no one ever *told* me?!'

After that, Uncle Mack had him hooked. He eased off on the criminal talk and, by the end of dinner, Uncle Mack was Kane's new favourite relative.

He had *never* been anyone's favourite in this family.

It was strange. Watching himself cheer up his nephew, he kept thinking back to what Shelby had said.

Everyone likes me?

It wasn't true. He had been run out of town. He was an outcast.

But perhaps things had changed. Everything had been re-arranged. Maybe in this world he was actually an okay guy? Maybe?

Maybe Big Mane was right. Maybe he *was* a good bloke?

After dinner Shelby and Fiona cleaned the table and Fiona stacked the dishwasher. Mackerel wanted to help, but the moment dinner was over Kane started pulling on his arm.

'Oi, Uncle Mack, come with me.'

He spoke with the ease of wealth – it wasn't a request, it was a command.

He led Mack down the stairs into the rumpus room, which took up the entire basement level. It had lush chairs, rich red carpet and two large TVs set up beside each other on the same wall.

'Dad bought two so that we could play Xbox together, but he was never very good at it,' said Kane. 'You know how to play, though, right?'

'I'll whoop your arse, kid,' said Mackerel, sitting down into a couch so comfy it was like being held by a shagpile rug. Shelby came down to check on them a few minutes later, bringing ice-cream for Kane and a beer for Mackerel.

Kane and Mackerel played for hours. Mackerel was genuinely having fun, and he played well. Kane had faster reflexes, but Mackerel had the patience and strategic thinking that came with age. Besides, he always played better when he was tipsy, and Shelby was vigilantly checking in on the rumpus room, always making sure he had a beer to hand. He wasn't sure why she was being so nice, after the way he'd behaved at dinner, but it was welcome.

Finally Kane's eyes began to slide shut, and soon he was snoring against Mackerel's shoulder.

It made Mack's heart twist up like a stone. He swept him into his arms and walked up the stairs to the living area. Fiona and Shelby had been deep in conversation but fell silent as Mackerel approached.

'Where's his room?' said Mackerel, a little resentful that Fiona was still there. He wanted to speak to Shelby about Davey once they were alone.

'I'll show you,' said Shelby, leading Mackerel up the stairs. It was a boy's dream bedroom – big bed, posters, toys and gadgets and a little bookcase, plus a gaming computer, and a charging station for his MacBook and iPad.

Shelby fluffed the pillows and he laid Kane down, stepping back to let Shelby tuck Kane under the covers. When Mackerel made to leave, Shelby grabbed his arm. 'Look at him. He's finally found a bit of peace.'

'Yeah,' said Mackerel, flushed with alcohol and a feeling of victory. 'We had fun.'

'He misses his dad,' she said softly.

'Yeah,' said Mackerel, 'I don't blame him. Poor kid.'

Before they left Shelby flicked on a nightlight. 'He still sleeps with it on,' she explained. 'He has nightmares without it. Don't tell him I told you. I think he's taking a liking to you.'

Mackerel didn't know what to say to that, but his chest swelled.

'He *needs* us,' said Mackerel.

'What he *needs* is his dad,' said Shelby, voice hard. 'C'mon.'

Halfway down the stairwell, lit by soft downlights, Shelby pointed at a portrait of Davey – good-looking, laughing – flanked by Shelby and Kane. 'Look at him,' whispered Shelby. 'He's still alive. He can still have this. It's killing me that I can't tell Kane he's not dead.'

Shelby still didn't understand. As painful as it was for all three of them, Davey had left so she and Kane could still have some semblance of normality.

'Shelby . . .' began Mackerel, but Shelby led him down the stairs.

'What do you want to drink? Anything out of the cupboard.'

'*Any*thing?' said Mackerel.

CHAPTER 31

AHAB

It was late at night, and Ahab strolled along one of Shacktown's beach-side streets. Wearing a singlet and shorts, he was barefoot and could feel the she-oak needles beneath his feet. Wealthy houses rose either side of him, but they were interspersed by fibro shacks, and even a large empty block, which was home only to a few tethered goats.

Up ahead was a huge whitewashed house set in the middle of a large block. It belonged to Chips, although she didn't seem to maintain it all that well – the walls were covered in moss, and the gutters needed clearing. But the yard itself was immaculate, the garden well tended.

He needed to speak to Chips about keeping Blackbeard from winning the loyalty of the crew. The more he sat with the thought, the more the danger of a drug war in Shacktown seemed to grow in his mind. The town wasn't big enough to handle it – the whole community would break.

But as he approached Chips's house, he could hear music coming from the backyard, and a burst of rowdy laughter. She had guests. Smoke from a fire pot was in the air, a glow trailing up it.

Whoever was with her, they were probably members of the Business. Would it be good if the crew saw him there?

Then he noticed the cars parked out the front. A Mustang and a Merc. Expensive cars were not *that* out of place in Shacktown, but their presence immediately put him on alert. Apart from those working senior roles at Dempsey Abalone, the crew knew not to flaunt their wealth – it always attracted the wrong attention. That meant these cars belonged to out-of-towners. *Rich* out-of-towners.

His mind went straight to Blackbeard.

Ahab hopped the front fence and slipped up the side of the yard. He spotted a sensor light mounted on the side of the house and hugged the wall, moving slowly underneath it to avoid setting it off. Once he was out of its range, he crouched and crept into the angular leaves of a squat white correa bush, sweet and heady, which afforded him a covert view of the backyard.

Chips had set the fire pot right in the middle of her overgrown yard. The smoke wafted across Ahab's face, the smell of burning pine just like the Darling's fireplace. She was in her familiar football jersey and baseball cap, but he didn't recognise the two strangers who were with her. They looked like hard men, both of them huge and muscular. One of them had two gold chains around his neck, diamonds in his ears, and a black Nike beanie. The other was tall, with a pockmarked face and burning orange hair. They spoke in loud voices that carried across to Ahab as they fed pages into the fire.

'. . . in that case, he won't come for the kid,' said the man with the gold chains.

'Lucky Forest, I guess,' said Chips. 'Reckon Blackbeard would've gone through with it?'

'He never backs out of his threats,' said the tall one harshly. 'That's why they're so effective. Good lesson to remember, woman. You wanna play with the big boys, you take him seriously.'

'*Don't* call me "woman" . . .' said Chips. 'I've played with plenty of the big boys.'

'Yeah, Vance, don't call her woman,' said the one with gold chains.

Vance laughed. 'Got some balls on her, doesn't she?'

'Laugh all you want,' said Chips. 'But it's a bit rich coming from the man who couldn't find Davey even after I told him *exactly* where his bolthole was.' She chuckled scathingly. 'Blackbeard needs me more than he needs *your* useless arse. So tell me, why does he want the kid left alone?'

Chips had betrayed Davey? No, Chips . . . not you . . .

'Not up to us to ask questions. No one in your crew touches the boy,' said the man with the gold chains, while Vance glowered and spat.

'I'm telling you, Tranquil, I can get the crew to accept Blackbeard's leadership,' said Chips. 'You don't need to go through Forest to make it happen.'

Gold chains – Tranquil – shrugged his massive shoulders. 'Blackbeard wants Forest left alone, so we leave Forest alone. Make sure *you* do too.'

So Chips really had defected to Blackbeard. That meant it was a dark day for Shacktown. Ahab expected to feel angry, betrayed, but all he felt was sad – sad for the town, but also for the young woman Chips had once been, lost to this new world.

But he wasn't beaten. The town would put up a fight, one way or another.

First of all, he needed to see what they were burning – was it evidence that could be used against them? Was it correspondence from the drug suppliers? Was it Davey's accounts?

The look of Tranquil and Vance gave him pause. They really were hard men; it'd be no good taking them on directly. What he needed was a distraction.

He crept back out of the white correa and around to the front of the house, to the Mercedes. It didn't take him long – jiggling the handle and rocking the car back and forth – to get the alarm blaring.

The moment it went off, he ran back down the side of the house, his footsteps masked by the car alarm. He set off the sensor light and flinched as he was bathed in light, but Chips and the men had run through the inside of the house to get out the front – guilty people had a habit of chasing any alarm they hadn't set off themselves.

He vaulted the bushes and moved into the yard, pawing through the paperwork in the box beside the fire pot, breathing in the smoke. They were just purchase orders and invoices for Dempsey Abalone, all signed by Davey. It wasn't unusual to use fraudulent invoices as part of a money laundering scheme, but why would Chips be destroying them?

Then it came to him. With those invoices signed by Davey gone, Chips would have to sign them for the money to go through. She was effectively holding the crew to ransom – if *she* didn't sign new invoices, they couldn't wash their drug money, and no one would be getting paid.

She was making herself indispensable. And proving it to Blackbeard's men while she was at it.

The car alarm was turned off, creating a ringing silence that left Ahab feeling dangerously exposed. He sprinted back into the correa bush, sprawling flat on the ground.

Chips and her new friends came back out into the yard.

Ahab noticed with alarm that Tranquil now had a sawn-off shotgun on his shoulder. He indicated the sensor light with a nod, raising a finger to his mouth, gesturing for Chips and Vance to help him search the yard.

Ahab lay quiet, his heart pounding. Mentally, he gauged the distance to the fence behind him – if he was discovered, he'd turn and sprint, making as much noise as he could. Surely they wouldn't dare shoot him with witnesses nearby . . . would they? Chips lived on such a large block, would the sound even carry?

Tranquil hesitated right by the bush where Ahab lay hidden. Ahab looked at the man's shoes, holding his breath, praying that he wouldn't look down . . .

'Probably the same possum that set off your car alarm,' called Chips.

Tranquil pointed the gun at her. 'Don't make jokes.'

'*Don't* point that gun at me.'

'He'll point it at whoever he wants to,' said Vance.

'Put it away or I'll tell Blackbeard how you nearly fucked the whole deal,' said Chips. She licked her lips.

'*You* aren't telling Blackbeard anything,' said Tranquil, laughing as he returned to the fire pot. 'You might think you're a big shot because you made it up high in Davey's crew, but you'll never get so far up in *our* crew that you'll meet Blackbeard. You're a small fish here, woman.' He waved the shotgun back and forth, like charming a snake, and Chips flinched.

'Oh, c'mon. You think I haven't worked out who Blackbeard is?' she said, voice cracking on the last word.

That caught Tranquil's attention. He stopped laughing and raised a challenging eyebrow at Chips. He lowered the shotgun. 'There's no way you'd know.'

She took a step towards Tranquil and spoke a word, but it was too soft – Ahab *strained*, but he couldn't hear it.

Tranquil did, however. His face went flat.

'Who told you?' His voice was dead of all emotion.

'No one. A woman has her ways.'

Vance looked shocked, turning back and forth between Chips and Tranquil.

Chips made to speak again, but it all happened so fast that Ahab couldn't even think about stopping it. Tranquil brought the gun up, leapt across the distance and *boom*, an instant later Chips was motionless on the grass, blood soaking her football jumper. He'd pressed the gun to her chest so the sound of the shot was softened, but not completely silenced.

She was dead.

The way she fell, it seemed to Ahab she was looking right at him. But no one living had eyes that dull. Blood seeped out of her open mouth, joining the pool gathering around her.

This is your fault. You brought her into this world.

'What are you *doing*?' shouted Vance.

'You heard what she said,' said Tranquil. 'She *knew*.'

'Yeah, but . . .'

'Congratulations, you've just been promoted again,' warned Tranquil. 'Now go find a blanket to cover her up. I'll call some of the boys to come and take her out to the continental shelf . . .'

A flame of murderous intent flickered in Ahab's heart, but he pushed it down.

He had to get out of there.

He waited until both of them walked inside, Vance still demanding answers from Tranquil. He took three long breaths, then wriggled out from under the bush, making as little sound as he could, and sprinted for the fence behind him. Up and over. On the other side, he stumbled through the scrubby dogwood and gumtrees of the neighbouring block, scrambled down a hill and onto the beach, and only then stopped to catch his breath.

Chips was dead.

Blackbeard will pay.

CHAPTER 32

MACKEREL

Mackerel, Shelby and Fiona sat on plush cushions on the built-in benches of the rooftop garden, the vertices illuminated with soft strip lighting, fairy lights draped from grape trellises and citronella torches keeping the bugs away. It was a sticky summer night and Mackerel had shed his shirt, enjoying the hotel feel of the garden. He was drinking his third glass of a whisky he would never have been able to afford himself. Davey's liquor cabinet was well stocked, and Shelby was still pouring him generous shots.

Shelby and Fiona were drinking mimosas from wineglasses, but from the way they kept nervously glancing at each other, he suspected they were more orange juice than champagne.

It hit him through his fog.

They're trying to get me drunk . . .

His mind was instantly filled with lewd scenarios. He pushed those thoughts away with a chuckle.

'What are you laughing at?' said Shelby.

'Just thought of something funny,' he said, letting his words slur. He'd let them think they'd succeeded and see what happened.

Fiona put her glass down. 'Tell me more about this Dread Pirate Blackbeard. Shelby says you're quite the authority.'

Whatever she'd been about to say, Mackerel had not expected *that*. He choked on his drink, spitting it back into his glass.

'Fiona knows,' said Shelby. 'Everything. About Davey, what he used to do, why he left.'

'What are you *doing*?' said Mackerel. 'You can't tell *anyone*!'

'Too bad, and too late,' said Shelby, sipping her mimosa.

'If Blackbeard is such a bad guy, then shouldn't someone like *you* step up and stop him coming in?' continued Fiona. 'Weren't you trained up the same way as Davey?'

'Shelby . . .' moaned Mackerel.

'I deserve to understand,' said Shelby.

'She does,' agreed Fiona. 'So please, explain it to us. How do we stop the Dread Pirate Blackbeard?'

Listen to them, casually asking how to kill the Devil. He needed time to think. And he needed to sober up. He raised his glass. 'I'll need another drink.'

Shelby made to pour him more whisky, but he stopped her. 'I'll go find my own. Who knows what you've been dosing me with.'

He was only half joking.

He walked down the stairs into the house and down to the kitchen, stumbling a bit on the bottom steps. He thought hard about how to get out of this conversation. He wasn't in the right state to be having it – he was bloody drunk *again*.

That's it. Starting now, I'm never drinking again.

He grabbed a bottle of vodka and tipped it down the sink – he winced at the waste, but desperate times . . . He refilled it with water and carried it back up to the rooftop. He couldn't just ignore them – he had to make Fiona understand that she *could not tell a soul*. And he needed his fucking shirt back on.

When he returned to the garden, Fiona and Shelby both stopped talking and pierced him with their eyes – Fiona's dark and attentive, Shelby's blue and triumphant. He looked around for his shirt, but it was gone. He sat down, feeling exposed.

'Well, Mackerel?' Shelby said. 'Don't you think I deserve to know more about this boogieman who's destroyed my family?'

'Alright,' he said gruffly, folding his arms over his chest. Feeling ridiculous, he uncrossed them and intentionally put his hands behind his head. 'Alright . . .'

He swigged from his 'vodka', feeling twitchy.

'Here's the truth, ladies. I know you're trying to think of a way to stop him, but you can't. That's because it's not just one person. The name Blackbeard gets passed down to whoever is the head of his drug syndicate. If Blackbeard gets arrested, or killed, his name lives on to inspire terror in the game. And, believe me, it works. There isn't any halfway-serious drug operation in this country that isn't afraid of Blackbeard.'

'There has to be a way to stop him,' said Fiona.

'There *is* no way,' said Mackerel angrily. 'Okay, so Davey was keeping him out of Shacktown, but now that he's gone, Davey's crew is weak. Blackbeard is already making his move. There's nothing any of us can do.'

'And Blackbeard is definitely worse than Davey?' said Fiona. 'If they're both drug dealers? No offence, Shelby.'

Shelby raised her glass in mocking acceptance.

What the fuck was going on? Why were they treating this like . . . like a bloody theatre show?

'Are you fucking insane?'

He was really getting angry now. Straight people just didn't understand how the underworld worked. And where the fuck was his shirt? He stood up, looking for it.

'Look, Blackbeard handles more than drugs. He's a human

trafficker. He does weapons. And he kills anyone in his way. *Anyone* in his way – women, children. He doesn't follow the code. Wherever he goes, bad things follow and good people disappear. He'll be bad for all of Tasmania – fuck, he'll be bad for Australia full-stop!'

'But what you're saying is, if Davey comes back, and runs the crew, Blackbeard can't establish himself here. Blackbeard needs a foothold first . . .' said Shelby.

'The crew lost faith in Davey the moment Forest came back. Blackbeard is dismantling Davey's crew as we speak. It's all over. Blackbeard has won.'

'Why can't another drug dealer just keep Blackbeard out?'

'*Davey* kept Blackbeard out because he already had the infrastructure in place! The Business took *generations* to build up! The buyers, the inner circle, the logistics, the bribed police . . . which, by the way, Blackbeard will commandeer for himself.'

'Okay, but what if we knew who Blackbeard was?' said Shelby. 'You said yesterday if we got close to him, we could take him down.'

'I said you *might* be able to,' he said. He couldn't find his shirt. He ripped at the leaves of a nearby grapevine. He wanted to throw something. He swigged more of his fake vodka, and tried to will his mind to sober up. 'But no one gets close to him, not without him finding out who you are and making you pay the price. The only way you could do it would be to find your way into his inner circle.'

He took another swig of whisky without thinking and put it back down.

'Where's my fucking shirt?' said Mackerel.

'No idea,' said Shelby. 'How does one get into Blackbeard's inner circle?'

'Become an important crew member,' he said. 'You'd have to be able to provide him with something.'

'Like what? What would *you* provide him with?'

'Shelby, are you sure you should be asking *Mackerel*?' said Fiona, saying his name like it was an insult. 'I'm not sure *Mackerel* would be able to provide *anything* to an important drug dealer like Blackbeard . . .'

He knew what they were doing, and it made him furious. He took another swig of whisky. Fuck them – if they wanted him to be drunk, he'd be drunk!

'I was brought up in a world of manipulation. You think I don't know what you're doing? No matter how drunk you get me, you're gonna have to work harder than that! *Yes*, I was a good drug dealer! And you wanna know why? Because I was always good with people. I could act professional, I knew how to run a business. I was actually pretty fucking articulate and presented like a normal fucking person.'

Fiona's delicate snort set him into even more of a rage.

'I was cooked on the ice down here when I tried to take over the Business, but if I *hadn't* been cooked, I would've succeeded!' Fuck, they must've been getting to him – he'd never admitted that out loud. '*That's* why they kicked me out of town, *that's* why my big brother gave me a belting, *that's* why he ruined my name and told me never to come back. Because he knew I could do it. I *did* do it. Went up to Queensland and fucking *proved* it.'

He drank another swig of whisky.

'If you can win people over, charm them, *that's* how you establish a *sustainable* operation as a drug dealer. You think I haven't thought about joining Blackbeard? Of course I have. If I started my own operation, I'd make sure I was moving enough product, and then I'd reach out. But I'd be different from the rest of the minnows trying to get his attention – I know how to make a drug business sustainable, that's where they all fall over. Criminals don't know shit about good business and good people management.'

'Yeah? And what drugs would you be selling?'

'Ice is where it's at, here in Tasmania – crystal meth, if you don't know what that is, Fiona.'

'I know what ice is,' said Fiona. 'I am a lawyer, Mackerel.' She leaned back in her chair. She was *literally* looking down her nose at him.

'So you'd cook ice?' prompted Shelby.

'Me?' He scoffed. 'Of course not. Blackbeard only deals in the really good quality stuff. He doesn't touch the gear from the shitty homecooks. So I'd have to get a good cook and make good product. And those are pretty fucking hard to find.' He looked over the ocean, the twinkling lights of the marina, thinking of all the shipments out over the horizon, just waiting for Dempsey Abalone workers to come and collect them. 'Davey never made the drugs, he just imported them. But that's no good. If Blackbeard's taken over the Business, he'll be importing it himself. So yeah, cooking would be the way to go. You just need to find a good cook . . .' His voice trailed off.

Looking at Shelby now, he had a fresh memory of back when they'd first met. She'd first been introduced to them at a party. Mackerel would have been eighteen, Davey twenty. Mackerel had been Davey's wingman, as usual, even though Davey was always surrounded by chicks without even trying.

Shelby had caught Davey's eye – he always liked the quiet, shy ones, because he liked anyone he could control. When Shelby's friend tried to embarrass her by telling everyone she'd just won some chemistry prize at the university, that really caught his attention. It was just a joke at first, even a game: could Davey make a girl fall in love with him enough that she'd try cooking ice for him?

But then they'd gone on a few dates, and Davey had loved her company, and for the first time in Mackerel's memory, he had respected a girl's intelligence. He'd come home, walk into Mack's room and sit on his bed, talking about how funny she was when she made that joke, how *clever* she was when she'd made this comment,

how she was even smart enough to have won some fancy scholar-
ship for an overseas trip . . .

By then, the game was over. Davey had genuinely fallen for her.

Why was it that even when Davey had bad intentions, good
things still happened for him? Why couldn't good things ever
happen to Mack?

A different memory came into his mind. Ivy had asked him to
run the Business. He had yet to give her a response.

Could he do it? Could he run the Business?

Of course he could. And better than Davey, too.

'Hell, if I was good enough, I could even become the next Dread
Pirate Blackbeard.'

'So it could be possible?' said Shelby quickly. 'If you were really
dedicated to this? You could become a drug dealer again, and somehow get into Blackbeard's inner circle and unmask him?'

It was what they were dancing around the whole night. Here it
was, the plan Shelby had come up with to save Davey and get her
family back.

He could be the hero. He could save the day. He could be the
man of the town.

He clenched his jaw. He wanted his shirt.

'No,' said Mackerel.

'Please,' said Shelby.

'*No*, Shelby.'

'The only way to bring Davey back is to bring down Blackbeard.'
Her eyes were bright, hopeful. 'The only way to win his trust is for
you to start dealing again. Please don't make me beg.'

'No, Shelby.' He said it softer this time. He felt for her, he
really did.

'So,' said Fiona, 'you're just going to let this *Blackbeard* monster destroy your lives. You're not doing anything to stop him?'
Fiona gestured to the mansion. 'Shelby doesn't care about all

of this, all she cares about is *that*.' She unlocked her phone and showed Mackerel a family photo of Shelby, Kane and Davey. They had really prepared for this. 'Or are you too selfish to see that, Mackerel?'

'How could you ask me that?' said Mackerel, folding his arms across his bare chest.

'If you won't do it, could you teach *me*?' said Shelby.

He'd stood up before he realised it. 'No fucking way. You'd put Kane at that much risk?'

'. . . Davey did.' She had cringed away from him. He realised he was standing over her and sat back down.

'Davey knew what he was doing,' said Mackerel.

'And so would you! That's why it's better you than me!' said Shelby.

'Shelbs, the cops would be onto me like a rash! No way! You will *not* —'

He cut himself off. Kane had appeared at the door to the rooftop, eyes squinting with interrupted sleep.

Davey's son walked across the deck, his eyes on his mum. 'I heard shouting.'

Mackerel waited for Shelby to do something, but all she said was, 'Do you want a hot chocolate, Kane?'

'Yeah,' said Kane. 'Why were you shouting?'

'I'll tell you later. Just rest there while I go make you some.'

Fiona pulled her phone out and scrolled her feeds, while Mackerel felt the alcohol dragging at his consciousness.

'Why are you shirtless, Uncle Mack?' said Kane with a frown.

'He was showing us how many push-ups he could do,' said Fiona. She yawned. 'I wasn't that impressed.'

A flare of anger. 'Fiona accidentally lit a stick on fire. I had to use my shirt to put it out.'

'A *stick*?' said Kane.

'Yeah, the one she usually keeps up her arse.'

Kane burst into laughter, and Mackerel grinned.

Fiona's face twitched in fury. She glared at him, then pointedly turned away with a muttering comment.

Shelby returned with the hot chocolate, but she wasn't in a rush to send her son to bed. She embraced Kane and comforted him, allowed him to stay up with them while they talked about more innocuous things. Mack went along with the ploy, quizzing Kane about the upcoming footy season, his teammates, his coach. In time the boy grew tired again, and before long he dropped his head onto a cushion on the bench and began snoring.

Shelby gave him a smile of triumph, holding Mackerel's eyes. *You could fix all this.*

That powerful protective urge was swamping him, but he tried to push it down.

'Mack. You'd have money and status. You'd have your own mansion,' said Shelby. 'You'd be the best guy in town.'

'Please don't start again,' he said. 'I can't . . .'

'Can't what?' said Fiona, as though it were the most casual conversation in the world. 'You said it yourself – all you've got to do is cook good quality ice, right? Get it into Blackbeard's hands, find out who he is, and get rid of him. We'll help you. Just break it down into steps.'

'You don't understand,' said Mackerel.

'We do,' said Shelby. She watched Kane's chest rise and fall in soft snores.

'Just stop, Shelby . . .' He shivered as a breeze blew in from the sea, setting the gum leaves to clattering, and cooling the sweat breaking out over his chest.

'You're an embarrassment, Mackerel,' said Fiona. 'You should've told Shelby years ago what was going on. You call yourself a man? You're going to prison anyway, right?'

'Why would you say that to someone?!' said Mackerel, his face growing hot.

'I told her about your case,' said Shelby.

'You don't know anything *about* my case!'

'When you go to prison, everyone will know it's because you tried to do the honourable thing for your sister-in-law. There's no down sides to this, just a bit of risk,' said Fiona.

'A *lot* of risk,' said Mackerel.

'For a much greater reward,' said Shelby, reaching out to grab Mackerel's hand and put it on top of Kane's shoulder.

'No. I said *no*,' said Mackerel, fighting the drunkenness, trying to hold his cracking resolve together. 'I can't go back to that world!'

'This is the only way to fix everything,' said Shelby, leaving her hand on his. 'Promise me, Mackerel. Promise you'll help.'

'Shelbs . . .'

'*Promise me.*'

This pull was stronger than any current he'd ever swum against. What would it be like if he just went with the flow?

The underworld.

The hunger to succeed in the game. The thrill, the danger, the power.

The risk, the reward. The success.

The sex.

He had kept those doors closed for so long, and now his defences were being breached.

He'd been alone for a long time, and now here were two women, asking for his help.

Telling him he could be a good man. A decent guy.

And a nephew beside him, a boy who would be growing up without his father.

Ivy would be happy again, Davey would be able to run the Business. Everything would be back to the way it was, except I'd be the hero. I could have a mansion. Or at least, somewhere to call home.

'No,' said Mackerel, trying to shake his emotions free from the foggy weight of drunkenness. His mouth had started to water. 'No.' He rose to his feet. 'I'm going to bed.'

He ignored the expressions on the women's faces – Fiona's disgusted, Shelby's devastated. The shame of letting her down hit him like a sucker punch.

It's insane. I won't do it, he told himself, even as the lure of the underworld filled his belly. *Not a chance.*

He walked down the stairs feeling like the worst human in the world.

I'm trying to be a good man.

I'm trying.

CHAPTER 33

AHAB

Ahab's clothes were soaked. After he'd seen Chips killed right in front of him, he'd gone straight down to the ocean for a swim – to calm himself in the bracing cold of the water. To stop himself from running straight back to Chips's house to . . . he didn't know what he wanted to do there.

Climbing the stairs from the beach to Ivy's place, he made his way around to the front so no one would misread his intentions. The police knew the two of them were not exactly on the best of terms.

It was Constable Linda, sitting in the marked car parked out the front. She climbed out, as though coming to speak to him, but he waved her back into the vehicle. He needed to focus on one thing at a time right now.

'Ivy!' He rapped his knuckles on the letterbox at the end of the drive. 'Ivy, I need to talk to you.'

There was no time for a family feud now. They needed to come together, for Forest's sake. Because if Blackbeard was inside Dempsey Abalone, but wanted Forest alive, it couldn't be for anything good.

Eventually the door opened. Ivy stepped out into the rectangle of light, wrapped in a dressing-gown. She walked down the footpath towards him. 'Will you be *quiet!* Forest is trying to sleep!'

'I need to talk to him,' he said without preamble.

'No,' said Ivy. Her tone was furious, her teeth bared. 'Go away.'

'You know I wouldn't ask if it wasn't important,' said Ahab.

'What do you need from him?' she snapped.

'I need to know what he's not telling us.'

'You think *you* can get it out of him? Give me a break.' She peered closer, seeing his drenched clothes. 'Why are you bothering an old woman at this time of night? The police are right over there – want me to call them over?'

She waved at the police car in a friendly manner, as though proving she could summon Linda if she so desired.

'We need to work together, Ivy,' said Ahab. 'Blackbeard *is* here. He's *inside* Dempsey Abalone. Forest is in danger.'

'The Business wouldn't let him in that quickly,' snapped Ivy.

'They have!' He fought to control his rising voice. 'I just saw Chips killed. By Blackbeard's men.'

That brought her up short. 'What?'

'She knew. She knew who Blackbeard was, and they killed her for it. I swear it on my mother's memory.'

That seemed to take her aback. 'She *knew*?'

'Ivy . . . Do you think it could be . . . Is Jesse Blackbeard? Is he back?'

'*Jesse* . . . My Lord . . .'

'It's the only thing that makes sense,' he insisted. 'That's why I need to speak to Forest. I need to know if Jesse's alive. I need to *protect* him.'

'Dear, *I* can protect him far better than you,' said Ivy. She had recovered her composure in an instant. 'You left the Business, remember?'

'You think you can protect him? Without Davey?'

Ivy's eyes flashed. 'Yes. I can.'

He punched the letterbox, leaving a dent. 'Come on, old woman, can you leave your grudge behind for a bloody second! I just *told* you he's inside the Business!'

'I'm working on that.' She backed up a step. 'It's been a while since I saw you lose control like this.'

'Chips is *dead!* This is serious!'

'*Davey* is dead. I am *well aware* of how serious this is.'

'Just give me a chance to speak some sense into the boy.'

'What do you possibly think you can get out of him?'

'Blackbeard wants Forest alive! Don't you get it?' He took a deep, shuddering breath. Ivy was right – the last time he'd lost control like this had been at his mother's funeral. 'I think it means Forest knows something that Blackbeard needs. Can we *please* work together? For Forest's sake.'

'You think I can't do it alone, don't you,' she said.

'Please, Ivy.'

She examined him. 'Beg.'

'What?'

'You heard me. Get down on your knees and . . . beg.'

'Ivy . . .'

'Do it, man. Wait, I want a witness.' She beckoned to Linda, who climbed out of the car and came wandering over.

'Don't do this, Ivy,' said Ahab.

'Get down and beg,' she hissed maliciously.

Slowly, hating her with everything in his being, he fell down to his knees. After all these years, she finally had Ahab where she wanted him.

His cheeks hot with humiliation, Ahab put his hands flat on the ground.

'Please, Ivy. Please help me.'

'Say it. Say you beg me.'

'Ahab, are you okay?' Linda came running – she probably couldn't compute why he was kneeling on the ground. 'What are you doing?'

'Ivy . . . I'm begging you.'

She laughed, loud and mocking. 'The great Ahab Stark, grovelling. My answer is no. I don't forgive you. I'll never forgive you.' She spoke loudly enough to make sure Linda could hear. 'Now go away.'

She turned and walked back inside.

'Ahab, mate . . . what are you doing?' said Linda.

Ahab pulled himself to his feet, a burning fury inside him warring with the humiliation and his despair at Chips's murder.

He should've known Ivy wouldn't help him. Every woman he'd ever known had let him down, starting with his mother – may she rest in peace. The only person he'd ever been able to rely on was himself . . .

It made sense that a woman like that had spawned the next Dread Pirate Blackbeard.

'I'm fine, Linda,' said Ahab. 'But keep a close eye on the place – Forest could be in more danger than we thought.'

He began the walk back to the Mermaid's Darling. He yearned for a cigarette, but he'd forgotten they were in his pocket when he went into the water – they were soaked.

Jesse had looked to Ahab as a father figure on occasion. All three of those Dempsey boys had – Mackenzie, Davey and Jesse.

Then Mackenzie had got lost trying to navigate the short end of the stick, Davey had become arrogant as he grew into his charm and his brains, and Jesse . . . well, the cracks had shown in Jesse the moment he'd become hooked on the ice. His father had been a bastard, and Jesse had grown up into the same angry man, but the ice addiction made it so much worse.

If Ivy wouldn't help him, then he'd have to find another way to get to Forest.

Because only one thing mattered now: Forest was going to tell Ahab what happened. One way or another, Ahab would make him talk.

CHAPTER 34

FOREST

Watching from the side of the house, fully dressed, barely able to breathe in the humid late-night heat, Forest first watched Ahab sink to his knees and then Ivy waltz back into the house.

He hadn't heard every word. Only parts of it. But he'd pieced it together.

Blackbeard . . .

Blackbeard wants something from me.

A thrill of fear ran through him.

What did the real Forest Dempsey know that was of use to Blackbeard?

With Ivy returning, he raced back inside, through the door to his room and beneath the covers.

Zeus flopped onto him, putting his leg over Forest as though he'd never left the bed. When he heard Ivy crack the door open and check up on him, he feigned a gentle snore.

He listened to the creak of her footsteps and, once she was gone, he was out of the bed again, grabbing a torch and shoes, and out the door, easily slipping down the stairs to the beach – really, what *was* the point of the patrol car when there were two ways to get to the house?

But rather than heading to Huck, as he'd been planning tonight, he now knew he had to get up to Homeward – Mackerel was the one he needed. It was the only way he could keep this going.

Walking along the sand, startling a group of gulls into flight, he could barely breathe, such was the panic within him. Blackbeard wanted something from Forest but, worse still, so did Ahab. All the research he'd done had made it clear that Ahab Stark was the biggest danger to his scheme – he was perceptive, confident, and if he had any mental cracks to exploit, Forest hadn't been able to expose them.

Stop. Calm down.

He rested a hand against a gumtree, looking up at the sky, full of moon-streaked clouds and a dusting of stars. He was at the end of a short driveway, and inside this house the people were still awake – through their open curtain he saw the whole family sitting at the table, chatting and laughing. It was comforting and yet at the same time it left him feeling incredibly lonely.

'You're okay, kid,' he said to himself, tearing his eyes away. 'You're okay. Quiet. Go quiet . . .'

Finally, letting the silence of the night sky fill his body, he fixed his mind on Homeward and continued on his way.

He reached the property and walked down the driveway, seeing Mack's car parked beside Shelby's Jeep. Mackerel was on bail, so Forest figured it was a safe bet he'd be the one answering the door himself, assuming it was the police coming to check on him.

He rang the doorbell and, a moment later, was proven correct.

Mackerel only opened the door a crack. 'Forest?' he said. His bleary eyes and heavy voice revealed either fatigue or drunkenness. Probably both. 'Why are you here?' He smelled of whisky.

Forest ducked past him. 'Take me to your room, we need to chat in private,' he whispered, faking confidence.

Mackerel, clad only in his jocks, led him to the bedroom he'd just moved into. Open suitcases lay on the floor, full of crumpled clothes. Deodorant cans were lined up on the table, and abstract artwork had been taken off the walls and piled up in the corner. It was *very* nice for a guest room, thought Forest, but Mack clearly didn't belong there.

'Why are you here, Forest?' said Mackerel, sloppily pulling on a shirt and shorts he'd found on the floor.

'Promise you'll keep it a secret,' said Forest. 'You're the only one I can trust.'

'Is it about Davey?' said Mackerel quickly. 'Has he made contact?'

'No,' he said. 'Ahab just came to Ivy's, and I overheard him telling her that Blackbeard wants to make sure I'm alive. But I don't understand *why*. What does he want from me?'

'Blackbeard wants you alive?' whispered Mackerel. He looked away from Forest – he had the feeling he was trying to hide the fear in his face. 'If he wants Davey dead . . . Then you're the heir to Dempsey Abalone. Maybe he wants to recruit you, so that the Business can keep the cover of being part of the abalone trade. I mean, it's good news if he doesn't want to kill you.'

Ahab said it might be something I know.

No, something Forest Dempsey *might know.*

The Treasure Cave . . . it might have something to do with the Treasure Cave.

'I need you to explain to me again how Davey moved his drugs around,' said Forest. 'You touched on it a bit in Seaglass with Shelby, but you didn't go into much detail.'

Mackerel twisted his mouth. 'It's not good for you to know that sort of thing . . .'

'If he tries to recruit me, I'll need to fake interest,' said Forest. 'It might be the difference between life and death!'

'How good are you at acting?' said Mackerel. 'This is *Blackbeard* we're talking about. All sorts of people will have tried to get one over on him.'

'I'm good enough,' said Forest, lying back on the bed, feeling the sheets. Yep, *silk* sheets. 'Tell me, Mack. Please. It could save my life.'

Mackerel took a bottle of spring water from his desk and took a swig. 'Alright, well . . . abalone fishing requires a diver to go down to the bottom of the ocean. If you mark out a spot where another boat, from anywhere in the world, could sink a barrel of product, then a diver could use the shot line to bring the barrel to the boat, hide it in a hatch . . .'

As Mack explained the complicated logistics, from falsifying warehouse inventory numbers to manipulating the gross weight of refrigerated trucks, Forest thought he saw a gleam of hunger return to his eyes, but the more he spoke, the gleam faded and was replaced by fear again.

Forest liked Mackerel. He wondered, again, how a family this dysfunctional had produced such a nice guy. He looked around the room, feeling intensely sorry that Mackerel clearly didn't fit in here.

He'd have to fix it, somehow. As Forest Dempsey, surely he had some sway? He had to find a way to look out for Mackerel.

Even though they weren't truly family, he'd do his best.

Once he'd farewelled Mackerel, Forest headed down to the beach and followed it to the abandoned boatshed. He found Huck reclining on the roof, smoking, watching the sky above.

He climbed up beside him, panting from the long walk from Homeward. He hadn't seen or heard any police cars racing around, so he suspected Ivy hadn't found him missing.

'Late night for a stroll,' observed Huck.

Forest lay down beside him with a sigh of relief. The sticky heat had begun to be dispelled by a soft breeze here by the water.

The moon had nearly set now, revealing more stars in the sky. Shacktown had little light pollution, save from the plaza near Overeem's Dive Centre, meaning when the stars were out, the Milky Way put on a show. Orion's belt, Sirius, Betelgeuse, the Southern Cross . . .

With his eyes on those sparkling points of light, Forest told Huck everything. About Davey being alive, about the drug business, about the Dread Pirate Blackbeard, how he might be Jesse.

Huck propped himself up on his elbow, taking the cigarette out of his mouth. 'You better not be making this up.'

'Why would I make it up?' said Forest irritably.

'Because you're so good at making stuff up, sometimes you fool even yourself. It's the Dempsey curse.' He put the cigarette back in his mouth. 'I don't want Jesse to find me.'

'I won't let him,' said Forest. 'But if I'd known the Dempseys were a criminal family . . . Can you tell me about the Treasure Cave now?' said Forest.

Huck was silent. He ground out his cigarette and, when he was sure it was out, flicked it onto the sand below.

'Why?' he said finally.

'I think that's what Blackbeard is after. It's the only thing that makes sense – something only Forest knows.'

'If Blackbeard really is Jesse Dempsey, then you have to kill him.'

Forest didn't know what to say to that, so he didn't say anything.

'I was at Forest's house one night,' began Huck, lighting a new cigarette. 'We were supposed to be up in his room, but we'd snuck out to go fishing off the jetty at the end of their property. We were coming back when we passed the kitchen window – Alexandra and Jesse were fighting. It was about some cave she'd discovered while diving. She said there was treasure in there, but Jesse didn't believe her. She told him to go see for himself. He . . . he got angry a lot, Jesse did. He was angry that night.

'Forest knew his mum wanted a divorce, so the next day he opened his big mouth. He told her that she should go get the treasure, and then the two of them could use that money to disappear. But Jesse overheard . . . He was violent when he was angry. I should've stayed, but I didn't. I ran.'

'It's not your fault.'

'Don't interrupt,' said Huck. He puffed on his cigarette, then shuffled, making himself more comfortable.

'The next day Forest came and got me. He was . . . pretty bruised. He said Jesse had something to show us. Another cave, one that he'd been keeping secret. Wanted to apologise for losing his temper . . . I should've known then something was wrong – Jesse *never* apologised. So Alexandra, Forest and me. All three of us went with him. He led us down near the boulder fields, and . . .' Huck's voice tightened.

'What happened?'

'He led us to a cave down by the water, and we all climbed in there . . . You've gotta understand, we were *excited*. There's nothing I loved more than exploring together with them like that, we did it all the time, going on walks or out on the boat. Alexandra was the nicest mum, and me and Forest . . . all we had was each other. But this time was different. Jesse . . . I could tell something was wrong, the way he kept looking through us rather than at us, but I didn't know what. I just figured he was high.

'Well, we were all down in that cave network. The three of us went into a cavern ahead of him, but instead of following us, he must've climbed up above and rolled down a boulder. All those rocks are loose . . . well, however he managed it, he blocked the entrance. Of course we scrambled back up, pushing at it, yelling for help – first from him, then from anyone. But . . . there was just silence. We were alone.'

Tears rolled down Huck's cheeks.

Forest could barely breathe, but Huck had stopped talking.

'And then?' whispered Forest.

'He'd planned ahead. When we climbed deeper into the cave, looking for another way out, we found Alexandra's scuba gear. He'd left it there beforehand. That's when she realised what was going to happen – he'd trapped us in a tidal cave. We were going to die. He'd put her gear in there so it'd look like she'd gone diving, or like she'd killed Forest and me in some kind of . . . murder–suicide.'

'Why did he do it?'

Huck turned to him, frowning, as though it were obvious. 'He didn't want anyone else to find the Treasure Cave. That's what Alexandra said, once the water started to rise.'

'He was evil,' said Forest. 'Pure evil.'

'Evil or not, he was gone. No one was coming to save us. Alexandra tried to put the scuba gear on Forest, but he refused. He . . . he put it on me instead . . .' Huck wiped his eyes. 'She used her diving slate to write a note, in case someone found us . . . after. We all knew we weren't getting out of there. I suppose she didn't want to die a meaningless death – she drew a rough map, leading to the Treasure Cave. Or maybe she just wanted revenge against her husband, her murderer . . .

'The water came so fast . . . We were all pressed up to the ceiling, thrown around by the current, taking our final breaths. But because the water pushed us up to the ceiling, I found an opening up there, a passage. It was a squeeze, it was so narrow, but I was just about able to get in. But . . . the other two didn't fit. I watched . . . I saw them . . . when the water came into the opening, I had to leave them behind. I dunno how, but I made it out.

'I ran all the way home. I've never been so scared in my life. I was going to get help from Dad, but when I got home, Jesse was there. He was at my dad's place. That's when I knew it wasn't safe for me. Not at home, not anywhere in Shacktown. And . . . and you know the rest. Dad got blamed for the disappearance, and he vanished himself. I've been hiding from Jesse Dempsey ever since.'

Huck finished talking. His story was over. He wiped at his eyes again.

Forest wrapped his friend in a hug, feeling sick. He couldn't believe he'd gone through this. He couldn't even imagine how scary it would be to be trapped like that, buried alive, left to drown . . . but Huck had stopped crying.

'Get off me,' he said, but without any force behind it. 'I don't need your sympathy. I just want to get back at Jesse. I want justice for Forest and his mum.'

'There might be a way. Do you remember the map?' said Forest, pulling away.

'What?'

'The map Alexandra drew, to the Treasure Cave. Do you remember where it pointed?'

'Do you have any idea how *scared* I was? How it felt to know that . . . that I would die? That map was the last thing I was thinking about!'

'But if no one's ever found it . . . the map would still be there.'

'In that cave? That *tomb*? Don't even think about it.'

He knew how painful this was for his friend. Telling that story must have felt like reliving it . . . but that was exactly why he needed the map: to make things right. 'I need that map,' said Forest.

'You've already stirred up Forest's ghost enough.'

'You said you'd be there for me, whenever I needed.'

'You're the one who broke the oath of secrecy!' said Huck.

'I haven't,' said Forest. 'I haven't told a soul what happened to Forest. Please. I'm doing all of this for *you*.'

'I never asked you to!'

'Then why are you still here?' demanded Forest. 'Why haven't you run away again?'

'Shut up!'

'Face it,' said Forest. 'I'm the only one you've got, in the whole world. It's you and me. Once I clear your name, we can . . .'

'What?' said Huck. 'Find a home? I'll come live with you in a drug lord's mansion? Don't you get it – you and me, we don't get to have happy endings.'

'I'm going back there,' said Forest. 'I'm finding that treasure and I'm clearing your name.' He looked down at the waves, gauging that the tide was heading out. No time like the present. 'I'll save you, whether you want it or not.'

He left before Huck could stop him.

Fog had come in from the sea by the time Forest reached the boulder field. He stood at the entrance to the cave, shivering in the sea breeze, the fog adding to the sense of menace. A tomb, that's what Huck had called it.

He climbed inside. Dead silence. No plants, no lichen or moss, no bugs. Only dirt and dolerite, the cold of the earth and water, his shaky breath and his dancing torch.

He found a rock he could use to mark the walls, deciding it would be unwise to not leave a path to follow out. But though the twisting passages promised labyrinth twists, there were no dead ends. The inside of the cave was more like a sponge than a maze.

But with that first step, panic flooded him. He couldn't do this, he was going to suffocate, he was going to drown . . .

He forced himself to think of Huck. He forced himself to think about what his friend had endured.

He took a deep, calming breath and continued on.

He went deeper, through the little corridors and the dank, dripping caverns, his torchlight sparkling off the walls. The further down he went, the wetter it became, with shells and seaweed gathering at his feet. That meant he had entered the tidal part of the cave. While he was confident it was low tide, he'd still need to proceed carefully.

He continued climbing even deeper, the heat long gone, replaced by damp cold, until his torch beam landed on the jagged entrance to another tunnel, the size of a fireplace. And there, at its lip, something square and flat and white. He approached it slowly, unsure if it was what he hoped it was, but, sure enough, it had writing on it.

This was Alexandra's diving slate.

The words written on it in waterproof pencil were a panicked scrawl, but readable enough: *JESSE DEMPSEY KILLED US BECAUSE OF THE BONE CAVE.*

And underneath those words, a roughly sketched map of Pirates Bay. An X in the middle of the water and coordinates noted down beside it.

He'd found it. He committed it all to memory, in case he accidentally wiped it clean, then picked it up.

Now Forest was certain what lay beyond that jagged slash in the rock. He almost didn't want to look, but he had to. He'd come too far. He imagined her, sticking her arm through after Huck, pushing the slate ahead of her, hoping that someone would find it . . .

He carefully poked his upper half through the narrow opening, scared of getting his shoulders stuck but finding he had plenty of room. He wondered how big Forest Dempsey had been that he couldn't fit through this space – unless erosion had widened the tunnel in the years since?

Through the gap was a drop down to a larger area, with water pooling at the bottom. It stank of brine and sea.

His torch beam landed on two corpses, arms and legs akimbo, picked clean of everything but their clothes and pieces of scalp by sea lice. The bodies were gunky, the larger one missing its bottom half, the smaller skeleton missing its bottom jaw. A rusting scuba tank lay in the corner, pitted and broken.

Here lay Forest and Alexandra Dempsey.

Don't be sad. It happened years ago. And it has nothing to do with you.

The thought came from a distance. Forest felt like he was seeing this scene through someone else's eyes. His own mind had disappeared way up into the stars, his ears buzzing, the taste of copper in his mouth.

Clutching the diving slate, Forest walked all the way back to Safe Harbour. His body was still shaking, his breath hitching in his throat. He tried to force himself to stay calm, but it felt to him that the whole walk happened in fast-forward, without conscious thought.

When he finally climbed into bed, it was only Zeus whimpering and licking his face that brought him back to his body, back to the present. He couldn't remember climbing out of the cave.

'How did I get out?' he wondered aloud.

Exhausted but uncertain of how much time had passed, he feared dawn would come all too soon.

He looked down at the slate. He had the coordinates to what Alexandra had labelled as 'the Bone Cave'. He didn't like that wording. He'd refer to it as the Treasure Cave.

But to see it for himself, to get down to the bottom of the ocean, he'd need to learn to dive. Mackerel would be the obvious choice for a teacher, but maybe there was a way to use this situation to his advantage . . .

Ahab was a trained scuba instructor, and he was very invested in protecting him.

For as long as he thinks I'm Forest Dempsey, at least.

Ahab was determined to get to him. And everything Forest had learned about the man suggested Ahab would get what he wanted, sooner or later. Even though he'd told himself earlier that night that he was going to avoid Ahab . . . maybe it was better that it happened on Forest's terms than his, where he could control the interaction.

And if the Treasure Cave was what Blackbeard wanted, if Forest and Ahab found it together, the old man might know what to do with that information. He might actually be able to keep Forest safe – he clearly thought he was in danger.

It was worth a shot.

CHAPTER 35

AHAB

The next morning, Ahab was on his balcony with De Corrado, Keegan at his feet. He felt gritty from lack of sleep – he'd had nightmares about Chips. Being with De Corrado didn't help, it only made him feel more guilty. He'd witnessed a murder and hadn't told the police. Chips's parents weren't around, as far as he knew, but she did have a big sister somewhere. She deserved to know. And the crew . . .

Well, Ivy knew. Ivy could tell them, if she felt it necessary.

If you tell anyone else, you'll only make things worse. You need to think this through. Chips can't get any more dead. You can't save her, but if you're smart about this, you might be able to save everyone else from Blackbeard.

'Are you sure you've got enough protection on Forest?' said Ahab suddenly. 'I went by Ivy's place last night. One officer doesn't seem like enough.'

'I heard about that,' said De Corrado delicately. 'I was wondering if you were going to bring it up. You never seemed like the grovelling type.'

So Linda had told De Corrado what she'd seen? Ahab couldn't be angry about that – she was doing her job well.

'I'm running out of options to talk to Forest. It seemed the only way.'

'You're also the one who told me that having someone tail Forest wasn't going to get him to open up to us,' she added.

'I know, I *know*,' muttered Ahab.

'Look, I'm going down to Hobart today,' she said. 'We're joining the team down there, following a lead from the Crime Stoppers hotline. I can almost guarantee it'll amount to nothing, but . . . do you want to come? Get you away from here for a while? You might need to bring your own car, I plan on staying there the night. Unless you want to stay too?'

De Corrado kept talking, but Ahab had tuned out when he noticed Keegan stirring, his hackles raised. He knew Keegan's moods – he'd spotted another dog.

Ahab's eyes caught on a small figure walking up the street, a dog at its heels.

A familiar dog, and a familiar figure.

Forest. And he was walking with intent, straight for the Mermaid's Darling.

Is he coming to see me?

'You want a coffee for the road?' said Ahab, lurching inside, beckoning De Corrado to follow before she spotted Forest herself. He didn't want her interfering, or sending him back to Ivy.

Ned had his instructions – if the boy ever came looking for Ahab, he was to keep him away from prying eyes.

'No thanks,' said De Corrado, stopping to peer closer at Ahab's board.

He looked across the mess of clues and rumours pinned to the corkboard. It all seemed so much less important now. He was no stranger to grief, but the manner of Chips's death . . .

'I might stay here,' said Ahab.

'Really? You don't want to come?' said De Corrado, putting her hands on her hips. 'I don't offer ridealongs to just anyone, you know.'

'You don't get it,' said Ahab, with a genuine chuckle. 'To us, going to Hobart isn't a fun daytrip. It's a bloody exhausting day.'

'Okay, old man,' she said. 'I'll see you tonight.'

Ned had ushered Forest around to the back of the inn, quiet at this time of morning, where he waited until De Corrado had got in her car and driven off. When Ahab finally got out there, he was surprised to see the boy looking so . . . comfortable. He looked tired, heavy bags under his eyes, especially for someone so young, but he leaned nonchalantly against a banksia tree, his dog's leash in his hands.

'Not here,' was all Ahab said, and the boy nodded in understanding.

They took the short walk down to the beach in silence, passing early morning joggers and other locals walking their own dogs. Ahab guided them to a picnic table on the foreshore, underneath tea-trees and jacaranda, a group of cockatoos strutting along the grass in front of them. Ahab felt weirdly excited. His instincts told him today was going to reveal something important.

Once they were sitting at the table, he stayed silent, waiting for Forest to volunteer something. But the boy gave him nothing. He watched the waves over Ahab's shoulder with a great weight of sadness.

'I missed the ocean,' said Forest eventually, bringing his eyes back to Ahab's.

Ahab was in no mood to play these games anymore. He'd been patient. They'd *all* been patient.

The boy had to man up. Was he a Dempsey or not? If he was, then he owed it to Chips's memory to help them stop Blackbeard.

'Forest, I'm so sorry for all you've been through but . . . I need to know . . . what happened to you?' said Ahab. 'And don't start making your —'

'I'll tell you,' said Forest.

'You *will*?'

'I will. But on one condition: first, you teach me how to scuba-dive.'

They were just heading inside Overeem's Dive Centre when a car came to a stop in the pedestrian zone. Out hopped Mackenzie, doing that awkward stumble-run he did when he was in a hurry.

'Forest!' he yelled.

When he reached them, he dipped his head to Ahab. Zeus strained at his leash to reach Mackerel, tail wagging so much his whole body was moving.

'Sorry, Ahab. It's just that Ivy is going crazy looking for him. She nearly told the *police*, that's how worried she is.'

'He's safe with me,' said Ahab.

'Right,' said Mackenzie. 'Sure. But . . . Forest, can you get in the car?'

'No,' said Forest, pulling Zeus back. 'I'm learning to dive with Ahab.'

'What? Why?'

'Forest,' Ahab held out a twenty-dollar note, 'go order yourself something from the café inside. Mackenzie and I need to have a chat.'

Forest's glare sent some unspoken message to Mackenzie, who flinched, and then he trotted towards the café, Zeus at his heels.

Ahab beckoned Mackenzie closer. 'What the hell is going on between you two? Don't even think about lying to me.'

'I don't know what you're talking about,' said Mackenzie.

'Yes, you do. I saw that look between you two.'

Mackenzie fidgeted.

'Look up,' said Ahab. 'Mackenzie, look at me, son. We're on the same side.'

'I know we are,' said Mackenzie, but struggled to maintain eye contact.

'Tell me, lad.'

'I promised I wouldn't tell.'

Now he made eye contact. Ahab felt a thrill – here, at last, an opening.

'Forest told you something, didn't he?' He gripped Mackenzie's arms. 'Tell me!'

'No. I made a promise . . . you're the one who taught me to be a man of my word,' said Mackenzie. 'Please.'

'*Tell* me,' said Ahab. 'It could be life and death for Forest!'

'What?' His fervour startled Mackenzie, who pulled away. 'No, it's okay, Ahab, it's not about Blackbeard wanting something from him.'

'What? How do you know about that?' said Ahab.

Mackenzie's face went red. He tried to stammer something, but now Ahab took a step closer, anger building. '*What do you know, Mackenzie?*'

'Leave him alone, Ahab,' said Forest – Ahab hadn't even heard him return. That was something to keep an eye on.

'What the *hell* is going on here?' said Ahab.

'Ahab . . .' began Mackerel.

'I heard you, last night,' said Forest. 'Ivy was right – you *did* wake me up.'

'You heard . . .?' said Ahab.

'About Blackbeard. About how he wants something from me.' Forest had moved so that he now stood between Ahab and Mackerel, as though protecting the bigger man. 'So I went to Mackerel, to ask him who Blackbeard is. Why he's after me. So now I know all about Davey's drug business.'

'You *told* him?' shouted Ahab, turning on Mackenzie. People turned at the sound of his voice.

'What makes you think I didn't already know?' said Forest. 'At least Mackerel is giving me the tools to protect myself, unlike the rest of you.'

'Well, if you'd *tell us* what happened to you, then maybe . . .' Ahab fought to control himself. 'You *can't* protect yourself from Blackbeard, Forest,' said Ahab. 'Go back to the café, your uncle and I need to talk.'

'Don't bully Mackerel, then,' said Forest.

'I'm not . . .' The passers-by still watched them. 'Enjoying the show, are you?' he called.

They scurried away.

'I'm not bullying him. Go, Forest. I need to talk to Mackenzie alone.'

'Anything you tell him, he'll just tell me,' said Forest. 'Right, Mackerel?'

Mackenzie grew flustered. 'I . . . I mean, I dunno . . .'

Ahab pointed to the café. 'Look, I'll keep you up to date, now that I know what you know. Now *get*.'

Forest looked to argue, but then turned and left, irritated, dragging Zeus by his lead.

'*Are* you going to run and tell Forest whatever I tell you?' said Ahab softly.

'No!' said Mackenzie. He looked miserable. He'd gone back to looking at his feet.

Ahab sighed. He knew his cousin wasn't stupid. So why was he making these kinds of decisions? 'Mackenzie . . . the Business is a man's game, you can't bring Forest into it.'

'The poor kid deserves to know a bit about what's going on . . .'

said Mackenzie. Surely he couldn't still be that naïve? Bloody hell, he was the child of Ivy and Joel Dempsey, surely any juvenile sense of right and wrong got beaten out of him years ago? 'How do *you* know that Blackbeard wants him?'

Well . . . maybe that sense of right and wrong was what was needed to combat Blackbeard. Maybe Mackerel should know what Ahab had seen . . .

'Let's sit in your car for a moment,' Ahab said. Without waiting he walked around to the passenger side and climbed in.

When Mackenzie got in beside him, Ahab told him everything that he'd gathered: the men working for Blackbeard, their deal with Chips, what had been on the burning papers. Mackenzie listened to the whole thing with growing horror, and groaned when Ahab got to Chips's murder.

'Chips, no . . .' said Mackenzie. 'Ivy asked me to take over the Business. But if Chips had turned . . .'

'Ivy asked *you*?' That gave Ahab pause. Then he considered it. Mackerel *was* the best option . . .

'I haven't given her an answer . . . but if they got to Davey's second-in-charge, Blackbeard is deep into the Business. There's no way they'd let me in now,' said Mackenzie.

'Unless we find out what Blackbeard wants with Forest. Then we might have a bargaining chip. *Might*.'

Ahab climbed out of Mackenzie's car.

'Ahab, I'll have to tell Ivy that you were with Forest,' said Mackenzie.

'No, you don't, actually. You never saw me. You know nothing. Roger?'

'. . . Roger, Ahab.'

CHAPTER 36

MACKEREL

After Ahab had gone inside Overeem's to dive with Forest, Mackerel sat in the car for a long time.

Chips was dead. Blackbeard had infiltrated the Business.

Forest was at risk of becoming a pawn in a much larger game.

And Davey was . . . *still alive*, but trapped, unable to return while Blackbeard was about.

Should he have told Ahab about Davey? No, he did the right thing – the fewer people who knew, the less risk to Shelby and Kane.

The drive up to Homeward took twice as long as it should have. Mackerel drove slowly, weighing up everything in his mind.

Shelby wanted Mackerel back drug dealing. And the thing was, the longer Mackerel sat with it, the more he realised she might be right: he couldn't see any other way of getting close enough to Blackbeard to find out his identity.

But if Chips had worked out who Blackbeard was, then maybe it wasn't as hard as he'd thought it'd be. That changed things . . .

Finally he arrived at Shelby's place. *His* new place. Although for how long?

He parked and limped down the crunching gravel to the door, still in two minds.

Shelby was waiting in the lounge, wrapped in a thin green cardigan. Ivy had instructed her to wait at home in case Forest showed up. Kane was out with Fiona and her kids, giving Shelby some space.

'Did you find Forest?' said Shelby, folding her cardigan across herself. 'Is he safe?'

'Yeah. He was with *Ahab*.' He sat across from her. 'He . . . had a lot to tell me. I know this will be hard to hear but . . . Chips is dead.'

'What? How?!'

'Blackbeard. Somehow, she learned his identity – she told some of his men, trying to intimidate them, and they . . . they killed her for it.'

Shelby's hand flew to her mouth, then began kneading her bottom lip.

'I know you knew her, that Davey brought her around here for dinner . . .'

Shelby seemed miles away. 'If *Chips* was able to work out who Blackbeard is . . .'

'She died because of that knowledge,' added Mack.

'No. No, that's not true – she died only because she told them . . .' Shelby nodded, as though making her mind up. 'Mack, I've been doing some research.'

He didn't like that tone in her voice. 'About what?'

'You know, you can find anything on the dark web . . .'

'Shelby . . .'

'And, I mean, I *am* a chemist . . .'

'No, Shelby, please don't —'

'You said so yourself last night.' She reached for her laptop. 'Crystal meth is the main drug in Tasmania. I'm going to head into Hobart and pick up the instruments I need from the uni – I've got a friend who still works there. I know that I'd get flagged if I tried to buy them myself, even with my background . . .'

'Stop it, Shelby!'

'I mean, I'm a bit rusty . . .' she said in a hushed voice. 'But . . .'

So, when it came down to it, she *was* scared. So why was she even considering this?

She turned the laptop around. 'I found a recipe for cooking ice. It's fairly straightforward. And I have an idea on where to get the precursors I'd need . . .'

'Don't do this,' said Mackerel. 'Not someone as smart as you. Don't throw your life away.'

Guilt boiled in his stomach. He was the one who'd told her about the ice. His presence in her life had probably inspired the idea. No wonder Davey wanted to keep him away! *Why* did he have to tell her about Chips?

'I wanted you to help me.' Her voice trembled. 'But if you won't, I'm going to do it alone. Just for a week. Just to see what I can find out about Blackbeard . . . if it becomes too dangerous, I'll stop.'

'No. I won't let you do this.'

'You can't stop me. All it takes is one call to the police. I could tell them I don't feel safe with you here, or that you've been breaking your curfew, or . . . or that you've been looking up recipes for ice . . .' She tapped the laptop. 'You'll go straight back to jail. Don't try to get in my way, Mackerel. I'm doing this, with or without you.'

He put his head in his hands. He pulled at his hair.

And then he sat up. 'Okay.'

'Okay what?'

If she wanted to come into the game . . . If he helped her, at least he could protect her from herself. Was that right? Could he?

'One week. You said it'll only be for one week. Right?'

'Yes.'

'Then I'll help you.' The words coming out of his mouth felt like spewing acid, leaving his throat raw. His whole body tensed up, a weight pressing on him like the pressure of the deepest ocean.

She sagged into the couch. 'Thank you, Mackerel.' She put her arm across her eyes. 'Thank you . . .'

CHAPTER 37

AHAB

Ahab's boat, the *Ambergris*, bobbed near the giant cliffs, anchored close to a reef in a guarded cove. The *Ambergris* was his great love. Built from Huon pine and celery, it was styled like a traditional rear wheelhouse fishing boat. Twenty-eight-tonne displacement, three cabins under the focsle hatch.

Unlike the rigid inflatable boat, which was good for quick trips and the only thing that could've handled the Black Wind, *this* was his true love. This design had been tried, tested and modified for Tasmanian conditions over a century by the Wilson Boat Yard on the Huon River. She had nice curves with a high flared bow, a broad beam, wide gunnels, panoramic views from the windows all around the generously sized wheelhouse. An artist had hand-lettered *Ambergris* and *Pirates Bay* on her stern.

He'd anchored her on a rocky reef he knew well, which would be a great place for Forest to learn diving. He peered down through the blue water, excited to get down there. He loved the ocean, always had, always would.

Zeus clearly didn't. He was curled up in the crate where Keegan usually slept – the dog looked miserable.

It would be Forest's first time scuba-diving in the ocean, but he'd given him a two-hour lesson in Overeem's Dive Centre and Ahab was satisfied. It wasn't strictly necessary – people ran scuba tours for tourists all the time with barely any preparation, but Ahab wasn't going to cut corners where the boy was concerned. No matter how impatient he was to hear what he had to say.

It'd be a fine thing if, when we're this close, I drowned the kid . . .

Forest had been surprisingly quick to learn. Ahab felt he should have expected as much – the boy was clearly smart, he never had to be told anything twice, *and* both Alexandra and Jesse had been at home in the ocean.

Ahab pulled the straps tighter on Forest's BC, then checked the seal on his cheap wetsuit. He'd hired the kit from Overeem's, and they didn't always take care of their rental gear.

'You do exactly as I say, or you'll die,' he said firmly. 'Okay?'

Forest nodded, sticking the regulator in his mouth as though to say, *Let's go, already*!

The glimmer of excitement behind his scuba mask was contagious, and Ahab himself was now eager to get in.

'Alright, sit on the edge of the boat, hand on your reg and your mask, other arm across your chest, and roll back. Careful – it's shallower than you think.'

Forest let himself fall backwards off the boat, exactly as instructed. Ahab waited until he'd surfaced and gave the *okay* symbol, then he followed him in.

The water was cold, as it always was, but touched only his hands and neck, his wetsuit keeping the rest of him warm. He inflated his BC and then said, 'Ready to go down? I'm going to see if you can clear your mask again, just like we did at the pool. Before we descend, what are the five steps . . .?'

But Forest had already released air from his BC, disappearing beneath the waves.

'Little mongrel,' muttered Ahab. He put his regulator in his mouth and went down after him.

Under the surface was like a fairyland. The music of water sloshing against sand and rock, the bubbles from the breather, the ebb and flow of the current, the cool water trickling ice-like down the back of his neck and up his sleeves.

When he caught up with the boy, Ahab roughly dislodged Forest's mask, flooding it with water. He watched as Forest pressed down on the seal and blew through his nose, filling his mask with air again and expelling the water – a standard scuba-instructor test.

Ahab gave him the thumbs up, the signal to surface, and they returned to the top. The sounds above the surface came back all the sharper for having been suppressed – the call of a lone seagull overhead, the snapping of the *Ambergris*'s mizzen mast sails.

'Alright,' said Ahab once the boy surfaced. 'Now point to every part of your equipment and tell me what it does again.'

'That was incredible!' said Forest, spitting out his regulator. 'That's amazing!'

'Yeah,' said Ahab, eyes crinkling in a smile. 'Now, tell me about your equipment.'

Forest pointed to the parts. 'Buoyancy release, weight pockets, spare regulator . . .'

When Ahab was satisfied, he nodded. 'Now, show me the hand signals.'

Forest reeled them all off perfectly.

Ahab had never had a student like him. He remembered everything Ahab said, word for word.

'If you're so good at remembering, show me the five steps for descent again,' he said. 'And if you do it properly, we can go for an explore – staying *shallow*, mind you, and *stick close* to me.

The currents around here are gentle, but that's no guarantee of anything. When in the ocean or on it, always stay alert.'

'Okay,' said Forest around his regulator. He demonstrated the five steps for descent – he signalled, oriented himself by a point of reference, checked his regulator was in place, looked at the time, and then . . . he went under the surface . . . and kept going down.

Cursing, Ahab dived after him, kicking harder when he saw Forest go right past the side of the reef and down, down towards the sand at the bottom. Ahab brought his hand to his nose, equalising the pressure in his ears as he went after him, shafts of light patterning the silt and the kelp.

Forest descended steady and calm. When he reached the sea floor he paused, then sat down flat on his rump. He picked up the sand, looking at it, letting it run through his fingers.

Biting his regulator, Ahab floated beside him, an expert hand on his buoyancy control device, lying flat so his fin kicks wouldn't stir up the sand.

Forest reached for a piece of kelp, tangling it in his fingers, and held it close to his mask. When he spotted a red weedy seadragon, slowly floating by the edge of the kelp bed, he went still.

Ahab floated closer, looking down at the seadragon, its tendrils and grace, the little fin fluttering like a hummingbird's wing. Silent and alone, the master of mimicry.

Forest was transfixed, perfectly still until the seadragon softly floated back into the kelp and was gone.

For a moment it looked like Forest wanted to follow, but he thought better of it and turned, swimming alongside the kelp bed instead.

Ahab followed above him, diving in and out of the giant kelp forest, showing off his dexterity. He could feel the excitement coming off Forest in waves, and he watched the joyous dips of the boy's hands as he manoeuvred through the water.

They spent a long time there, on the seabed, until Ahab checked his watch and indicated it was time to surface. He took them up slowly, making sure that they had enough safety stops – time floating at different depths – just to make absolutely sure Forest decompressed properly. Ahab hadn't intended for them to go so deep, but he had to admit the boy was a natural.

When they'd both climbed back aboard the *Ambergris*, shivering but invigorated, Forest surprised Ahab with a quick hug. 'Thank you. That was the most amazing thing I've ever done.'

Ahab pushed him gently away. 'Yeah, righto,' he said, scruffing the boy's hair. 'You did good.'

Ahab got the motor started and steered them out of the cove, Zeus whimpering in the crate.

'Yes, alright, poor old fella. We're heading back,' said Ahab. 'Here, Forest, hold the wheel and keep us steady as we head for the marina. I'll put a brew on.'

Forest looked at home standing at the sassafras wheel, gazing out over the decks like an old salt. He made small corrections as the hull moved with the swell and the currents – like it was second nature and he'd been doing it all his life. A true Dempsey.

Ahab watched him from the galley as the kettle boiled – the sound of the diesel engine purring below – and wished that the two of them could just keep steaming along, out to sea, away from the mess that awaited them on shore.

When all this was over, he was going to get away for a while, aboard *Ambergris*. A week, a month. Ned could look after the inn. He'd bring the boy and they'd fish, dive, cook up a storm. They'd sit by the wood heater in the wheelhouse and Ahab would tell him stories about his family, tell him everything he'd missed and more.

———

They washed their gear with fresh water from the marina tap, then hung it up to dry back in the *Ambergris*'s warm engine room, a promise of another dive either later that day or tomorrow. Zeus stood trembling on the jetty, shell-shocked by his first boat ride.

Forest had a fresh energy about him as they dodged and weaved around people haggling for fish, a group of teenagers sitting on the edge and listening to music, a family who wanted to stop and pat Zeus – who had quickly recovered and was now barking at birds and straining at the leash like a gambolling puppy.

Ahab had planned to get Forest back to the Mermaid's Darling for lunch, to get him somewhere quiet so he could finally get the answers the boy had promised him in return for the dive . . . But Forest looked so happy and peaceful, laughing at Zeus's antics, even chatting with strangers.

And did Ahab really want to throw himself back into that world right away? The world where Chips could be murdered in front of his eyes, and all of this, the marina and the tourists, was threatened by the Dread Pirate Blackbeard?

It could all wait half an hour longer.

'Want an ice-cream?' said Ahab gruffly.

Forest beamed.

Man, boy and dog walked along the sand, heading back to the inn. Ice-cream dripped down Ahab's hand; Forest had nearly finished his already. Zeus was off his leash, although it got him no closer to the seagulls he was chasing.

When they got to the path leading up from the beach, towards the Mermaid's Darling, Forest hesitated, then stopped.

'I wanted to say thank you,' he said.

'That's okay,' said Ahab. 'It was my pleasure —'

'Not the ice-cream. I mean taking me diving.'

'I knew what you meant,' said Ahab.

Forest smiled weakly, his mind seemingly elsewhere.

'Listen, there's something I've been wanting to say . . . is it right that Aunty Miriam could talk to shells?'

Ahab went still – he didn't like talking about his mother. 'Yes, she thought she could —'

'Well . . . so can I . . . can I show you?'

'That's not funny, boy,' said Ahab.

'I know it's not funny,' said Forest. 'Do you want to see me do it or not?'

'No,' said Ahab, 'I don't.' He continued walking, knowing his tone had shifted. Forest had flinched as though struck.

Forest caught up to him. 'I really can talk to shells, you know,' he muttered.

'Let's get back to the inn,' said Ahab. 'You owe me some truths.'

'Alright,' said Forest, now matching Ahab's tone. 'But I'm still hungry.'

Talking to shells . . .

Ahab pushed the emotions down. 'I'll get you some food,' he said. 'And some for Zeus, too.'

He'd set Forest up at a corner table of the inn's restaurant.

'Order anything you'd like, but I'd recommend the seafood chowder. Best in Tasmania. We have the award to prove it.'

Zeus was tied up outside, by the kitchen door, where one of the staff had given him some offcuts and a bone.

Ahab walked around the pub, greeting the regulars in the lunch-time crowd, pouring a few beers. He kept an eye on Forest at the other end of the room, but gave him space while his food was prepared.

Forest, who had clearly been expecting Ahab to sit down to interrogate him immediately, frowned.

Ahab's mind was still on what the boy had said down on the beach. The same thing he'd said in the ambulance.

I really can talk to shells, you know . . .

He could remember his mother doing exactly that, ever since he was a kid. He'd loved the way that he could whisper into a shell, give it to her, and she'd tell him what the shell said in response. It was like believing in Santa Claus – he'd clung to the belief his mother was magic for a long time. Even when she was deep in the drug-induced psychosis of ice addiction, paranoid and then euphoric in dizzying cycles.

When she'd first landed in hospital, they found it so hard to identify her, it was a long time before they were even able to reach out to let him know she was there. They claimed she had a grandson who came to visit her, but then the police had come asking questions and they realised she wasn't who she said she was . . .

From what he'd pieced together after that, in the later years of her life she'd been living in Hobart, moving from drug house to drug house . . . Ahab had always tried to stay in touch, but he'd lost contact with her well before that. Her disappearance had been the final straw – that was when he resolved to drag himself out of the Business.

And then, just as she was dying, she was back in his life.

Hooked up to those machines, she was in withdrawal, and her mind was gone. She was dosed up and asleep most of the day. But there on her deathbed, an infection in her blood caused by a dirty needle, in one of her rare moments of lucidity, she'd told him the truth about the shells.

'I need to tell you, my boy . . . the shell-speaking was a trick.'

Ahab was a grown man by then, and he had known for some time that there must have been a trick to it, but part of him had still clung to the idea that his mother *did* have a spark of magic. That maybe she was part-siren.

'It's just lip-reading, Ahab. That's all it is.'

She must have seen the disappointment in his face, because she'd reached for his cheek and then entered a coughing fit. He'd had to leave the room while the nurses came to assist. But when he'd come back, that was when she'd made him promise never to turn on his family. To always be there for them.

After Miriam had died, Ahab did a lot of research into shell-speaking – the folklore behind it. It wasn't long until he stumbled upon a book about mentalist tricks, which explained the lip-reading 'Jar of Secrets' trick in detail.

So if Forest claimed he could talk to shells . . .

Either he really could, in which case his mother's magic might have been real – unlikely – or he was just lip-reading, in which case he was trying to trick Ahab.

Was he trying to manipulate Ahab in some way? Or was it just a childish prank? What could he hope to gain?

Uncomfortable thoughts entered his mind. Why did Forest know a conman's trick like that in the first place? When would he have learned it?

He did his best not to stare at the boy, sitting placidly at that corner table. All this time Ahab had been trying to reach Forest, but in the end the boy had chosen the time and place to come to him. What was his motivation? He wanted to win Ahab's trust, win his confidence, to convince him of . . . what? That he was magic? That Dempsey blood flowed through his veins?

One particular thought wrestled its way to the front of his mind.

What if he's not Forest?

Impossible. How would he know all those things only Forest could know?

He worked the bar, silently pulling pints on autopilot while his mind raced through the possibilities. He'd have to be smart about how he did it, but he would need to test the boy.

Finally, Forest's chowder was ready. Ahab took a seat, pretending to read the newspaper while Forest ate. He couldn't eat himself, his mind was spinning too fast. What would it mean if this wasn't Forest? What should he do if that was the case?

Stop it. You saw him underwater. He was a natural. He has to be Forest Dempsey. Snap out of this. Maybe he really believes he can talk to shells.

'So . . . my dad?' said Forest tentatively.

Ahab lowered the newspaper. 'Yeah?'

Forest leaned forward. 'What was he like?'

Ahab held his eyes, searching for something in them. 'Surely you remember enough to know what he was like?'

'I remember some . . .'

If this kid wasn't the real Forest then he was a damn good actor.

So Ahab told Forest the stories. Stories of Jesse's childhood. Of Jesse running amok at school, always in trouble with his teachers. Long days fishing, up early to beg Ahab to take him out. Girls who fell for him, swooned over his looks and charm, only to be left heart-broken.

He also used to hit you, Forest, thought Ahab. *I didn't find out until years later, but you and Alexandra were terrified of him. All of the Dempseys are bad dads, but he was a real bastard of a father. And I never did anything to stop him.*

But that was never common knowledge. You'd only remember that if you were really Forest, wouldn't you?

He searched Forest's eyes for any recollection of his father's abuse. The boy had been six when he disappeared – surely he couldn't have repressed it completely.

'I'll show you some photos,' he said eventually.

There was a barely perceptible pause before Forest said, 'Sure.'

'They're upstairs in my rooms – take your time with the food, enjoy it. I need to go ahead anyway,' said Ahab.

He went upstairs while Forest finished his chowder, giving Keegan warning once inside: 'Visitor is coming, old boy.'

The dog wouldn't let anyone in without Ahab there, not unless it was Ned, and even that had taken a while.

Keegan waved his tail in acknowledgement, but gave a soft growl nonetheless.

'None of that. Go.'

He climbed out of his bed and stood guard by the door, ready to inspect the newcomer. Ahab pulled photo albums out of the cupboard and had them waiting on the coffee table. He used to take them out all the time, but now he tried not to spend too much time dwelling on the past. He kept them in a special order now, based on how happy they made him feel. Some years had been better than others. The worst years were kept at the end of the line, only brought out rarely . . .

Before long he heard Forest climbing the steps outside; when he knocked on the door, Keegan growled. Ahab opened it, a hand on the dog's collar. But as Forest stepped into the room Ahab's supposed guard dog wagged his tail at the sight of the boy, and even began licking his hand.

'He likes you,' said Ahab, surprised.

He knew his dog like he knew his own self. That lick and tail-wag combo was reserved for people he particularly liked. Which was impossible, because Keegan had never met Forest before.

'I'm good with animals,' said Forest easily. 'Maybe he can smell Zeus on me.'

'Maybe,' said Ahab.

Suspicion took over once more. Keegan definitely seemed to know Forest. Something wasn't right.

Ahab gestured the boy over. He pointed out interesting photos, all scrapbooked once upon a time by Alexandra Dempsey. Gifted to him – he always figured it was because she knew about the child he'd lost, and felt sorry for him, having no family of his own.

He turned the pages, handwritten captions alongside the pictures. Forest with their old dog, Roxy. Forest curled up with Jesse in front of the TV. Forest with his little space backpack, with the caption in Alexandra's careful hand: *Given to Forest, 6yo, by Ivy, after he informed her he wanted to be an astronaut when he grew up. She told him he was born for it, and bequeathed this backpack. How time flies.*

Forest touched the page. 'I remember this.'

Ahab turned away, clearing his throat, overcome with emotion warring with paranoia. It wasn't fair on the boy that Ahab was feeling this way! Why did Dempseys *always* have to assume something bad was going on?

As if on cue, the phone rang. He picked it up. 'Mermaid's Darling.'

'I told you to stay away from Forest,' came Ivy's hard voice.

Ahab gripped the receiver tighter. 'You should've known you couldn't keep him from me forever.'

'I want him back within the hour, or I'm sending the police.' She ended the call.

Ahab turned, watching the boy. What to do? He still hadn't got his answers. It was now or never – it was time to find out what had happened to Forest, Jesse and Alexandra.

Forest sighed sadly. 'Ivy, yeah?' He gathered up the photo albums, walked to the cupboard and opened it, weighing each album in his hand before sliding it into place.

In the exact right order.

Exactly how they'd been before.

How did he know *that*?

He hadn't been in the room when Ahab took them down.

Ahab's eyes flicked down to Keegan, who was following Forest around, snuffling at his pockets. He was looking for treats. He only did that with Ahab, or when Ned brought him bacon – his favourite.

'Are you okay, Ahab?' said Forest, watching him.

There was something new in the boy's face, something in his voice. He glanced at the cupboard, then back at Ahab.

Forest knew.

Forest knew he'd made a mistake, but he wasn't sure what.

All of the facts started to join together in Ahab's mind.

Keegan has seen Forest before.

Forest has taken down the photo albums before.

Forest has been here before.

He might not have been so suspicious if Forest had not wanted to do that trick with the shells, down on the beach.

It's not really Forest Dempsey.

The thought hit Ahab in the belly with physical force. He had to sit down.

Forest's forehead was a sheen of sweat. He approached. 'Ahab?'

Ahab had to look away.

But what about the tattoo on his back?

Suddenly he was certain. The tattoo was perfect. The words brooked no argument.

THIS IS FOREST DEMPSEY

It was genius.

It was diabolical.

Ahab couldn't remember grabbing the boy by the collar, but the next moment he'd slammed Forest against the wall.

'*Who are you?*'

'Put me down, Ahab.' The boy spoke calmly, with an even tone, as though to a spooked animal. He didn't resist, but it must've been hard to breathe. 'You're not making any sense, Ahab.'

Where was the supposedly traumatised boy? There was no sign of him now.

Ahab's anger filled the room, his fury like a tidal wave. '*Who. Are. You?*'

Keegan growled, catching on to Ahab's mood.

'Put me down,' whispered the boy, 'or you'll regret it.'

Ahab could have been a statue. The boy's face turned red as Ahab's forearm further constricted his breathing.

'Why did you do it?' snarled Ahab. 'For the money?'

The boy stayed silent.

'Or are you working for Blackbeard?'

A flutter of an eyelid. *No.*

'Are Jesse and Alexandra dead? Is Forest?'

The boy kept his gaze.

'Who. Are. You?' growled Ahab. 'A DNA test will prove you're an imposter.'

'No it won't,' said the boy with an uneasy smile. 'Forest was adopted.'

Ahab dropped him.

'Keegan, *sic.*'

Keegan snarled and leapt forward, keeping the boy backed against the wall.

Slowly, Ahab lit a cigarette and walked out on the balcony to smoke it. Stupid. How could he have been so *stupid*?

This changed everything. *Everything.*

It wasn't even Forest Dempsey!

Eventually he turned back and stepped inside. The boy still stood against the wall, frozen. Keegan, still snarling, was close enough to chomp the boy's fingers off if he moved.

The boy didn't look so assured now. He looked up at Ahab. Ahab said nothing.

'Keegan, calm.'

Keegan changed instantly, returning to his bed.

Forest let out a huge breath.

'Forest wasn't adopted,' said Ahab.

'You mean Jesse never told you? I thought you were close.' There was no mistaking the salt in the boy's voice. 'Forest knew, you know? His mother told him.'

'You're lying.'

The boy smiled. 'Guess you'll never know, will you? Without a DNA test you can't prove anything, and, well, everyone already believes I'm Forest, don't they?'

The boy who Ahab had seen below the ocean, enamoured by the weedy seadragon, was nowhere in those cold, calculating eyes.

Ahab parked out the front of Ivy's house. He walked the boy up to the door, dragging Zeus behind. He and the boy said not a word to each other and, once he let go of him, the boy walked inside without a backwards glance.

Fake Forest *wasn't* Ahab's problem. He turned to leave, all the while thinking, *Except that he might be the only leverage we have against Blackbeard, who wants him alive for some reason. Does Blackbeard know he's a fake? Or does Blackbeard think he's the real Forest?*

All his plans were falling apart. They were no closer to working out who Blackbeard was.

He sighed angrily, spun back towards the door. He set his jaw.

Then he shook his head and turned again to leave.

I need space to think.

That's when he saw Ivy, sitting in the shade under an archway of trailing greenery. She had knitting on her lap, bees buzzing around her feet, her fox-like eyes on him.

'You look like you're trying to make a decision, Ahab,' she said.

'I brought the boy back like you wanted. I have nothing to

say to you,' he said. He stomped past her, trying to work out what to do.

'Such grief. I haven't seen you this sad since Miriam's funeral. Did the boy tell you Jesse was dead?'

'No,' snarled Ahab. 'He didn't.'

'Ah, so the boy told you something else,' she said pointedly. 'That he's not the real Forest, perhaps?'

He froze. 'What?'

'So he has told you. I wonder why? But yes, he's an imposter.'

He felt like the earth fell away from him. Ivy *knew* he wasn't the real Forest? How?

'Imagine what would happen to that boy,' said Ivy, rising to her feet, putting her knitting on the seat, 'if Blackbeard finds out he isn't the real Forest. He *will* kill him.'

'How do you know he's not the real Forest?' said Ahab.

'Forest and Alexandra have been dead for years,' said Ivy. 'You think I wouldn't know what happened to my own grandson?' She wiped away the tears that had formed on her otherwise stone-cold face. 'Don't worry, Jesse paid for what he did. I made sure of it. But now, if Blackbeard wants Shacktown, I'll do whatever it takes to keep it from him. Including keeping *his* secret.' She cocked her head towards the house, meaning the fake Forest. 'But if it gives me the chance to put a knife in Blackbeard's heart, I'll kill the boy myself and hand him to that pirate on a platter.'

The boy appeared at the door, Zeus at his side. He had been listening, and Ahab saw that he had turned deathly pale.

'Ahab?' The boy's voice sounded strangled.

Ivy smiled warmly. 'Hello, Forest.'

'So you don't care for the boy?' said Ahab.

'Of course I do,' said Ivy. 'Back inside, Forest.'

'I don't think so,' said the boy. He stepped closer to Ahab. 'I think I'll be staying at the Mermaid's Darling for a while.'

What? No, Ahab didn't need to be babysitting a conman.

Ivy smiled. 'If that's what you want. But you'll be back.' She picked up her knitting and sat back down. 'Ahab can't protect you like I can. Don't forget to go to Frankie's on your way – if you don't, the police will want to know why.'

Ahab's knees felt weak. He walked quickly to his ute.

The boy and the dog followed.

'What are you doing?' said Ahab. 'Go back.'

'I'm staying with you.'

'No, you're not,' snarled Ahab, walking around to the driver's side.

'I can tell you the truth,' said the boy in a low voice. 'That's what you want, isn't it? I'll tell you what happened. If you protect me.'

'We already had a deal once. As though I could believe anything you say.'

'No, but there might be someone else you'll believe,' said the boy. He opened the passenger door and jumped in, Zeus settling beside him.

'Get out,' said Ahab, coming around to that side of the car and pulling open the door.

'Get in and listen to me. If it isn't what you want to hear, I promise I'll go back to Ivy.'

Ahab scowled, but he shut the door and walked back around to the driver's seat.

'Okay, imposter. Who do you think is going to convince me to trust you?'

'Davey Dempsey,' said the boy. 'He's still alive.'

What? No, not a chance. What kind of game was he playing *now?*

'You're lying,' said Ahab.

'I'm not, and Mackerel can prove it.'

'Davey . . .' Ahab laughed harshly. 'I saw Davey's body with my own eyes.'

'Ask Mackerel if you don't believe me.'

Ahab frowned. Was it possible?

This was all too much.

'Fine.' He turned the ignition. 'We're going back to the Mermaid's Darling, and then you're going to tell me everything.'

'No, old man,' said the boy. 'I'll tell you only what you need to know.'

The way he spoke, the words he chose . . . even his voice was different now. 'Who the hell are you?' said Ahab.

'I'm Forest Dempsey. And if you don't want me telling the whole world Davey Dempsey is alive, you'd do well to remember that. Which means you use my name. Say it. *Forest*.'

'Why would I care who you tell about Davey?' said Ahab, rapidly getting the sense that he'd lost all control of this situation.

'Because if Blackbeard finds out Davey is alive, Shelby and Kane will be in danger. And you wouldn't want their deaths on your conscience, would you?'

Ahab's knuckles were white where he gripped the steering wheel. 'You'd put them at risk?'

'Not unless someone put *me* at risk,' said the boy . . . no, *Forest*, if he insisted on being called that.

'Where is Davey?' said Ahab.

'Take me to Frankie, and then let's head back to your place,' said Forest. He rummaged in the centre console of the car until he found a cigarette and a lighter. Rolling down the window, he lit it up. 'Let's go. It's been a long day.'

CHAPTER 38

MACKEREL

Mackerel drove the Jeep towards Hobart, Shelby scrolling on her iPad beside him, her feet up on the dash.

'It sounds so easy,' said Shelby. 'And *anyone* can just . . . download instructions for how to cook this stuff.'

'Why would they want to?' muttered Mackerel.

'Because look how much you can *sell* it for. No wonder Davey never worried about money.' There was a forced lightness to her voice. Or at least, he hoped it was forced. 'There's plenty of recipes,' said Shelby, still scrolling. 'Not all of them are dangerous. Some of these are so simple . . . I wonder if everyone else knows ice is this easy to make?'

'It's not easy, it's fucking dangerous. You've heard of homecook lab explosions, right?' said Mackerel. 'Besides, most of it's cut with shit that will erode you from the inside out.'

'This recipe is the safest,' she said, flashing the screen at him. 'It's exactly right for what we want to do. But we'll need pseudo-ephedrine . . . Although I have some ideas . . .' Shelby swiped across to her notepad app, typing ingredients and quantities.

'You really shouldn't be putting that on the iPad. The cops can pull up the data even if you delete the note.'

'Relax, Mackerel. You've briefed me enough on how to stay safe. This is brand new, paid for in cash, and not linked to any existing account.'

He'd taught her everything he could think of about being safe in the digital world. To her credit, she seemed to be taking it in. He could do this. If they went slowly, and he kept her as safe as he could . . . They'd even left their phones at Homeward. If their phones were tracked later on, at least there would be no evidence they'd come into town together – Mackerel could claim he'd acted alone and leave Shelby out of it. He was going to jail anyway.

The bridge into Hobart was packed with traffic – nothing like Brisbane, but enough to grate on Mack's already fraying nerves. He was on the lookout for police cars, even though there was no way they'd know what they were up to. By the time they'd driven through the CBD and out to Sandy Bay, Mackerel was wound so tight that even Shelby was telling him to relax.

They pulled up outside the leafy university, after doing two blockies just to find a park. Mackerel waited in the car – the odds were slim, but if someone he knew saw him buying a bunch of chemicals and lab supplies, alarm bells would ring. Shelby Dempsey, on the other hand – a grieving widow, rekindling her love for chemistry – that was another story.

They sat at a café on the pier in Hobart – Shelby had insisted she treat him to a meal. He'd just wanted to go home to Shacktown, but she wouldn't take no for an answer. She had no fear – that wasn't a good sign. Shelby had all the equipment and chemicals stashed in the car, and she didn't seem to think that was an issue.

'My car has never been searched in my entire life. You have *got* to calm down.'

He poked at his fish and chips, leaving his coffee untouched. The water lapped at the wood and it stank of brine. A seagull strutted nearby, eager for an easy meal. He thought about throwing it a chip, but didn't want the whole flock coming down on them.

Then he saw a scruffy man walking past, dragging a shopping trolley full of bedding and plastic bags, and Mackerel had an idea. 'Do you still have some of that cash?'

'Yeah . . .'

'Give me three hundred,' he said. 'Quickly.'

She obeyed, handing over the notes. Mackerel chased after the homeless guy. 'Hey, brother.'

The man turned, wary, and Mackerel showed him the cash. 'I'll buy your phone off you.'

The man nodded wearily. This wasn't a completely abnormal request for someone on the street. After ensuring Mackerel memorised the passcode, he wished him well and the money disappeared into his pocket.

Mackerel breathed easier. Three hundred bucks for an ancient, cracked Samsung. But at least now Shelby had a burner phone she could use. It wasn't worth the risk for Mackerel to source one for himself – it was against his bail conditions for him to have more than one phone.

'There's this saying,' he explained to her. 'Two phones and you're a businessman, three phones and you're a drug dealer.'

'Okay,' said Shelby, eyes on the screen. She opened a browser and tapped away. 'Do you have any idea how we can buy a houseboat without anyone knowing?'

'*What*?'

'I want to buy this liveaboard converted ferry.'

She put the phone on the table and twisted it around so he could see it.

'And . . . why are you going to do that?'

'It's advertised down at Fortescue Bay. Listen: "Old and rickety, not good for much. It's the old Isle of the Dead ferry from Port Arthur." Some bloke converted it into a houseboat years ago and now it's falling apart. We own a block down there with its own jetty – it's barely ten minutes from Shacktown. Davey and I were gonna set up a little retreat there for ourselves, or for Kane to use when he's older and wants to throw wild parties. We can moor the boat there.'

'Why do you want a houseboat?'

Shelby glanced off across the water. 'Because it'll make a good lab.'

'Oh,' said Mackerel. 'Of course.' He slammed his fork down a little too hard.

She sighed. 'What are you upset about now?'

'Nothing,' said Mackerel.

'Why are you sulking? Did you think I was going to cook it in the rumpus room at Homeward?'

'No,' said Mackerel. 'I didn't.'

'Then *what*?' said Shelby.

'I'm not upset with you, okay!' he said. 'It's just that . . . I shouldn't have dragged you into this. Setting up a lab – if the cops don't catch you first, what will happen if Blackbeard finds out you can cook?'

He realised he was rambling and took a drink from his coffee to stop himself. He wanted a beer, but reminded himself that he wasn't drinking anymore.

'Let's make one thing clear, Mackerel Dempsey. You did not *drag* me into anything. I'm here of my own free will.' She fixed him with a convincing stare. 'Now, tell me what *will* happen if Blackbeard finds out I can cook?'

Mackerel held his tongue. It wouldn't do to scare her. 'Let's just go home,' he said.

'Fine,' said Shelby, throwing her napkin on her plate and rising from the table. 'But we have one more stop to make first.'

'We do?' said Mackerel.

'My aunty's an end-time prepper,' she said, with a hint of mischief. 'You know what that means? She's a hoarder. She's got boxes and boxes of Sudafed.'

'Shelby, no. We can't.'

She slipped her arm through Mackerel's playfully. 'You said it yourself, to win Blackbeard's business, we need the best ice on the market. The only way we're making that is with pseudoephedrine.'

CHAPTER 39

AHAB

Ahab paced his room as far as the landline cord would allow. Mackenzie wasn't picking up his phone.

Forest sat on the end of Ahab's bed, his arms folded around himself.

Ahab hung up the phone with a curse.

'So let's say I believe you, and Davey's alive,' he said.

'I know you're upset with me, but —'

Ahab cut him off. 'Yet conveniently, you don't know how to find him.'

'I'm sorry, Ahab, but Davey didn't run through his itinerary with me,' said Forest wearily.

Damn the boy was frustrating. And so bloody confident now!

'Just be patient,' said Forest. 'Mackerel will be able to tell you all about it. He heard most of our conversation.'

'Heard? So Mackenzie didn't even see Davey?'

'He would have, except Davey locked us in and ran away.'

'Locked you in where?' said Ahab.

Forest seemed reluctant to answer, cracking his knuckles and looking away.

'Don't try me, boy. Locked you in *where*?' said Ahab.

'In the pump shed behind Overeem's Dive Centre. That's where he met me.'

'The pump shed?'

Overeem's Dive Centre . . .

Surely that was no coincidence. Davey knew the place well, but so did Ahab. There weren't too many places to hide.

'I might know where he'll be.'

'Then I'm coming,' said Forest.

'No, you're not.'

'Just try to stop me,' said Forest. 'I'm the only bargaining chip you've got.'

The dive centre had closed for the day, but that wasn't about to stop Ahab. He'd dug out his boltcutters from the tool shed at the inn and now, together with the boy, he walked around the back of the main building like he belonged there. Much better than sneaking around in the dark.

But when they got to the pump shed, he stopped in his tracks. The door was closed, but there wasn't even a padlock on there. That wasn't right – there was thousands of dollars of equipment in there.

He flicked on his torch and stepped inside, sweeping the light around the room, the smell of chlorine filling his nose. Searching behind the boxes of discarded pipe ends and bottles of cleaning chemicals, it didn't take him long to find what he was looking for: the trapdoor.

In another life, when Overeem's had just opened, he and Davey had been two of their casual dive instructors. It was how he'd gained his dive master certification. During his time working here, he'd spent a bit of time in the maintenance tunnels that ran under the whole centre. This is where all the pipes that fed the different aquariums and pools ran. Once upon a time they'd had public facilities down here, but they'd been replaced by fresher change rooms when the aquarium wing was added.

Forest had followed him into the pump shed, but Ahab ordered him into the corner. 'Stay put. I'll be back.'

'I'm coming too.'

'Too dangerous. Don't worry, I know I need you to get Davey to talk. Assuming he's here. Assuming you're telling the truth.'

'Just wait until Mackerel answers your call,' said Forest, crouching in the corner. 'He'll confirm it.'

'Stay,' said Ahab, as he began climbing through the trapdoor. Forest did as he was told. 'There's a good boy.'

At the bottom of the ladder, his torch revealed wide tunnels lined with dirt and cobwebs. The concrete walls were covered in moisture that caught the torchlight; a steady dripping echoed from somewhere.

He crept along, covering his torch with his hand. No need to give anyone else down here forewarning of his presence.

A little further along he found an old storeroom. A printed 'OUT OF ORDER' sign was tacked to the door, but it had none of the patina of age and wear that everything else down here had.

A flimsy disguise.

He listened at the door, staying still for the longest time, taking calm breaths.

He stayed that way for one minute.

Then two.

Then three . . .

There. A shuffle inside. A cough.

He kicked the door open and quickly scanned the room with his torchlight.

A man gave a holler and backed away, shielding his eyes. He was dressed in a raincoat, dishevelled, his hair matted, his beard thick and scruffy.

Davey Dempsey.

'Bloody hell . . .' said Ahab.

So he *was* alive.

This changed everything.

'Wha— *Ahab*?' said Davey.

'Hello, Davey.' Ahab grinned. A fearsome, terrible grin. 'Let's have a chat.'

Davey looked back and forth. '*You're* Blackbeard?' He groped around in a pile of filthy clothes behind him, then pulled out a dive knife. 'Stay the fuck back.'

'Of course I'm not Blackb—'

Davey lunged forward with the knife, shouting.

Ahab leapt out of the way and scrambled back out the door, slamming it shut and putting his foot against it, trapping Davey inside.

'Calm down, Davey!'

His cousin pounded on the door. 'Fight me like a man, Ahab! It's the least you can do! You've taken *everything* from me!'

'Will you shut up! Do you *want* someone else to find you? Obviously I'm not Blackbeard – do you think I'd have come alone and unarmed?'

The pounding on the door slowed, then stopped.

'Why are you here? How did you find me?'

'Forest told me you'd met him in the pump shed. I put two and two together.' He adjusted his stance – Davey was still pushing on the door. 'Son, if I open this door and you still have a knife in your hands, I'll be very upset. Put the knife on the ground and back away. Call out when you're touching the back wall.'

'Why should I do anything you say?'

'I'm losing my patience. I'll give you to the count of three.'

'Alright, alright . . .' Davey's voice had lost all its fight – Ahab knew the sound of a broken man when he heard it. A moment later he called out from further away. 'I'm touching the back wall.'

Ahab wrenched the door open, his torch ready to strike, but Davey was against the back wall, the knife on the floor between them. Davey raised his hands. 'I'm unarmed.'

He really was the picture of a defeated man. Now that Ahab's adrenaline had eased off, the stench coming from the room was overpowering. Rotting food was piled in the corner – it looked like it'd been pulled from the café's skip bin. Davey's face was smeared in mud, his eyes dark from lack of sleep. A bucket that might have been his chamber-pot buzzed with flies in the other corner. That nearly made Ahab gag.

'Hell, man. How long have you been living like this?' Ahab stepped into the room, kicking the knife away. 'I'll admit, this is going a long way towards helping me forgive you.' He'd imagined this moment so many times – he'd always been suspicious that Davey knew something. And now, after he'd thought Davey was gone forever, here was a chance to ask everything he wanted to. Would he ever get an opportunity like this again?

But with everything going on . . . he didn't even know what to ask anymore.

'You should've told me that Jesse chose to leave. You know how crazy I went trying to work out what happened.'

'So you've finally found out?' said Davey. 'I'm sorry, mate. He made me promise to never tell you. He was afraid of what you'd do to the Business while he was gone.'

'Even when I turned suspicion for his disappearance on you?' said Ahab. 'You could've told me then.'

'Even then. I knew no one would believe you: Jesse had told the crew himself – that's why they never doubted me. And Jesse said he was coming back. I didn't want him thinking I hadn't followed orders.'

He ran a desperate hand through his matted hair and slumped to the ground, pulling his knees to his chest.

'Well, you were right about one thing.' Davey's voice was still trembling. '*Something* must have happened. The state that Forest is in . . . All these years, the crew has been waiting for Jesse to return. So the moment Forest Dempsey showed up . . . showed up the way he did, I was a dead man walking. They all thought I'd deceived them. That you were right – that I'd stabbed Jesse in the back.'

'None of that matters now. Without you to hold the crew together, Blackbeard wins,' said Ahab. 'They need you, man. Damn me for saying this, but it's true – *Shacktown* needs you.'

'Blackbeard! Ahab, that bastard has been sniffing around for a long, long time,' said Davey. He sounded tired now. It wasn't just these last few days, he realised. Davey had been fighting a losing battle for years. 'He's so intent on setting up here, I've never understood it. I guess it's the curse, right? Something had to bring me undone . . .'

'You're still here,' said Ahab. 'It hasn't brought you undone yet.'

'Only because I'm weak! I can't bring myself to leave my family.'

'We should go to the police,' said Ahab. 'There's a detective here, a good one. I trust her. She'll be able to protect you. Protect your whole family.'

'Ahab, I'm a drug baron! I'll go to prison forever.'

'Not forever. There might be some kind of deal you can strike.'

'Yeah, in exchange for being a dog. I'd be killed before I even go to trial.'

'*Blackbeard* will kill you.'

'And so will my crew,' said Davey. 'You're not getting it. I'm fucked either way.'

'I'll have Forest tell them you weren't involved.'

'Forest hates my guts – you didn't hear the way he spoke to me. He blames me for whatever happened to him.'

'Except he's not the real Forest,' said Ahab.

'. . . What?'

'He's not the real Forest, Davey. He's up there right now, in the pump room, but he's an imposter . . . I think he wants your money.'

Davey's expression changed from disbelief to relief, to horror, to fury.

Realising what was about to happen, Ahab stepped forward to grab the knife just before Davey could.

'Davey, you can't hurt him . . .'

'He ruined my life! He's taken everything from me!'

The two men wrestled in the doorway, Davey's stink sharp and acrid in Ahab's nose as he tried to squeeze past him. Davey was bigger and stronger, but he'd been living on rotten café food and sleepless nights – Ahab was able to hold him off without much trouble.

'Please, Ahab, get out of the way. I'm gonna kill him.'

'I can't let you do that. We need him – *you* need him,' said Ahab. Then he grimaced. 'Although maybe you can scare him a little . . .'

Ahab let Davey climb through the trapdoor first, up into the pump room, where Forest was waiting.

'You ruined *everything*,' Davey roared. He launched himself at the boy.

Unsure if Davey would keep his word to not hurt the boy, Ahab swiftly clambered up after him.

Davey had Forest pushed into the corner, but Forest didn't back down, holding his chin up defiantly.

'Don't you dare judge me.' Forest's voice had taken on a harsh edge. For the first time, Ahab wondered if he was actually older than he looked. 'You, a drug dealer, bringing that poison into people's lives, bringing that world close to your *family*!'

'You don't know anything about this world, you little rat. I was *protecting* this town – before you came along and ruined everything!'

Forest laughed. Davey looked about ready to knock him out.

'Enough,' said Ahab. 'Both of you.'

'If I didn't run the Business, someone else would,' said Davey, ignoring Ahab. 'Someone worse. So you don't get to lecture *me* on ethics.'

'Yes, actually, I do,' said Forest. 'Imagine me as karma. I've come to fix your mess. I *am* Forest Dempsey, and neither of you can prove otherwise.'

'*Enough*,' said Ahab, letting his voice fill the whole room. Both of them turned towards him. 'You're both responsible, and both of you will help me sort this out.'

'How can we possibly do that?' said Forest.

'We find Blackbeard. We protect Shacktown. That way, we get Davey back to his family safely.'

'You want to take out Blackbeard?' said Davey. His voice broke. '*How?*'

Forest wrenched himself free of Davey's grip.

'We find out who Blackbeard is; we get into his inner circle,' said Forest.

'And just who do you think is going to manage that?' said Davey. 'There's no contacts of mine I can trust. Unless *you're* getting in the game, Ahab?'

'Of course not,' said Ahab, frustrated with himself. The boy had the right of it, but that didn't mean it would be possible. 'I need to think it through. I can't think of anyone who we can trust with this.'

'Idiots,' said Forest. 'You're both idiots. *Obviously* there's someone you can trust.'

CHAPTER 40

MACKEREL

Mackerel was awoken by something patting against his window.

He was a light sleeper these days, something in his subconscious always waiting for the police to knock. But as he groggily came to, something tweaked that the noise was coming from his window, not the door.

Suddenly he was wide awake. He scrambled for the cricket bat under his bed and in moments his back was against the wall, ready for the intruder to enter. His thoughts flashed to the man who'd been in the roof, searching for Davey's bolthole . . .

Another soft knock against the window.

This wasn't someone breaking in.

He edged over and pulled back the curtain.

He yelped – a ghostly face leered back at him.

Forest Dempsey.

It took him a moment to make sense of what was happening, and then he was pulling his clothes on and heading for the door.

'What the hell are you doing out here alone?' whispered

Mackerel once he was outside, his hand still on the doorknob, easing the front door closed.

'We found your brother. He's at the Mermaid's Darling right now.'

'Davey?' His hand fell off the doorknob. 'Wait, who's "we"?'

'Me and Ahab,' said Forest.

Mackerel felt dizzy.

'Listen, Davey has a plan,' said Forest. 'Your brother needs you – he just doesn't know it yet. Will you come?'

Mackerel looked up towards Shelby's room. This was perfect – if Ahab had a plan, Shelby might not feel the need to cook ice after all.

'I better tell Shelby,' he said.

Forest gave a small smile, with a knowing look in his eyes. 'Good.'

Mackerel, Shelby and Forest drove into town, towards the Mermaid's Darling. Fiona had agreed to come and sleep in the house, in case Kane woke up. She understood that Shelby couldn't wait until morning to see her husband.

'Of course Davey is staying at Ahab's inn!' Shelby was ranting. 'Why didn't I think of that sooner? Every Shacktown citizen with a pair of testicles hero-worships that man.'

'Actually, he's only just —' began Forest.

'Not now, Forest.' Shelby turned a corner too tight and too fast, pushing Mackerel up against the door. 'Adults are talking.'

Mackerel had been worried about the change in Shelby, but this was something else – she was a force of nature, animalistic. The thought of seeing Davey inspired a ferocity in her that he'd never seen before in his whole life.

When they arrived at Ahab's place, Forest glanced back at Shelby before heading up the stairs. 'You should know that Ahab's not expecting you, Shelby. Nor is Davey.' The thought seemed to give him pleasure.

'Take me to my husband,' was all she said.

Forest led on.

When Ahab opened the door to his room, he immediately zeroed in on Shelby.

'You brought a woman into this?' he said angrily to Mackerel.

'The woman brought herself into this,' retorted Shelby, shoving past him. 'You're not keeping me from my husband!'

Mackerel followed sheepishly.

Davey sat hunched on a stool, a beer in his hand. He wore some of Ahab's clothes, hair lank from a recent shower, dark circles under his eyes. He looked nothing like the bold leader Mackerel had known him to be.

He stood up, spilling his beer. 'Shelbs?' he said in a strangled voice.

She walked right up to him and punched him in the gut. Then she grabbed his collar and pulled him in for a kiss.

Within seconds the two of them were tearing each other's clothes off, Davey wincing as Shelby caught skin with her nails. Forest quickly fled. Ahab, after a series of protests that went ignored by the couple, finally left the room too, dragging Mackerel with him, who was watching events unfold with horror.

Seated at the bar of the Mermaid's Darling, with Forest and Ahab beside him, Mackerel received a text from Shelby: *You can come back up now.*

Ahab entered the room first, his anger filling the space. Davey put his hand protectively over Shelby's leg at the sight of him.

'If you ever, ever do that again – in *my* room – I'll castrate you,' said Ahab.

'Oh, I'm terribly sorry,' snapped Shelby. 'I just found my husband *returned from the dead*.'

Her husband looked like a beaten dog. 'He's right,' said Davey. 'We can't do this . . . you should go.'

Shelby's eyes went so wide Mackerel thought she might pass out with rage. '*Excuse* me? You're lucky I don't throw you out that *window*. If you're talking about Blackbeard, I'm staying. I can help.'

'Everyone shut up,' said Ahab.

'Well, if we're telling secrets,' said Davey, 'I've got a pretty big one too.' He glanced across at Forest.

'*Enough*. Don't you *dare*,' thundered Ahab. 'I didn't invite you here for a happy reunion. We have a *mission*.'

'To kill Blackbeard,' said Forest quickly.

'No,' said Ahab. 'To find Blackbeard and then tell the police.'

'We're already doing that,' said Shelby. 'We have a plan.'

'Shelby,' said Mackerel, 'don't . . .'

'I'm starting my own drug cooking business. Mackerel and I are going to infiltrate his organisation and take Blackbeard down from the inside,' said Shelby.

Silence greeted her words, and Mackerel groaned. 'She . . . it's not like that.' Except it *was* like that. He prepared himself for Davey, or Ahab, to come at him. Would he even fight back?

Davey turned to Mackerel, his hand back on Shelby's thigh. 'What is she talking about?'

'I'm gonna cook ice,' said Shelby easily. 'It's going to be the best product Blackbeard's ever seen.'

'*Are you insane?* Do you know what he'll do if he finds out you can cook?' hissed Davey.

'You don't get to tell me how to live!' she shouted back. 'Not anymore!'

'You're actually going back to this life, Mackenzie?' said Ahab, making his disappointment clear. '*And* dragging Shelby into it?'

'It's the only way,' he muttered, feeling miserable. He could've told Ahab it was all Shelby's idea, but that felt weak, not taking responsibility for his decisions. Even though he hated Ahab being disappointed in him. 'Only for a week. Just one week, then we're done.'

'You knew about this?' Ahab had turned on the boy.

'No, but . . . it makes sense,' said Forest. 'Who better than Mackerel? I can't think of another way to find Blackbeard.'

'It's madness,' said Davey.

'It's *illegal*,' said Ahab.

'It's the only way,' said Mackerel again, desperately, hoping they'd understand.

Davey yanked at his hair. 'Shelby . . . you can't.'

'I don't need your protection anymore!' snapped Shelby.

'Yes —' began Davey.

'— you do,' finished Mackerel.

The two brothers caught each other's eye, and Mackerel felt a shiver run down his spine. The last time they'd seen each other had been underwater in Devils Kitchen. Davey must've been thinking something like that too.

Mackerel missed his brother so much. Even though he was standing right there in front of him.

'Thanks for the ladder,' said Mackerel.

'Thanks for jumping into that ocean to try to save me,' said Davey.

An awkward silence filled the space. Davey seemed to take a moment to really think through what they'd told him. He turned on Shelby. 'There's no way you're cooking ice. I forbid it.'

'Fine,' said Shelby through clenched teeth. 'In that case I want a divorce.'

'So what next?' said Forest over all the cross-talk, trying to keep them on track.

'What's next,' said Davey, his angry eyes now flicking to the boy, 'is you come clean about who you really are.'

'*Don't*,' said Ahab.

'We don't even know who he is!' said Davey. 'For all we know, *he's* working for Blackbeard!'

Mackerel didn't follow. With a plummeting feeling in his belly, he sensed that something bad had gone down before he and Shelby had arrived. 'What are you talking about?'

'He's not the real Forest Dempsey. He's an imposter!'

'*Shut your mouth, Davey!*' boomed Ahab.

This silence filled the room like a rung bell.

Turn by turn, Mackerel looked at Ahab, then Davey, and finally Forest.

'He was just after the Dempsey fortune,' finished Davey.

'No,' Mackerel said. 'No, not possible. How could he have known everything about Forest? About us?'

Ahab was tense. He walked over to a cupboard, pulled out a stack of scrapbooks and dropped them heavily onto the table. 'Because he did his research.'

Mackerel turned to Forest, who was flushed with what he could only assume was shame. Or was it victory?

Everyone in Mackerel's family had let him down. Had fucked him over. Now, for once, he thought he'd formed some kind of connection with someone, and *it was all a fucking con!*

'I'm not working for Blackbeard,' the boy said hurriedly. 'I promise! In fact, I want to help you bring him down. He's a danger to me too!' He sighed. 'And honestly, without me, you probably have no hope . . .'

Mackerel felt something brewing inside him. His whole body felt hot.

'How . . . So you're not even Forest Dempsey?' Shelby turned to Davey. 'Ha! And if he *hadn't* come back, you'd still be leading your double life, your idiot wife none the wiser.' She gave the boy a warm smile. 'Thank you for that, Forest. I owe you.'

'*What the fuck, Ahab?*' roared Mackerel, standing up.

Everyone fell silent again.

'You *knew*? And you were just gonna let him keep pretending?' Mackerel's chest felt hot, his hands tingling. They curled into fists. He advanced on Ahab.

'Who do you think you're talking to?' said Ahab, rising as well. 'Sit back down, boy, before I make you.'

He didn't look at Forest. He'd kill him if he did. He hadn't felt this angry in a long time. Finally, he had someone to blame.

'Chips is *dead* because of him!'

Ahab grimaced and Mackerel realised Davey didn't know. Typical – his cousin talked a big game, but he kept secrets that worked to his advantage, just like the rest of them.

'Chips . . .' said Davey, his eyes cold. 'Who?'

'I was going to —' began Ahab.

'*Tell him, Ahab!*' Mackerel's voice echoed around the room.

'Blackbeard's men. I was there, I saw it. I . . . Davey, if I could have stopped it, you know I would.'

Davey stared hard at the floor, massaging the palm of his hand, arms trembling. He stood beside Mackerel, putting an arm on his brother's shoulder. 'Easy there, Mack.'

Forest had moved to hide behind Ahab, watching Mackerel warily.

'I'm gonna kill him. This is all his fault.'

'We'll kill him later,' said Davey. 'Do you get it now, Shelbs? Chips died, and she knew the game. This is what I was protecting you from. What I'm *still* trying to protect you from. It's real. This is what happens when you play with the big boys. You can't possibly think that —'

'Listen,' said Forest directly to Mackerel, 'if I keep pretending to be Forest, we actually have a chance of stopping Blackbeard.'

'You caused *all of this!*' shouted Mackerel. 'And for *what?* How long did you think you could keep this up?'

Davey and Shelby were now yelling too.

'You have a dinghy's chance in a Black Wind!' he shouted.

'*You* left to play dead! *You* don't get to —' Shelby roared back.

Ahab had stepped between Mackerel and Forest. 'Mackenzie, he's just a kid.'

'Everything was fine until he came along!' Mackerel wondered if he could risk pushing Ahab to the side – he was much bigger and stronger, but Ahab was a force to be reckoned with if you got him offside.

'Wait, wait, *wait*. Mack! As Forest, I can win the loyalty of the Business . . . Right? Davey's crew? I can speak to them, convince them. Promise them a future without Blackbeard!'

'A *boy* kingpin?' said Davey, checking back into their conversation. 'Face it, kid, you've fucked us all. Including yourself. You've brought the monster of Blackbeard on us all.'

'Then help Shelby, who is the one idiot in this room who's actually got a plan to *stop him*!' shouted Forest.

'You don't get to say anything!' shouted Mackerel.

Someone started hammering on the door and they all fell still.

'Ahab? Are you okay?' It was Ned's voice. 'I'm sorry, but the noise is waking the guests. Won't be long until someone calls the police.'

'They can't catch me out after curfew,' said Mackerel, thinking, *I can't go to prison now.*

He fled the room, leaving Shelby behind.

Mackerel was smoking his vape on the front porch of Homeward. He'd checked on Kane and, once he was assured he was all fine and well, he'd come back out to calm down and wait for Shelby.

When Ahab's ute pulled up, Shelby climbed out first, giving

Mackerel a quick squeeze of the arm and heading inside to be with her son.

Ahab approached him slowly, coming to stand beside him and lighting his own cigarette.

After a moment, he said, 'Are you going to be able to stop? When the temptation is real, when it's right in front of you? When it comes down to it, will you be able to walk away?'

'Me walking away isn't the problem,' said Mackerel. 'I know exactly where that path leads. I've been there.'

'Okay,' said Ahab, turning, the cigarette between his teeth. 'But will you be able to stop *her*?'

That's what he was worried about. Haltingly he said, 'She just . . . wants her life back. She's not doing this for money, she's doing it for Davey.'

'Which means she won't walk away until she gets what she wants.' Ahab held the cigarette in his teeth a bit longer. 'How is that any different from Blackbeard?'

'Are you crazy?' Mackerel had to look at him. 'It's completely different. Nothing like Blackbeard!' He couldn't believe Ahab would even make that comparison. 'Chips was *murdered* in cold blood!'

'You think whatever product she cooks won't hurt people? Of course it will. How is that different from Blackbeard?' said Ahab. 'And if someone finds out Shelby can cook, how long until they have her locked up in a shipping container somewhere, forced to cook ice for one gang or another?'

'We were both brought up in this world. You know that if anyone can do this, it's me.' He hoped that didn't sound arrogant. It was just the truth. 'There's risks, but it's the only way to get everything back to how it was. If *she* can't decide to take that risk, then who can?'

'You don't believe that. That's her talking.'

'And it's her decision to make.'

'Every man can find a way to justify what he wants to do. What will be her next excuse, once a week is up? Once she has a taste for the easy money of the game?'

'I'll be able to stop her,' said Mackerel. 'I know that I will.'

'Swear it,' said Ahab, his eyes lit up from below by the glow of his cigarette. 'Swear to me you'll stop her if this gets too big.'

'I swear,' said Mackerel.

'Alright.' Ahab ground out his cigarette on the gravel drive, appearing to come to a decision. 'Then I'll stay out of your way. *For now.* Forest will be staying with me. You're not to hurt him.'

'Why do you call him Forest? That's not his real name.'

Ahab gave a wave and climbed back into his ute.

'You should've told me!' he shouted. But Ahab was gone.

CHAPTER 41

AHAB

Ahab's mind turned over events as he drove back to the Mermaid's Darling. He'd surprised himself with the way he'd spoken to Mackenzie. Was he growing too trusting in his old age . . .?

No, he wasn't *that* old.

But the Business is the cause of all of this, he thought, pulling into his parking space at the inn. *The Business is what brought Blackbeard here. So how could I allow him and Shelby to start another one?*

Why don't I put a stop to it now?

Usually he knew instinctively what the right thing to do was. Right now, he felt adrift.

But one thing seemed the right thing to do.

Shelby, who had lost the most, deserved to at least try.

Upstairs, he'd put Davey and Forest into a shared room – he wanted them to keep an eye on each other.

When he got up the stairs, he wondered briefly if they had killed each other while he was gone.

He was relieved to find Davey lying on the bed, looking at the ceiling, and Forest in the armchair reading one of the children's picture books left in the rooms for guests.

'If it's true what those two are saying . . .' began Ahab. 'If becoming a supplier to Blackbeard is the only way to find him —'

'It's true,' said Davey before he'd finished.

'But you're against it,' said Ahab.

'How could I support it? Of course I can't. Shelby . . . it's too risky. We should just cut our losses and run.'

'Then why don't you?' said Ahab. 'Take Shelby and Kane, and run?'

'That's no life for her . . . on the run with me.'

'And being an ice cook is better?'

'I tried to talk her out of it!' said Davey. Ahab felt sorry for his cousin. The spark he'd gained at seeing his wife had gone, leaving him even worse than before. 'You need to put a stop to it!'

'No,' said Ahab, but not unkindly. 'You had your chance. Now it's theirs. It's only for a week.'

Davey whimpered. 'Please, Ahab . . .'

'And you,' he said, pointing at Forest. 'You're coming with me. We're going for a walk.'

'Then I'm coming too,' said Davey, sitting up.

'Great idea,' grumbled Ahab. 'Let's parade you for all of Shacktown to see.'

Davey slowly lay back down.

'Where are we going?' said Forest, following Ahab.

Once he'd closed the door and they were halfway down the stairs, Ahab said, 'We're going for a drive. To Hobart.'

'What? Why?' Forest pulled up short.

'We're going to find Detective De Corrado and tell her that you're not Forest.'

'What?' hissed Forest. 'Wait!' He grabbed Ahab's arm.

Ahab pulled away. 'If Shelby and Mackenzie are going to try

this, then they can't have the police watching them. Right now, everyone around you is vigilant. We can remove that by you coming forward with the truth. You owe my family that much.'

'What about Blackbeard? What about what he wants from me?' The boy had grown panicked. But he had nowhere to run – the only way out of the inn was through Ahab, unless he wanted to break a leg jumping out a window.

'Whatever it is, *you* can't help!' said Ahab.

'Wait! Wait, wait, wait . . . I know.'

'You know what?'

'I know what Blackbeard wants from Forest,' said the boy. 'Promise me you won't go to the police and I'll show you.'

'No, boy, you tell me first.'

'Fine.' Forest's shoulders dropped. 'I'll show you where the bodies of Forest and Alexandra are.'

'. . . Forest and Alexandra are dead?'

'Here will do,' said Forest in a quiet voice. 'Park here.' He had Zeus in his lap, insisting that he come – Ahab had thought it part of his ploy, but now he wasn't so sure. The boy was terrified of wherever they were headed, and the dog went some way to calming him.

They were in the carpark of another of Shacktown's geomarvels, a boulder field of fallen dolerite pillars that would have once been a sea cliff.

Ahab had been silent for the whole drive, wrestling with this new information. After all these years, they'd been this close? That felt the biggest betrayal of all. Unless Forest wasn't telling the truth, which was the most likely option. Should he be on guard in case the boy was dangerous? How mad did you have to be to get a tattoo of a dead boy's name?

Forest was dead. This boy had made him hope for a moment he was alive. Now he would need to mourn the real Forest all over again.

Ahab slammed the door shut. Forest scurried after him, dragging Zeus on his leash. Ahab had found them a headtorch each, and they flicked them on as they headed down the path to the boulders.

'If there aren't any bones down there —' began Ahab.

'There are,' said Forest. 'Keep your voice down. Have some respect for the dead.'

They walked along a path through the scrub, insects buzzing around their headtorches, before the track opened out onto the boulder fields and the renewed sound of waves. Clouds covered the sky, bringing darkness save for the small twin circles of light offered by their torches.

Across the angular planes of the fallen stones they went, Ahab crawling on all fours when it was too steep, cursing the lack of visibility, stopping once to have a cigarette. The boy was more limber than him, scampering ahead and waiting for him to catch up, but the dog was ill-suited to rock climbing and Forest demonstrated remarkable patience when coaxing him along, finding passageways the dog could wend through when the path was too steep. Ahab took his time, his shoes now wet from stepping in a rockpool. He wasn't surprised the tide reached all the way up here – these fallen rocks created all sorts of channels for water.

He stopped for another cigarette.

'Can I trust you, Ahab?' said Forest from atop a boulder Ahab was yet to scale. Zeus had slipped through a tunnel and made it to the other side already, barking for his master. 'Before I tell you what really happened . . .'

'What are you playing at, boy?'

'You want to know why *I'm* here, don't you? You think I'm just after the money. I'll give you a clue . . .'

He disappeared down the other side.

Grumbling, Ahab climbed up after him.

Forest was waiting for him at the foot of a nearby tree. He rested his hand on a stone that appeared to make the crossbeam of an arch. He took a deep breath of salty air. 'The truth is in the story everyone believes about what happened to Jesse, Alexandra and Forest.'

'No one knows what really happened,' said Ahab.

'But who do they blame?'

'Jonah Donnager.'

'Good. Remember that name. We have to go inside here,' said Forest, crouched, his forearm resting on the mouth of what Ahab now saw was a cave. 'You're sure it's low tide?'

Ahab nodded, gesturing for Forest to continue.

Forest pulled Zeus's leash from his pocket and tied the dog to the roots of the tree. 'It's alright, boy, I'm not taking you inside.' He pressed his face into the dog's fur and rubbed his ears, then faced the mouth of the cave again. He took another deep breath, steeling himself, then walked inside.

There were no plants down in these caves, not even moss – the only life was cave spiders, their webs shimmering from their head-torches. Silent, his breath in his ears, the cold pressing down on him, Ahab followed the boy's lead.

He didn't mind caves, but night-time would not be his chosen time to go exploring in tidal caves, following a mysterious boy, on a quest to find what Ahab was quickly realising must be a tomb . . .

'How much further?' said Ahab.

'Only a little way . . .'

Easy enough for the boy to say – he was small enough to move comfortably.

Stooped over, Ahab noticed footsteps and scuff marks in the dirt.

'You've been here recently.'

'The other night. Don't worry, old man, we're not lost.' His voice had taken on an odd, dead tone.

They moved deeper into the cave network, and he saw the seaweed on the walls – they were in the tidal section of this tangle of tunnels.

'And here it is . . .' said Forest. 'Stick your head in. Have a look.'

The crack in the wall was slight – you would have missed it if you didn't know to look for it. Ahab hesitated only briefly, wondering about the wisdom of turning his back on the boy, then squatted in front of it and smelled the damp, salty brine beyond. Whispering air and echoes suggested a larger space beyond.

He stuck his shoulders through, but that was as far as he could get – he could feel the rock pressing on his back.

He'd been right: it *was* a tomb.

The cave was wide and long, and his headtorch cast jagged glistening shadows. On a floor of tightly clustered boulders there were two gluggy corpses, splayed out, thrown about by years of ebbing and flowing tides. The remains of one set of scuba gear were wedged in the rocks between them.

Alexandra and Forest.

He'd tried to prepare himself, but that sight still ruptured something deep inside him that he'd been trying to protect for years.

He tried to fight them but tears blurred his eyes. He blinked them away, moved his torch beam back and forth between the two bodies. It wasn't hard to determine what had happened. Trapped, when the tide filled the chamber, they had drowned here. He couldn't allow himself to look away from that. It was important to bear witness, to pay his respects and, in a way, make his apologies for his failures.

Then something caught his eye.

He backed out carefully, pulling himself together as best he could.

'Get in there, boy,' he said gruffly. 'I need you to bring me Forest's skull.'

'Are you kidding? No way am I touching his body!'

'It's not like that,' said Ahab. 'It's . . . I don't think that's Forest in there.'

'. . . What?' The boy looked horrified. 'Who else would it be?'

'The skull,' said Ahab. 'It has a cleft palate. Forest didn't have a cleft palate.'

Forest looked at him blankly, failing to comprehend what Ahab was trying to tell him – Ahab could barely believe it himself.

'But another boy did,' said Ahab. 'Jonah's boy. Huck Donnager.'

Forest went very still. He turned to look at the crack as though seeing all within it anew. 'Huck?' he whispered.

He pushed past Ahab and into the hole.

Ahab stuck his head back through, watching as Forest picked his way down the wall.

'There hasn't been a confirmed sighting of Huck or Jonah since Forest went missing,' said Ahab. 'I thought the boy was on the run with his crooked old man, but . . .'

When he reached the skull, Forest seemed loath to touch it. He took a gulp of air, then picked it off the floor.

'It's damp,' he groaned, as sludge fell away from it.

Dry-retching, he clambered over and handed it up to Ahab.

It was a child's skull, and he'd seen right: it had a cleft palate. Ahab shuddered himself as he cradled the skull, imagining Alexandra and Huck drowning in that cave. He could almost hear the memory of their screams.

He pulled out of the crack and a moment later Forest followed, face pale in the torchlight.

'You're sure it's Huck?' said Forest, shaking uncontrollably.

'I'm sure . . .' Ahab put the skull down on the ground. 'Let's get out of this place.'

'You're not gonna bring him with us?' said Forest. He couldn't take his eyes off the skull. 'You're *sure* it's Huck?'

'We'll tell the police it's here. They wouldn't want it moved far, and I don't know what the outside air will do to it.' His voice echoed in the cave, sounding foreign to himself.

Forest didn't seem to hear him. He had crouched beside the skull, arms folded to try and stop himself from shaking.

'But why didn't Huck escape? Why didn't he climb out?'

'Huck had a bone deformity and an intellectual disability. In a dark cave, once it started filling with water, I imagine he would've panicked . . . knowing Alexandra, she would have comforted him in those last moments . . .'

He closed his eyes, just for one breath, in memory of her. She had been the best of all of them.

'Right. Time for the truth. Why were the two of them here? How did Alexandra fit through that crack, and why did they only have one set of scuba gear?'

'You're not going to like the answer,' said Forest.

Ahab had had enough of games. 'Out with it.' His whisper hissed and echoed in the cave.

Forest sighed, took a deep breath. 'It was Jesse. Jesse trapped them in there.'

'Jesse? Are you sure?' But even as he said it . . .

'Jesse killed them. Jesse led them down there. He wanted them to die. He wanted to kill Forest too, but . . . I guess he escaped.' There was a catch when he said that, but Ahab barely registered it.

Ahab's ears were ringing. He felt as though he was sinking, or the caves were somehow coming unmoored.

'It's the truth, Ahab.'

'That's – he wouldn't do that to his own family . . .' he managed to croak. He couldn't even convince himself.

'Yes, he would,' said Forest, his teeth chattering. 'You know it's true. He was brutal, he was selfish, and he never loved Forest.'

Ahab fell to his knees, the cold rock cutting at his hands as he braced himself. The boy was right. Of course he was right. Jesse would have done anything to save his own skin, Ahab knew that to be true. He'd just always hoped . . .

'Tell me,' he said. 'How do you know this?'

'Because I met Huck Donnager. He told me everything.' Forest looked down at the skull. 'At least, that's what he told me his name was. Now I think it's clear who he really is.' Forest wiped at his eyes. 'It looks like Forest is alive after all. He just calls himself Huck.'

'Tell me everything.'

Crouching on the floor with him, Huck's skull between them, he told him the story. The cave Alexandra found and the rage it inspired in Jesse. Their trip to the caves and Jesse's betrayal. The diving slate, the rushing water – Huck's escape. The boy who claimed to be Huck, anyway . . .

If Ahab had had the strength to lift his hands over his ears, he would have.

'Where's that boy now?' said Ahab.

'I don't know,' said Forest. 'Haven't seen him in years. Figured he was dead.'

Now Forest stayed silent. He was giving Ahab time to process it all, but Ahab wasn't sure he'd ever be able to comprehend what had happened. How wrong he had been about Jesse's true character.

I could have helped them . . .

Suddenly Forest sprang to his feet, hunched in the small space.

'Do you hear that?'

Ahab was ready to snap at the boy, but then he heard it too. A distant drone.

The Black Wind.

Leaving the skull where it was, they fled up through the passages, Ahab following the boy's lead, pushing him to speed up.

He told himself he wasn't panicking, he was just moving quickly because it was the sensible thing to do. The Black Wind's waves filled ocean caves fast. But . . . there was something dark about the Black Wind coming when it did. Right as they had moved Huck's skull.

Black Wind at morning, sailors take warning.

Black Wind at night, death is in sight.

Soon the two were in the open air, panting.

Ahab felt sick, Forest still shook.

So this kid calling himself Huck Donnager . . . was that the real Forest?

He'd come back to that later. This fake Forest claimed he hadn't seen him in years, but there might be a trail there to follow. But first . . .

Forest had a map to a cave that Jesse was willing to kill for . . .

'We can't tell the police just yet,' he said, hating himself even as he said it.

I'm sorry, Alexandra, but I need to know what was in there that Jesse was willing to kill for . . . if it's about the Business, it could put Shelby and Mackenzie at risk now . . .

'The diving slate,' said Ahab. 'Show me.'

CHAPTER 42

FOREST

The boy who called himself Forest and Ahab Stark drove towards Ivy's.

Could Ahab be lying? The boy asked himself, over and over. *That can't be Huck in there. Huck is in his boatshed. Who else would it be? Huck is waiting for me. Huck is alive.*

All of this can't have been for nothing!

At least he hadn't told Ahab about Huck still being nearby. That wasn't his secret to tell.

He'd ruined his friend's chances, now. By pretending to be Forest Dempsey, he ruined his friend's true claim. Who would believe Huck now? (He would still call him Huck, until Huck himself told him his real name.)

And with Blackbeard around, wanting Forest . . .

This was all his fault!

No. He wouldn't think about it. All he could do was show Ahab the slate, get the coordinates, and then the two of them could go to the Treasure Cave. Once Ahab knew what was in the Treasure Cave, things would begin to make sense.

He clung to that. He could still save his friend. Somehow. Whatever was in the Treasure Cave would solve everything . . .

By the time they reached Ivy's street the Black Wind's drone was as loud as a beehive. Forest was grateful – it'd mask any noise he'd make in the house.

The police car was still parked out the front of Safe Harbour, so clearly Ivy hadn't told the police that he wasn't staying there anymore. Ahab pulled up a few doors down.

'I'll go in and grab it,' said Forest.

'I'm coming too, boy,' said Ahab gruffly. He'd calmed down since the agony of the tomb, and there was a new energy about him.

Forest led them both through the neighbouring yards of manicured lawns, scraggly beach shrubs and plastic play equipment until they stood in Ivy's yard. But when he tried the door to his room, he found it locked.

Without hesitating Ahab took his shirt off, wrapped his fist in it and cracked the glass of the door. He reached in to unlock it and then eased it open.

'Not exactly stealthy,' said Forest.

'Where is it?' was all Ahab said.

The slate was where he'd left it – hidden behind the wardrobe in his room. He retrieved it and mutely handed it to Ahab, who studied the writing on it, face unreadable.

They left the door open, heading out into the humming wind.

Forest lay awake on the hard bed of his room in the Mermaid's Darling, listening to Davey's snores.

No. He thought he could sleep, but he needed to solve the mystery of the boy in the boatshed. He needed to be sure.

But when he slipped out of bed and moved to the door, he found that it was locked. From the outside.

He scurried to the window and looked out – far too high to jump.

'This is a fire hazard,' he muttered to himself. 'He can't just lock us in here . . .'

Davey's snoring ebbed, and a second later his bedside lamp lit up the room.

'What are you doing?'

'Just looking out the window. Can't sleep.'

Davey frowned, then fiddled with something under his pillow before lying back down.

Ah, not locked in then . . . Davey has a key.

Forest looked out at the sea, his chin resting on the windowsill. The Black Wind beat against the glass.

Who is the boy in the boatshed?

He tried to remember their first meeting. The details were hazy in his mind.

It had been in the backyard of the broken-down house on Sutton Place. Forest had had a different name then. He'd had several over his lifetime – that was one of the things the Witch had taught him.

There were a number of adults staying in that house, but only one of them cared for him like she was his mother – he called her the Witch. He'd stumbled into her life straight out of the bush, somewhere far away from that house, half-starved and close to death. She'd nursed him back to health, and showed him the wonders of her potions.

He was old enough now to know that her potions were actually drugs, but as a young kid, searching for safety, he'd taken everything she'd given him – and been grateful for the oblivion they brought. In return, she'd taught him how to retrieve her drugs and make sure the money was right, how to cut a sad figure while panhandling, how to trick addicts into handing over their money or their drugs using the shell-speaking con . . .

She'd taught him other things, too – ways to hide and protect himself from the world, just like she had done. When bad people came to her beach shack, looking for him, she'd hidden him under the deck and sent them on their way empty-handed. After that they'd left that house behind and fled to Hobart.

It wasn't until a few years after she'd found him that he realised she was crazy, but by then he was as close to her as if she was blood. She kept him fed, tucked him in at night; other times he did the same for her. When she'd grown really sick, somehow they'd ended up at the house on Sutton Place.

That was where he'd met Huck – the same week the Witch died. He couldn't remember it exactly, because Forest hadn't slept for days after her death, courtesy of one of her gifts. She'd left him two presents in parting: a dog named Zeus and a bag of bliss salt. Everyone on the street called it ice, but the Witch was more romantic with her names.

He couldn't say what it was about him, but seeing Huck in the corner of the yard that night, smoking his cigarette, scowling at all the other kids drinking and joking – he just seemed different. Almost free.

Kids were commonplace in that house because they made the best drug runners – police rarely searched them, and even if they did, they didn't get the same harsh penalties as adults. All the kids in and around Sutton Place were trapped in that world, doing whatever the adults said – Forest learned that the hard way – but Huck ignored the grown-ups and yet never seemed to get belted.

That's why Forest had first approached him. Started a friendship. Without the Witch to protect him, he needed someone else in his corner. Zeus was great, but Zeus couldn't talk.

It took a long time before Huck had opened up about who he was . . . and about everything he had lost. That's how Forest came to know that Huck had a home, somewhere, and that it had been ripped away from him.

Forest had decided he was going to do whatever it took to clear Huck's name. He'd seen enough bad stuff in the world, and once he was old enough, he resolved to do something to fix at least some of it. He would steal back the home and fortune that had belonged to Forest Dempsey. Because, according to Huck, the real Forest Dempsey was dead in a cave. He didn't need it anymore.

But now here he was, furious at Huck. How could he not have known that Dempsey Abalone was a front for a drug business? After all his work to get away from that world, he was deeper in it than ever.

And, even worse, Huck wasn't even *Huck*!

But there was just one more hurdle and he'd be in the clear. Blackbeard. And the adults were dealing with that.

He turned from the windowsill towards Davey.

The head of Dempsey Abalone. The head of the Business.

Did Ahab have the right of it? Should they just go to the police and have them sort it all out? Throw Davey in a dark hole he'd never get out of?

You're just tired, he chided himself. *Get some sleep or you'll go crazy like the Witch.*

He had to see what this Treasure Cave housed. That was the next step for his side of things. Let the family figure out Blackbeard.

He climbed into bed, but sleep wouldn't come. His mind kept turning back to the boy in the boatshed.

It would explain a few things about his behaviour, his anger, about why he thought Forest Dempsey haunted him . . .

Poor Huck.

But why hadn't he trusted Forest with the truth?

CHAPTER 43

MACKEREL

The morning after reuniting with her husband, Shelby was full of a new fever.

The sun was shining on Homeward – the Black Wind had eased by daylight. The locals called it a False Wind. But nearly always, if a Black Wind began at night and ended before the dawn, that meant it'd come back twice as strong within the week.

Black Wind at night, death is in sight.

A False Wind meant Shacktown locals started battening down the hatches. Mackerel felt like he should be out there doing the same for Homeward.

But right now he nursed a coffee, willing his eyes to stay open. Last night he'd stayed up late with Shelby, answering more questions about the world of drug dealing. Today, she wanted to try cooking for the first time.

'Are you sure you're ready, Shelbs?'

Kane was going on another daytrip up the coast with Fiona's husband and sons. Fiona herself would be rejoining them at Homeward soon.

'I have to try. We can't afford to waste time.'

'You're sure you know how to do it?'

'Please, Mackerel. Who's the chemist here? But I thought of . . . another ingredient that will help us. I'm going to have to head back to Hobart. But while I'm gone, I have a surprise for you . . .'

Mackerel did not trust Shelby's surprises. 'What now?'

'You said that status and image are important in this world, right? That's why Davey always insisted on showing off how rich he was. Expensive clothes, heavy jewellery, had his hair and beard trimmed fortnightly . . . I thought bling was just a Hollywood thing, but I did some research last night – did you know there are some *fascinating* journal articles about the sociology of drug culture?' She tried to hide a yawn and failed.

'How much sleep did you get, Shelbs?' She must've been reading well into the early hours.

She flapped his remark away. 'Long enough that I heard the False Wind stop. Anyway, if we're to be taken seriously, *you* need a makeover.'

'What?' said Mackerel. He could see where this was going and he hated it. 'No.'

'Yes, Mack, you're the one who said that the way we look goes a long way in the drug world. You said you used to show up in your suit and company car, right? That's how you got so far?'

'Yeah, but we're not here to make money, we're here to —'

'We're here to build a brand, so . . . look, your clothes are old and saggy, your hair looks like you did it yourself as a drunken dare. If I saw you in the street I'd probably think about giving you some money so you could find a new sleeping bag.'

He put his hand to his hair. 'I didn't do it myself.'

'And while I like the stubble, it needs to go. Fiona is bringing our friend Richelle over. She's a hairdresser. We all used to be in the same mothers' group. She's gonna tidy you up a bit. While she's doing that, Fiona and I will pick up some new clothes for you in town.'

'No, I'm not —'

'You're my partner in a business venture,' said Shelby, 'so you're gonna look the part.'

'This is *not* a business venture!' Mackerel stood up.

'I know it's not,' she said, standing as well, 'but it helps me to think about it that way! You think I *like* becoming a drug dealer? No, this is a simple case of supply and demand – the right product for the market. And for that to work, we need to be professionals – you're the one who told me that – and that means we *all* have to do our bit. That begins with *you* looking the part!'

Mackerel was still arguing with her when the doorbell rang. Red-faced, he followed Shelby all the way to the door.

Fiona led Richelle in. She was older than Mackerel expected, with short grey hair and heavy make-up. She quickly caught Mackerel's mood.

'So you're the man we're cleaning up? Well, no use arguing. We'll set up in the bathroom. Besides,' she eyed him up and down, 'I'm curious to see how you scrub up.'

Hours later, Mackerel stood outside, smoking his vape. The sun was bright and in one of Shelby's prickly wattles he heard the sweet song of an olive whistler. His cheeks felt raw – after his shave, Richelle had insisted on using a pore-cleansing face mask. Mackerel was no stranger to those – at the height of his game, he'd had his own skin care regime morning and evening – but now it all felt alien. He touched the sides of his head, where she'd given him the close-cut fade.

He hated how good it made him feel. It made him feel in control. Respectable.

When Shelby finally got home, she lowered her sunglasses and gave a low wolf-whistle.

'Look at *you*, Mack! *Now* I see the resemblance between you and Davey.'

He wanted to fall into a crack in the ground. He also wanted to see what was in all those shopping bags she and Fiona had brought back from Hobart.

He walked out of his bedroom feeling ten feet taller. He wore a tailored button-up shirt, the collar still starched cardboard stiff, as well as expensive designer slacks and calf-leather boots. Adrenaline spiked through him as he headed into the dining room, where Fiona and Shelby were waiting for him.

'Give us a spin, sweetheart!' cried Fiona.

'Going my way, darling?' added Shelby with a laugh. 'You look good, Mack. Really good. And now . . .' She fished around in one of the bags. 'The final piece. I remember you used to wear one all the time.'

In her hands, shimmering and reflecting light, was a thick gold chain. It must have been at least 20 inches of 14-carat gold.

'Shelby . . . this must've cost . . .'

'More than that shitbox car you drive, yes,' said Shelby. 'Probably worth about five of them. Do you like it?'

Did he *like* it? It was worth more than any jewellery he'd ever owned before, and he'd owned some heavy chains.

Mackerel touched the precious metal. He felt sick; he felt hungry. He wanted his old life back. He wanted to be in penthouse suites, surrounded by people who respected him. *He* wanted the money to buy this chain, not have his brother's wife do it for him.

She reached forward to clasp it around his neck, taking the

time to linger and whisper in his ear, 'We'll take Blackbeard down. Forever.'

The lure was too much. He was going to drown in this.

'I can't do it.'

'What?' said Shelby, pulling back, alarmed.

'I can't. I can't do this.'

'Mackerel? Calm down.'

'No,' he shook his head, 'I can't.'

He ran out the door, the world spinning, only to realise he'd forgotten the car keys. He could hardly go back in there and grab them.

If he'd ever had a dad who gave a shit about him, he might've gone to him for advice.

The closest thing he had was Ahab. Maybe his cousin would be able to save him from that world clawing him back.

He ran for the Mermaid's Darling.

CHAPTER 44

AHAB

Ahab sat out on the deck of the *Ambergris*, in the middle of the bay. The water sparkled in the gentle swell, lapping at the hull, but he couldn't enjoy it – he kept an eye on the skies and an ear out for the drone. The Black Wind would be coming back any moment, and it would be ferocious.

He checked the GPS and confirmed again they were in the right spot, even though he knew they were. These were the coordinates Alexandra had written on her slate. They were above what Forest called the Treasure Cave.

They had come out here at first light, and ever since had been taking turns to dive, exploring the ocean floor, searching for the cave. Forest was diving right now – there were plenty of rocky crags and reefs to work through.

A yellow float bobbed on the surface, tied to Forest below. The boy really was remarkably good at diving, and Ahab knew that for all his cockiness, he had the right instincts to take care of himself down there. Still, Ahab kept an eye on the float as it moved around while he took a much-needed break.

He heard the dinghy powering out towards him before he saw it. For a wild moment he thought it was the Black Wind, but then he saw Ned's boat. Except it wasn't Ned steering it, it was Mackenzie Dempsey.

He pulled the little dinghy up alongside the *Ambergris*, on the opposite side to Forest's buoy, tethering it to the larger vessel and lowering a curtain of foam down over the side so the hulls wouldn't scrape against each other.

Mackenzie climbed up the ladder, his movements setting it to *tink* with each step. When at last he stood before Ahab, he wouldn't make eye contact. He'd had a haircut, a shave, and his clothes were not exactly seafaring gear. They were the clothes of a man with money. Mack wore them well, but something in his face told Ahab they weighed heavy on his shoulders.

There was a splash off the other side of the boat, where Forest had surfaced, having heard the boat approaching. He made the *okay?* sign.

Okay, Ahab signed back.

'Ned told me where to find you,' said Mackenzie. 'Let me borrow his boat.'

'I can see that, son,' said Ahab.

Mackenzie looked up. Ahab saw now that his eyes were bloodshot and his chin wobbled. That face told him everything he needed to know.

'Ah, mate,' said Ahab. 'Did you bite off more than you can chew?'

'I c-can't do this,' said Mackenzie. 'I can't.'

'Why not?' said Ahab, gesturing for him to take a seat.

Mackenzie did so, crumpling in on himself.

'I left that world behind once already – I can't go back! I've got court coming up soon!'

'Then don't,' said Ahab. 'No one is forcing you to.'

'But Shelby can't do it without me,' said Mackenzie. 'Blackbeard is —'

'Blackbeard this, Blackbeard that,' interrupted Ahab. 'The man's reputation is bigger than he is. I promise you he's flesh and blood, just like you and me.'

'You don't get it,' said Mackenzie. 'He's more dangerous than that.'

'You have a choice, you know?'

'I can't. I'm not strong enough. It's too tempting.'

'What is?' said Ahab. He found it hard to imagine, after all he'd been through, that Mackerel could still be seduced by it all. 'What's tempting about it?'

'The rush. The power. The . . . the clothes, the toys, the girls. The respect.'

'Not the drugs themselves?' said Ahab.

'No,' said Mackenzie firmly, 'if I touch ice again, I'll lose my mind.'

Finally he was showing some steel. Ahab even believed him.

'But you'll willingly let that drug loose on other people?' he said.

'We don't have a choice. It's the only way.'

He could have thrown him overboard for that. The Business ran on unexamined assumptions, the path of least resistance, handed down from generation to generation.

'I'm sick of hearing that there's no other way. What if you worked with police?'

Mackenzie shook his head furiously. 'Are you insane?'

'Why not? Why shouldn't we?'

Mackenzie put his head in his hands.

'So what do you want me to tell you?'

'I need . . . different advice.'

Ahab considered the man in front of him. He had new clothes, a new haircut, even an expensive gold chain around his neck, but he looked terrified, like a scared little boy. Yet the man was built like a brick shithouse. *And* Ahab had seen how aggressive he got when angry. Why was he always so timid?

But Ahab knew. Between his father and his brothers, they'd really worked a number on the boy.

'Alright, I'll give you some advice . . .' said Ahab. 'Tell me your name.'

'What . . .?' He looked confused. 'It's Mackerel.'

'Really? It says that on your birth certificate?'

'No . . . it says Mackenzie Dempsey.'

'Mackenzie. So why do you call yourself Mackerel?'

'It's just my nickname.'

'And why is it your nickname?'

He shrugged. 'Dad gave it to me. I'd caught a mackerel, but I thought it was a tuna.'

'Tell me that story,' said Ahab.

'Me and Davey went with Dad on a fishing trip. I was only little. He said that we were gonna catch a tuna – it was an initiation thing. He'd done it with Jesse, and now he was gonna make men of us two.'

'Go on.' Ahab already knew the story. Mackenzie's father had told it to an appreciative crowd at the pub that very night, and many nights thereafter. The nickname had stuck to the poor boy as firmly as a Greenlip abalone to a rock.

'I caught a mackerel, but . . . I thought it was a tuna. I was so proud, and Dad let me believe it. When Davey caught an actual tuna – it was huge, biggest fish I'd ever seen – I just thought mine was a smaller one.' There was a clarity in Mackenzie's eyes, as though this memory were seared in his mind. 'We came back to shore and I showed my fish to Mum, my "tuna", and that's when Davey and Dad started laughing and told me it was only a mackerel. Dad said I didn't pass the initiation. I wasn't a man, would never be the man Davey was. Started calling me Mackerel from that day on.'

'How did that make you feel?' said Ahab.

Mackenzie shrugged. 'It's just a joke.'

'Not a very funny joke for a little boy,' said Ahab. 'Do you tell people the story behind the name?'

'Yeah,' said Mackenzie. 'They always ask.'

'Your father,' said Ahab, 'was a cruel man.'

Mackenzie's face went red with shame. 'No, he wasn't.'

'And you've caught tuna since?' said Ahab.

'Oh yeah,' said Mackenzie. 'I've caught 181 tuna since that day.' The speed and precision of his response told a whole story in itself, one that Mackenzie couldn't even see.

There came the sound of scrabbling on the ladder and Forest appeared, pulling his heavy scuba gear up with him. Mackenzie lurched, not realising he'd been out there in the water, then scowled at the boy. Forest gave him no greeting either, but had the good sense to look mildly embarrassed about it.

That's unlike the boy I've seen these last twenty-four hours. Maybe he does have some sort of moral compass . . .

An idea came to Ahab. He held out his hand to Mackenzie. 'Pass me that gold chain.'

Mackenzie's hand went to it immediately before he thought to hesitate.

'What? Why?'

'Pass it here.'

Mackenzie's shoulders drooped. He reached around to the back of his neck, unclasped the chain and handed it over to Ahab.

'I need you to witness this too, Forest,' said Ahab.

He walked to the rail and held the gold chain out over the water.

'W-wait a minute,' choked Mackenzie.

Ahab dropped it.

Mackenzie didn't have time to react, the chain barely making a sound as it disappeared beneath the surface. He took one step forward, then looked at the deck, cowed. 'I'm sorry.'

'My father never made me catch a fish to prove my manhood,' said Ahab. 'He was only interested in bravery and determination. So that's what I'm doing for you now.'

Mackenzie looked back up.

'Dive down there. Now. No mask, no gear. Bring that gold chain back. Then you'll have the right to wear it. You'll reclaim the right to the name on your birth certificate. You'll be a true man.'

'Ahab,' said Forest in disapproval.

But without question Mackenzie stripped down to his underwear and stepped up to the side of the boat. He peered down at the water, taking deep breaths, over and over, oxygenating his body. He entered the water with a perfect dive and disappeared from view.

Ahab sensed Forest's glare.

'You have something to say, boy?'

'That was cruel,' said Forest. 'You know how deep it is right here?'

'The question that sits at the heart of a man is always the same: am I a true man?' Ahab watched the water. 'Am I strong enough? Brave enough? Mackenzie's father chose to answer that question for him long ago – even worse, he shared that answer with anyone who would listen – and Mackenzie has held on to it ever since. To undo that, he has to be given a different trial.'

'You don't need a trial to prove yourself a man.'

'Of course you do. A boy isn't a man *because* he doesn't yet know the important things a man needs to know. To be a man is to be useful, and to be useful is to put into practice everything you've ever learned. That's why I'm not going to set him a task as chancy as catching a fish. He needs to be measured by what he's learned, and Mackenzie is one of the best divers I've ever seen.'

'He doesn't need to pass a test to prove he's a man,' said Forest again.

'Every culture in the world has an initiation rite for passage into manhood,' said Ahab stubbornly.

'Whatever, old man,' said Forest. He peered over the edge. 'He's been down there a long time.'

'It's not so far down,' said Ahab.

'What if he can't find it?' said Forest.

'He will,' said Ahab.

'And if he can't?'

'He will,' insisted Ahab.

The boat rose and fell with the surge of the swell, creaking . . .

'He's not gonna make it,' said Forest.

A bubble surfaced, and then Mackenzie followed, gasping for breath. He coughed and spluttered, reaching for the ladder.

'Did you find it?' said Forest.

Mackenzie shook his head, sucking in air.

'Tell him to come back up, Ahab,' said Forest. 'Tell him.'

'Try again, son,' said Ahab.

Mackenzie nodded, shivering in the water, and dived under.

Forest pulled his scuba vest back on. 'I'm going down to help him.'

'Don't you dare.' Ahab's voice cracked across the deck. 'He won't thank you.'

'He's going to drown trying to impress you!'

'Boy, he's trying to impress *everyone*. He's trying so hard it's killing him.'

'Then why are you feeding into it?' said Forest.

'A man needs a witness. Someone to whom he can *prove* he's a man. Otherwise, he'll always question it.'

'That just sounds like a self-fulfilling prophecy, Ahab,' he said.

Mackenzie surfaced again. 'I can't find it,' he choked. He took shuddering, shivering breaths.

'We're not leaving until you find it,' said Ahab. 'Again, Mackenzie.'

Mackenzie gave him a helpless look. 'Please, Ahab.'

'You're not a man until you find it,' said Ahab.

Mackenzie took another run of breaths and then dived down.

'Now you're definitely being heartless,' said Forest with heavy disdain.

Ahab didn't reply. The truth was, he doubted that Mackenzie could find the chain that far down. But when Mackerel finally stood up to Ahab and refused to dive down again, Ahab would say that Mackenzie had passed the real test: standing up to him. Or maybe he'd tell Mackenzie that the test was giving up something that cost that much. It didn't matter what the test was, only how Ahab delivered his judgement afterwards, making sure someone else was there to witness it so Mackenzie knew it was the real thing.

A full minute passed.

And Ahab began to grow a little worried.

Another minute passed, and still no sign of Mackenzie.

And then Mackenzie surfaced, gasping and clamouring for air.

He held the chain aloft in his hand.

Like Poseidon with his trident. Like a man who'd found a name.

Forest jumped up and down, cheering and shouting.

Ahab smiled to hide his surprise. It had seemed an impossible feat. There was kelp covering the ground, and the sand down there shifted minute by minute . . .

Mackenzie climbed shakily up the ladder and turned to Ahab, his eyes red from the salt water.

'Here,' said Mackenzie, holding out the chain, shivering. 'I found it.'

'It's not for me,' said Ahab, pushing Mackenzie's hand back to his chest. 'Put it on. You've earned it.'

With trembling hands, Mackenzie clasped it around his neck.

'What's your name, son?' said Ahab.

'Mackenzie,' he said. 'Mackenzie Arlo Dempsey.'

'And don't you forget it.'

CHAPTER 45

MACKENZIE

Mackenzie steered the dinghy back to the marina. His body ached but his mind was clear, the gold chain cold around his neck.

Mackenzie.

It made sense. Why had he ever doubted he was a man? He'd been a millionaire, for fuck's sake. He'd been to prison. He was tougher than almost all the men in this town.

Now he was doing the world a favour. He was going to save his brother, and he was going to protect his home town from Blackbeard. And he wasn't going to listen to the siren's call of the drug world, now that he knew he was strong enough to resist it, and while he was at it he'd protect Shelby from it too.

He drove up to Shelby's house, his mind turning with ideas and potential. He glanced over at the security men who were still working to turn Homeward into a veritable fortress, ensuring no one would be able to enter the place without Shelby's say-so ever again.

When he limped in, it made Shelby look up. She caught his new energy immediately.

'Mackerel?' she said uncertainly.

'I don't like that name,' he said. 'Call me Mackenzie from now on.'

'What happened to you?' she said.

'Have you got all your equipment?'

'Yeah, it's out in the car.'

'Then let's go see what you can do.'

CHAPTER 46

FOREST

Ahab watched Mackenzie's boat until it had rounded the cliffs and was out of view. Forest thought on what Ahab had said.

'You've never mentioned your father before today,' said Forest.

'Why would I? You've never mentioned yours.' Ahab turned. 'I'm assuming you do have parents, somewhere? Waiting for you to swindle the Dempseys out of everything they have?'

'No parents. Just me.'

'What was your father like?' said Ahab.

'Honestly, I don't remember much,' said Forest. 'I remember he used to hit me.'

Ahab snorted in sympathy. 'At least you've got that in common with us Dempseys.'

'Are we looking for this cave or not?' said Forest. He slipped his BC back on, tightening the straps.

'Let me check your air first,' said Ahab.

'I've already checked it.'

'Well, let me check it *again*.'

'It's almost like you don't want me to drown,' said Forest lightly.

'Couldn't care less,' said Ahab.

'Okay, then I'll leave my marker buoy behind,' said Forest. He hopped up on the rail and let himself fall into the cool press of water.

Kicking his grey fins, he dived down into the colourful world. The water was soft and heavenly cold against the skin not covered by the thick wetsuit. He loved the pressure of the mask against his face, the tang of oxygen from the regulator in his mouth.

He let himself sink all the way to the sea floor. Down here the fish-filled reef gave way to a comparative wasteland of rippling sand. With a hand at his buoyancy control, which even Ahab said he was near-perfect at using already, he swam a lap around the bottom of the reef. He'd already done this, in the other direction, but there was no harm in . . .

There was a dip in the sand here. If he'd seen it before, he hadn't noticed it. Looking at it now, there was something about this little crease in the sand that was different. He swam towards it, holding on to the reef as the surging current tried to wrest him away. He ran his fingers through the dip . . .

An opening.

He released more air from his buoyancy, sank down to swipe the sand away, revealing a gap under the craggy reef. He shone his dive torch in – the kelp was hiding the entrance to a larger space.

A cave. This has got to be it.

There was no time for celebration. Now Forest was all business. *Time to see what treasures this cavern holds.*

A clunking caught his attention. Sounds travelled better underwater, and Ahab had come down after him, trailing the rope attached to the buoy he'd left behind. The old man was tapping his dive computer against Forest's oxygen tanks to get his attention. He showed a message written on his dive slate: *WEAR YOUR BUOY!*

Forest simply used his index and middle fingers to gesture to his eyes, then stabbed his finger at the cave, making the scuba signal of *Look here.*

Ahab floated down beside him, peering into the opening. He rubbed out the message on his slate and wrote: *TOO DANGEROUS FOR YOU, HEAD TO BOAT.*

They'd already had this conversation. Ahab had espoused the dangers of cave diving, explaining that a large percentage of diving fatalities was the result of people attempting to dive in caves without the proper training. That the way water moved in smaller spaces caused people to get stuck in crevices, that the walls scraped against equipment, that the lowered visibility set people into a panic, making them unable to orient themselves to the surface, a slow death by depleted oxygen tanks . . .

But Forest hadn't made it this far by playing it safe.

Before Ahab could stop him, he was inside the opening.

Instantly the sounds of the ocean were softened, echoing, eerie. The kelp tickled him as he moved further.

If there was something in here valuable enough for Jesse to kill Alexandra . . .

The passage angled upwards, burrowing into the reef itself, and . . .

Stale air touched his face.

His torch lit up the inside of a cavern the size of a large room. He took his regulator out and took a breath.

Immediately his lungs tightened. He coughed, grabbing his throat, gasping, coughing again . . .

A second later Ahab had pushed Forest's regulator back in. He held his own breather aside and whispered out the side of his mouth, 'Breathe, Forest, the air is toxic in here . . .'

Eventually the terror eased and Forest was able to breathe deeply through his regulator again. He made to reach under his mask to wipe at the tears, but Ahab grabbed Forest's wrist and shook his head, tapping the mask.

Mask stays on.

Forest had felt a lot safer under the water than in this cave with its dead air.

He shone his torch around, trying to get a better sense of what they'd uncovered. At first he thought the floor was covered in sharp rocks, but he peered closer, trying to pin down the irregular shapes of those stones. They certainly weren't man-made, but they weren't typical stones, either . . .

He backed away with a yelp through his regulator, dropping his torch and sending frantic shadows jumping all over the ceiling. He bumped into Ahab, who gripped Forest's arm to help him find his balance.

The floor of the cave was completely covered in bones.

Forest had a sickening sense of déjà vu, as though they were back in Alexandra and Huck's tomb.

Ahab gave his arm a comforting squeeze.

Why is he so calm?

Ahab reached into a nearby pile and pulled out a small flat object. He touched his bare thumb to the sharp edge and it came away with a prick of blood. He swept his torchlight around the area while Forest slowly eased back into the water. All those bones, the toxic air, the blood on Ahab's finger . . .

He let the water support him, already feeling better. Ahab, without straying far from the pool of water that was their exit from this death trap – moving expertly even in his fins – scanned through some more of the debris.

When the old man returned, Forest went first, swimming back through the tunnel, eyes straight ahead, then straight up to the boat.

He gasped for breath once he was out of the sea, clambering up onto the boat and taking in the cool fresh ocean air. He'd never take that for granted again. He felt like vomiting.

All that, and not even a hint of treasure. He could barely begin thinking about what happened next, but that cave had not been what he'd been hoping for. What he needed it to be. Not even close.

Ahab was not far behind. Once he was on deck he took his mask off and pulled that flat round stone out of his diving pouch. His beard was dripping wet, his eyes shining as he held the stone up to the light as though it were made of gold.

'It's another tomb,' said Forest.

'They weren't human bones, son.'

He put the stone carefully back into his pouch.

'What's so special about a bunch of bones and rocks?' asked Forest. 'That's not *treasure*!'

'We need to get back to the Mermaid's Darling, son,' he said, distracted. 'Hold on to something.'

CHAPTER 47

MACKENZIE

Mackenzie stood at the prow of the old houseboat, the MV *Anne*, watching the wide blue waters of Fortescue Bay, which reached out from the mouth of the tidal river where they were moored. The bay was cupped between giant sea cliffs that levelled out to the flatlands of the peninsula.

The *Anne* bobbed gently in the current, moored beneath overhanging myrtle beech branches that offered a sense of privacy. Its sides green with mould and decay, the converted ferry had the charm of all things rustic and abandoned. A rickety wooden pier led from the open doorway up to the Dempseys' empty block of land.

As far as ice labs went, it wasn't the most secure – it was clearly visible to any traffic on the river – but who would want to snoop on a houseboat? Still, while Shelby set up her equipment, Mackenzie had spent his time installing heavy curtains and new deadbolts on all the doors just in case.

He turned back from the ocean and pulled on the pink coveralls and face mask that Shelby had left for him. The mask smelled like new plastic, and the eye-guard immediately fogged up. He unbolted the outer door, stepped through and locked it again from the inside before heading down into the lab. A solid bar of tension sat between his shoulder blades. There was no going back now if they were caught.

But also . . . he was excited. Since Ahab's boat, all those other feelings were still there, the worry about getting caught and the fear for Shelby, but . . . they were lessened, somehow. He felt confident. He could give himself permission to be excited about how this might turn out. He'd done this many times before – there was something about it that brought you face to face with your humanity.

Shelby stood in front of the lab she had created, which had once been the houseboat's dining room; it wasn't the biggest room in the place, but the range hood provided good ventilation without raising any suspicion.

She was clad in her own coveralls, hair safely tied back into her hood. On the table before her were beakers, vials, tubes and Bunsen burners. The boxes of Sudafed were lined up against the wall, alongside bottles of powders and liquids labelled in Shelby's careful handwriting.

Mackenzie stepped up beside her. 'You ready for this?'

'Easy as pie.'

'There's no going back,' he said.

'I know!' she snapped. 'But I'm making it as pure as possible. Then it won't hurt people as much.'

'It's still gonna hurt people,' said Mackenzie. He'd seen first-hand the desperation of those willing to do *anything* for another score. Hell, he'd been one of them.

'Ice only hurts people because of the acidic nature. If you can get the pH levels right, it doesn't eat away at the body,' she said crisply.

'Chances are that eventually they'll put enough through themselves that sooner or later the acid eats part of their flesh. They're not always going to be using your stuff, Shelby. If they go long enough, they all end up looking like skeletons. Besides, it's not the acid that hurts them, it's the sleep deprivation.'

Mackenzie remembered *that* season of his life all too well. Ice was like coffee with the volume turned up to a thousand. It was a euphoric lava flow just beneath your skin. It could keep you awake for days, and the brain is just not meant to be awake for that long. The body needs sleep more than it needs food.

'Ready, set, go,' said Shelby with a huff of air.

She crushed up a whole box of Sudafed pills with a mortar and pestle, then tipped them into a glass beaker. She poured in a solvent from a marked bottle. 'You've got to separate out the pseudo-ephedrine,' she said. 'We mix it with a solvent at low temperatures to remove it.'

She began setting up other vials, beakers, a Bunsen burner.

'Once the pseudoephedrine has been distilled and it's risen to the top of the solvent, it'll be oil, and then we'll burn it off with this: a reflux condenser. The steam runs up, gets cooled, then drips down here.' She traced the path with her finger through the glass tubes.

Mackenzie had seen part of this process before, but with different chemicals. There were a hundred different ways to cook ice. He'd never seen it done this way, but he made it a habit not to watch the product being made. If people thought you knew how to cook, you became one of two things: a god or a slave.

But in Shelby's case, he'd let her explain it to him. It seemed to help her work, and he didn't want her feeling alone as she stepped into something so major.

'After it turns into liquid,' Shelby pointed to where the steam was condensing, 'you run red phosphorous and hydrochloric acid through it. That's where you have to get the pH level right. This is where ninety per cent of people muck it up. If the pH is way too high, it'll just burn. But even if it's just a little too low or too high, it'll hurt your body.'

Mackenzie peered closer at the red phosphorous. 'Where did you get this? I thought you couldn't buy this stuff.'

'Get too close and you'll be sorry,' she warned. 'No, you can't buy it. It's illegal to have red phosphorus without a good reason. So you can spend weeks scraping it off matches . . . or you can have friends who work in the chemistry department at the university.'

'Shelby, you can't do that! You'll lead them straight to us! Police monitor chemicals like this!'

'I'm going to make it as safe as possible, and we're not doing this long-term, right? So we'll be fine.' She stepped away from her work. 'Damn it, Mackerel, now I'm shaking.'

'Don't call me Mackerel,' he said. 'My name is Mackenzie.'

'Fine, yes, don't make me screw it up, *Mackenzie*.' She stepped back to the lab. 'Okay, after that, you filter out the phosphorus and add a lye solution to neutralise the rest of the acid.' Now she paused. 'Here comes the gamble. The science is sound, it *should* work.'

'What should work?' said Mackenzie. 'Shelby, don't take chances . . .'

'I have something that should bind to the ice without affecting . . .' She poured a few drops of golden liquid into the mix from a glittering, unmarked bottle. 'Then we drain the liquid meth out.' She poured it into another beaker. 'Now we bubble hydrogen-chloride gas through it, which will turn it into crystal – *crystalline hydrochloride salt*.'

Once it was ready, she poured it through a filter cloth. 'Now we leave it on here until it dries.'

The crystal was a rich golden yellow, transparent as stained glass.

'You turned it gold?' Mackenzie was on the edge of a pit of despair. He couldn't believe he'd let her blow their one chance at this. 'Shelby, the purest ice is translucent. No one is gonna buy this!'

'I know what I'm doing,' she snapped, wiping sweat off her forehead. She waved the glittering bottle. 'This is what's going to distinguish us from the competition. I bet no one else is cooking golden ice.'

'No one will buy it, either,' said Mackenzie.

'They will once they try it.'

The sun shone down on them as they sunbaked on the deck, waiting for the ice to set. Mackenzie was shirtless and Shelby had stripped down to her bra. He pointedly looked away, which made her give an earthy chuckle.

When the timer on her phone went off she busily pulled her shirt back on.

'Let's go have a look, then.'

Mackenzie dressed and followed her back inside.

The crystals had dried and cracked. The shards looked like delicious toffee. Mackenzie's mouth watered. He hadn't been this close to ice for ages . . .

Fight it, said one voice in his mind.

But another, dangerously rational-sounding voice betrayed him . . .

'I'll have to try it,' said Mackenzie.

'Don't be stupid,' said Shelby.

'We can't give Blackbeard ice that's bad. It'll ruin everything.'

He'd already begun rummaging in the kitchen cupboards. He soon found what he was looking for: a wineglass with a long bowl and a narrow rim.

'I don't think so,' said Shelby, holding out a shaking hand. 'My creation, I'll be the one to trial it.'

'Not a chance. I won't let you expose yourself to that. We need your brain more than we need mine.'

'And I've done the research, Mack. You've had psychosis before. If you smoke ice, you could easily lose your mind again. My brain is fresh as a daisy.'

'This is one argument you won't win,' said Mackenzie, as he picked up a small shard of the ice. It was golden and clear like honey. Now his mouth went dry.

'Give it here, Mack!' she snapped, trying to take the wineglass off him.

He pulled away and dropped the shard into the glass. If they tested him for his bail in the next few days, he'd fail. But there was no other way. He was struggling to even swallow. He crouched down over a Bunsen burner and, holding the stem and turning the bowl over the flame, put the rim to his mouth.

'Mack . . .' she whispered. 'Be careful.'

He took a deep breath of the vapour, and . . .

Nothing happened.

Some ice hits you slow and lasts longer, he remembered, and some hits straight away and burns off fast.

But then the hit came hard, and it had weight.

It came in his hearing first – a ringing like tinnitus that grew as loud as cicadas. Yet he could hear perfectly every breath he took. The glub of water on the hull, the tap of the willow on the deck.

The world shifted from fuzzy edges to minute detail. He could've sworn his muscles swelled, his skin rearranging itself until it felt, finally, like it belonged to him again. Even the pain in his leg was gone.

Heat rushed into his face, his cheeks, his chest, his toes. Warm little waves lapped at his skin, and then an angry ocean of passion, almost knocking him off his feet. He was excited – so excited, everything was exciting. He couldn't remember feeling so good ever before.

They say there's nothing like the first hit, and after so long . . .

'Mack?' said Shelby uncertainly.

He laughed, sweeping her up in a hug.

'You're a genius,' he said hotly, then realised he was far too close to her. He wanted to kiss her, but he was dimly aware that wouldn't be a good idea.

She backed away from him. 'Is it . . . are you okay?' she said.

'This,' he announced, 'is the best ice I've ever had.'

He wasn't sure if that was true – he hadn't had a hit in so long, and the first was always the best, but . . . this one hit him *everywhere*. In his eyes, in his throat, in his belly, in his groin . . .

He put his hands down in front of himself to clumsily hide his growing arousal.

Shelby saw what was happening and a strange expression rolled over her face. That look on her face went some way to reminding him why he was here.

He was no stranger to drugs – he'd trained himself to keep a level head while under the influence, especially when paranoid customers demanded he try some of the product before they bought it. The trick was to fake being sober. Just do what you thought a sober person should do. Then, when you finally did sober up, you found that those actions were nearly always the right ones.

Of course, faking it took a lot of energy when your body felt like a galloping horse and your brain felt ten times smarter and fifty times chattier than normal.

But perhaps his subconscious knew enough to be worried. A voice chattered in the back of his mind, spewing facts that had been drummed into him during his drug rehabilitation course in prison.

. . . mirrors the natural neurotransmitter for pleasure so completely, your brain can't tell the difference. It both imitates dopamine and stimulates your brain to release more of its own, flooding your brain, overloading you with pleasure . . .

'Take this off me,' he said, handing over the wineglass. Acting how a sober person would act. 'Before I take another hit. We have all the proof we need.'

Shelby mutely took the glass off him and dropped it into the bin.

Mackenzie heard that other voice still chattering away:

. . . causes damage to the production of natural dopamine, until you rely on the substance just to feel normal. It's like a nightmare you can't wake up from. You'll never get that same feeling as the first rush. And yet, you'll never stop chasing exactly that . . .

Shelby busied herself breaking up the crystallised ice and weighing it out into ziplocked bags.

'It needs a name,' said Mackenzie. He still had his hands over his groin. Was that what a sober person did?

'What does?'

'The ice,' said Mackenzie. 'You said it yourself, it's a brand. Marketing is everything. What do you want to call your creation?'

'Is now really the time to be talking about this?'

'Yeah. Great time to talk about it. Do you need help bagging that?'

'No!' said Shelby, but she didn't move as he came to help. He pressed up against her. 'Hell, Mack – you're sweating like crazy. Is that normal?'

'I'm okay,' said Mackenzie. He was too close. He stepped back and wrapped his arms around himself as he watched her work. 'But when you finish that, can you take us home?'

'You want to go home?' she said. 'What if Kane sees you like this?'

'I think the safest place for me right now is in the rumpus room, playing Xbox,' he said. 'Please.' He was aware that his eyes were darting all over the place and he couldn't stop them. He was fidgeting with his hands, his clothes, his hair, his . . .

He yanked his hands away from his crotch. His cheeks burned with embarrassment and arousal in equal measure.

'Alright, why don't you go to the car and I'll meet you there,' she said, blushing. 'I'll just lock all this away . . .'

The coastal roads back to Shacktown were bumpy, wending through cleared paddocks edged with common heath and tea-trees. He felt at complete peace there in Shelby's Jeep, fiddling with his gold chain. He hadn't said anything – he wasn't sure if a sober person would speak right now, with so much illegal product in the back seat.

'Don't laugh,' said Shelby, 'but, lately, I've been trying to imagine Davey's face if the roles had been reversed. If I had come out and told *him* I was some drug queenpin.'

Mackerel chuckled. Now he was fiddling with his seatbelt, pulling it in and out, in and out . . . 'Just happy little daydreams, hey?'

'Yeah, well,' she said, embarrassed. 'In my daydreams, one day I decide to become a queenpin myself. Persephone. Like the queen of the underworld? Bit of a joke – Persephone was married to Hades, lord of the dead.'

Mackenzie kept his eyes out the window. 'Davey didn't tell you the truth because he wanted to protect you.'

'Yes, Mackenzie, you've told me a hundred times. But he shouldn't have married me if this was the life he chose. Not without telling me.'

'He wanted to tell you,' said Mackenzie.

'A lot of stuff makes sense now.' she said. 'He wanted to recruit me, didn't he? When we first started dating?'

'He loves you.'

'What made him think I'd *ever* want to cook ice?' said Shelby.

'People don't usually turn Davey down . . .' said Mackenzie. 'We'd never met a proper chemist before. Plus you were smart, funny, drop-dead gorgeous. He had this picture-perfect plan for you and him. I think, in the end, that's why he didn't tell you.'

'He didn't trust me?' said Shelby.

'He couldn't face the danger of you becoming a cook.'

'I mean, *you* survived prison. That can't have been fun, but I'm sure I could've handled it.'

'I'm not talking prison, Shelbs,' said Mackenzie. 'Ice cooks . . .'

'You keep saying it's dangerous, but you never tell me why, exactly. We're in this together now. Stop keeping things from me.' Even while driving, she was able to glance across and pin him down with a fearsome look.

He sighed. 'A friend of a friend was a genius with ice. She could cook it from stuff you buy at Woolworths, a real miracle worker . . . They found her three years after she was abducted. She'd been kept in a shipping container in the Victorian bush, chained to her lab by her ankle. She lives in a support home now. She's never recovered.'

Shelby cursed. 'Tell me you're joking.'

'*That's* why Davey's scared of you getting involved in all this,' said Mackenzie.

Silence filled the car. Mackenzie was full of blinding self-loathing – ice enhanced your emotions, and he regretted bringing it up. Images of Shelby held captive in a cellar somewhere filled his mouth with bile.

'One week,' said Shelby, drumming a single finger on the steering wheel. 'I'll be an ice cook for one week, and then . . . then I'll leave it all behind.'

'Okay,' said Mackenzie. 'Deal.'

One week.

'But to get Blackbeard's attention in just one week . . .' said Shelby. 'The ice needs a name. It needs some prestige.'

One week. We can do that. Nothing bad will happen in one week. Everything will go back to the way it was, but better.

'Persephone brought the springtime,' said Shelby. 'I think we should call our ice Golden Sunshine.'

The image of Kane in an empty house, calling for his mum, came into Mackenzie's head, and he put a knuckle in his mouth as he fought off sobs.

'Mack . . .?' she said.

'I'm sorry, Shelby!'

He began to cry.

CHAPTER 48

AHAB

Ahab and Forest sat in the corner of the pub, Zeus at Forest's feet. Ahab was cold and his hair was wet – they'd come directly from the boat – but a steady excitement built within him.

He leaned closer to the laptop screen. He wasn't very good at technology or the internet. It took him a lot longer to find what he was looking for than it would take others, but he'd finally got there.

Kutikina.

Triumph.

He glanced up at the boy. 'Who are you waiting for?' he said impatiently.

'What?' said Forest.

'You keep looking at the door. You're skittish. You haven't touched your drink.'

'I need to go for a walk,' said Forest.

'You're not leaving my sight,' said Ahab. 'Not until we come up with a plan.'

'A plan for *what*?' moaned Forest. 'We found a cave full of bones and sharp rocks. So what? I was expecting treasure. What I got was another tomb.'

'*This* is what,' said Ahab. He spun the laptop around.

Forest pulled the laptop closer to him to read. '*Kutikina Cave* . . .?'

'It's a cave on the Franklin River, in the south-west – one of the richest Aboriginal artefact deposits ever found. It was key to the Franklin Dam controversy.'

'Controversy over a dam?' said Forest.

'There's *always* gonna be controversy over a dam,' said Ahab, laughing despite himself. 'This time, a cave was used to show how important that part of the river was, which would've been destroyed if the dam had gone ahead . . .'

'So . . . those bones down there . . .? You think they're *that* old?'

'It's above my paygrade to answer that question. But this . . .' Ahab spun the stone chip on the table. 'This is called a scraper. *These*, at least, were among the tools recovered from Kutikina Cave.'

'I don't understand,' said Forest. 'I thought we were looking for a reason someone would kill Alexandra. I wanted *treasure*, damn it!'

'We've found it, lad. Don't you get it?' He couldn't understand why he was getting so angry with the boy. Of course he wouldn't understand, how could he? 'That cave is a massive find. It asks so many questions – probably answers a few, too. It'll draw researchers from all over Australia . . . we'll have divers *everywhere*, looking for more finds. They might turn this place into a national park.'

'And that's bad?' said Forest.

'It is if you're running a drug trade out there. The Business would end overnight. *That's* why Jesse wanted it kept secret. That's why he killed Alexandra. She would've told the whole world – she would've *had* to. It's an incredible find. And she knew about the Business, how much this place would lose – what her husband would lose. She probably saw this as a way to end it permanently. Clever girl.'

'And then Jesse murdered her,' said Forest.

'If she died for this cave, it won't have been for nothing.' After all these years, Ahab had wanted to find Jesse because he thought something terrible had happened to him. Now he wanted to find Jesse so they could have . . . words. Stern words. Words one of them may not survive. 'We need to tell someone. I don't even know who you're supposed to tell when you find things like this. There must be some government department you're supposed to call.'

'We need to be careful who we tell . . .' said Forest. 'That cave wouldn't be hard to destroy. Or block up the entrance. Or . . . just kill us, to keep it a secret.'

But the cave was still there for us to find . . . so Alexandra mustn't have told Jesse the coordinates. Or she gave him the wrong ones.

If Jesse believes this boy is the real Forest, then that's *why he wants him alive – he wants the cave.*

The door opened and in walked Shelby. She took her sunglasses off, scanning the room until she saw them. She walked over, heels clicking. Ahab put the scraper in his pocket.

'I need to talk to Davey,' she whispered. 'Where is he?'

'What's happened?' said Ahab. She looked either nervous or excited, he couldn't tell which.

'The product is ready. Now we need to make sure the next part is right. We're going to try and make contact with Blackbeard . . .'

Ahab glanced at Forest. He thought again about what the boy had said.

If Ahab told Shelby about the cave, and they went straight to the government, then how long would it take for it all to be sorted out? Days? Weeks? Months? With the resources Blackbeard had at his disposal, would the site even remain intact that long?

No, they had to find another way to take down Blackbeard. They had to save the cave for when he was out of the picture.

'Ahab, I want that product out of my house!' said Shelby.

'Let's grab Davey on the way and talk in my room,' said Ahab. 'Be careful, De Corrado is back.'

Forest made to follow, but Ahab gave him a stern glance. 'No. You stay put. This doesn't involve you.'

At least he could try to keep the boy out of this side of things. As much as possible.

Once they were in Ahab's room, Davey and Shelby embraced and then sat beside each other.

'We've got the product,' said Shelby, her hands in Davey's. 'Now we have to decide who should take it to Blackbeard. Mack says it should be him, but he's not . . . thinking clearly right now.'

'Not a chance,' said Davey.

Ahab stood at the doorway to the balcony, smoking furiously. Shelby had explained what had happened in their lab. It was stupid of Mackenzie to try the ice. What if he got hooked again? At least Shelby hadn't felt the need to hide the truth from him, so presumably Mackenzie was showing restraint.

'Mackenzie is the *only* choice,' said Shelby. 'Who else could it be?'

'He's living in our house!' said Davey. 'Blackbeard will know you're involved. He might even work out you're the cook!'

Ahab nodded in agreement, then stepped outside to discard one cigarette and light another. Davey had his eyes on him when he came back inside. 'Shelby's right,' said Ahab. 'It has to be Mackenzie.'

'It could be you,' said Davey.

Ahab scowled. He should have seen that coming. 'I already told you, I'm not getting involved.'

'I had the same idea,' said Shelby. 'But Mackenzie said everyone knows Ahab's straight now. Blackbeard's crew would never buy it.'

'Straight people become crooked,' said Davey.

'Not this one,' said Ahab. 'I'm not peddling your ice.'

'We need to hire someone, then,' said Davey. 'A middle-man to work as a drug runner.'

'And who do you suggest?' said Shelby. 'Is there anyone you used to work with who you're sure isn't working for Blackbeard? Who the hell can we trust?'

'Trust a hundred per cent? Only the people in this room . . . and the fake Forest. If he was working for Blackbeard, I'd be dead by now.'

Ahab felt a sinking feeling in his gut. He didn't want them getting the boy involved. 'No. You're not using him.'

'Why not?' said Davey, voice rising. 'He's the reason we're in this mess.'

'And he'd be safe,' said Shelby thoughtfully. 'We know Blackbeard doesn't want him dead.'

'But if Blackbeard finds out he's involved in a drug syndicate, that could change. And he's only a *kid*!'

'We ran drugs as kids,' said Davey. 'It's not that hard.'

'No,' said Ahab. 'Forest is not an option.'

'There's no one else who we can guarantee isn't already in Blackbeard's crew,' said Shelby.

'We should let Forest decide what he wants to do,' said Davey stubbornly. 'Give him a chance to prove himself.'

'There . . . is someone else . . .' said Ahab. They looked at him expectantly, but he himself could hardly believe what he was about to say. 'Ivy.'

'What?' snapped Davey.

'We know she's not with Blackbeard, and she'd do anything to bring him down. If she knew you were alive, she'd be desperate to have you back as head of the Business. Plus she's a Dempsey – her name carries weight.'

'You can't bring my mother into this!' said Davey.

'Why not? When you said you used to run drugs, *she's* the one who taught you that, isn't she?' said Ahab. 'An old woman, trying to regain some of what her son has lost? With a killer product? The story makes sense.'

'I'll speak to her,' said Shelby. 'It's brilliant, Ahab.'

'No, please – I don't want her to know I'm alive. It'll kill her . . .' said Davey. His head turned back and forth between them. 'Please. She's been through enough.'

'I have to ask my mother-in-law to sell my drugs,' said Shelby. 'I'm not exactly looking forward to it! But I can't leave you out of it. She's never respected me. We have to tell her you're involved, or she'll never do it.'

Davey looked at her, broken-hearted.

Ever the mummy's boy . . .

'You'll have to be the one to convince her,' said Shelby. 'If she survives the shock of seeing you alive.'

CHAPTER 49

FOREST

Ahab had made a mistake in letting Forest out of his sight. The moment he and Shelby climbed up the stairs, Forest was out the door.

He tied Zeus up out by the kitchen door. 'I'll be back soon.' He gave him a pat, then set off at a sprint.

He took an inventory of everything he now knew.

One, there was no Treasure Cave, just a cave full of bones. No, he was being petty – there was something important about them. Just not anything that would save his friend.

Two, Huck was actually Forest Dempsey. He had to find him and confirm that. But what if he wasn't able to acknowledge who he was?

He ran along the beach, feet sinking in the wet sand that had been stirred up by the Black Wind's waves overnight. He headed for the boatshed first – even though Huck didn't spend much time in the shed during daylight, it was worth checking.

A young couple were manoeuvring a boat into a shed a few doors up. The man was cursing as the trailer caught on something.

Forest waited until he was sure they were distracted, the woman giggling at her partner's frustration, before he fell to his stomach and slid underneath Huck's shed.

Inside, he found the remains of a small campfire, a rusty pot and billy, a canvas sack, and nothing else. Where was the rest of Huck's stuff? The pack with all his clothes? His sleeping bag, or the store of firewood, or . . .?

This was a bad sign. Why had Huck removed all traces of himself?

No, he must've been out fishing. That made sense.

Forest roamed over the shoreline, tripping over ocean-weathered rocks, to the fishing point. But there was no sign of him there either.

He took a different path back, looking through the scrub along the edge of the beach, then walked among the sightseers around the blowhole, down to the bustling marina, scanning faces. He even approached strangers and asked if they'd seen a tall, tanned boy with curly brown hair who looked like he'd been sleeping rough. No one had seen him. He sweated in the heat of the day, eventually returning to the boatshed.

He couldn't lose Huck. He couldn't . . .

He made his way back to the Mermaid's Darling and sat down beside Zeus, pulling the dog's head into his lap. He was grateful to see one of the kitchen staff had given Zeus food and water.

Huck and Zeus – they were all Forest had.

His mind turned briefly to Mack and Ahab.

He remembered the hurt on Mack's face when he'd realised that Forest had been lying to him all this time.

He thought of the way Ahab had said, *You're not leaving my sight* . . . He'd lost the man's trust.

Even though those relationships hadn't been real, it still hurt to lose them. He'd liked the way they'd tried to protect him, when they thought he was one of their own.

But now they didn't care about him . . . and he couldn't care about them. How could he? They were just . . . a means to an end.

Huck was all he cared about, and Huck deserved to have back everything that he'd lost. That had to still be in his power. Somehow.

Untying Zeus, he led him down the streets of Shacktown. The dog was happy for the exercise, sniffing at whatever he found in bushes and gutters, cavorting with other dogs out for a walk. Forest let him have his fun. There was no need to rush now. There was no turning back after what came next.

When he arrived, he knocked on the door until she came and answered.

'Good to see you, Forest,' Frankie said warmly.

'Call De Corrado,' he said, gruff in the face of her cheeriness. 'She's gonna want to hear this, too.'

Frankie sat back in her chair, relaxed and placid, but the detective sat with her elbows on her knees, leaning forward. There was a lean hunger in her eyes. 'Well? What do you have to tell us?'

'I'm afraid I have bad news and good news, followed by more bad news,' said Forest carefully, eyes focused solely on De Corrado's. 'The bad news is I'm not really Forest Dempsey.'

'*What?*' said De Corrado, eyes bulging. She sat back and then laughed. 'Okay, you got me, that was good. Did your grandmother put you up to this?'

'The good news is, the real Forest Dempsey has been in Shacktown for the last week or so.'

'What do you mean you're not the *real* Forest Dempsey?' demanded De Corrado. 'This *is* a joke.'

'I knew Forest was adopted. I knew that I could pretend to be him and no one could prove otherwise with a DNA test. And I did my research.' He tried to put as much arrogance into his voice as he could. He had to convince them he was the opportunist they would imagine him to be.

'How did you . . .? Ivy said you didn't know about the adoption.'

'The *real* Forest did know. Because his dad never let him forget it.' This had been one of the first things Huck had told him – that Jesse had teased Forest mercilessly about being adopted, about not being a true Dempsey.

He hated the expressions crossing the detective's face, shock and anger and confusion. She landed on a glare that seemed reserved for something you'd find beneath your shoe.

She turned on Frankie. 'Did *you* know?'

Frankie shook her head, mute, a horrified expression on her face. She hadn't spoken a word. She'd spent all this time thinking she was psychoanalysing Forest Dempsey, only to find out all of it had been a lie.

'The bad news is, the real Forest Dempsey has gone missing. I need your help to find him.'

'The *real* Forest Dempsey?' said De Corrado. She stood up and walked to the window. After a moment, she punched the wall. 'You little *bastard*! Who else knows?' She was shaking her hand, wincing.

'I can prove it. There's a cave nearby with . . . with Alexandra's body.' That's all he had to say. He could keep Davey, Shelby and Mack out of it all.

'What? Where?' said De Corrado. 'Tell me everything, you little rodent!'

'I . . . I think I need a moment,' said Frankie, trembling. 'I'm sorry, detective. Just . . . give me a moment.' She fled the room.

Forest knew he shouldn't feel good about how his one-time therapist was reacting, but it *did* feel good. He'd got the better of her – he'd come out the victor in their private war.

'So how did you fake it?' De Corrado sounded disgusted. 'All those things about Forest's childhood?'

Forest shrugged. He wasn't proud of how he'd gone about it, but it hadn't been difficult either. 'There's endless news articles from back then. And Ahab has the family photo albums in his room . . .'

There was a spark of recognition on De Corrado's face. 'You little cocker.'

'. . . and I've been friends with the real Forest Dempsey.'

'Inserting yourself into a family desperate to believe it's all true . . . It's evil. *Genius*, but evil.'

'I'm not evil,' spat Forest. 'I was just trying to help him.'

'And who the hell are *you*?' said Frankie. She came back into the room with two steaming cups. 'Here, detective. Thought you might need a coffee. I sure do.'

De Corrado took the coffee, sipping it distractedly. 'You've been playing us like puppets on a string! Tell me how you met the real Forest. Tell me everything.'

'You have to promise me you'll help find him.'

'Obviously! Now tell me.'

'He's tall, he's got dark hair. I can help someone sketch a picture. He can't have gone far, if we spread his picture around . . .'

'It goes without saying you're in big, big trouble for this. And so is anyone who's helped you.'

He looked at the ground. 'No one helped me. I did this alone. None of the Dempseys know.'

'I might even believe that.' She looked up at him, but her eyes seemed unfocused. 'Putting two and two together . . . Davey killed himself because you . . . Which raises more questions than . . . but . . .'

There was a dull thud as De Corrado's coffee cup hit the carpet. She slid out of her seat, convulsing.

Forest sprang to his feet, shouting for help, just as Frankie screamed, 'Now! Grab the kid!'

Two men ran into the room – one clamped a sweaty hand over

Forest's mouth, then roughly pulled his arms behind his back and zip tied his wrists together.

Forest panicked, struggling to pull away, but the men were massive. He bit the hand covering his mouth and the tall redhead released his grip with a curse. Forest screamed for help.

'Shut up, kid,' said the other man, delivering a blow to the back of Forest's head that left him seeing stars. 'Fuck me, can we kill him now, Frankie?'

He felt far, far away. He slumped to his knees, struggling to focus.

Frankie was on her phone. 'Blackbeard? Yes, Tranquil and Vance are here. The kid told De Corrado the truth, but it gets worse – he said the *real* Forest Dempsey is alive somewhere!'

'No . . . no, don't . . .' Forest tried to right himself. The man with the gold chains pressed his knee into the back of his neck.

'Yeah. A tall kid with dark hair. That's all he said, but he reckons he can't have gone far . . .' said Frankie. 'I'll get Vance on the lookout.' Frankie nodded, with a smirk in Forest's direction. 'Got it. Find the boy. Kill him on sight.'

'Ahab,' he croaked, disoriented. 'Ahab will stop you.'

The man with the gold chains laughed. 'No one can hear you, mate.'

He dragged Forest into one of the bedrooms, still laughing. He grabbed a pillow case and made to put it over Forest's head, but Frankie stopped him.

'Just one more thing.' Frankie's grinning face was the last thing Forest saw. 'I win.'

CHAPTER 50

AHAB

Ahab sat on one of the beds in Davey's room, Davey sat on the other.

Ahab licked his lips. His mouth was dry. 'Nervous?'

'What do you reckon?' muttered Davey. He turned his head. 'You?'

'She'll find a way to make me pay for not telling her you were alive,' said Ahab.

'Don't worry. She'll be too busy punishing me . . .'

Someone began pounding on the door and didn't stop.

Davey hesitated too long and Ahab got up to answer it instead.

The moment he turned the knob, Ivy came bursting through, pushing Ahab out of the way. She took in her son. '*You!*'

'Hi, Mum,' he said quietly.

Ivy's eyes overflowed with tears, but her mouth was set in an angry line. 'You *dare* do that to me?' She crossed the gap between them and pulled him in for a hug. She burst into loud, wet sobs. 'You *stupid* boy! You absolute *idiot*!'

Shelby was hovering in the doorway, not wanting to intrude, but Ahab pulled her inside so he could close the door.

'What should I do with this?' whispered Shelby. She pulled a zip-lock bag out of her pocket. It was full of golden shards.

'Bloody bliss salt,' muttered Ahab. He leaned against a wall, wanting nothing to do with this scene.

'What's that?' said Shelby.

'My mum used to call it that . . .' said Ahab. 'Get it out of my sight.'

'You think I like it?' said Shelby. 'Mackerel was a mess after one smoke.'

'Don't call him Mackerel,' growled Ahab.

Ivy continued to hold Davey, loud sobs still escaping her stony demeanour, slapping him on the back of the head every now and then.

Eventually she composed herself, straightening her dress and her hair. She sat on the bed next to Davey and turned to the room. 'Right. Show me.' Her voice was hoarse from crying, but like usual she was taking control.

Shelby held out the bag. 'We're calling it Golden Sunshine.'

Ivy refused to take it, clasping Davey's hands instead. 'I just don't understand. Why are they involved? What on earth do you think you're doing?'

'Trying to unmask Blackbeard,' said Davey. 'It could work, Mum. Blackbeard needs locals he can trust. If we can work our way in, it won't be long until we figure out who he is.'

'And that's why . . .' Shelby swallowed, unable to say it. She gestured for Davey to continue.

Her husband shook his head, eyes wide, looking terrified. *You ask her!* he mouthed.

'Spit it out, woman!' snapped Ivy.

'They want to know if you'll take this "Golden Sunshine" to Blackbeard,' said Ahab, pushing away from the wall. 'They want you to tell him you're cooking ice. That you want to go into partnership with him.'

'Me?' said Ivy. She pulled her hands out of Davey's and stood, brushing out her dress. She began to pace the room. Ahab could imagine her mind following the same paths theirs had gone down. 'And *you* made this, Shelby?'

'I'm only cooking for a week,' said Shelby flatly. 'After that, I'm out.'

Ivy snorted. 'Of course, dear,' she said wryly.

Next she turned on Ahab. 'And what exactly are you going to do if you *do* find out who Blackbeard is?'

'Tell the police,' said Ahab.

All three Dempseys looked at him.

Ivy began to laugh. Soon she was clutching at the curtains, bent over in mirth.

'I'm serious,' said Ahab. 'This ends. It *has* to end.'

'I thought . . . once we knew, we could blackmail him into leaving Shacktown,' said Shelby.

That made Ivy laugh some more. She rubbed her eyes. 'Davey has a better idea. Don't you?'

'I don't know what you're talking about, Mum,' said Davey carefully.

'Give me some credit – I know that look in your eyes, and I know you're not stupid enough to think that Blackbeard will bow to blackmail. And it's a death wish to tell the police. Go on, boy. You know what you have to do.'

'What's she talking about, Davey?' said Shelby.

'I'd like to know that too,' said Ahab. He took a step towards him.

Davey flinched from the heat of Ahab's anger. 'Mum, I can't.'

'Don't tell me what you can and can't do. You're Davey Dempsey.' Her chin wobbled again. 'You're *alive*, and that means everything is fine. You can do it. This is what you were born to do.'

'*What is she talking about?*' said Shelby.

'Davey will take over his crew. He'll become the next Dread Pirate Blackbeard.'

'*What?*' cried Shelby.

Davey and Ivy looked into each other's eyes, and Davey seemed to grow a foot taller. Some of the fire that had been missing was back.

'You're right, it's the only way,' said Davey.

'Over my dead body,' said Ahab.

'That can be arranged,' replied Ivy. He shot her a furious glare, but she only raised an eyebrow in amusement. Her hand was possessively across Davey's leg.

'What is *wrong* with you, Davey?' said Shelby. The Golden Sunshine lay forgotten on the floor beside her. 'I'm trying to get our family *back together*!'

'That *is* what we're doing,' said Davey. He knelt down to grab the ziplock bag, offering it to Shelby on one knee as though proposing. 'You're giving us a chance to get our family back together. We'll be able to go anywhere you like. Anywhere in the world. I can do it. It won't be hard – it's easy to take over a drug crew. You saw how quickly he took over mine!'

'No, actually, I didn't – because you *never told me about it!*' said Shelby shrilly. 'No! No, no and *no!*'

'I will *not* allow it!' said Ahab. 'And neither will Mackenzie. We'll both stand against you.'

'Speaking of my halfwit son . . . Mackerel can come with me,' said Ivy.

'What? Why?' said Shelby. 'No. We don't need to get him involved.'

'He's staying at my house, Mum,' said Davey. 'I don't want Blackbeard, or anyone from the crew, thinking Shelby's involved.'

'Fine, we'll have his bail address moved to mine if that makes you happy.' Ivy's nostrils flared as though she'd just had a whiff of something disgusting. 'I might make him sleep in a tent.'

'He won't want to stay with you!' said Shelby.

'*Enough!*' said Ahab.

'If I see you approach a police officer, Ahab, I'll kill you,' said Ivy. 'I will *not* lose my son again. We're doing this. We'll take over Blackbeard's crew. I'll take Mack with me, we'll have the whole family together.' She gestured to Shelby. 'Well? Call him and tell him to come here!'

Ahab tried to think fast. 'You *can't* do that to him, Shelby.' She was the last person he could appeal to.

Shelby wiped her nose, her make-up running. 'Ahab, does it look like we have a choice?'

'Mackenzie will not be part of this,' said Ahab. 'You leave him alone.' The man had suffered more than his fair share, and now they were dragging him back in . . .

'By the way,' said Ivy, looking at her nails. 'You're looking after the imposter boy, right? On our way here I saw him jogging towards the boulder field. Looked like he was searching for someone.'

That jarred Ahab. The little conman, what was he up to now? Why couldn't he have just stayed put?

'Forest?' said Shelby. 'I didn't see him.'

'That was why I was on the phone to Frankie in the car, dear,' said Ivy, but her amused eyes never left Ahab's. 'Well, aren't you responsible for him? You better go get him.'

Ahab stalked out of the room, slamming the door behind him. He *was* responsible for Forest.

But before that, he was responsible for his family. He had to talk Mackenzie out of joining Ivy's plot.

Ahab pounded on the door to Homeward. 'Mackenzie!'

He kept pounding until the door was yanked open. It was Kane.

'He's gone,' he said. He wiped his eyes. 'I think he was on something.'

'Why are you crying?' He felt a chill. 'Did Mackenzie do something to you?'

'What? *No*,' he snapped. 'I just don't want him to become addicted to ice again! Dad told us all about our ice-addicted uncle.' He caught Ahab's expression and rolled his eyes. 'He wasn't dangerous! All he did was play Xbox, and then he got a call from Mum and basically sprinted out the door.'

Kane took a moment longer to appraise him. 'But why are you here?' he said. 'Are you part of it too?'

'Part of what?' said Ahab.

'Whatever secret stuff is going on between Uncle Mack and Mum,' said Kane. 'I know something's up, I'm not an idiot. Are they having an affair? Mum looks at him sometimes the same way she used to look at Dad.'

'They're not having an affair,' said Ahab firmly.

'So why are you looking for him?'

'It doesn't matter,' said Ahab, turning to leave.

'Don't leave me here alone!' said Kane. 'I'm coming with you. Someone needs to tell me what the fuck is going on.'

'Language,' warned Ahab.

He didn't want to bring the kid with him. The last thing he needed was someone else to take care of, asking him questions he didn't want to answer. But he also couldn't leave him behind either. If something went wrong with Ivy's attempt to sell the Golden Sunshine, if Blackbeard traced it back to Shelby, he'd have to get Kane out of this house anyway.

And if Ivy had already called Mackenzie . . . when all of this was over, Ahab would have to swallow his pride and buy a mobile phone.

'I'm looking for Forest. You can help me search.'

'Where is he?' said Kane.

'If I knew that, I wouldn't be searching for him,' said Ahab testily.

CHAPTER 51

MACKENZIE

The high had faded at last, midway through an Xbox session with Kane, and he'd fled to his room. He was exhausted, thirsty and filled with shame.

Lying back on the plush bed, fiddling with his gold chain, he remembered everything he'd done – he groaned, remembering the houseboat and his arousal. What would Shelby think of him? Would she have told Davey?

His phone rang. An unknown number. The cops sometimes called to check in on him . . . he answered.

'Davey was alive and you didn't tell me?'

It was Ivy.

He'd never heard this sound in her voice. So defeated. So . . .

He sat up on the bed, pressing the phone against his ear. 'How?'

'He's gone. Blackbeard found him. My son was alive, and now he's . . .'

'What happened?' He rose, fear flooding through him. Blackbeard had found Davey?

'The imposter. The fake Forest. He was working for Blackbeard.'

Mackerel shook his head. 'No. No! We were sure he wasn't . . .'

'There's only one way to get Davey back. Blackbeard wants the ice Shelby cooked. You and I have to deliver it to him. In exchange. Right *now*.'

'Okay. Okay, what do I do?'

'You cannot, on any condition, tell another soul. If you do, Davey's dead. Not even Ahab. Do I have your word?' Her voice was watery and full of pain. 'Promise me, Mackenzie.'

He'd been a small boy the last time she'd called him Mackenzie.

'What do I need to do?' he said again.

Mackenzie met Ivy at the entrance to the marina. He was dressed in a silk shirt, expensive slacks. He let his gold chain hang on his chest, top buttons undone, glinting in the sun.

'Well,' said Ivy, squinting. She wore a pantsuit he'd never seen her in before and a red headscarf. Almost like an old-timey aviator. 'You certainly look the part.'

Yes, he did. And he hated it.

He forced himself to smile.

'Blackbeard is sending someone to pick us up from the end of the third pier.' She held out her arm. 'Let's go, Mackenzie.'

Arm in arm, tripping over his bad leg, he let her lead him. He expected her to berate him, or tease him for losing his footing, but all she did was clutch him tighter.

He caught sight of a speedboat headed towards the end of the pier. It pulled in and he climbed down into it, helping Ivy find her feet as she stepped aboard. He didn't recognise the driver, but the driver recognised Ivy.

'Thank you, dear,' she said to the driver, in her normal manner. 'Take us where we need to go.'

She sat down beside Mackenzie, pulling his hand into hers. 'Thank you. Together, we'll save Davey.'

His heart swelled.

And then . . . slowly, like a balloon with a small leak, deflated.

This was what he'd always wanted. His mother, affectionate, valuing him. And he, riding in to save Davey.

So why did it feel so wrong?

They dipped through the waves, Ivy's headscarf flapping in the wind, the driver shooting glances back at them. They followed the coast until they came to a quiet bay, where the driver pulled them up alongside a large cray-fishing barge. Mackenzie instantly set about memorising identifying features – its rusted-red colour, the tyres tied in a line right at water-level, and especially the name: *Margot's Revenge*.

A big man with a beanie and two gold chains was waiting for them at the top of the ladder, with two more rough-looking men beside him. 'Hello, Mrs Dempsey. I see you've got something for us?'

'Who are you?' said Mackenzie, stepping in front of Ivy protectively.

'You can call me Tranquil.' He smiled widely. He lifted his shirt to show he had a pistol tucked into his belt. 'I hear that someone wants to do business with the Dread Pirate Blackbeard?'

'We have a product for you,' said Mackenzie. 'Show them, Mum.'

Ivy pulled the golden ice out of her handbag.

'The purest you'll ever try,' called Mackenzie. 'We call it Golden Sunshine.'

'You'd better come up, then,' said Tranquil.

He threw a rope down and their driver set about pulling them up against the tyres of *Margot's Revenge*.

'You stay here, Mum,' said Mackenzie out the corner of his mouth.

Ivy chuckled. 'I'm not that old, yet.' She moved ahead of him, scaling the ladder. He wondered if that was why she'd worn a pantsuit – did she know she'd be climbing?

He followed after her, the iron rungs cold against his palms, feeling the sway of the larger boat.

Tranquil met them sitting on an upturned crayfish pot. The other two men hovered nearby, but aside from them, the deck was deserted. Crayfishing gear, ropes and cables, and countless crayfish pots lay all about. Tranquil winked at Mackenzie as he held his hand out and Ivy passed him the little bag.

'Why is it gold?'

'Unique strain,' said Mackenzie.

'Why is this one doing all the talking for you?' said Tranquil.

'Because he's dying to try some,' said Ivy with a slow smile. 'To prove to you it's not dirty.'

Mackenzie stiffened. 'No!'

'Is that so?' Tranquil pulled an ice pipe out of his pocket – an instrument that looked like a glass lollipop, but with a thick hollow stick instead of a stem, and a hole in the ball. Tranquil dropped a few shards of the ice into the hole and handed both the pipe and a lighter to Mackenzie. 'In that case, smoke it.'

Mackenzie's mouth was so dry he couldn't swallow. 'I don't . . . I don't want to.'

'If you don't, I'll assume you're trying to fuck me over and I'll beat you bloody. Smoke it.'

Mackenzie took the pipe and the lighter. He turned to Ivy. She nodded encouragingly. 'It's okay. Go for it.'

Slowly he lit the lighter underneath the glass ball. Sweat broke out on his forehead. It *was* possible that taking another hit this soon could plunge him back into psychosis.

Remember, act like a sober person . . .

He breathed in the smoke that rolled down the pipe.

A moment or two later and the feeling hit him hard. It was as before. So sweet it was sickly: corrupt and coppery. A buzzing thrill like termites in his veins. Euphoria like sex. He fought to find his fake-sober thoughts.

'Damn, it looks like good shit,' said Tranquil. 'Look how hard it's hit the man.'

He made to take the pipe from Mackenzie's stiff fingers, but Ivy stopped him.

'No. Make him smoke it all.'

'Please,' croaked Mackenzie. Why was she doing this?

'All of it,' said Ivy. 'Do it.'

'It'll kill me.' Already the edges of his vision were growing white. The Golden Sunshine was too strong – it wasn't cut with anything – and he had only just come down from the last hit.

Tranquil pulled the pistol from his belt. He aimed it at Mack's head. 'Smoke it. All.'

Mackenzie tried to catch his eye, but he couldn't. Why was Tranquil so eager to do what Ivy said? He put the glass to his mouth but he didn't suck in another breath. He held the pipe to the side.

'You think I won't shoot you?' said Tranquil.

'I'd rather be dead,' said Mackenzie. He closed his eyes, fighting off the feeling. Pushing it away. He'd never smoked ice only to then try to *fight* the high. It was like pushing against an immense wind. He thought of Shelby. He thought of Davey. He thought of Kane. He thought of Ahab. He even thought of the fake Forest.

He threw the ice pipe into the ocean.

'I smoked your ice. You know it's good. Now where the fuck is my brother?'

Tranquil observed him, then broke out in laughter. He dismissed the other men from the deck.

'What did you tell him?' Tranquil asked Ivy.

'What he needed to hear,' she replied.

What were they talking about? What did she mean by . . .

Through the glow of the ice inside him, he realised.

'You're Blackbeard.'

Ivy, observing him with her head cocked to the side, didn't dignify him with a response.

'Why?' moaned Mackenzie.

'Beat him black and blue,' said Ivy. 'Don't let him leave the ship, but let him keep his little gold chain. I'm heading back to shore. Have someone else try the Golden Sunshine – let me know if it's as good as they're claiming it is.'

Mackenzie didn't see the first punch, but he saw the rest.

He moaned, wordless, raising his arms for forgiveness, or mercy.

He received neither.

CHAPTER 52

AHAB

'So where are we gonna look first?' said Kane from the passenger seat of Ahab's ute. The kid had rolled down the window, slicing his hand through the air as they drove down the hill, away from Homeward.

Ahab had lit a cigarette, his own window rolled down too. If they pulled this off, how would Kane react when Davey re-entered his life? Ahab hadn't given thought to it, but now it was front and centre. His dad might return, and continue to run the Business – and with Shelby knowing about it too, how long could they keep Kane in the dark? He and the kid weren't close anymore – not since Ahab had accused his father of being behind Jesse's disappearance – but that didn't mean Ahab had stopped caring about him. But Kane was a Dempsey to his bones. He even *looked* just like Davey, and he wasn't stupid either. Did that mean he'd take to the Business too?

Would the curse come for him?

The Bone Cave. Once Ahab told the right people about it, the ocean around here would be safe from harm. He was sure of it.

And then, without Dempseys being able to plunder the ocean, the curse would be lifted. Right?

Ahab thought back to that little coffin, so many years ago. Had he been a coward, not to try for another child? Would any kid of his have turned out like Kane?

'Ivy said she saw him walking towards the boulder field,' said Ahab, as they rumbled down the road.

'The boulder field?' said Kane with sharp suspicion. 'Is Forest involved in all of this, too?'

'No,' said Ahab.

'Liar,' said Kane waspishly. 'I'm sick of you all keeping secrets. You *know* who killed Dad.'

Ahab took a puff. 'You think he was murdered?'

'Dad would never dive during a Black Wind, everyone knows that,' said Kane.

Ahab drove the rest of the way without answering questions or letting himself be goaded into conversation. He couldn't understand why Forest would have gone back to the boulder field – they'd already explored that cave together, and the boy had been there by himself before that.

He'd soon find out, he supposed.

He pulled up in the boulder field's gravel carpark with a skid.

'You stay here,' he told Kane.

'Like hell,' said Kane. 'I'm coming.'

'You're staying here, boy,' thundered Ahab.

Kane sat back with a grunt. Ahab didn't have time to babysit someone else's kid. It was already indignity enough to be chasing after Forest like this. But he still felt a moment of pity. He thought his dad was dead, after all. He didn't know what Ahab knew.

'Look, kid,' he said. 'Chin up. Things aren't as bad as you think they are. Watch the car.'

He jogged along the path to the boulder field. The daylight made it a different world to the one he'd seen the night before. The side of the track was scrubby with cutting grass and Bushman's Bootlace, tall smoky tea-trees looming over him. He passed a couple of hikers – this was the beginning of a much longer trail – who were sitting on a bench, fixing their gear. Insects buzzed and a lull in the ocean breeze rendered the tea-tree smell heady and muggy.

No breeze?

That was one of the few signs that occasionally came before a Black Wind. Was it brewing even now? Ahab glanced at the sky. No rippled clouds. Yet.

He turned off at one of the sandy paths that led down into the boulder field, onto the rocks.

'Forest?' he yelled. His voice carried easily without any wind.

He climbed over a few rocks, orienting himself to the direction of the tomb cave. Would Forest be there? Why would he be there?

How did Ivy know he was headed towards the boulder field? thought Ahab suddenly.

Ivy would have to have been at least in that carpark to guess Forest was headed to the boulders, and there was no reason for her to be there. And no way would Forest have told her where he was going.

That woman was up to something. All that time he'd foolishly assumed Ivy was sitting in that mansion, watching events unfold, but of course she'd been playing her own angle behind the scenes. He just had no idea what that angle was . . .

'Found him yet?' came Kane's voice.

Ahab spun with a growl. 'Go back, boy.'

'No,' said Kane. 'Something is going on here.'

Ahab turned and began walking back to the carpark, following the line where scrub met boulder. 'Back to the car. Now.'

'No,' said Kane, hurrying to catch up with him.

Ahab came around a bend in the banksia scrub and pulled up short. Kane bumped into him from behind.

'Don't move, boy,' said Ahab, reaching out to grab him.

Before them stood one of Blackbeard's men – the tall one with red hair and a pockmarked face. Vance. The man who'd been there when Tranquil shot Chips. He wore a long jacket – in this weather? – and it had the telltale shape of a firearm. Ahab's mind turned back to the sawn-off that had killed Chips.

'Hello, Ahab,' said Vance. He smiled, showing little studded jewels in his large teeth. 'You were supposed to be alone, but I see you brought a friend. Come out, boy. You're a tall one, aren't ya? I think this must be my lucky day.'

'Stay behind me,' hissed Ahab.

Kane stepped around him. 'What's going on here?'

Ahab grabbed his shoulder, his eyes never leaving the man.

Kane shrugged out of Ahab's hold and skipped over to the man.

'If you won't tell me, maybe he will,' said Kane. 'Who are you?'

'Who are *you*?' said the man.

'Who do you think I am?' said Kane. 'Look me in the eyes.'

The boy had courage, Ahab would give him that, but he was stupid. He thought his money made him invincible – he got that from his father.

Ahab took a step forward, and Vance raised his eyebrows in warning. He smiled again, showing those studded jewels, and put his hand inside his jacket.

He wouldn't . . . not a child.

Ahab gauged the distance. Could he tackle the man before he drew his weapon?

'I was expecting to find Ahab with *Forest Dempsey*.' He cocked his head, studying Kane. 'Are you him?'

'Well,' said Kane, 'I'm definitely a Dempsey.'

The way he said Forest's name, Ahab realised Vance wasn't looking for the imposter Forest – Blackbeard had sent him to look for the *real* Forest.

How did he know the truth about Forest? Why had Ivy led them here?

Something was about to go terribly wrong.

'Boy, run!' shouted Ahab, dashing forward.

But Vance was too quick. He pulled the shotgun from his jacket, levelled it, and fired.

Kane's body jolted, then slumped down over the boulders, sliding into a gap between two rocks.

Ahab's vision grew dark, then blindingly white. He yelled in agony.

No . . . it couldn't be . . .

Vance looked from Kane's lifeless body up to Ahab.

Again, he levelled the shotgun. And Ahab, somehow, brought his body into a pause.

He was looking down the barrel of the gun. The sound of the shotgun blast had left an imprint on his hearing; all he registered was Kane's blood on the man, splattered all over his face, still grinning.

Kane is dead. Another boy dead. Because of you.

He knew he had to put that aside for now or he'd be just as dead. This man in front of him would not hesitate to kill him.

Kane is dead.

What will I tell Shelby?

What would Ivy do?

'You realise what you've done, don't you?' said Ahab, raising his hands in surrender.

'I've killed the *real* Forest Dempsey.' He smiled wider. 'Now Dempsey Abalone will be ours.'

'That's not Forest Dempsey,' said Ahab. 'That's *Kane* Dempsey. You've just killed Davey Dempsey's son. *His* crew will kill *you*. Ivy Dempsey herself might kill you.'

Confusion rolled through Vance's face. He looked down again at Kane's body.

'Kane Dempsey?' Horror replaced confusion.

He let the shotgun dip, and Ahab leapt forward to tackle the man to the rocks.

As they crashed to the ground, Ahab's temple hit a boulder and his vision darkened. Vance's knee caught him in the guts, but Ahab was as tough and wiry from his daily swimming as he'd ever been. And although this man was younger, he could not match Ahab's desire to avenge Kane and Chips.

He hit Vance in the chest, blocked Vance's next punch and used the momentum to get beneath his guard, punching him again. Vance's long legs twisted up to wrap around Ahab's waist, but Ahab took both of their weight and rolled to the side, scraping himself on the rocks as they tumbled into the same crevice as Kane's body. Slipping in Kane's blood, Ahab smeared a handful of it over Vance's eyes, blinding him. As Vance's hands went to his eyes, Ahab pulled away, gathered up the shotgun, and rose to his knees.

When Vance opened his eyes, he was looking right down the barrels of the shotgun.

And Ahab, teeth bared, covered in Kane's blood, wanted him dead.

'Go ahead, kill me,' he moaned. 'She'll skin me alive.'

'She?'

'Blackbeard . . .'

Blackbeard's a woman?

He felt like the world was tipping away from him, but he kept the shotgun steady.

Distant voices, calling. The hikers he'd passed! Of course they'd heard the echoing blast of the shotgun, and Ahab's shouts.

He needed to check on Kane. He needed to call the police.

'I'll tell you where they're keeping the detective,' whispered Blackbeard's henchman. 'If you promise to kill me.'

'De Corrado?' said Ahab. '*You've taken her?*'

'Hey!' shouted one of the hikers. 'Are you alright?'

'He's got a gun!' screamed his partner.

'Call an ambulance!' Ahab shouted at them. 'Call the police!'

'Everyone says you're a man of honour,' said Vance. 'Promise me you'll kill me if I tell you.'

Ahab stared down at the man, adjusting his grip on the shotgun. He'd rather die than face Blackbeard's punishment. That alone chilled him to his core.

Could he do it? Could he kill a man? Especially when he made it this easy – *begging* Ahab to do it.

Vance had just killed Kane. He'd been there when Chips died.

One of the hikers had approached, feeling Kane's neck for a pulse. The other hiker had disappeared back up the path – hopefully to call someone.

Can I shoot a man in cold blood?

I have to know what's happened to De Corrado. She's the only one who can fix this without more bloodshed.

'I promise,' said Ahab.

The man relaxed, letting his head fall back. 'She's at Frankie's house. The counsellor. The detective is at her house. Now *kill me.*'

Frankie? Frankie was Blackbeard?!

'The police are coming!' The other hiker came running back down the trail. 'They said they're nearby!'

But Ahab was barely listening. There was something else, swelling up from underneath all the other sounds.

A distant drone. The sirens were singing.

The Black Wind.

'Kill me! You promised!'

'That's the thing about us Dempseys,' said Ahab, ejecting the second cartridge and throwing the shotgun out of the man's reach. 'We lie.'

CHAPTER 53

FOREST

Forest sat on a rail-back chair, his arms bound behind him, a rag in his mouth and a silk pillowcase over his head. He could see the pillowcase billowing in and out with his rapid breathing. He was trying to stay calm but he was failing. Oh, was he failing.

He was still at Frankie's. He could hear seagulls through the window. His wrists were chafed raw from the zip ties.

Someone else was in the room with him – he could hear shallow, gasping breaths in the pattern of fitful sleep. He guessed it was De Corrado. He wished he could help her – this was all his fault. All of it. His fault.

And now they were going to kill Huck.

Footsteps approached, familiar voices.

The pillowcase was pulled from his head almost tenderly.

Ivy and Davey stood in front of him, the pillowcase in Davey's hand. Ivy, dressed in a pantsuit with a red scarf in her hair, appeared triumphant. Davey, now dressed in a tailored shirt and expensive slacks, was fidgeting with uncomfortable awe.

Forest looked around the room, trying to grasp the situation. It *was* De Corrado, lying on the bed, her arms and legs bound.

Forest shouted through the rag. His words were muffled. '*Wake up, detective!*'

'You're sure about this, Mum?' breathed Davey. He glanced between Forest and Ivy, wringing his hands.

'He has to die,' she said. 'He knows too much.'

Through the gag, Forest forced out: 'Why?' Tears sprang into his eyes, but he felt no sadness, only hate. 'Why, Ivy?'

She looked down at him as one would examine a particularly troublesome puppy. She spoke to Davey. 'Jesse told me he'd drowned Alexandra and Forest, right before he lost his mind at what he'd done, poor dear. I think there'd be some poetic justice to you drowning this imposter in Jesse's stead. You deal with the boy, and I'll deal with the detective. That way we both have skin in the game, should anything go amiss.'

Davey visibly swallowed, licking dry lips. 'Mum . . .'

She put a hand on his shoulder. 'You've killed men before, Davey.'

'Not by my own hands!'

'You can do this.' Her fingers were a claw. 'I'm your captain, now.' She caressed Davey's cheek. 'Chop chop, dear.'

The pillowcase back on his head, Forest let himself be led through the house by Davey. By the time he realised he'd been taken into the garage – the stink of petrol in his nostrils – he was being forced down into the boot of a car. The door slammed shut and plunged him into blackness, and he screamed and beat against the inside hopelessly.

They drove for a while, and Forest began to feel his body grow sluggish. Was he suffocating? He couldn't breathe. He was going to suffocate in the car! What if Davey never took him back out, but simply pushed the car off a cliff? He had to get out of here!

He was able to get the pillowcase to catch on the locking mechanism of the boot and, pulling his head away, managed to get it off. At least now he could see. Light came in around the edges of the boot door, so that meant air could get in. He wouldn't suffocate.

He whimpered as they went over a bump, and the timbre of the wheels against the road changed. They were on gravel.

They were headed to the shore.

He tried to pull his arms in front of him, but they were too tightly bound.

He was still struggling to loosen his restraints when the car rumbled to a stop.

This is where I die.

The sounds of footsteps outside, the lock turning – breeze and light flooded the boot. Davey, looking like he'd aged ten years, wrenched Forest out. He didn't seem concerned about Forest having wriggled out of the pillowcase. In fact, he pulled the gag away.

'Help!' shouted Forest. *'Help me!'*

Tall eucalypts rose around them, dense scrub. They were deep in bush.

'No one can hear you,' said Davey quietly. 'It's just you and me.'

'Please, Davey. Please!'

'I don't have a choice,' said Davey, pulling Forest into the thicket. 'Neither of us have a choice.'

Forest made himself heavy, letting his feet drag as Davey hauled him along.

'You're not a murderer! You're not, Davey. Think of Kane! What would he think, knowing his dad killed me?'

Davey screwed his eyes shut, his every step crunching in the undergrowth. Insects buzzed and a rosella's fluting warble rose up somewhere ahead of them. The heat was sticky-close.

Davey pulled Forest inexorably forward.

'Ivy is Blackbeard. Why? It doesn't make sense!' shouted Forest, trying to pull himself free of the big man's grasp. 'I refuse to die just because she said so!'

'You forced her hand,' said Davey.

'But why?' said Forest. '*Why*?'

Davey stopped and threw him to the ground, planting his foot on Forest's chest.

'If I tell you, will you stop struggling?' He looked ghastly pale, nothing like the man in the photos at Ivy's place.

Forest stopped squirming and simply nodded.

Davey sighed.

'Jesse said he was coming back one day,' began Davey. 'Before Jesse left he had been . . . dangerous. Unhinged. Violent. The things he did to his family, to little Forest . . . it kept me up at night.'

Davey was looking off into the bush. Forest tried to turn his head to follow his line of vision, to show some kind of common feeling, mirror him, try and get on his side . . . but no, whatever it was, it was beyond him. Davey kept on.

'Once, he shot Forest full of ice right before a football game, just so he'd perform better. Jesse didn't like to lose, and little Forest losing reflected badly on him. He was six! Shooting up a six-year-old with ice! Forest was awake for days after that. Jesse thought it was funny. After that, he used ice to make the boy do what he wanted. It cooked his head. Cracked him right down the middle. We were all happy to see Jesse leave, but of course we were worried about Alexandra and Forest going with him . . .'

Forest thought of Huck, thought of his pain and suffering. It burned his fear away with white-hot anger. 'And you didn't stop it? You're as bad as him, then! You're *worse!*'

Davey flinched at that. He hauled Forest back to his feet and kept dragging him through the bush, but he kept talking.

'I figured he really would come back one day. I knew I'd have to give the Business back to him – Jesse never liked sharing things. But Mum knew . . . she *knew* Jesse was coming back one day, and worse, he'd lost his mind. He'd told her, you know? He told her the day he killed Alexandra and Forest, just to keep the Business going.

'Well, she was worried that when he returned he might . . . arrange for me to get out of the way. So from that day *she* began spreading the myth of Blackbeard, as a contingency plan, without telling me. She could do it – she knew the Business, knew all my contacts. She has a certain way with people, as you've seen. She began bringing people over to Tassie, starting her crew. She knows what she's doing, she's been helping Dempsey men peddle drugs since before I was born. She had the resources, the knowledge, the . . . grit.' Even now, a proud smile crossed his haggard face. 'She's an incredible woman, my mum.'

'She didn't trust you enough to tell you,' sneered Forest, still scrabbling.

'Yeah. Well. I'll admit, she changed her mind. She liked being the boss. She wanted to do it alone. She didn't trust me enough to just ask me. Or maybe . . . I think she just wanted to prove that she could. It must get boring, being that old, with all the money you could want . . .' He cocked his head. 'I suppose I should thank you. If not for you, I might never have found out.'

'She clearly didn't want you to know! Can't you see she's playing you?' He could smell the ocean now, hear the lapping of waves. The ground was sloping down. He grabbed at a tree, but Davey wrenched him, *hard*, and he was being dragged again.

'You're wrong. The moment we were alone, Mum told me. Everything.' He swiped at his eyes. He took a few breaths to calm himself, then continued. 'I should've trusted her. Should've told her I was alive. But I didn't want to break her heart twice if Blackbeard ended up finding me.'

They came to a steep bank that descended to a rocky beach. Hidden under a spreading willow was a small aluminium boat with an outboard motor on the back.

Davey hauled Forest down the bank and tossed him in. With an ear-splitting scrape of hull against rock, he pushed the boat into the water. His legs splashing through the murky, leaf-covered water, he followed and hopped in.

'I used this boat that first day, when I put the body in Devils Kitchen. I've always had it hidden here in case I ever needed to flee up the coast. Lucky for me that I kept it aside – much easier than rowing.'

He's gonna take me out on the ocean and throw me in, Forest realised with grim certainty. Panic was settling over him again. 'Help! Help!'

Davey heaved on the starter cord a few times and the engine spluttered into life. They set out onto the water.

As they left shore, Forest could see that they were in a small bay lined with sea cliffs so high he had to strain his neck trying to spot the top of them. The boat cut through the rolling sea, land far behind, and with it Forest's last hope of rescue. 'Help! *Help!*'

'Please stop,' said Davey. 'You don't want to spend your last moments like this, begging for help. Take it like a man.'

As they got further out, Davey cranked up the motor, making Forest's hair blow around wildly and the air sting his eyes. Davey steered expertly up and down, cresting blue waves. More panic settled like a suffocating hand across Forest's mouth. And with it came grief.

He thought of the Witch. She'd taken him in when he was scared for his life. She'd given so much for him.

He thought of Huck. In danger. He'd never be able to become the man he was destined to be.

Mackenzie and Ahab. Forest would never get the chance to redeem himself for lying to them.

They rounded the edge of the bay, where waves beat against tall pinnacle rocks. Davey had gone quiet again – he could've been made of stone, and Forest of crumbling sand. Everything faded in and out. Terror . . .

And just like that, it was gone. He imagined himself far away, floating above it all.

Here, at the end of all things, down in the deep. Death.

Without warning, Davey changed course, veering towards the base of the cliffs. But then Forest could see it – a small archway above the rolling water.

Davey slowed the engine and they pottered into the cavern. The sounds of the motor echoed back off the jagged edges of the cave and the plane of the water. He threw a loop of rope over a rock, drew it tight, and then pulled his lifejacket on. He grabbed Forest by the back of his collar and leapt into the water.

Forest struggled under water, wrenched back into his own body. The cold water had woken something in him. Davey wasn't simply going to drown him; whatever he was doing would be much worse.

Davey swam into a smaller tunnel, once again dragging him, gripping rocks to pull himself along. Kelp tickled Forest's legs and he screamed.

'Me and Mackerel used to come here,' said Davey conversationally. 'At high tide, this place is submerged. There's heaps of these little mermaid grottos. We figured it's where the sirens used to live.'

Light was fading the deeper they went. Water occasionally filled the entire space, pushing his head against the ceiling and covering Forest's mouth and nose. Davey didn't panic – whenever the waves filled the cave, he took a breath and let the space fill, then when it pulled back he'd continue swimming on as normal. Forest had to do the same the further along they went, the cave growing narrower and narrower, kelp on all sides, squeezing and constricting. It was now completely dark ahead, but from the sounds of the water, they had emerged into a larger space.

'Jesse found this place originally. As a kid I thought he was reckless. Now, I think he was suicidal.' Forest could see nothing anymore, and Davey's seemingly disembodied voice echoed all around him. 'He was the first to swim in here. Scuba gear, of course. I came along a few times after that. Mackerel, once. Jesse could always get me to do things I didn't want to. Mackerel thought he had it rough? Getting picked on by his brothers? At least nothing Jesse did to him was as dangerous as what he'd get *me* to do.'

He slowed and fiddled with Forest's bonds, freeing his arms.

'If you swim straight ahead you'll come to a little gravelly island in the middle of the cave. When the tide comes in, it'll fill up with water. There's worse places to die. When the wind hits this place right, it sounds just like music. That's why we called it the Siren's Cave. If I were you, I'd fill my pockets with stones, let them pull me to the bottom, and then take the biggest gulp of water you can. You'll panic for a minute or so, and then you'll be dead.'

'No. No! *No!*'

Davey shoved him forward. 'Goodbye, nameless boy. For what it's worth, I'm sorry it had to end this way.'

'Davey! *Please, Davey!*'

But Davey was gone.

Forest huddled in the middle of the gravel cave. He could hear glubbing and splashing all around him. This would be his tomb. Just like Alexandra and little Huck. He was going to drown.

Was there a way out? No, he'd already felt the tide rising. He couldn't get back through that tunnel.

And he was tired. So, so tired. Tired of running. Tired of pretending. Tired of the madness. Everything he'd set out to do had blown up in his face. He made everything worse for everyone he'd ever met. It would've been better if he *was* swallowed up by the ocean. Forgotten.

Nameless.

Now, knowing he was about to drown. Knowing there was nothing else he could do to stop it . . . he let go.

Instantly there came the sound of settling gravel. Then he heard familiar breathing beside him. With the click of a lighter, a little flame appeared. It cast no light or shadow, save to reveal his face, but it was fuzzy. Weird. In and out of sight.

He lit his cigarette and puffed a cloud into the damp air.

'Huck?' said Forest.

'No more pretending,' said Huck. 'We go to our deaths as men.'

Forest shook uncontrollably. His teeth were clenched so hard they hurt.

'How are you here?' said Forest.

By the light of the cigarette tip, Huck turned on him. 'You're about to die the same way I did. I'm here to help you. I don't blame you. It was good you listened to your mum. It was good that you left me.'

A memory echoed around the cave. Alexandra's voice. 'Go, Forest!' She was panicked, but her voice was calm. Her diving torch lit up the cave. Little Huck whimpered in the corner, eyes wide and unseeing, terrified out of his wits. 'You can't help him. Get out of here!' She'd handed him the slate, brushed his cheek. 'You'll be fine. I love you. Don't let your dad find you! Just go!'

'I'm sorry!' said Forest. That memory, suppressed for so long, surged through him like a tidal wave, running through muscle and vein until his bones felt loose. 'I let you to die! I'm *so* sorry!'

'It's okay, Forest. I'm not here. I'm not even real. I never was.' He gripped Forest's arm. 'But don't worry. I'll stay with you. We'll go under together.'

Somewhere at the edge of his awareness, he could hear a droning.

He listened. It grew louder.

The Black Wind.

And, with it, the cave sang, the acoustics like a choir of eerie voices.

Tears rolled down Forest's cheeks. He was alone in here. And he was about to die. Drowned, in a cave. Just like his father had wanted.

'No, shhh, none of that,' came Huck's voice. The flame from his lighter was gone. 'We're together until the end.'

The singing grew louder. Little waves lapped at his feet, rolling the rounded stones back and forth.

He pressed the scar on his forearm. An oath he'd made to himself. The Witch's face loomed in his mind. She gave him safety, sedatives. 'Pretend it never happened,' she advised him. 'Pretend it never happened. It's better that way.'

Pretend it never happened.

No. He couldn't. Not anymore.

This *was* real. This *was* happening.

And as the waters rose, Forest Dempsey curled into a ball and cried for his mother.

CHAPTER 54

MACKENZIE

Mackenzie stood at the prow of the *Margot's Revenge*, watching the morning sun rise out of one eye, the other puffed closed from the beating he'd received. The sky was a bright red. In the distance he could see the rooftops of Shacktown.

Mackenzie had spent the night locked in a storeroom on board, nothing but a mattress on the floor and a thin blanket, nursing his bruised ribs. His nose had been broken, he'd lost a tooth, and his bung knee was worse than ever before. Tranquil hadn't been kind to him.

All around him was the activity of a legitimate, working crayfish boat. It didn't have the same simplicity as abalone, but he grasped at once that the crayfish pots would still be effective drug-smuggling vessels. Rough jokes, the glint of gold chains, men and women Mack hadn't seen before, with the wild dark edge of sunken eyes and worry lines, evidence of methamphetamine abuse.

There was a joviality to it all. News had spread that Davey Dempsey was still alive and would be joining the crew. Their take-over of Shacktown was nearly complete.

He needed to get off this boat and warn Ahab and the fake Forest – he could see the marina from here. If Ivy really was Blackbeard, both of them were in danger.

Who was he kidding? If Ivy was Blackbeard, both of them were probably dead by now.

Mackenzie gripped the rail, digging his nails in, scratching at the metal. His limbs felt tightly strung, like the ropes of a taut sail – any tighter and they might break. He needed his painkillers. He needed his opiates. He needed to get off this boat . . .

'You've got the look about you,' said Tranquil, stepping up beside him. 'You're gonna try to escape.'

Mackenzie kept silent. All his bruises felt sore anew next to the man who'd inflicted them.

'It's okay. I would too.' Tranquil spoke low. 'Blackbeard has some *bad* things planned for you. Says she's finally gonna make a man out of you.'

That comment made Mackenzie's blood fizz with anger. That woman . . . he would never forgive her. He'd hate her until his dying day.

'But hey, I'm feeling generous.' Tranquil spun to lean against the railing, arms nonchalantly folded behind his neck. 'I just don't trust Blackbeard to not change her mind about you. She's big on "family is family". I'm already her second-in-command – I don't need you coming in and fucking that up for me. Davey will be bad enough.' He gestured back to shore. 'You think you can swim that far?'

'You'd help me?' He said the words before he realised it must be a trick.

'I'd help *myself*,' corrected Tranquil. 'You know how it is. I mean, the best outcome for me is you drown on the way. But Blackbeard wouldn't like me killing you, so the only other option is you conveniently escape, and run far, far away and never come back. Like the coward we all know you are . . .' He grinned, his eyes intense.

'Is there scuba gear?' said Mackenzie.

'Yeah. At the back.' He gestured to the stern of the ship. 'Want me to create a distraction for you?'

Before Mackenzie could answer, a low hum echoed across the deck.

Tranquil sprang into action, genuinely alarmed. 'Black Wind incoming!' he shouted, sending the boat into a scurry of activity.

Mackenzie felt a tremor run through him.

'Couldn't ask for a better distraction than that,' said Tranquil. 'Let's go, mate.'

Tranquil dragged him to the rear of the boat, where a bolted-in stand offered oxygen tanks, vest, fins. No wetsuits, though.

'No suit, but you'll be okay,' said Tranquil. 'It's not that far.'

Mackenzie knew that hypothermia could kill you just as well as drowning. But he hadn't come this far to give up now.

Mackenzie pulled on fins and a mask, while Tranquil attached an oxygen tank and BC to a diving vest, then helped Mack slip into it. He stepped up to the edge, unclipping the cable that guarded the gap in the rails over the hull-side ladder. Below, the crests of the waves were sharper than before, textured with weird ripples. He swallowed his fear, remembering the last time he'd swum in the Black Wind.

'Jump now,' said Tranquil. 'While no one is looking. Just step off.'

Mackenzie prepared to jump, but then something stopped him. There had been an undertone in Tranquil's voice – the barest hint of humour. Mackenzie had grown up attuned to people taking the piss out of him. Years of being bullied and teased by his family meant that knowing when someone was making fun of him had become a survival instinct.

'Go, Mack!' said Tranquil, urging him over the edge. 'I can't protect you if someone else sees you!'

Trusting his gut, Mackenzie quickly checked every part of his equipment that he could see. When he got to the pressure gauge on his oxygen tank, he took a step back.

The tank was empty.

'Ah, you fucking idiot,' said Tranquil, seeing what he'd done.

He shoved Mackenzie from behind, but Mackenzie was ready for him. He grabbed the railing and slammed his body backwards, knocking Tranquil on his arse.

A dazed Tranquil tried to pull himself to his feet, swearing, holding a nose blooded by the oxygen tank. 'Help! He's trying to get away!'

Mackenzie scrambled to grab another tank from the rack, praying that it was full. There was no time to attach it.

He threw his arms around it and leapt out into the ocean.

The moment he hit the water he felt the weight of all that gear dragging him down. Cold water rushed over his skin and he gasped for breath. No one would be foolish enough to follow him into this water, but he'd need to be swift anyway – the cold would overwhelm him before long.

He tried to inflate his BC, forgetting the current tank was empty, and endured a brief moment of panic when nothing happened.

He forced himself to calm down, feeling his confidence surging back with the rolling waves. *Remember, the water is where you're at home. You're safe here.*

Calm returning to him, he expertly detached the empty tank from his BC, then hooked up the tank he'd grabbed before it sunk under the surface. The waves had pushed him away from the boat, threatening to pull him under, but Mackenzie was strong, the cold water easing his aching body as he kicked his fins, favouring his sore knee.

The new tank was attached, the BC settled across his shoulders, the regulator was in his mouth, and he was descending, down to where the Black Wind's dangerous currents weren't as strong.

Breathe in, bubbles out.

Before long, an all too familiar hum filled his ears. He could see the surface rocking with it, and he felt himself pushed to the side by weird currents.

Breathe in, bubbles out.

He kicked towards shore, his fins biting into the water. He watched the silt moving in the current, seeking the places that looked gentler, like steering a boat through rough water.

Breathe in, bubbles out.

The drone resonated through the water. It was all around him, consuming everything, the whole ocean trembling in anticipation of what would come next.

CHAPTER 55

AHAB

Constable Linda had just dropped Ahab off at Ivy's house, her lights flashing and siren still sounding. He still had blood on him. No time to wash. No time for anything but to find Ivy. She'd hired Frankie. Ivy knew Blackbeard better than anyone – he had to find out what she knew.

He walked through the front gate, fringed blue butterflies in the flowers of the daisy bush along the path, the heady scent of ocean and breeze. Safe Harbour. The end of an era.

Linda hadn't noticed anything different about Ahab. She was devastated by Kane's murder, and carried along by the frantic search for De Corrado. She'd brought Ahab here as a personal favour, but she wanted him out of the car. 'I'll go to Shelby's place and . . . break the news.' She'd looked like she was in shock herself. 'I'll wait there for you to arrive – she'll want someone she trusts there.'

During the last hour – had it really been that long? – the police had listened to the hikers' testimonies, but they'd grasped right away that Ahab was not the aggressor. Vance was being taken to the station in the back of another squad car at this very moment, but Ahab knew the man wouldn't talk. He was scared enough of Blackbeard as it was.

After they'd taken Vance in, the police had taken photographs of Ahab and evidence swabs from his clothes and fingernails, as well as impounding his ute. But in the end they'd believed him when he said he needed to be with the grieving family – news of Kane's death would soon spread like wildfire. For Ahab, there would be more police interviews to come, official statements, a criminal trial . . . a funeral.

But for now, he had to talk to Ivy.

He pounded on the white timber door, dried blood on his knuckles. A kookaburra laughed in the gumtree. The Black Wind bellowed.

Most of the Shacktown police force were out scouring the town for De Corrado and the fake Forest, and as they'd driven up to Safe Harbour Linda had let him listen in on the police radio. The pair hadn't been found at Frankie's house – nor had Frankie – but there were signs of a struggle.

He'd warned them during the preliminary interview at the boulder field that he suspected Frankie was a dangerous drug baron who was staking out a claim on Shacktown. Linda had made a sceptical face, and he'd heard the doubt in her colleagues' voices, but he didn't care. He'd told them the truth; it wouldn't take much investigating to prove him correct. He wondered how long it would be before the link to the Dempseys was fully investigated? No matter how this day ended, the Dempsey dynasty was at an end.

He knocked on the door again. 'Ivy! It's Ahab, let me in!'

Still no answer.

He walked around the house, to the front door. The path from the beach, white gravel lined with life rings.

At least he hadn't broken his promise to his mother. He hadn't betrayed his family. He'd simply pointed the police in the direction of Frankie. But his priority *was* getting back to Ivy and Davey – Frankie must have been a master manipulator to get herself onto Ivy's payroll.

That's when he spotted Mackenzie, dripping wet, staggering up the stairs from the beach below.

'Mack?' said Ahab.

Mackenzie's face was mottled with bruises. His shirt and trousers were ripped and bloodstained. But, though he was limping worse than Ahab had seen before, he walked like he owned every step he took. And he still wore his gold chain.

'What happened?' said Ahab.

'Ivy happened.'

He sounded calm. No, he sounded furious. No . . . he sounded ready for murder.

'Ivy? What . . .?'

'Yes,' said Mackenzie softly. 'Ivy.'

With those two simple words, everything fell into place in Ahab's mind.

Ahab had said it himself. *That's the thing about Dempseys. We lie.*

Vance's voice: *She'll kill me!* Why'd he been so scared?

Because he'd just killed Ivy Dempsey's grandson.

How had he been so blind? Why hadn't he seen it sooner?

'Ivy is Blackbeard,' said Ahab.

'Yeah,' said Mackenzie. He wiped his nose, stopping to take a breath. 'We have to stop her. Whatever it takes.' He spoke softly, but there was no weakness in his words. That man who'd shown up on Ahab's boat, panicked and confused, was gone. In his place was someone else. Beaten, bruised and hurting, yes . . . but someone resolute.

Ahab had sent the police after Frankie. He needed to call them back. 'We should call the police,' said Ahab.

Before they could do anything, the front door swung open. Ivy stood there, wearing an immaculate apron, a knife in her hand.

'Hello, dears.' She looked the picture of control. 'Why don't you come inside.'

It wasn't a question.

'We need to go, Mack,' said Ahab, backing away from Ivy. 'We have to tell the police.'

'If you want Detective De Corrado to make it to the end of the day, you'd best come inside, dear,' said Ivy. 'Both of you. C'mon now, and don't get blood on anything.'

De Corrado? 'What have you done with her?' said Ahab.

Now Mackenzie approached her, with a heavy limp and a dark expression. With his eye swollen shut, he made a grim picture. 'Hello, Ivy.'

'Wait, Mack!' said Ahab, following behind. 'We can't just walk into her house —'

'Come in. Take a seat. Lunch is nearly ready.'

Mackenzie walked in first. Ahab followed behind, searching for a weapon.

There, in the wide open living area of Ivy's house, was the massive driftwood table, with two people already sitting there.

Bound by zip ties to a dining chair was Detective De Corrado. Her face was pale, her eyes bloodshot, and fear and fury were clear on her face. She caught Ahab's eyes.

'The whole family is here,' she croaked. 'Beautiful.'

'Yes, just a happy little family, all together at last.' Ivy moved to stand behind her, holding the knife to her exposed throat. 'Let's all sit down, shall we?'

Beside De Corrado sat Davey, kneading his temples. There were deep lines beneath his eyes, and he kept pulling at his chapped lips. Was he being held against his will too?

'Have you heard the news, Davey?' said Ahab.

Davey winced at the sound of his voice. He didn't look up. 'What news?' he mumbled.

'Sit *down*,' spat Ivy.

Mack sat across from Davey. He didn't take his eyes off Ivy.

Ahab sat, too, right beside De Corrado, steadying himself against the table as he pulled the chair out. He trusted Ivy would take a seat as well. That would even the playing field – he was more nimble than her, and once she sat, he could leap across the table to grab her knife.

Or . . . the dining table, in a macabre tableau, was set for family lunch, with silverware and a flower arrangement and glasses of red wine. A roast chicken sat in the centre. Loaves of bread, a bowl of butter, steaming vegetables . . . and sharp cutlery. He managed to slip a knife into his hand as he steadied himself on the table.

'Now, dears, I'm so pleased you were able to make it to my victory feast,' said Ivy to the group, as she took her place at the head of the setting. She pulled a shotgun out from under the table, ruining Ahab's plans, and let it rest on the table. 'Let's eat, as a family, shall we? Plus guest.' She set the carving knife down within easy reach and raised a wineglass in toast to De Corrado, her other hand on the shotgun.

'Don't worry,' said Ahab evenly to the detective. 'It's going to be okay.' Under the table, he'd already begun sawing at the zip ties that bound her arms.

'Yeah, I can see that, everything's *clearly* under control, isn't it?' De Corrado said, but she gave nothing away as he went to work.

'Where's Shelby?' said Mackenzie.

'She should be back at Homeward by now,' said Ivy. 'I think it's best we leave her out of this unpleasantness. Don't you? Can't have our naïve little cook getting her values all mixed up.' She tapped her fingers on the shotgun. 'Our plans are on the edge of a knife right now. You bungling your way in here doesn't help us.'

Ahab snuck a glance at Davey. Whatever was going on here, it seemed he was part of her 'us'. Typical. When it came down to it, the man was weak at heart.

Ivy gestured at De Corrado with her wineglass again, then took a sip. 'I *had* planned to kill the detective. But now I figure we might need a hostage to use as leverage, especially if we can't track down the real Forest Dempsey.'

'You can't hope to get away with this, Ivy,' said Ahab. His mind hummed as he thought through his options. When should he tell them about Kane? That would upset them enough that they'd lose focus, surely?

'No. You're right. We'll need to leave Shacktown. But I have resources. I'm the Dread Pirate Blackbeard, remember? Ask my dimwit son – he's just had a taste of what my empire has to offer.'

Mackenzie stretched his jaw experimentally and put a hand to the bruising on his face.

'How *did* you get off *Margot's Revenge?*' she asked him. 'Which of my crew do I need to . . . release from their service? I might even have you do the honours —'

'Speaking of your crew . . .' said Ahab. 'Kane is dead.'

All eyes snapped to him.

'Your man Vance killed him,' finished Ahab, staring straight at Ivy.

'You're lying,' she said instantly.

'What the fuck are you playing, Ahab?' said Davey, some fire returning to his eyes. 'That's a sick thing to say.'

'You gave your man instructions to kill the real Forest if he found him, right? Well, he got it wrong. Kane was with me. Your own grandson.' He wiped at the tears rolling down his cheeks. He let them see the dried blood on his hand, while the other hand still furiously sawed at De Corrado's ties. '*This* is what your empire has to show for it! This is what —'

'No,' croaked Davey. 'No! *No!*' He stood up. He looked between Ahab and Ivy. 'He's lying. *He's lying.*' His eyes had gone so wide Ahab could see the whites all the way around. 'If he's not lying, I swear I'll . . .'

'He *is* lying,' confirmed Ivy, but her face had lost all colour. 'Vance is not an idiot. He wouldn't . . .'

'I need to know. I need to go find him!' shouted Davey.

'You can't be seen,' said Ivy. 'Sit back down, dear.' She put a shaking hand to her forehead. 'Ahab, I don't know what game you're playing, but —'

While he looked as shocked as the rest of them, Mackenzie was alert to the opportunity. He lunged across the table and grabbed the shotgun. In an instant, he was levelling it at Ivy with steady hands.

Everyone went still.

'You killed Kane. This is all your fault,' said Mackenzie. 'What have you done with our boy? Where's *our* Forest?'

Davey leapt up and moved towards the door, but Mackenzie turned the gun on him. 'Stop or I'll blow your head off, Davey.'

'I have to go to Shelby,' Davey moaned. 'Please . . . *please*, bro.'

'You're not going anywhere,' said Mackenzie. 'Where's our boy?'

'My son . . . I have to see my son . . .'

Ivy licked her lips and gave a piercing whistle.

Two men appeared from the bedrooms at the back of the house. They had rifles, and they aimed them at Mackenzie.

Mackenzie's arms didn't move an inch. 'I hear a gunshot and he dies.' He kept his shotgun trained firmly on Davey. Something really had changed in him – he looked like a different person. 'Don't test me.'

Ahab stopped cutting at De Corrado's bonds, and she went still too. He held the knife aside – if they started shooting, he'd have to throw her to the ground with him and try to find cover under the table.

'What should we do, Blackbeard?' asked one of the men, slowly, as though Mackenzie were a horse that might be spooked easily.

'Don't worry. He won't shoot anyone,' said Ivy. Her voice had lost its playfulness, but not its authority. 'He's never killed anyone. He wouldn't have the balls to shoot his own brother.'

Mackenzie shifted his grip on the shotgun, but the barrel never swayed. His eyes remained level. 'Davey, she's evil. *She* did all of this to us.'

'Kane can't be dead . . .' said Davey. 'I need to get to Shelby.'

'Go,' said Ivy to one of the armed men. 'Find out if what Ahab says is true and report back. If my grandson has been killed, bring the man responsible to me. By any means. I'll deal with him myself.'

The man didn't hesitate, dashing out of the room, but his mate stayed behind, his gun still on Mackenzie.

Ahab felt like the room was an overfull balloon – about to pop – when the front door slammed open.

Light footsteps pattered down the corridor, and then there she was. Shelby Dempsey.

Her chest heaving, her eyes wild, she took in the whole scene. Mackenzie with the shotgun on Davey, Ivy's henchman with his own gun, Ivy with a knife, Davey halfway to the door, De Corrado bound.

Shelby simply fell into an empty seat at the table.

She sought out Ahab's eyes. 'Was he in pain, at the end?'

So Linda had told her . . . at least Shelby had known to leave her out of whatever came next.

'It happened in an instant,' said Ahab. 'He wouldn't have felt a thing.'

Davey howled, but Ivy snapped, '*Shut up, Davey.*' Tears had pooled in her own eyes. 'Just . . . just shut up!'

Under the table, he finally cut through one of the ties binding De Corrado's arms. He passed her the knife and she quietly began sawing at the other tie. Ahab felt sweat pouring down his sides – if they saw what she was doing, Ivy wouldn't hesitate to kill her.

'Pass me the butter, please,' Shelby said to Mackenzie, as she took a bun from the centre plate. What was she doing, playing along with Ivy's game?

Mackenzie didn't move. His eyes were firmly fixed on the other man's gun.

'Mack! Sit *down*.' Shelby slammed the table with her fist.

'You too,' said Ivy to her henchman.

Slowly, Mackenzie eased into a chair beside Shelby, still holding the shotgun. His eyes were flicking around the room now – an edge of uncertainty. Ahab was praying the way he was holding himself now wouldn't translate into him doing something rash.

The henchman sat down beside De Corrado. He put the gun flat on the table, but left his hand resting on top of it.

'Pass me the shotgun, Mack,' said Shelby.

Mackenzie hesitated.

'Mack . . .' said Ahab. 'Don't.'

'Relax, Ahab,' said Shelby. Though her face was a mask of anguish, her voice was collected.

Mackenzie handed the shotgun over.

'There we go. Calmly now,' said Shelby. 'Thank you, Mackenzie. Now please pass me the butter.'

Davey folded his arms across the table, lowered his head into them, and began to cry in heaving sobs.

Mackenzie looked as puzzled as anyone, but he did as Shelby asked and handed her the butter.

She put the shotgun on the table in front of her and began to spread the butter on her bun. The smell of melting butter was warm and inviting.

'Who killed my son, Ahab?' Her voice was light, conversational, but her hands were shaking so much she had to put the knife down.

'One of Blackbeard's men,' said Ahab. 'Vance.'

'And *who* is Blackbeard?' said Shelby. 'Do we know now, at least?'

'Yes,' said Ahab.

Ivy observed Shelby closely. 'I . . . I will make sure that man is executed. I'll have him tortured to death. I'll do whatever it takes.'

'So you *are* Blackbeard?' said Shelby, not sounding all that surprised. She must have suspected as much. The detective tied up at Ivy's dining table was probably a good indicator.

'Yes,' said Ivy. 'I'm the Dread Pirate Blackbeard.'

'For how long?' said Shelby.

Ivy shrugged casually. 'I started the rumour seven years ago.'

'So, do you traffic children? Do you kill people?' said Shelby.

'No. Just part of a brand.'

'A brand that killed my son.'

'I can explain everything, my dear,' said Ivy.

'I doubt it.'

'Jesse was always going to come back one day. And he's a maniac,' said Ivy frankly. 'When he came back, I expected he'd kill both Davey and me. Probably you, too.'

Shelby said nothing.

'But Jesse was always paranoid. I figured if I created a villain scary enough, I could keep him at bay. Until the fake Forest ruined *everything*.' The last words were a bite.

'And where is he? The fake Forest?' said Shelby.

Ivy opened her mouth – to spin some lie, Ahab thought – but Davey spoke first: 'I left him to die in the Siren's Cave.' He said it without lifting his head, his voice hollow.

Mackenzie stiffened. For the first time, Ahab sensed fear in him. 'How long ago?'

'About an hour . . .'

Ahab could see Mackenzie's mind working. 'When's high tide?'

'Black Wind will fill any cave up long before the tide will,' said Ahab. He dug his fingers into the arms of his chair.

'If he hasn't drowned himself already . . .' said Davey pathetically.

Shelby looked at Davey as though she'd never seen him before. 'You *murdered* the boy?'

Ivy raised her hand, trying to placate her daughter-in-law. 'I know you never intended to marry into this kind of family, but Davey has a job to do. Everything, all of this, it's been about protecting you! Keeping everything —'

In one movement, Shelby swung the shotgun towards Ivy and squeezed the trigger.

The sound filled the entire world, and everything that followed was still and empty.

Ivy was blown backwards in her chair, then fell to the ground.

Three times Ahab had heard it recently. Three deaths. Chips, Kane, and now Ivy . . .

The end of an era . . .

At the same moment, De Corrado tore free of the last zip tie and tackled the henchman to the ground before he could reach for his gun. The shotgun blast still pressing on his eardrums, Ahab grabbed the man's firearm from the table.

Mackenzie scrambled around the table as fast as his bad leg would allow and helped De Corrado subdue the man.

Davey was looking at Shelby with abject horror.

Shelby was taking deep, panting breaths. 'What are we waiting for?' she huffed. 'The boy is going to drown in that cave.'

'You shot her,' said Davey. 'You just —'

'*She killed our son! Go save that boy!*'

'Shelby . . .' He looked at the man De Corrado was subduing. 'He saw you shoot Blackbeard . . .'

Ahab read his thoughts. 'No, Davey. No more killing. We're not hurting him.'

'You knew all along, Ahab!' said De Corrado. 'Whatever the hell's going on, you *knew*!'

'Mum . . .' Davey's shaking hands raked his scalp in agony, eyes rolling around the room. 'If we don't kill this man, even from prison, he'll tell the crew Shelby killed their Blackbeard. We'll *all* be dead.'

'As far as I see it . . .' said Shelby, her composure shot. 'I killed Blackbeard . . . so . . . I've taken the mantle. I'm the next Blackbeard.'

'No,' said Mackenzie, the fear in his voice startling Ahab. 'No, Shelby!'

Mackenzie climbed off the henchman, whom De Corrado had secured with strips of torn tablecloth. He made to move towards Shelby, but was stopped in his tracks when he saw the spreading pool of blood around Ivy. Ahab saw the light in his eyes change, as he began to truly grasp what had happened.

'Save the boy, Mack,' said Shelby. She held the shotgun loosely at her side. 'Go save the boy. Please.'

'Mackenzie?' said Ahab, trying to shake him out of his thoughts. 'We might still have a chance. Can you take us to the cave?'

'Y-yeah,' said Mackenzie. He tore his eyes away from Ivy. 'R-right, yeah. It's down by Cape Pillar.'

Shelby pushed the shotgun into Davey's hands and approached Ivy's body, kneeling down to rummage in her pockets.

'What are you *doing*?' said De Corrado. 'This is a crime scene. No one's leaving! No one touch anything!'

'Something Mack taught me. Two phones, you're a business-man. Three phones, you're a drug dealer.' She pulled the phones out of Ivy's pockets. She lifted Ivy's dead finger to the sensor and unlocked it. 'Meet me at the lab when you're finished,' said Shelby.

Everything was spinning out of Ahab's control, but two things pressed on his mind: save Forest, and get De Corrado to safety. 'C'mon, De Corrado, let's go find Forest.'

'I'm afraid the detective will need to stay here with us,' said Shelby. 'If you tell the police . . . please don't tell the police.' She wiped at her cheeks, leaving a red smear of Ivy's blood. She looked perfectly calm.

'I'm not leaving her here like this,' said Ahab.

'It's fine, Ahab,' said De Corrado. 'I'll be fine. *Go*. Save the boy.'

'We don't have time for this,' said Mackenzie, grabbing Ahab's arm. 'We need to *move*.'

CHAPTER 56

MACKENZIE

Mackenzie and Ahab ripped through bushland hiking trails on dirt bikes, the tyres gouging through the rain-muddied soil of the national park. Every bump jolted through Mackenzie's aching ribs. At least the swelling in his eye had gone down, and he could see out of both.

Ned had brought his bikes down to the marina, where they'd frantically pulled together three sets of scuba gear from the *Ambergris*. They had to save the boy, but there was no way they were getting to Siren's Cave by sea – not with the Black Wind in.

Instead, they were going overland, to the top of Cape Pillar. Once they got there they'd have to make their way down to a nearby beach via an abandoned 'path' climbers had once hammered out of the cliff face, back in the sixties.

If they survived that, they'd have to dive to the cave in the middle of a Black Wind – and, unlike the relative shelter of Devils Kitchen, this time they'd more or less be out in open water.

He could hardly focus on what lay ahead – Davey was trying to kill a *child*. How had it come to this? Or had Davey always been like this and he'd just never seen it?

Ivy is dead.

Kane is dead.

Davey is trying to drown our little imposter.

As they neared the top of the cliffs, the Black Wind grew stronger, buffeting them and making the speeding bikes wobble dangerously. When the bush finally thinned out and they reached the brink of the cliff at Cape Pillar, it turned ferocious: just as strong as it would be at sea. The sky was menacing, rain pounded down, and the waves below roared with anger.

'We have to climb down that?' shouted Ahab above the tempest. 'We'll break our necks!'

The rocky path switchbacked down the cliff, barely a foot wide, leading to a tiny gravelly beach battered by the ocean. The only safety on the way down was rusted metal poles that might once have supported a chain-link fence.

'First rule of scuba diving,' said Mackenzie with a rueful smile. 'Just breathe!'

Ahab wiped the freezing rain from his eyes. 'Then let's go!'

Mackenzie went first, taking both his gear and Forest's. He gripped rocky edges, smoothed and eroded by years of exposure, willing his limping feet to find purchase, trying to keep the rain from his eyes as he took each step after gruelling step. He glanced back to be sure Ahab was still following. He'd never realised how old Ahab looked, but he saw it now, with the wind and rain lashing the man's face.

Distracted, his foot slipped on the rain-slick rock, and for a horrifying instant he felt himself hanging out over the edge, before he pulled himself back to the cliff face using one of the rusted poles.

Down, down, down they went, each step as terrifying as the last. The weight of the gear pulled at Mackenzie's arms, his sides stiff and sore from the beating Tranquil had given him on *Margot's Revenge*. His emotions rolled and pinwheeled, the last of the Golden Sunshine leaving his system. Ivy's violent death at Shelby's hands, the fact that Kane had been caught up in the dangers of the drug game . . .

Don't think about it. Save the fake Forest. One thing at a time.

Breathe in, breathe out.

They sat on a narrow outcrop above the gravel beach and got ready. Mackenzie pulled on his BC, mask, headtorch. They couldn't have brought wetsuits too, it would've been far too heavy – they'd just have to make it work without them. They'd brought a length of diving rope and he used that to tie Forest's gear to his front, trying to balance out the weight of his own gear on his back.

Mackenzie eyed the ocean, whipped into crosshatch waves by the Black Wind. It was worse than it had been that day in Devils Kitchen, filling him with dread. The water rolled up over the beach. It would suck the feet from under them if they weren't careful.

Ahab gripped Mackenzie to help him balance while he pulled on his fins. Then Mackenzie returned the favour.

When they were ready, the two men grasped hands.

'Black Wind at morning, sailors take warning,' said Ahab.

They jumped into the hungry ocean.

Instant chaos. The pull of the water, the agony of crushing pressure and howling waves. Freezing cold, salty, loud. Mackenzie was flipped upside down, his side bashing into rocks, but he kicked and kicked and kicked, deeper and deeper, releasing buoyancy . . .

Breathe in, bubbles out.

Finally he reached a depth where the current wasn't pulling him in the wrong direction, but the water was darkly twilit. Mackenzie switched his headtorch on and shone it around. Kelp and sand and silt swirled around him.

Close by, an answering beam. Ahab's figure loomed out of the muck.

Mackenzie felt a surge of unease – how could the current be so strong? What hope did they have?

Ahab swam closer, making the *okay?* gesture.

Mackenzie responded in kind.

He turned and kicked, sweeping the base of the cliff with his torch. He looked for places where the patterns in the silt suggested calmer water, at the same time scanning for the entrance to Siren's Cave.

He found it before long. A maw of darkness in the wall of the cliff: the crevasse that led to the cave. He pointed it out to Ahab, and the two of them swam in, staying low, using the kelp to pull themselves forward.

The torchlight leading the way, they kicked and steered their way into the tunnel, fighting the surges that tried to flush them back out into open water. It was like being in a stone oesophagus – the current was breathing, and the kelp moved with each inhale and exhale.

When the water was being sucked out, Mackenzie had to kick like mad just to stay in place, and then when it rushed back in he was thrown forward dangerously fast. Sometimes Ahab slammed into him, caught up in the current and out of control.

The tunnel was smaller than he remembered, but luckily the kelp made it slippery and soft. Otherwise they'd have been torn to shreds by the rocks.

Mackenzie's chest felt like it was going to burst, and his legs were leaden. He wasn't sure how he was going to make it through this tunnel if this went on much longer . . . And if the current was this fierce going *into* the tunnel, how could they possibly push against it on the way back out?

Finally he shot out into a peaceful bubble of water. His fins met rocks below him and he was able to stand up, chest-deep in water, his headtorch lighting the way.

The cave was cramped and arched, carved by centuries of high tides. Geologically, this was the beginning of what would one day become another Devils Kitchen. But for now it was a round cavern with a swirl of gravel rising in the middle of it, volcano-like. On that small rise sat a thin, shivering boy, arm raised against the blinding torchlight.

All through the space, the drone echoed and overlapped, sounding eerily like singing.

Mackenzie spat out his regulator. 'It's okay, Forest! We're here!'

'M-Mack?' Forest pulled himself to his feet. 'Is it . . . Are you . . . really here?'

'Mack, look at the water,' came Ahab's harsh croak. His teeth were chattering from the cold, but there was no doubting the urgency in his voice.

Mackenzie saw what had distressed him. The water around them was beginning to swirl. It was still slow, but it wouldn't take long before the filling cavern became a whirlpool.

Mackenzie, desperate to get the scuba gear on Forest, stumbled up the hill towards him. The boy threw himself into Mackenzie's arms.

Ahab staggered up beside them, taking the spare scuba gear off Mack. 'There's a good lad. You're doing great,' he said to Forest. 'We've got to get this gear on you, but you're gonna be fine.'

The singing-drone came to a crescendo, and a giant wave exploded out of the tunnel, completely submerging all three of them. Mackenzie clung to the others, rooting himself in the gravel with his fins.

It seemed like hours but could only have been seconds – finally, the water receded. All three of them gasped for breath.

'Mack! The gear!' coughed Ahab.

Mackenzie saw that his hands were empty.

All the spare scuba equipment was gone. Washed into the dark water of the cavern.

'We have to find it!' said Mackenzie.

Ahab turned once on the spot, then looked Mackenzie in the eyes. 'We don't have time.'

'He's not getting out without it!'

The singing-drone grew louder again, but this time they were ready for the surging water, bracing against each other until it passed.

'We're going to die here,' spluttered Forest.

'Not all of us,' said Ahab. He began unstrapping his BC. 'You and Mackenzie are the ones with the future.'

'No,' said Mackenzie.

'Yes, son!' said Ahab. 'Get yourself ready, before another wave comes.'

'No!' shouted Mackenzie. 'We're not leaving you!'

'Yes,' said Ahab. 'You are.'

He strapped the BC across Forest's back.

Mackenzie tried to argue, but Ahab raised his voice. '*Enough, Mackenzie.*' He grabbed Forest by the collar and pulled his face close. 'Forest, listen to me. You'll need to kick . . . *really* kick. Like your life depends on it.'

'I have something to tell you, Ahab. It's important!' said Forest.

'There's no time,' said Ahab roughly. 'Don't argue with me.'

The singing-drone was louder than ever – a huge wave was forcing itself up the tunnel. Ahab and Mackenzie gripped each other's arms, keeping Forest in between them. When the wave came, it came with such force it ripped Ahab's headtorch from his head, swirling it away into the water.

When the water levelled out, Ahab yanked his fins off and helped Forest into them. They were too big, but he pulled the straps as tight as they could go. That was the last of his gear.

'Well,' said Ahab, a sorrowful smile on his face. 'I suppose this is goodbye.' Even the drone had dimmed, as though honouring their farewell.

This couldn't be happening.

I can't let Ahab die in here!

Mackenzie unclasped his gold chain – it still hung around his neck – and handed it to Ahab. 'Take this!'

Ahab grabbed the chain, exasperated. 'Mackenzie . . .'

But Mackenzie didn't let go of his end of the chain. 'You said I was a man! You said when I brought this chain back from the bottom of the sea, I was a man! You were *both* there when that happened!'

'Mackenzie, this really isn't the time —'

'This is *exactly* the time!' roared Mackenzie. He clasped the chain around Ahab's neck. 'I'm not gonna let this cave, my brother, my mum, the whole damn ocean, take anything from me ever again! It doesn't matter if you don't have a mask. You don't need one. You just follow me – I'll get us out of here.' He yanked at his spare regulator, also attached to his oxygen tank, and shoved it into Ahab's mouth. 'Because I'm not losing that gold chain ever again!' He pounded Ahab's shoulder. 'Keep your eyes closed, and trust me!'

Mackenzie pushed Forest, Ahab and himself into the water. He guided Ahab's hands to the side of his BC, looped the rope around him, and then Mackenzie – with powerful kicks – set off into the tunnel, holding on to Forest to guide him and dragging Ahab behind.

CHAPTER 57

AHAB

Ahab clung to his cousin and kicked as best he could as they fought their way out of the tunnel. He kept his eyes shut against the rushing water. The rope cut into his side, the regulator in his mouth the only safe thing in this terrifying world, reduced to the tiny space around him.

It was cold, claustrophobic, horrific. There was none of the magic of diving. In its place was only terror. Sometimes, when he brushed the side of the cave, he felt something like a static shock rushing through him, pressing on his ears, making him nauseous.

It was useless – he might as well give up. Out there in the currents of the open sea, what would they do? It would be impossible to find their way back to the gravel beach with the path to the cliff. Ahab was blind. Ahab was dead weight. It wasn't fair on Mackenzie or the boy for him to keep holding on. He'd only end up killing them.

He heard the singing-drone intensify – the sirens' song – and then he felt the three of them being sucked back towards the cave, the whirlpool growing stronger. Eyes tightly shut, breathing with

Mackenzie's safety regulator, Ahab gripped the kelp and wedged himself in place, trying to stop them all getting sucked back into the cave.

When it finally passed, he felt Mack pulling forward. He added his own kicks, fuelled by the adrenaline of survival.

A sudden swirl of current – Ahab's head pounded into a rock. Even as stars sparkled in his vision, he fought it off, fighting for consciousness.

And then, just like that, he sensed a shift in the current. They were out of the tunnel, out into the wide-open water. Clinging to Mackenzie, he felt them being thrown around by the currents. For a long while he kicked in the dark, limbs growing sluggish.

Then there were heavy rocks against his legs, and waves pounding on top of him. He felt someone shaking him, saying something he could barely make out. He opened his eyes, blinking against the light. The waves were pulling at him. He was tired, just . . . so tired. It'd be beautiful to just let the waves take him out to sea. He was done, so done . . .

Mackenzie grabbed him and he felt himself being dragged along gravel, then pushed up against cold rock. Mackenzie was shouting in his face, ripping the BC off him, but he had to concentrate to understand what he was saying.

'C'mon, Ahab! C'mon! We're on land, we're safe, we just have to get up this switchback!'

But Ahab was too exhausted to ever move again.

CHAPTER 58

FOREST

'He's not too good,' shouted Forest over the thundering sound of the waves crashing into the cliffs. He was holding Ahab against his chest. An almighty storm raged all around them, the rain driving down in sheets, flashes of lightning off on the horizon.

They were pushed right to the back of the gravel beach, each surge threatening to pull them in. Forest's heart was pounding from the effort of swimming out of that cave, his throat was raw from exertion, and he was freezing.

Above them was a switchback path up the cliff, narrow and wet with rain. It looked like a deathtrap.

'I need you to play the hero this time, Forest,' said Mackenzie. 'Go up the path, take the bikes, and go get help. Can you do that?'

'No, Mack!' Forest swept his sodden hair out of his face. 'No way are you carrying him up there alone. And I'm not leaving either of you behind!' He climbed up onto the first overhang, bringing the coil of rope with him. 'Pass him up to me!'

'I can't,' said Mackenzie. 'My arms are like jelly. I'm done, Forest. I'm cooked.'

'You saved me!' shouted Forest. 'I thought I was dead, but you saved me! We made it out! This next part is easy. C'mon, you big lump, *move!*'

Suddenly a large roller plunged onto the beach. Before Forest knew what was happening, the two men, and all the gear, were wrenched from the beach, back into the waves.

Just like that, they were gone. He was alone on the beach.

'*No!*' screamed Forest. '*No!*'

There was no sign of them on the surface. The two of them would have no oxygen, no energy, no hope . . .

Forest shouted at the ocean, raising his voice in defiance: '*I will not let you drown my family! Never again!*'

He still had the rope. He tied it to a rusted metal pole, and the other end in a loop around his waist. Then he leapt out into the icy, boiling sea.

There was nothing. Salt and silt, sound and wind and the drone.

Forest kicked out, full of fury, fighting the wave . . . The water pushed the rope down his waist – he hadn't tightened it! He reached for it and it looped around his leg. Twisting, he clung to the rope, reminded of clinging to the kelp when he'd first let himself wash up on the shore. He looped it three times, four times, until it was tight around his ankle. Not as good as his waist, but . . .

What did it matter? There was no one out here. Nothing. He was going to drown alone in the heavy swell.

Then, a head surfaced at the peak of a wave. Mack, holding Ahab. Forest kicked and kicked towards them, but they went under again. He dived, grasping, feeling something – hair? – and then he was on the surface again.

They were being sucked out to sea. Waves on all sides. He had Mackenzie's hair in his grip.

The rope yanked on his foot. Hard. He felt a popping and then fiery agony.

The pain made him queasy, but his whimpering brain was awash with the knowledge of death.

'I've got the rope, hold on to me!' shouted Forest into Mackenzie's ear. 'We can do this!'

Mackenzie's grip on him tightened, pressing Ahab between them. Forest clung to his family as another wave set them tumbling, the force as heavy as a whale, the rope twisting and twisting around his foot, the pain increasing ten-fold, a hundred-fold, and then the resistance was completely gone.

He gasped for air, swallowed water, and everything went black.

When Forest opened his eyes, he found he was at the top of the cliff, sheltered behind a copse of scrub and two dirt bikes.

Agony at the end of his leg. He couldn't breathe from the pain.

Mackenzie poked at a campfire that was burning hot, setting their wet clothes to steaming. Ahab, pale and half-drowned himself, was crouched over Forest, a damp but burning cigarette between his lips. Pain pushed into the area behind Forest's eyes, deep into his brain. He smelled burning meat.

Ahab gripped his chin and forced it up, into his eyes. 'Look at me. Don't look at it. Look at me.'

Forest looked into his eyes. He trusted him. He wouldn't look at the end of his leg. His mind felt funny. Delirious?

'Thanks for coming for us, lad.'

'Without that rope we'd be dead,' said Mackenzie. 'You saved us.'

'I have one more secret.' He leaned forward. 'I'm Forest Dempsey.'

'Yes, son. It's okay,' said Ahab, putting his hand to Forest's forehead, testing for fever.

'No, Ahab. Listen.' He grabbed Ahab's hand to push it away.

If he died today, they'd never know. 'I was with her when she died. Your mum . . .'

He had to get it out. All of it.

'Miriam – I knew her as the Witch. She was the one who took me in, after my father tried to kill me. She . . . she hid me, when the police came looking. She saved me, but she also . . . She knew that my dad got me hooked on the bliss salts – the ice – and she was able to . . . I went crazy.'

Ahab's face filled with confusion. 'Bliss salts? You're burning up, lad. You need to stop talking.'

'No, *listen* to me! Huck's skull in that cave – I was there. I was Forest. I *am* Forest.' He reached for his shoulder. 'I knew it all along, it was just . . . hidden. I am Forest Dempsey. Be careful what you wish for . . . what I wished for . . .'

Another burst of fire from the end of his leg.

He was rambling now. 'She was in a bad way, but she saved my life, Ahab. The way she did it . . . but she was a good person. The best. She took me to Hobart and gave me a new life. She always said that she – she loved you, Ahab. She wished she could have been there for you, but the ice . . . she couldn't escape the hold it had on her . . .'

Mackenzie had come over to listen, the gold chain back around his neck, and he put his arm around Ahab's shoulders. The older man was completely still, shock in his face.

'When she died, I was confused, lost. I thought I was . . . claiming someone else's life. With everything that's happened . . . you've lost everything,' said Forest. 'I've ruined it all.'

'No,' said Mackenzie. 'You haven't. Blackbeard is dead – you're safe.' In a lower voice, he said, 'Could it be true? Could he really be Forest Dempsey?'

Ahab shook his head, shrugging Mackenzie's arm off him, trying to regain his composure.

'The cave,' he said, taking a big breath to still himself. 'The Bone Cave will change everything. The Business.'

Mackenzie gave him a confused look.

'We found a cave, out in the ocean,' said Forest. 'It's full of bones, artefacts.'

'They're ancient, Mackenzie,' said Ahab. 'Who knows what they mean for the history of this place. But it'll have to be protected. That will change Shacktown. The tourists . . . the fishing . . .'

'You're right, it'll make the Business unviable,' said Mackenzie. 'It's perfect. And Dempsey Abalone belongs to *you* . . . Forest. You'll never need anything ever again. We're here. We'll help you.'

Then his face darkened. 'Davey won't like it.'

CHAPTER 59

MACKENZIE

The fire helped warm them up enough to ride back. It would've been dangerous to attempt it while they were still cold and wet – between the Black Wind and the rush of wind from the speeding bikes, the risk of hypothermia would have been all too real. At least the next band of rain hadn't hit yet, but they could see it on the horizon.

As it was, he was worried about all the blood Forest had lost – Davey's attempt to kill the boy might yet succeed. Ahab had cauterised that ragged stump where his foot used to be with the fire, but he needed an ambulance and fast. He'd offered to let Forest ride with him, but Ahab had found some strange second wind and his protectiveness over the boy was fierce, so he was sharing his bike.

The boy. The true Forest Dempsey? Seeing him now, filled out since that first day in the hospital, his hair now lightened by the sun, his face freckled and tanned . . .

Mackenzie knew that Jesse had been a bastard, but he'd never believed the rumours he'd dosed his own boy with ice . . . He should have done more to protect his nephew back then, rather than turning a blind eye. How much responsibility was on his shoulders? A child suffering from drug-induced psychosis . . . the lifelong trauma that would follow . . .

They'd already agreed to meet Shelby at the MV *Anne*, their houseboat lab, so that's where they were headed. When they passed a police car on the way, Ahab slowed, and Mackenzie thought he was about to flag it down, but then he sped up again, sticking close to Mackenzie. 'We need Shelby to see he's safe first!' he shouted.

Finally they pulled into the Dempseys' bush block, where the *Anne* was moored.

When they came to a stop, Forest vomited on the sodden ground. 'It hurts,' he croaked.

'We're getting you out of here as fast as we can,' said Mackenzie.

A fleet of vehicles was parked right on the beach, forming a circle, a bonfire burning on the sand.

Ahab lifted Forest from the bike and let it fall to the ground. 'Here he is! Here's the boy, Shelby.' He carried him tenderly, careful of his leg. 'Just a moment longer, Forest, then we'll get you to an ambulance.'

Mackenzie limped after them.

Shelby emerged from the middle of a huddle of people, men and women, all with that same wary look on their face from years spent working in the underworld. Mackenzie recognised some of them from *Margot's Revenge*, most notably Tranquil. They waited a respectful distance, Davey among them.

His brother wouldn't meet his eyes.

So Shelby had really done it. She'd summoned Blackbeard's crew. From where she was situated in the middle of them, it was clear she was in control. She'd taken on the mantle.

Shelby looked like a sick caricature – the shotgun strapped across her back, two holsters criss-crossing her chest, handguns in place. Shelby had learned quickly about how important optics were in the drug game – she was demonstrating to the crew she was not someone to be trifled with.

Mackenzie couldn't believe it. She'd fallen so far, so fast.

The Black Wind droned, and Mackenzie's heart was a storm.

'Here he is,' shouted Mack. 'He needs the hospital.'

'Shelby?' said Forest from Ahab's arms.

She looked between the three of them. 'So you really did it. I can't believe it.'

'Where's De Corrado?' said Ahab, stern as ever.

'She's safe – she cooperated well. She's in the back of that car,' said Shelby, pointing at a sedan. Dim thumps could be heard from within. 'Naturally we can't let her out until we're long gone. You three can take that car to get back. Although I'll have to insist you let me and the crew have a head start.'

'Shelby,' said Ahab. 'You're not seriously . . .?'

'Not what, Ahab?' Shelby's voice was cold. 'De Corrado saw me shoot Ivy. She knows about the Business. Either I become Blackbeard or I kill her. We have no *choice*.'

They all said that, time and time again. Davey, Mack, even Ivy. They all wanted to believe they had no control over the pain they were bringing into the world. But Shelby did have a choice. She could escape this world, right now, before it was too late. What could he do, though? How could he show her a way out?

Forest was gawping at her, his eyes on the shotgun. 'Can we go, Ahab?' His whisper carried to Mackenzie.

Is he right to be afraid?

Shelby stepped closer, her voice cracking. 'With Davey at my side, I'll be able to do it. Without Kane . . . But we're still a family.' Mackenzie saw it in her eyes – she was terrified. She was grieving. 'But I won't be Blackbeard. I won't have *anything to do* with that woman. I've told them to start calling me Persephone . . . bringer of the Golden Sunshine. Queen of the Underworld.'

'You don't have to do this,' said Mackenzie.

'Grow up, Mack! What else could I possibly be good for now? My son is dead, I *killed* my mother-in-law! Maybe this is *all* I'm good for.' She gestured to the crew. 'I'll take them far away from here. Shacktown will be safe. We'll leave Tasmania. Ivy had assets like you wouldn't believe – Tranquil, he knows where and how to use them.'

'This is bloody stupid, Shelby!' said Ahab. He looked between her and the sedan, torn.

'Take Forest and go, Ahab,' said Mack. 'I'll handle this.'

'No. It's possible. Me and Davey can do it. Together.' Shelby's voice was full of sorrow, but that gave it weight, too. She was scared, but she believed in what she was doing.

Mackenzie felt cold.

He had to save her.

'Go, Ahab.'

Shelby was in grief and in pain. She was making an irreversible decision, but she wasn't thinking clearly. She needed time and perspective. But life and death in the drug world moved fast. He understood why she felt she needed to make a decision now.

'I got you into this . . .' he murmured. He turned. 'Ahab, take Forest and get out of here. Keep De Corrado safe.'

'You can't let her —'

'I'll handle it,' said Mackenzie. '*Go*, Ahab.'

'Mack . . . be careful. She's not . . .' Forest ran out of words.

Ahab pierced Mackenzie with a stare. 'You know what you're doing?'

'Yeah,' said Mackenzie. 'I do.'

Ahab took him at his word. Without looking back, he carried Forest to the car in a hurry and then drove off in a swirl of gravel.

Watching the sedan's tail-lights disappear down the road, Mackenzie knew Ahab would let De Corrado out as soon as he thought they were a safe distance away.

So did Shelby – she was already gesturing at her crew to get in their vehicles.

'Meet at the rendezvous point!'

Car doors slammed, and in a swirl of screeching tyres, roaring engines and spraying sand, the vehicles headed out onto the road after Ahab.

The only members of her crew who remained were Tranquil and Davey. They stepped up to flank Shelby. It was just the four of them on the beach now.

It began to rain. Heavy coastal rain, slanted sideways by the Black Wind. It ran down into Mack's eyes, as he stood there, one against three.

'We need to go, Shelbs,' said Davey, still avoiding his brother's eyes. 'Now.'

'I'll find a way to contact you,' said Shelby to Mackenzie.

No, she wouldn't.

Mackenzie mourned all the things he'd never get to have. A home to call his own. A wife, children . . . a picket fence, and a dog to sit at his feet . . .

But some things just couldn't be helped. He'd always been a realist. Cut your losses and run. That was the only way to survive in this world.

And when your time was up . . .

'Just one last piece of advice,' said Mackenzie. He stepped in for a hug, pulling Shelby tight. She held him just as close, her fingers pressing into his back. He could feel her pulse pounding in her chest. 'That story about Persephone . . .'

'It's just a name,' said Shelby, now trying to pull away.

He put his mouth closer to her ear. 'Shelby, Persephone only had to spend half her life in the underworld because she was married to Hades.'

'Mack,' said Shelby, slumping a little. 'I know.'

'Okay. Good.' Mack was whispering as low as he could. 'Do me a favour . . . bury me at sea.'

He pulled away from Shelby, one of her pistols now in his hand.

'No, wait!' she screamed.

He pointed it at Davey and pulled the trigger.

His brother's eyes showed the barest hint of surprise as the bullet caught him in the middle of his chest. He slumped to his knees.

Tranquil's gunshot hit Mackenzie a second later, with such force he was knocked off his feet, red-hot agony flaring in his side.

He felt no fear as he fell to the ground. No sorrow.

Shelby was free of the underworld.

Mackenzie felt only peace.

CHAPTER 60

FOREST
One Month Later

Forest sat on a stool at the bar in Mermaid's Darling, Zeus asleep on the floor. He was with Ahab and De Corrado, and he was happy.

The light of early autumn shone in through the windows, the fire burning merrily in the corner, chatter and clinking cutlery echoing all around. The Mermaid's Darling was rarely empty, these days. The smell of spilled beer, the busy kitchen, woodsmoke . . .

The only thing that marred it for Forest was the ache where the bottom of his right leg had once been. He was supposed to be on painkillers, but he didn't take them. Any drugs affected his mind in weird ways now, making his head feel like he was on the precipice of a big hole. Dr Joseph, his psychiatrist again, now that Forest was able to tell the whole truth, said his neurochemistry was still fragile given the drug abuse he'd suffered, first under Jesse, then the Witch.

He figured the pain would ease once he got his prosthetic leg. Although he had to admit, the temporary solution Ahab had come up with *was* growing on him: a wooden peg leg.

All the doctors said they were impressed by Forest's resilience. He'd had three journalists approach him, wanting to write his biography. 'A remarkable young man. An inspiration.' He was putting these journalists off – he wouldn't mind writing the book *himself* one day, when there were a few more happy stories to put in there. Moments like this one right now – safe, warm, full, and with family.

And they were family. Blood. The police had insisted on a DNA test, and it had shown that Forest really was a Dempsey. Jesse's insistence that he was adopted was another of his merciless tortures – Forest's identity built on shifting ground even in childhood.

Ahab stood behind the bar, in a bartending apron, smiling as he pulled De Corrado a beer, making a wisecrack.

'Thank you, *Master Pubman*,' said De Corrado. She wore a flowery dress, and her hair was tied back. The way they looked at each other, Forest suspected there was a romance brewing. That would explain why Ahab looked happier these days – and why he had started keeping his beard and hair neatly trimmed.

The door to the Mermaid's Darling opened, and a familiar figure limped in, wearing a well-fitted white shirt. Forest's mood improved even more.

Mackenzie had lost a lot of weight in hospital, surgery saving his life after he was shot. Not that Mackenzie Dempsey was one to let things keep him down. Not anymore.

Forest waved him over, but Mackenzie was immediately stopped by two men. One slapped him on the shoulder, the other shook his hand. Mackenzie tried and failed to palm them off – it looked like they were offering to buy him drinks. Big Mane followed him into the pub, dressed in boating gear, and pushed the other men away cheerfully, his booming voice reaching across the room, 'He's busy, pester him for a job later.'

As Ivy's only remaining son, Mackenzie had inherited Safe Harbour and all her assets. He'd soon be ready to dive again, his FLAD registration restored.

Not that he'd ever need to dive commercially again. Ivy had been smart enough to have the abalone business set up in a family trust. All the legitimate assets had no link to the Business – the Proceeds of Crime Act couldn't touch them.

But, even better than that, until Forest was old enough, Mackenzie would be helping manage Dempsey Abalone – a job that came with a generous salary. And there was a lot of work to do for the company to adjust to the new landscape. Mackenzie was excited about the idea of converting some of the abalone fleet into running conservation and diving tours. The town was excited by that too. The Bone Cave was drawing people from all over the world to Shacktown – more sites and artefacts were being discovered almost weekly.

There was no chance of Mackenzie going back to prison. De Corrado had spoken to the prosecutor, and they'd agreed to drop the charges against him. They'd all been in the hospital room when De Corrado broke the news. Although it was expected, in that moment Mackenzie seemed to regain some of his lost youth. Ever since then, it'd been hard to find Mackenzie Dempsey without a smile on his face. A genuine smile.

Mack came limping over to the bar and slid a large white envelope across the desk. 'She's signed it.'

She.

Shelby.

He'd just come from the remand prison.

'How was she?' asked Ahab.

'Better today. She's looking forward to seeing what this does.' He tapped on the paperwork. 'Fiona was with her, so she wasn't too bad. It's exactly one month today.'

The four of them fell silent. A month since Mack had killed Davey. Only Ahab and Forest knew the truth; De Corrado believed it had been Tranquil, and Shelby hadn't said anything to contradict that version of events.

Shelby was looking at serious prison time for killing Ivy, but with all the extenuating circumstances, there was the potential for a lighter sentence, or at least bail. Fiona was acting as her lawyer, and this had been her idea. The paperwork Mackenzie had brought was the key.

Forest opened the envelope and pulled it out: forms that would make Shelby his legal guardian.

With Forest to look after, and the high-profile nature of the case, Fiona thought Shelby had a chance of having the murder charge reduced to manslaughter. Of course, Forest planned to live with Mackenzie, even if Shelby did get bail. But for now he'd agreed to pretend, to help her case.

Thankfully, none of the other crew had come forward, or mentioned anything about her. Forest felt angry knowing all of Ivy's crew were out there somewhere, including Tranquil, but especially Frankie. He hoped one day he'd be able to find her and repay her for what she'd done to him, but he suspected De Corrado would find her first.

De Corrado had understood right away that Shelby wasn't some criminal mastermind – she was a mother pushed to the brink by the secrets her family kept from her, and then driven over the edge by grief. Terrible grief over the murder of her son.

Between De Corrado and Fiona, they'd even arranged a number of speaking engagements for her once she made bail – she'd already appeared via video-link to speak to community groups and rehab clinics – as a way to bring some good from her story.

Early on, Ahab had made a comment that it was all for show, trying to impress the courts, and Forest thought the three women were going to lynch him: with De Corrado at the front of the line.

Forest hadn't gone to visit her. He wasn't sure he wanted to, just yet. But from what De Corrado told them, although Shelby was still raw from everything she lost, she was desperate to put things right. Forest was willing to let this guardianship agreement go ahead; he thought of the memorial service for Kane and Davey, and how Shelby hadn't been able to attend. Shelby had lost more than anyone.

Well, maybe her losses and Forest's were about equal. Not that it worked like that. But who knew, maybe they'd even get along? He missed having a mother, and he thought Shelby might need him for the years ahead. She had suffered trauma that would haunt her for the rest of her life, but so did he, and look at him now . . .

Not long ago, he'd been trapped in a dissociative mental snap. Now he had his name, a house, Dempsey Abalone. He'd wanted to clear Huck's name . . . well, he'd done that. Somehow. In a weird way. If Jonah Donnager was still out there, he hoped he'd feel safe to come forward now.

He reached a hand to his shoulder blade, where those tattoos still showed on his skin.

THIS IS FOREST DEMPSEY
BE CAREFUL WHAT YOU WISH FOR

What had he wished for? To save Huck . . . Dr Joseph said that drive was probably his subconscious wanting him to save himself. And he'd done it. He'd lost a leg, but he'd gained everything.

He looked down at the paperwork again. All it needed was his signature.

A pen appeared under his nose. Mackenzie, watchful as always, had read his mind. Forest took the pen with a grateful smile and signed his name.

Forest Dempsey.

'It needs a witness,' he said.

'I'll do the honours,' said Ahab, standing directly across the bar now, leaning on his fists. 'Mack got to deliver it – it's my turn to sign it.' He took the pen, twisted the paperwork around so it faced him, and signed it with gravitas.

Ahab had spread the story around Shacktown in such a way that Forest was considered the hero. Because of Forest's bravery, the mystery of what happened to Alexandra and Huck had been solved. All those who knew Ahab understood how important that was to him. Ahab also gave Forest the credit for the archaeological find of the decade – what was now being called Alexandra's Cave – *and* for being instrumental in dismantling the local drug cartel.

That news had turned heads. Some members of the Business still walked the streets of Shacktown, but most had left town for pastures new. When Mackenzie had asked Ahab what he planned to do about that, Ahab had shrugged. 'They don't have a leader. The oceans around here are becoming a national park, so they can't operate as they used to. They're harmless. And they know what will happen if they ever try something in my town again . . .'

These days, Forest was more grateful than ever that Ahab was on *his* side. And Ahab, from what he could see, was as content as it was possible for the man to be. Even now, he was stealing a glance at De Corrado. Forest loved that.

Mackenzie winked at him. Clearly he saw it too.

'Stop it, you two,' said De Corrado, meaning Mackenzie and Forest, but she wasn't even looking their way. 'I know what you're thinking.'

'Let them think what they want to think,' rumbled Ahab.

The story grew more complicated as far as Blackbeard's crew was concerned. De Corrado's team hadn't been able to track down many of them, and Shelby had conveniently forgotten any names or identifying features.

From what Mackenzie had told him, after Davey's death, Shelby had spun a quick deal with Tranquil. He could have the crew and she wouldn't give up the location of the rendezvous, or anything else that would implicate them. In exchange, she wanted Pirates Bay and Shacktown left alone. Tranquil was only too happy to take that deal.

Ahab suspected it was because Ivy had been so well respected – Tranquil wasn't keen on having any of her family around, should any of his crew decide the operation should revert to Dempsey ownership.

Forest shifted a little closer to Mackenzie.

'How was Shelby today? I mean . . . with you.' He kept his voice low.

Mackenzie nodded. 'Oh, yeah, she still hates me. I don't think she'll ever forgive me for taking Davey from her – how could she? But I think she loves me, too, you know what I mean? One day she'll work out which feeling is stronger, and we'll see what happens then. It's not for me to decide.'

He looked out across the bar for a moment, lost in thought. Then he smiled that new authentic smile of his, made whole.

'You know, I picked something else up while I was in Hobart visiting Shelby. He's waiting in the truck. He's a bit shy at the moment, though.'

Forest's eyes lit up. Over the past week, Mack had been taking loads to the tip, getting rid of all sorts of things at Ivy's house, starting with the decorative life rings. The sign that read *Safe Harbour* had come down too, with a new sign announcing it as *Huck's House*. Mack had installed a wraparound deck, a new attic room with perfect 360-degree views, and . . . dog doors in every entrance. He'd also enclosed the whole property in a canine-proof picket fence.

'So you got him?' said Forest.

'Not the one in the pic,' said Mackenzie. 'There was another in the litter – he just came up and flopped on my shoe. Not as cute as the one in the pic, but I like him, I'm pretty sure he's the runt but it's hard to tell, they were *all* pretty small . . .' Mackenzie was already up and limping towards the door, eager to show off his new puppy friend.

Forest moved off his stool carefully, distributing his weight across his good leg and the wooden peg-leg.

Forest limped out after Mackenzie, following in his footsteps.

Tail wagging, Zeus stirred from his spot and trotted behind.

EPILOGUE

The red double-decker tour bus rumbled down the hill, into Shacktown. The side of it read:

SEE TASMANIA? SEA TASMANIA

The top section, open to the elements, was at full capacity, as it was most days now. Since the discovery of Alexandra Cave, the scuba-diving tourism had boomed. Even those who couldn't dive still came with snorkels and fins, searching the shallower and calmer waters, caught up in the treasure hunt.

The bus came to a halt, right near Overeem's Dive Centre. The sound of seagulls, the smell of the sea, the heat of the autumn sun . . .

A man sat right at the back of the bus, sunglasses on his face, a cap pulled down low. He appeared to be asleep.

Two women, freshly flown in from Sydney, rose, backpacks on their shoulders. 'Excuse me, mate?' one of them called to him. 'We're here.'

He stirred, looked around himself. He took a deep breath, smelling the air, and gave a sigh. 'Home,' he said, with a wry smile.

'Oh, you're a local?' said the woman politely.

'Not anymore,' said the man, taking off his sunglasses as he stood to stretch. He had the most startling blue eyes, the colour of ocean water.

'*We're* here to dive in Alexandra Cave,' said the woman.

'Is that so?' he said softly.

He looked out over the marina, over the ocean, and up towards a mansion set high on the hill.

'I'm here looking for my son,' he said. 'Forest Dempsey.'

ACKNOWLEDGEMENTS

Ali Watts, publisher. Thank you for continually bringing my dreams into reality. At the beginning of this publishing journey I had no idea how important you were to every part of the writing voyage, but as I've gained understanding about it all I've realised how lucky I am to have you.

Johannes Jakob, editor. Same as with Ali, I had no idea how lucky I am to have you until this book, and I've only just begun to realise how much of a madly complicated and highly specific skill set you have as an editor. But as well as that, thanks for the encouragement throughout every conversation.

Matthew McDonald, for all those initial phone calls that set in my mind the first ideas for *The Deep*, and for giving me the bones and a heartbeat to build Mack around. Thank you for being so generous with your stories.

Haylee Kerans, for being the first person to read *The Deep* and helping me whip it into shape, and then for being one of the last people to read it and close the loop. And as always, thanks for setting my feet on this journey.

Andrew Herring, for all those late-night chats, for helping me stay grounded and keep my emotions regulated when navigating how to write another book while riding the high from my last book, and for the writer's studio.

To my secret police contact, Jack. You've done it again! Thanks for the back-and-forth messages, for giving me specific descriptions to include, and for all that brainstorming over beers.

Blair Harding and Craig Oosthuizen, for being the best colleagues a man could ask for and for teaching me how a drug dealer thinks, how drug psychosis presents and the best way to steal money from rival outfits. Most importantly, thanks for teaching me how to relate to people who use drugs and for breaking down all those false ideas I had, even as a professional in the sector.

KC McDonald, for the insight into the criminal mindset, the introductions to people and places that taught me a lot about what I needed to know, and for all the coffees you joined me for mid-writing session. Thanks especially for always providing encouragement and good energy to keep me focused.

Tom Costello and Ryan Bester, for letting me into your world. Thank you for those scary tales of dependence on amphetamines, for the long conversations about life and meaning and the future, and for answering my questions, like, 'What, specifically, does a hit of ice feel like?', 'What's the best way to steal a car?' and 'What's the best way to make an impromptu ice pipe?' (Thanks, Tom – a wine glass! Bloody genius.)

To the Kouncil of Kyle, our massive online community of thousands of people all named Kyle, and particularly Kyle Clayton, who allegedly took about three minutes to allegedly find me an ice recipe on the dark web and then allegedly got it to me in an undisclosed way. NDH.

To my three main beta readers, Rebecca Thomson, Jacqueline Saward and Shantelle Perry. Without your insights, feedback, comments, detailed responses, phone calls and suggestions, this book would not be what it is. Indebted to you! Without beta readers, the world stops turning.

To Jessica Malpass, publicist, for being the most famous person I know, and for always making the wheel turn and yet still going above and beyond. Thank you especially for the late-night advice when I was getting frantic.

Emily Hindle, marketing executive. Thanks for the support, the hype messages, holding my hand through all the digital assets stuff, and then for *leaving me* – I can't believe it! I hope you hate your new job.

To Nerrilee Weir, Alice Richardson, and the whole rights team – thank you for the phone calls, the wisdom, and for helping me set out into the final frontier!

Adam Laszczuk, cover designer, for two knock-out covers. On behalf of not only myself but all the people who have picked up *The Bluffs* and *The Deep* based purely on how eye-catching you made the books, thank you!

Deb McGowan, Tassie sales rep. Where would we be without you? I've no idea, but sometimes I have nightmares about it. I don't even want to think about it. Thank you for being the shining star of this outfit.

Janine Brown and the sales team, thank you again and again, over and over, for everything you've done to support me. Thank you for your time and energy, I am so grateful.

To the booksellers all over Australia, and especially the Tasmanian booksellers, *thank you*. You're such great people and I love how you've all welcomed me into your community.

Cheryl Akle and the team at Better Reading. Receiving that groundswell of support from you and your community at the very beginning of my journey went a long way to making me feel like I'd finally arrived, and I am forever grateful for such a beginning to being an author.

To the four big-time authors who listened to my insecurities and gave me advice for tackling the notoriously difficult second book. Jane Harper, particularly for the advice, 'All this book needs to be is something you are proud of and something that supports your overall goals for the kind of author you want to be.' Trent Dalton, particularly for the summary of your advice in, 'What I'm trying to say, mate, is it really doesn't matter because you've already lived the dream!! You did it!! The rest really is gravy!! So go for it with no second thoughts.' Craig Silvey, particularly for the advice, 'It's the story that matters more than anything . . . listen to your authorial instincts.' And Chris Hammer – thank you for reading *The Deep* and loving it enough to provide a cover quote!

Gabrielle Barber and the team at Agapé Hair Hobart, for having a copy of *The Bluffs* on the front desk of your salon and talking about it to patrons. Those moments of support have great power for me, and remind me why I love the reading community. Thanks for getting copies of my book into the hands of so many readers.

To my family, for being the best team I have, for the cheerleading and hyping, and for liking all the screenshots of reviews that I put in our FamJam group chat. Thanks especially to Dad who helped go through my manuscript for me when I had damaged my arms.

And finally, thank you, God, for the gifts you gave me, the people you surrounded me with, and that stubborn streak that wouldn't let go.